喚醒你的英文語感！

Get a Feel for English !

喚醒你的英文語感 ！

Get a Feel for English !

附 MP3

難易：英檢中級至中高級程度

大師獨門記憶術無私公開

翻譯大師教你記單字 進階篇

作者/詹婷婷、解鈴容、吳岳峰
企畫主編/郭岱宗

- 聯想串單字，說故事般自然就記住！
- 嚴選 31 類進階知識單字，學到的保證幫你英文加分！
- 傾注半甲子教學功力的單字筆記，變身英文達人超效首選！

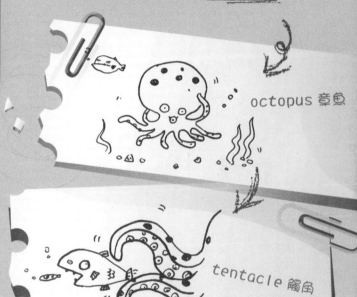

octopus 章魚

tentacle 觸角

prey 獵物

貝塔語言出版
Beta Multimedia Publishing

主編序—薪火傳承

我一個卑微的火苗如何去照亮別人？

我短暫的生命要如何激起下一代的努力？

當我頭髮漸白、體力漸弱時，

心愛的孩子啊，只要你們成長茁壯！

當我聲音沙啞、老態畢露、演講不再魅力無限時，

心愛的孩子啊，只要你們個個神采奕奕、出類拔萃！

一個平凡的我，若能成就不平凡的你們，

我的生命就已不平凡。

這群優秀、努力、令人疼愛的年輕作者，日後必將成為具真才實學、言之有物、教之有效、能夠激發學生學習之火的良師！

郭岱宗

作者序

很多人從小學就開始參加坊間的美語課程，但是多年之後，說英文卻還是支支吾吾。我們不禁自問，到底什麼時候才可以輕鬆地和外國人溝通？什麼時候才能使用道地的口音及速度與他們交談呢？

我們發現，學了至少六年的英文後，之所以仍然無法使用流利的英文對答，問題在於教材及學習方法。CD 速度太慢及單字實用性偏低是市面上教材的普遍問題，以致讀者真正和外國人對話時，通常只有傻眼的份。光埋頭苦讀而不開口練習、只會寫考卷而不講究正確的發音，等到用時舌頭一定會打結。

大多數的台灣學生都認為國內沒有學習英文的環境，一定要花大把鈔票出國留學，像是到美國、英國、加拿大等國的語言學校，才能把英文學得呱呱叫。好英文其實不必遠求，環境是可以自己創造的。如果學習的方法不正確，就算出國深造多年，回國之後的英文程度恐怕還是在原地踏步。

大學時期，我們一票人多年選修郭老師的各項課程，包括發音、會話、演講及口譯課，受過郭老師與眾不同的英語教學風格洗禮後，有一天突然發現我們的英文實力大增，而且說起英文竟然可以行雲流水，連自己都難以置信。

「愛的教育，鐵的紀律」是郭老師威震四方的座右銘。上郭老師的課，我們絕不敢遲到，因為她要求我們嚴格自律；老師常耳提面命：「我們的生命要發光發熱，照亮別人！」因此同學之間只有相互鼓勵與關懷，沒有惡性的競爭。她是絕對地專業、絕對地嚴厲，卻又那麼善良溫暖，我們每一個學生都因而對她又敬、又愛、又怕。就算最頑皮的同學，也會在老師的教誨下，成為孜孜不倦的好

學生。擔心多縱容我們一分，我們日後的競爭力就會少一分，是老師堅持一貫嚴格教學的理由。你們一定以為郭岱宗老師很兇吧？其實郭老師從來不罵人，若有同學達不到老師所要求的完美標準時，她只會慈祥地說一句「You failed.」。不過，雖是輕輕一句話，卻是我們每個人心中的痛！

　　修郭老師的課雖然很辛苦，卻絕對不會痛苦。正是這種魅力，讓老師的課堂堂爆滿，也讓我們不敢懈怠。而這一切努力都沒有白費！今天的我們開口說英語時，總能侃侃而談，感覺好像上知天文、下知地理，連外國人都以為我們是ABC 呢！

　　書中收錄生活及新聞中最常見和最實用的內容，並藉由 CD 的示範幫同學們有效提升口語實力（發音、語調、速度），讓你擺脫「說不出口」、「說不標準」的惡夢！書中所有單字皆經過精心設計，採用人類與生俱來的邏輯概念，透過「聯想線」的連結，與其死背單字不如靈活運用。系統化的單字群組讓你輕鬆學習、輕鬆聯想，不只快速擴充字彙的深度及廣度，更能有效記憶。背單字再也不是一件苦差事了。

　　感謝恩師淡江大學郭岱宗教授和貝塔語言出版社給我們這個機會，讓我們能和許多積極想學好英文的朋友分享所學。本書將為你打造進階的英語字彙實力，讓你成功掌握成熟、精準的語彙，進而大幅提升整體的英文實力！

詹婷婷　解鈴容　吳岳峰

單元說明

① 單元目錄
② MP3 軌數

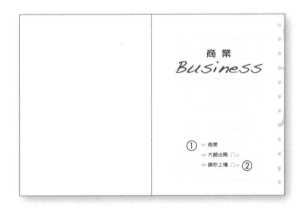

① 單字主題
② 藉由聯想，擴充、記憶主題
　 單字。
③ 大師小叮嚀：
　 提點、說明關鍵單字用法和
　 注意事項。

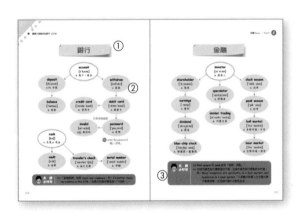

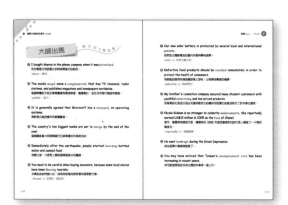

大師出馬：
道地例句，示範單字用法。

換你上場：
豐富練習，進一步示範單字用
法並驗收學習成效。

略語說明

n. = noun（名詞）

v. = verb（動詞）

adj. = adjective（形容詞）

adv. = adverb（副詞）

sth. = something（某物）

sb. = somebody（某人）

ph. = phrase（片語）

【美】：美式用法

【英】：英式用法

搭：搭配詞

同：同義字

反：反義字

補：相關字補充

Contents

PART 1

食物
FOOD

海 鮮
Seafood

甲殼類、貝類

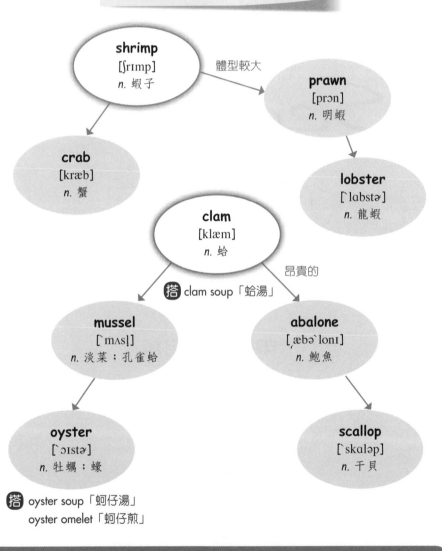

shrimp
[ʃrɪmp]
n. 蝦子

體型較大

prawn
[prɔn]
n. 明蝦

crab
[kræb]
n. 蟹

lobster
[ˋlɑbstɚ]
n. 龍蝦

clam
[klæm]
n. 蛤

昂貴的

搭 clam soup「蛤湯」

mussel
[ˋmʌsl̩]
n. 淡菜;孔雀蛤

abalone
[͵æbəˋlonɪ]
n. 鮑魚

oyster
[ˋɔɪstɚ]
n. 牡蠣;蠔

scallop
[ˋskɑləp]
n. 干貝

搭 oyster soup「蚵仔湯」
oyster omelet「蚵仔煎」

大師
小叮嚀　☞ Prawn 是體型較大的蝦種,在餐宴中常可見到。

魚類

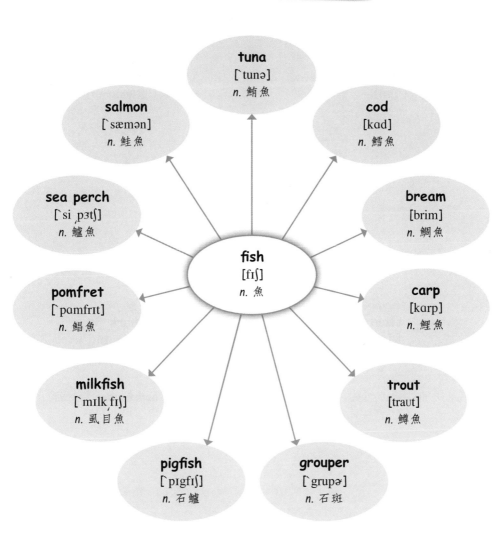

tuna
[ˋtunə]
n. 鮪魚

salmon
[ˋsæmən]
n. 鮭魚

cod
[kɑd]
n. 鱈魚

sea perch
[ˋsiˏpɝtʃ]
n. 鱸魚

bream
[brim]
n. 鯛魚

fish
[fɪʃ]
n. 魚

pomfret
[ˋpɑmfrɪt]
n. 鯧魚

carp
[kɑrp]
n. 鯉魚

milkfish
[ˋmɪlkˏfɪʃ]
n. 虱目魚

trout
[traʊt]
n. 鱒魚

pigfish
[ˋpɪgfɪʃ]
n. 石鱸

grouper
[ˋgrupə]
n. 石斑

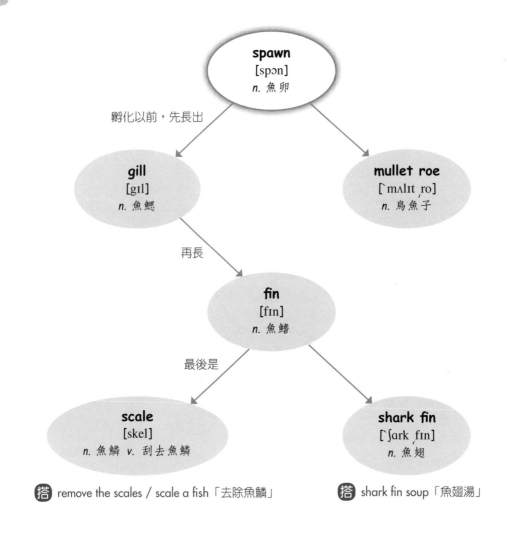

spawn
[spɔn]
n. 魚卵

孵化以前，先長出

gill
[gɪl]
n. 魚鰓

mullet roe
[ˋmʌlɪt ˏro]
n. 烏魚子

再長

fin
[fɪn]
n. 魚鰭

最後是

scale
[skel]
n. 魚鱗 v. 刮去魚鱗

shark fin
[ˋʃɑrk ˏfɪn]
n. 魚翅

搭 remove the scales / scale a fish 「去除魚鱗」

搭 shark fin soup 「魚翅湯」

大師
小叮嚀 | ✎ Scale 當名詞也有「秤；規模；刻度」等意思。

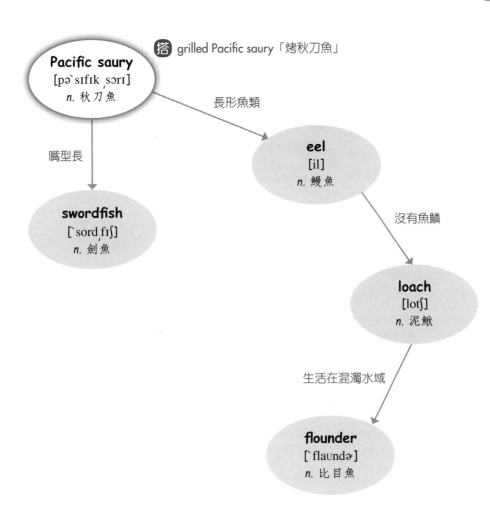

搭 grilled Pacific saury「烤秋刀魚」

Pacific saury
[pə`sɪfɪk͵sɔrɪ]
n. 秋刀魚

長形魚類

eel
[il]
n. 鰻魚

嘴型長

swordfish
[`sord͵fɪʃ]
n. 劍魚

沒有魚鱗

loach
[lotʃ]
n. 泥鰍

生活在混濁水域

flounder
[`flaundɚ]
n. 比目魚

大師 小叮嚀 ✏ Grill 當名詞也有「烤架；燒烤店」之意；當動詞則有「烤」之意。

軟體動物

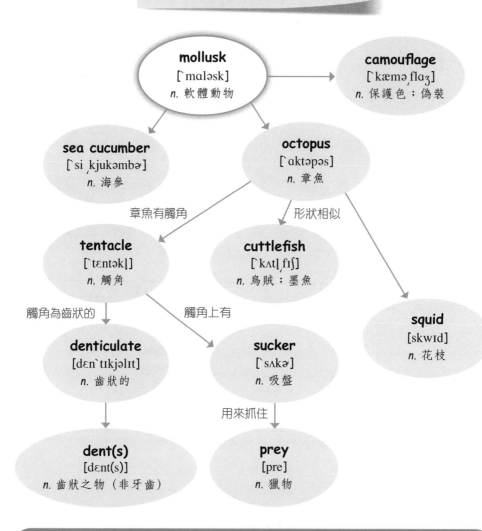

mollusk
[ˋmɑləsk]
n. 軟體動物

camouflage
[ˋkæmə͵flɑʒ]
n. 保護色；偽裝

sea cucumber
[ˋsi͵kjukəmbə]
n. 海參

octopus
[ˋɑktəpəs]
n. 章魚

章魚有觸角

形狀相似

tentacle
[ˋtɛntəkḷ]
n. 觸角

cuttlefish
[ˋkʌtḷ͵fɪʃ]
n. 烏賊；墨魚

觸角為齒狀的

觸角上有

squid
[skwɪd]
n. 花枝

denticulate
[dɛnˋtɪkjəlɪt]
n. 齒狀的

sucker
[ˋsʌkə]
n. 吸盤

用來抓住

dent(s)
[dɛnt(s)]
n. 齒狀之物（非牙齒）

prey
[pre]
n. 獵物

**大師
小叮嚀**

- 章魚、墨魚等軟體動物的觸角上都有齒狀的 (denticulate) 吸盤 (suckers)。
- 花枝、章魚等冷血動物的皮膚能變成保護色 (camouflage)。例: This is its camouflage.「這是牠的保護色。」

大師出馬

單字用法看這邊！

❶ Salmon is a popular food, because it's high in protein and low in fat.
鮭魚是很受歡迎的食物，因為牠含有豐富蛋白質和低脂肪。
（protein *n.* 蛋白質）

❷ Groupers are a kind of fish that have a stout body and a big mouth. Because of the black spots covering their body, the Chinese name is "stone spot."
石斑魚是擁有龐大身軀和嘴巴的魚種。由於身上佈滿黑色斑點，所以中文名稱為「石斑」。
（stout *adj.* 結實的；粗壯的）

❸ Milkfish is a very common kind of fish in stores and markets in Southeast Asia. My mom usually cooks it with black beans and pineapple.
虱目魚是東南亞店家和市場很普遍的魚種。我媽媽通常會用黑豆和鳳梨來料理牠。

❹ Flounders are very different from other fish. They have both eyes situated on the same side of their head. Furthermore, their **camouflage** allows them to blend in with their environment just like **cuttlefish**.
比目魚和其他魚類非常不同。牠們的兩顆眼睛都位於頭的同一側，而且，牠們的保護色可以讓牠們與周遭環境合而為一，就像墨魚一般。
（situate *v.* 位於　blend in 與……混合）

❺ Open a **scallop** and you'll see it has two parts: the meaty, white scallop and the soft, red **roe**.

打開干貝殼,你會看到兩個部分:又白又多肉的干貝和紅紅軟軟的卵。

(meaty *adj.* 多肉的)

❻ **Mussels** and **clams** are bivalves and cannot be eaten uncooked, because their shells stay tightly closed until they are cooked.

淡菜和蛤都屬於雙殼貝,不能生吃,因為牠們的殼在未煮熟前是緊閉的。

(bivalve *n.* 雙殼貝類)

❼ From little **clams** and **abalones** to bigger **squid**, cuttlefish, and **octopi**, **mollusks** can look quite different from each other, but they all share many similar traits.

從小小的蛤、鮑魚到較大的花枝、墨魚和章魚,軟體動物看起來彼此不同卻又有著許多相似處。

換你上場

學習成效知分曉！

⟜ *Exercise* ⋯⋯ 根據你所聽到的對話完成填空。

(Tina and Evelyn are at the 1. 水族館 .)

Tina:　Which area do you want to go to first?

Evelyn: Let's go to the 2. 軟體動物館 . I like them a lot.

(After arriving at the 2. 軟體動物館)

Tina:　Why do you like 3. 軟體動物 ? They're so ugly and scary.

Evelyn: I don't think so. They're interesting animals. Look! The 4. 墨魚 is 5. 用牠的手抓捕獵物 ! That's cool!

Tina:　Yuck! I don't like 6. 牠們的手 at all. They've got all those scary 7. 吸盤 ! Wait! 8. 我是不是眼花啦 ? Why does it have ten arms? I thought they only had eight arms, just like 9. 蜘蛛 .

Evelyn: No! 10. 那是章魚 ! Cuttlefish and 11. 魷魚 are different. They have eight arms and two 12. 觸角 , just like what you see in this 13. 水族箱 . That's how people distinguish cuttlefish from octopi.

Tina:　You're the expert. I am only interested in how to eat sea creatures. 14. 鰻魚 is my favorite fish. I order it every time I go to a BBQ restaurant. 15. 龍蝦, 16. 干貝, and 17. 海參 are really delicious, too. That's one of the reasons why I like to go to wedding banquets so much.

Evelyn: Yeah, there's always good seafood at weddings.

Tina:　You bet!

⊱ *Answer key* ···

1. aquarium
2. mollusk zone
3. mollusks
4. cuttlefish
5. securing its prey with its arms
6. their arms
7. suckers
8. Am I seeing double
9. spiders

10. They're octopuses/octopi
11. squid
12. tentacles
13. tank/aquarium
14. Eel
15. Lobster/Lobsters
16. scallops
17. sea cucumbers

⊱ 中譯

（*Tina* 和 *Evelyn* 兩人在水族館。）

Tina： 妳想先看哪一區？
Evelyn： 我們先去軟體動物館好了，我很喜歡軟體動物。

（到了軟體動物館。）

Tina： 妳為什麼喜歡軟體動物？牠們又醜又嚇人。
Evelyn： 我不這麼覺得，我覺得牠們是很有趣的動物！妳看，這隻墨魚正在用牠的手抓捕獵物，超酷的！
Tina： 好噁！我一點都不喜歡牠們的手，上面都是恐怖的吸盤。等等！我是不是眼花啦！為什麼牠有十隻手？我以為牠們跟蜘蛛一樣，只有八隻手。
Evelyn： 不！那是章魚，但墨魚和魷魚就不同了。牠們有八隻手和兩隻觸角，就像妳在這個水族箱裡看到的一樣，這就是如何分辨墨魚和章魚的辦法。
Tina： 妳真是牠們的專家啊！說到海底動物，我只對如何吃牠們有興趣。我最喜歡吃鰻魚，每次我去燒烤店都會點。龍蝦、干貝和海參也都很好吃。這就是我為什麼喜歡去喝喜酒的原因之一。
Evelyn： 對，喜宴上總是有好吃的海鮮。
Tina： 沒錯！

著名菜色
Well-Known Dishes

中式料理

full Manchu-Han banquet
[ˋfʊl mænˋtʃuˏhan ˋbæŋkwɪt]
n. 滿漢全席

豬

雞

roast suckling pig
[rost ˋsʌklɪŋ ˋpɪg]
n. 烤乳豬

drunken chicken
[ˋdrʌŋkən ˋtʃɪkɪn]
n. 醉雞

Mongolian barbecue
[maŋˋgoljən ˋbarbɪˏkju]
n. 蒙古烤肉

kung pao chicken
[ˋkɔŋˏbaʊ ˋtʃɪkɪn]
n. 宮保雞丁

鴨

Peking Duck
[ˋpiˋkɪŋˏdʌk]
n. 北京烤鴨

大 師
小叮嚀 ✐ Suckling 指的是仍在吃母乳的幼獸。

猪肉料理

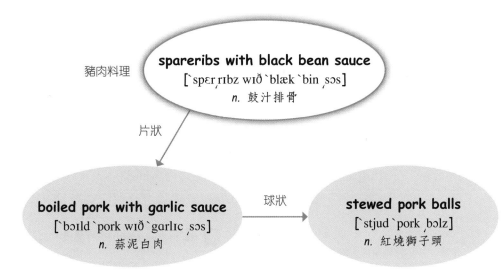

spareribs with black bean sauce
[`spɛr͵rɪbz wɪð `blæk `bin ͵sɔs]
n. 鼓汁排骨

片狀

boiled pork with garlic sauce
[`bɔɪld `pork wɪð `garlɪc ͵sɔs]
n. 蒜泥白肉

球狀

stewed pork balls
[`stjud `pork ͵bɔlz]
n. 紅燒獅子頭

魚類料理

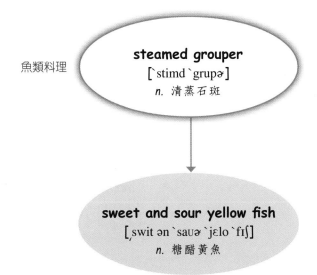

steamed grouper
[`stimd `grupɚ]
n. 清蒸石斑

sweet and sour yellow fish
[͵swit ən `sauɚ `jɛlo `fɪʃ]
n. 糖醋黃魚

大師小叮嚀 🗨 從上列單字可以推出「糖醋排骨」怎麼說嗎？答案就是 sweet and sour spareribs。

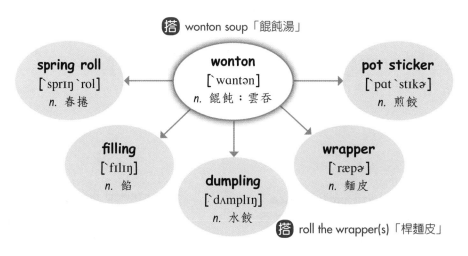

搭 wonton soup「餛飩湯」

wonton
[`wɑntən]
n. 餛飩；雲吞

spring roll
[`sprɪŋ `rol]
n. 春捲

pot sticker
[`pɑt `stɪkə]
n. 煎餃

filling
[`fɪlɪŋ]
n. 餡

dumpling
[`dʌmplɪŋ]
n. 水餃

wrapper
[`ræpə]
n. 麵皮

搭 roll the wrapper(s)「桿麵皮」

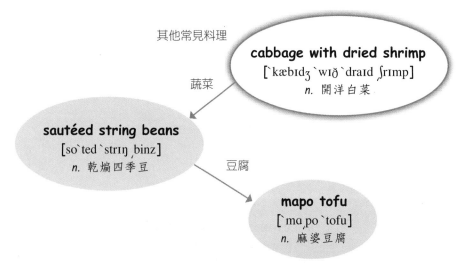

其他常見料理

cabbage with dried shrimp
[`kæbɪdʒ `wɪð `draɪd `ʃrɪmp]
n. 開洋白菜

蔬菜

sautéed string beans
[so`ted `strɪŋ ˌbinz]
n. 乾煸四季豆

豆腐

mapo tofu
[`mɑˌpo `tofu]
n. 麻婆豆腐

大師小叮嚀

➾ Sauté [so`te] 是嫩煎或炒。

➾ 水餃或包子的內餡為 filling；壽司、pizza 或冰淇淋上的餡料為 topping；沙拉上的醬料則為 dressing。

➾ 水餃常會沾醬食用，可用搭配詞 dig in the sauce「沾醬」來表示。

日本料理

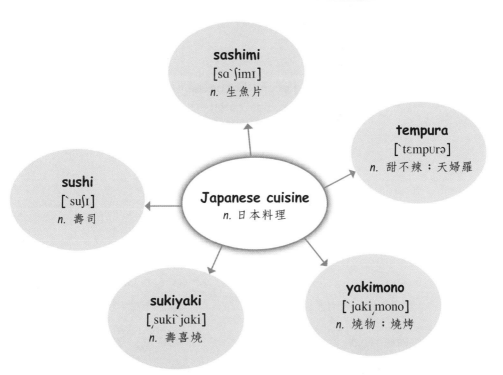

sashimi
[sɑˋʃɪmɪ]
n. 生魚片

tempura
[ˋtɛmpʊrə]
n. 甜不辣；天婦羅

sushi
[ˋsuʃɪ]
n. 壽司

Japanese cuisine
n. 日本料理

sukiyaki
[ˌsukiˋjaki]
n. 壽喜燒

yakimono
[ˋjakiˌmono]
n. 燒物；燒烤

大師
小叮嚀

- Sushi 是由 vinegared rice（用醋浸泡過的米飯）製作而成，可分成很多種：
  1. 用海苔包飯捲起，再切成一小圈的捲壽司為 maki-sushi 或 rolls。
  2. 飯上面有生海鮮的握壽司為 nigiri-sushi。
  3. 稻荷（豆皮）壽司為 inari-sushi。
  4. 手捲為 temaki-sushi（或 hand roll）。
  5. 加州捲 (california roll) 的外圍常包裹橘色魚卵，內餡有海鮮、蔬菜。
- 燒物指的即為「燒烤類食物」。
- 壽喜燒的材料主要以牛肉、青蔥、蔬菜、蒟蒻、豆腐為主，在鍋中以醬汁烹煮。

韓國料理

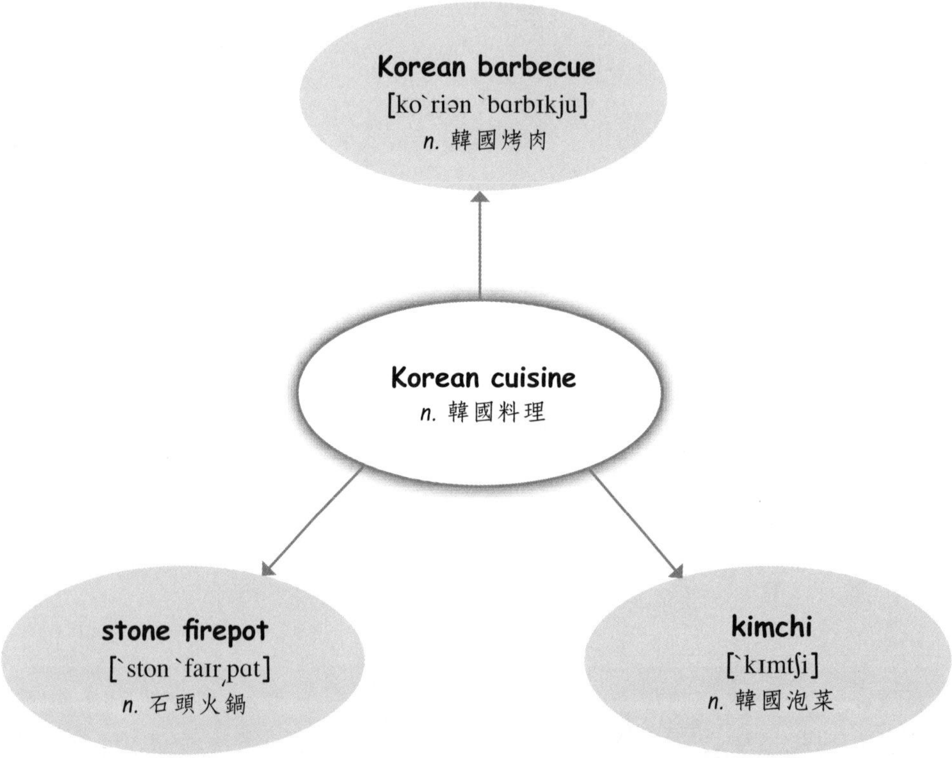

Korean barbecue
[koˋriən ˋbɑrbɪkju]
n. 韓國烤肉

Korean cuisine
n. 韓國料理

stone firepot
[ˋston ˋfaɪrˌpɑt]
n. 石頭火鍋

kimchi
[ˋkɪmtʃi]
n. 韓國泡菜

義式料理

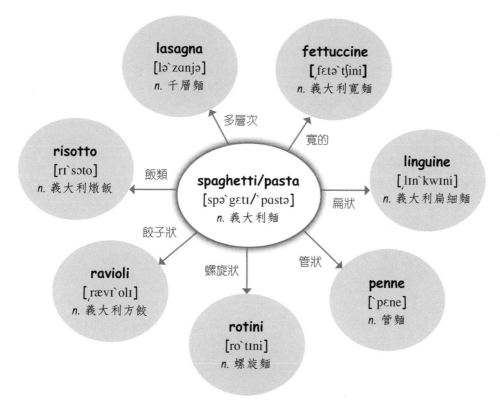

lasagna
[lə`zɑnjə]
n. 千層麵

fettuccine
[ˌfɛtə`tʃini]
n. 義大利寬麵

risotto
[rɪ`sɔto]
n. 義大利燉飯

spaghetti/pasta
[spə`gɛtɪ/`pastə]
n. 義大利麵

linguine
[ˌlɪn`kwɪni]
n. 義大利扁細麵

ravioli
[ˌrævɪ`olɪ]
n. 義大利方餃

rotini
[ro`tɪni]
n. 螺旋麵

penne
[`pɛne]
n. 管麵

多層次
寬的
飯類
扁狀
餃子狀
螺旋狀
管狀

法式料理

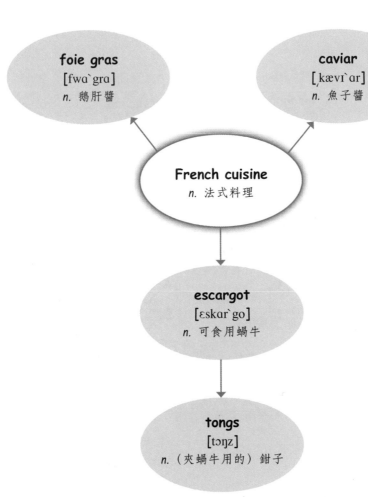

foie gras
[fwɑˋgrɑ]
n. 鵝肝醬

caviar
[͵kævɪˋɑr]
n. 魚子醬

French cuisine
n. 法式料理

escargot
[ɛskɑrˋgo]
n. 可食用蝸牛

tongs
[tɔŋz]
n.（夾蝸牛用的）鉗子

墨西哥料理

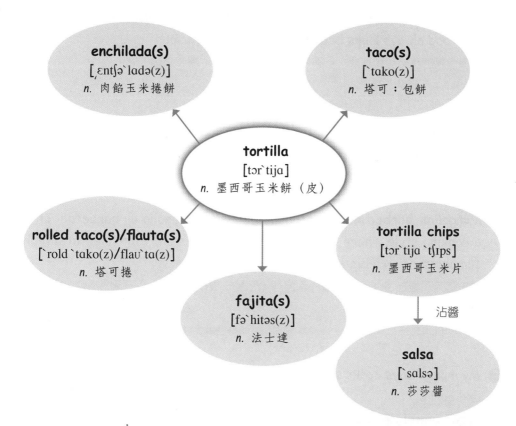

enchilada(s)
[ˌɛntʃəˈlɑdə(z)]
n. 肉餡玉米捲餅

taco(s)
[ˈtɑko(z)]
n. 塔可；包餅

tortilla
[tɔrˈtija]
n. 墨西哥玉米餅（皮）

rolled taco(s)/flauta(s)
[ˈrold ˈtɑko(z)/flauˈtɑ(z)]
n. 塔可捲

fajita(s)
[fəˈhitəs(z)]
n. 法士達

tortilla chips
[tɔrˈtija ˈtʃɪps]
n. 墨西哥玉米片

沾醬

salsa
[ˈsɑlsə]
n. 莎莎醬

 大師 小叮嚀

- Salsa 是一種以蕃茄和洋蔥做成的辣味醬汁，吃玉米脆片時常會搭配食用。
- Enchilada 和 taco 都是用玉米餅或麵皮包裹內餡的墨西哥食物。前者狀似春捲；後者則有點像韭菜盒子。
- Fajita（法士達）是用 tortilla 做為外皮，食用時加上青椒、肉、洋蔥……等內餡包裹而成。

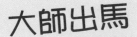

① The materials used to cook a **full Manchu-Han banquet** are varied, but the food always looks beautiful and tastes delicious.

滿漢全席的食材包羅萬象，但食物總是看起來漂亮，嚐起來也美味。

（varied *adj.* 各式各樣的）

② **Peking Duck** is famous for its thin and crispy skin.

北京烤鴨以又薄又脆的鴨皮聞名。

（crispy *adj.* 酥脆的）

③ **Mongolian barbecue** has nothing to do with Mongolia or barbecue. It is a cooking style where the meat and vegetables are stir-fried at a high temperature on a big iron griddle.

蒙古烤肉和蒙古及烤肉一點關係都沒有。它是一種在大鐵鍋上以高溫翻炒肉和蔬菜的烹調方式。

（griddle *n.* 淺鍋）

④ My mom always cooks **sweet and sour yellow fish** with ketchup, vinegar, and garlic.

我媽媽都用番茄醬、醋和大蒜來料理糖醋黃魚。

⑤ Many materials can be used for **wonton** and **dumpling fillings**. Some options are Chinese cabbage, leek, pork, or shrimp.

許多食材都可做為雲吞和水餃的餡料，白菜、韭菜、豬肉或蝦子是其中一些選擇。

（leek *n.* 韭蔥）

❻ When it comes to Japanese cuisine, **sashimi** is often the first thing that comes to mind.

每當提到日本美食，總是第一個想到生魚片。

❼ **Kimchi** is rich in vitamins and calcium, and it also contains dietary fiber, all of which have well-known health benefits.

泡菜含有豐富維他命、鈣質和膳食纖維，這些對健康都有為人熟知的好處。

（dietary fiber *n.* 膳食纖維）

❽ **Escargot** is a dish of cooked snails that are eaten with a special snail fork and snail **tongs**.

法式蝸牛是用特殊叉子和鉗子來食用的蝸牛料理。

❾ **Enchiladas** are made by wrapping **tortillas** around a **filling** of meat, vegetables, or cheese.

墨西哥捲餅是以玉米薄餅包裹肉、蔬菜或起士等內餡製成的。

❿ **Lasagna** is an Italian dish made with layers of pasta, cheese, and sauce.

千層麵是一種用層層麵皮、起士和醬汁做成的義大利麵食。

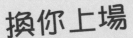 

☞ *Exercise* ······ 根據你所聽到的對話完成填空。

(Tina and Evelyn are in a Japanese restaurant.)

Tina: Wow, all the food on the menu looks so delicious! What are we going to order? The 1. 生魚片 looks fresh and I heard the 2. 天婦羅 is tasty, too.

Evelyn: How about some 3. 壽司 ? I'd like to eat some cold food first. We shouldn't eat cold and hot food at the same time though. It's bad for our stomachs.

Tina: Do you want some 4. 握壽司 ? That way we can have rice and sashimi together.

Evelyn: 4. 握壽司 is fine. I'd like some 5. 豆皮壽司 and a 6. 鰻魚手捲 as well.

(While waiting)

Tina: My cousins came back from Canada on their summer vacation last week and I took them to a 7. 中國餐廳 yesterday.

Evelyn: Had they ever had 8. 中國菜 ?

Tina: They sometimes eat 9. 水餃 , 10. 鍋貼 , or 11. 雲吞 . But they eat 12. 速食 most of the time.

Evelyn: You mean 13. 漢堡、薯條 and things like that? Wow! 14. 那類食物膽固醇很高喔 , and 15. 可能會造成心血管疾病 .

Tina: Yup. That's why my aunt has started to teach them how to cook, so they can make some 16. 清淡的食物 for themselves.

Evelyn: What did you eat yesterday?

Tina: Some traditional Chinese food: 17. 宮保雞丁 , 18. 紅燒獅子頭 , and 19. 麻婆豆腐 .

Evelyn: Do you like Chinese food? I like 20. 墨西哥菜 better. It's a little spicy, but really flavorful. I like to eat 21. 雞肉捲餅 and 22. 鱷梨沙拉醬 .

Tina: Hey, the food is here. I guess we should start eating before it gets cold.

Evelyn: It's already cold!

☞ *Answer key* ┈┈┈┈┈┈┈┈┈┈┈┈┈┈┈┈┈┈┈┈┈┈┈┈┈┈┈┈

1. sashimi

2. tempura

3. sushi

4. nigiri-sushi

5. inari-sushi

6. eel temaki-sushi

7. Chinese restaurant

8. Chinese food

9. dumplings

10. pot stickers

11. wontons

12. fast food

13. hamburgers and fries

14. Foods like that are high in cholesterol

15. that could lead to cardiovascular diseases

16. light food

17. kung pao chicken

18. stewed pork balls

19. mapo tofu

20. Mexican food

21. chicken enchiladas

22. guacamole

↩ 中譯

(*Tina* 和 *Evelyn* 在日式餐廳用餐。)

Tina： 哇！菜單上的食物看起來都好好吃喔！我們要點些什麼呢？生魚片很新鮮，聽說天婦羅也很好吃！

Evelyn： 來點壽司如何？我想先吃點冷的食物，冷食跟熱食最好不要一起吃，這樣對胃不好。

Tina： 妳要握壽司嗎？那樣就可以一起吃到飯和生魚片！

Evelyn： 好啊，點握壽司，我還要豆皮壽司跟鰻魚手捲。

(等待餐點的時候。)

Tina： 我表兄妹上星期從加拿大回來過暑假，我昨天帶他們去一間中國餐廳用餐。

Evelyn： 他們吃過中國菜嗎？

Tina： 他們有時候會吃水餃、鍋貼或雲吞，但他們最常吃的還是速食。

Evelyn： 妳是指漢堡、薯條之類的東西嗎？哇！那些膽固醇很高喔，可能會造成心血管疾病。

Tina： 對啊！所以我阿姨最近開始教他們做菜，這樣他們就可以替自己煮一些清淡的食物。

Evelyn： 妳們昨天吃了什麼？

Tina： 一些傳統中式料理：宮保雞丁、紅燒獅子頭和麻婆豆腐。

Evelyn： 妳喜歡中國菜嗎？我比較喜歡墨西哥菜，有點辣，但是很好吃。我喜歡雞肉捲餅和酪梨沙拉醬。

Tina： 嘿，菜來了。我想我們該開動了，不然它們會冷掉。

Evelyn： 它們本來就是冷的啊！

零嘴和點心
Goodies & Desserts

蜜餞

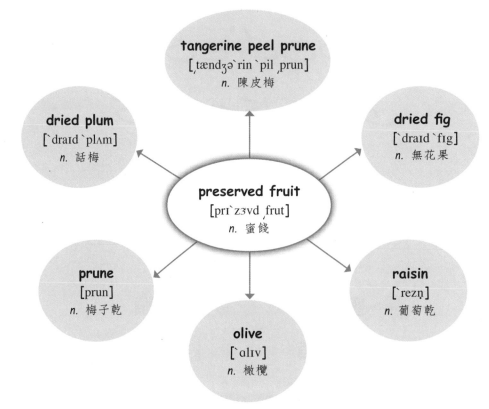

tangerine peel prune
[ˌtændʒəˈrin ˈpil ˌprun]
n. 陳皮梅

dried fig
[ˈdraɪd ˈfɪg]
n. 無花果

dried plum
[ˈdraɪd ˈplʌm]
n. 話梅

preserved fruit
[prɪˈzɝvd ˌfrut]
n. 蜜餞

prune
[prun]
n. 梅子乾

raisin
[ˈrezn̩]
n. 葡萄乾

olive
[ˈɑlɪv]
n. 橄欖

 大 師 小叮嚀 ☞ 蜜餞的製作通常是將水果以特殊方式除去水分、醃漬或以糖汁包裹，使其得以保存較久時間，所以稱為 *preserved fruit*、*candied fruit* 或 *glacé fruit*。

乾果類

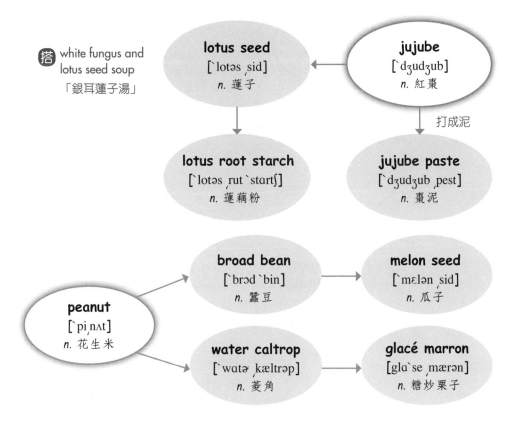

搭 white fungus and lotus seed soup
「銀耳蓮子湯」

lotus seed
[`lotəs ˌsid]
n. 蓮子

jujube
[`dʒudʒub]
n. 紅棗

lotus root starch
[`lotəs ˌrut `startʃ]
n. 蓮藕粉

打成泥

jujube paste
[`dʒudʒub ˌpest]
n. 棗泥

broad bean
[`brɔd `bin]
n. 蠶豆

melon seed
[`mɛlən ˌsid]
n. 瓜子

peanut
[`piˌnʌt]
n. 花生米

water caltrop
[`watə ˌkæltrəp]
n. 菱角

glacé marron
[glɑ`se ˌmærən]
n. 糖炒栗子

大師小叮嚀

- 一般常見的黑瓜子是特別栽種，做為食用的西瓜子（watermelon seed）；若是向日葵子則為 sunflower seed。
- Jujube 是中藥或調味常用的紅棗，煙燻過後（be smoked）成為黑棗，更具風味。中國糕點中的棗泥內餡就是由黑棗製成。
- Paste 通常指將蔬菜、水果煮爛成泥的糊狀物。

糖果類

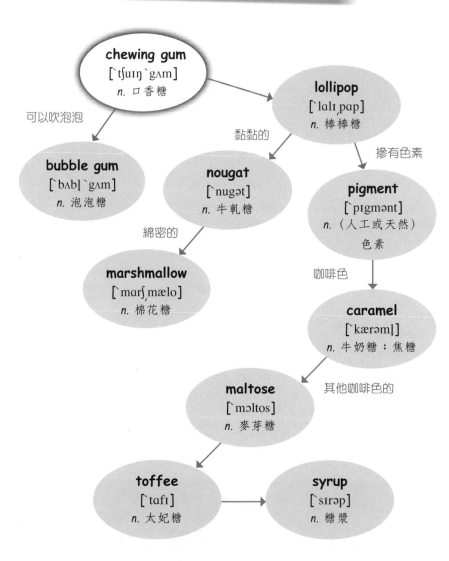

chewing gum
[`tʃuɪŋ `gʌm]
n. 口香糖

lollipop
[`lalɪ͵pap]
n. 棒棒糖

可以吹泡泡

黏黏的

摻有色素

bubble gum
[`bʌbl̩ `gʌm]
n. 泡泡糖

nougat
[`nugət]
n. 牛軋糖

pigment
[`pɪgmənt]
n.（人工或天然）
色素

綿密的

咖啡色

marshmallow
[`marʃ͵mælo]
n. 棉花糖

caramel
[`kærəml̩]
n. 牛奶糖；焦糖

maltose
[`mɔltos]
n. 麥芽糖

其他咖啡色的

toffee
[`tafɪ]
n. 太妃糖

syrup
[`sɪrəp]
n. 糖漿

肉乾類

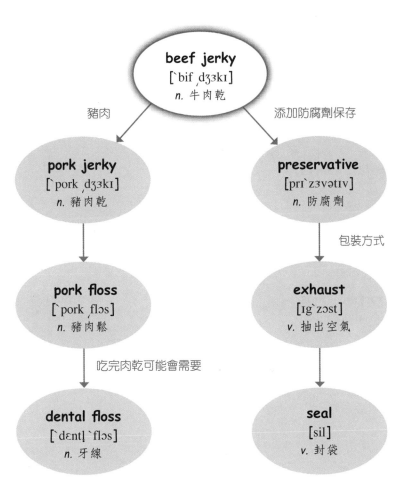

beef jerky
[ˋbif ˏdʒɜkɪ]
n. 牛肉乾

豬肉

添加防腐劑保存

pork jerky
[ˋpork ˏdʒɜkɪ]
n. 豬肉乾

preservative
[prɪˋzɜvətɪv]
n. 防腐劑

包裝方式

pork floss
[ˋpork ˏflɔs]
n. 豬肉鬆

exhaust
[ɪgˋzɔst]
v. 抽出空氣

吃完肉乾可能會需要

dental floss
[ˋdɛntl̩ ˋflɔs]
n. 牙線

seal
[sil]
v. 封袋

脆片類

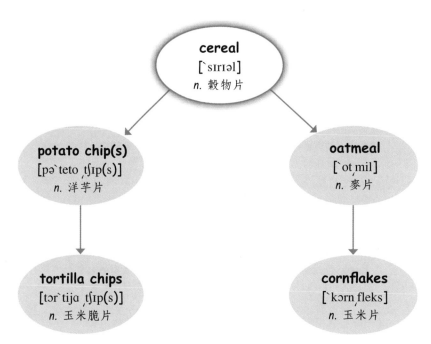

cereal
[ˋsɪrɪəl]
n. 穀物片

potato chip(s)
[pəˋteto ˏtʃɪp(s)]
n. 洋芋片

oatmeal
[ˋot͵mil]
n. 麥片

tortilla chips
[tɔrˋtija ͵tʃɪp(s)]
n. 玉米脆片

cornflakes
[ˋkɔrn͵fleks]
n. 玉米片

餅乾類

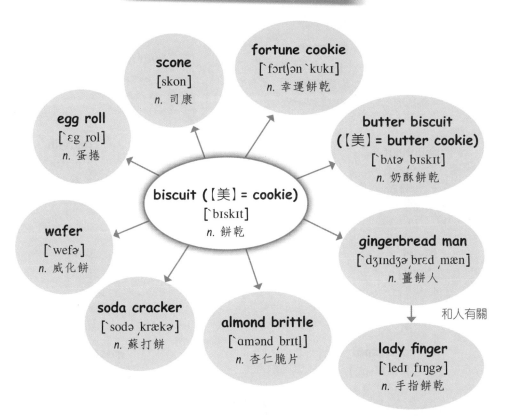

scone
[skon]
n. 司康

fortune cookie
[ˈfɔrtʃən ˈkʊkɪ]
n. 幸運餅乾

egg roll
[ˈɛg ˌrol]
n. 蛋捲

butter biscuit
(【美】= butter cookie)
[ˈbʌtə ˌbɪskɪt]
n. 奶酥餅乾

biscuit (【美】= cookie)
[ˈbɪskɪt]
n. 餅乾

gingerbread man
[ˈdʒɪndʒə ˌbrɛd ˌmæn]
n. 薑餅人

和人有關

wafer
[ˈwefə]
n. 威化餅

soda cracker
[ˈsodə ˌkrækə]
n. 蘇打餅

almond brittle
[ˈɑmənd ˌbrɪtl]
n. 杏仁脆片

lady finger
[ˈledɪ ˌfɪŋgə]
n. 手指餅乾

大師
小叮嚀

- 早餐搭配牛奶食用的現成穀類也叫做 cereal。
- Biscuit 和 scone 在不同國家代表不同的食物。Biscuit 在英國指餅乾（例：英國著名的 digestive biscuit「消化餅」），相當於北美的 cookie 或 cracker；在北美 biscuit 則為速食店常見的附餐 (side dish)，國人常譯為「百斯吉」。而司康 (scone) 則為英式百斯吉，常見於英國下午茶。
- Lady finger 是指狀餅乾，常與 tiramisu「提拉米蘇」搭配食用。
- Egg roll 也可指常當成早餐的煎蛋捲。

糕點、麵包類

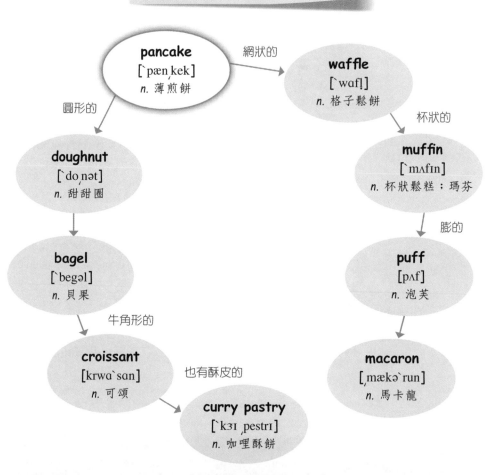

pancake
[ˋpænˌkek]
n. 薄煎餅

網狀的 →

waffle
[ˋwafl̩]
n. 格子鬆餅

圓形的

杯狀的

doughnut
[ˋdoˌnət]
n. 甜甜圈

muffin
[ˋmʌfɪn]
n. 杯狀鬆糕；瑪芬

bagel
[ˋbegəl]
n. 貝果

膨的

puff
[pʌf]
n. 泡芙

牛角形的

croissant
[krwaˋsɑn]
n. 可頌

也有酥皮的

macaron
[ˌmækəˋrun]
n. 馬卡龍

curry pastry
[ˋkɝɪ ˌpestrɪ]
n. 咖哩酥餅

大師小叮嚀

- Pancake 與 waffle 兩者外型不同。前者為薄扁型，蛋餅也稱作 pancake；後者有網狀格紋。
- Muffin 是帶有甜味的杯狀小蛋糕，有人譯為「瑪芬」。
- Macaron 是源於法國的小點心，圓圓膨膨像小餅乾，中間有夾心，在西點麵包店可見到。

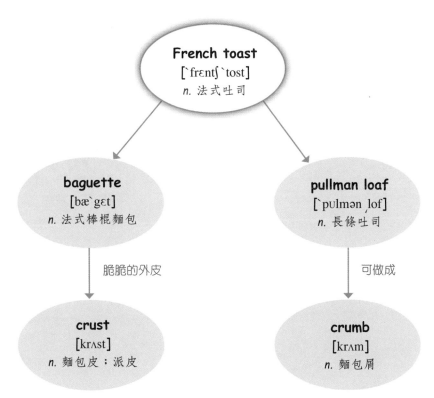

French toast
[ˋfrɛntʃ ˋtost]
n. 法式吐司

baguette
[bæˋgɛt]
n. 法式棒棍麵包

脆脆的外皮

crust
[krʌst]
n. 麵包皮；派皮

pullman loaf
[ˋpʊlmən ˌlof]
n. 長條吐司

可做成

crumb
[krʌm]
n. 麵包屑

大師 小叮嚀

- 法國吐司與我們常吃的吐司不同。法國吐司是將吐司沾裹蛋液再油煎，然後佐以楓糖或糖霜。
- Baguette 常用來做潛艇堡，從中間切開再放入餡料。

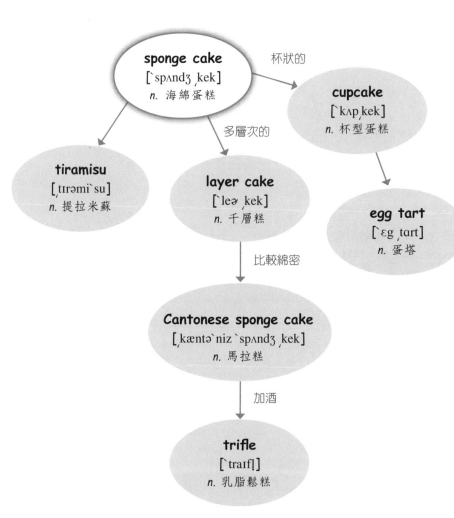

 大師 小叮嚀 | ✎ Trifle 是西方人聖誕夜不可或缺的甜品,通常以酒、水果製成。

冰品類

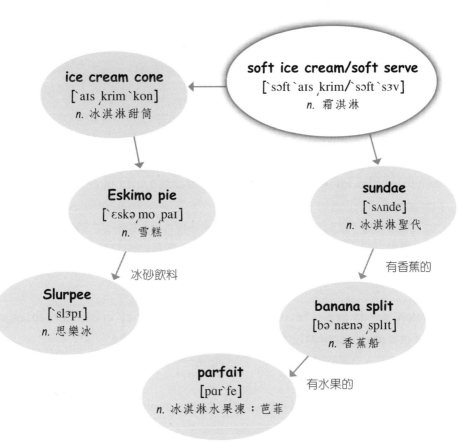

ice cream cone
[ˋaɪsˏkrim ˋkon]
n. 冰淇淋甜筒

soft ice cream/soft serve
[ˋsɔftˋaɪsˏkrim/ˋsɔftˋsɜv]
n. 霜淇淋

Eskimo pie
[ˋɛskəˏmo ˏpaɪ]
n. 雪糕

sundae
[ˋsʌnde]
n. 冰淇淋聖代

冰砂飲料

Slurpee
[ˋslɜpɪ]
n. 思樂冰

有香蕉的

banana split
[bəˋnænəˏsplɪt]
n. 香蕉船

parfait
[parˋfe]
n. 冰淇淋水果凍；芭菲

有水果的

大師
小叮嚀

- ☞ Parfait 是混合冰淇淋和水果等材料的杯裝甜點，源自法文，意思是「完美的」。
- ☞ 包裹冰淇淋的錐形餅乾，北美稱為 cone，英國人稱作 cornet。
- ☞ Eskimo pie 是雪糕創始人的註冊商標，後人沿用來指稱「雪糕」。

① **Jujubes** are used in traditional Chinese medicine and are believed to calm the nerves and purify the blood.

紅棗被使用在傳統中藥當中，一般認為它可以穩定神經和清血。

（calm *v.* 使平靜）

② Although the **olive** and **plum** look similar, they do not belong to the same family. The former has been a source of edible oil since ancient times, whereas the latter has long been fermented into plum wine, plum juice, or jam.

雖然橄欖與梅子看起來很像，但它們不是同一科水果。前者從古早時代就一直是食用油的來源之一；而後者則是長久以來被發酵製為梅酒、梅汁或果醬。

（ferment *v.* 使發酵）

③ **Melon seeds** are a favorite snack in China. They are often eaten with tea and are frequently served at wedding banquets.

瓜子是中國人最喜歡的零嘴之一。它們常搭配茶一起食用，也常作為婚宴點心。

④ After all the air is sucked out, the bag is **sealed** to keep the flavor in.

空氣完全被抽出後，袋子被密封來保持風味。

⑤ Although **marshmallows** tend to be white, they can be made in different colors with the use of food coloring.

雖然棉花糖一般是白色，但可以食用色素加工把它們做成不同顏色。

（tend to *v.* 趨向；趨於）

換你上場

⇨ **Exercise** ······ 根據你所聽到的對話完成填空。

Evelyn: Yummy ...

Tina:　 What are you eating? It smells so good.

Evelyn: I'm eating 1. 甜甜圈 , I just bought them from 2. 對街的商店 . 3. 我可是排了很久的隊才買到的 . What are you reading?

Tina:　 I know that store—it's always full of people. I'm reading a recipe for 4. 提拉米蘇 . Do you know what 5. 手指餅乾 are ?

Evelyn: Of course I do! 6. 妳不記得我超愛吃甜食的嗎 ? It's a kind of cookie that is always eaten with 7. 提拉米蘇 , and, just like the name, it's shaped like rather large, fat fingers. Why don't you make 8. 奶油泡芙 or 9. 瑪芬 ? I like them better.

Tina:　 You like them better?! 10. 拜託 , you like all kinds of 11. 點心 . I bet you would eat anything as long as it was sweet.

Evelyn: Maybe you're right!

Tina:　 12. 如果妳不節制一點 , your fingers will become as big and fat as 13. 手指餅乾 sooner or later. Anyway, I'm going to the supermarket to get some stuff, do you want to eat anything?

Evelyn: 14. 妳真了解我 .

❧ *Answer key* ··

1. doughnuts
2. the store across the street
3. I had to stand in line for a long time
4. tiramisu
5. lady fingers
6. Don't you remember that I have a sweet tooth
7. tiramisu
8. cream puffs

9. muffins
10. Come on
11. desserts
12. If you don't control yourself
13. lady fingers
14. You know me so well

❧ 中譯 ··

Evelyn： 好好吃喔……

Tina： 妳在吃什麼啊？聞起來好香喔！

Evelyn： 我在吃甜甜圈啊！我在對街的商店買的。我可是排了很久的隊才買到的，妳在看什麼啊？

Tina： 我知道那家店，常常都擠滿了人！我在看提拉米蘇的食譜，妳知道手指餅乾是什麼嗎？

Evelyn： 當然啊！妳不記得我超愛吃甜食的嗎？那是一種經常搭配提拉米蘇吃的餅乾，就像它的名字一樣，看起來像又粗又肥的手指。妳為什麼不做奶油泡芙或瑪芬？我比較喜歡吃這些。

Tina： 妳比較喜歡吃那些？！拜託！妳什麼點心都喜歡吧。我猜只要是甜的，妳應該都會吃。

Evelyn： 妳說的也許沒錯。

Tina： 如果妳不節制一點，妳的手指很快就會像手指餅乾一樣又大又肥。不說了，我要去超級市場買一些東西了，妳要吃什麼嗎？

Evelyn： 妳真了解我。

PART 2

人物
PEOPLE

描述人物
Describing People

人物形象

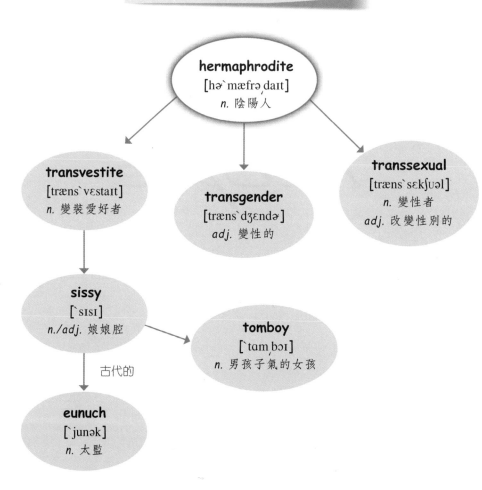

hermaphrodite
[hə`mæfrə,daɪt]
n. 陰陽人

transvestite
[træns`vɛstaɪt]
n. 變裝愛好者

transgender
[træns`dʒɛndə]
adj. 變性的

transsexual
[træns`sɛkʃuəl]
n. 變性者
adj. 改變性別的

sissy
[`sɪsɪ]
n./adj. 娘娘腔

tomboy
[`tam,bɔɪ]
n. 男孩子氣的女孩

古代的

eunuch
[`junək]
n. 太監

大師
小叮嚀

✑ Transvestite 的字首 trans 為「轉換；轉變」之意，vestite 則為「衣服」之意。

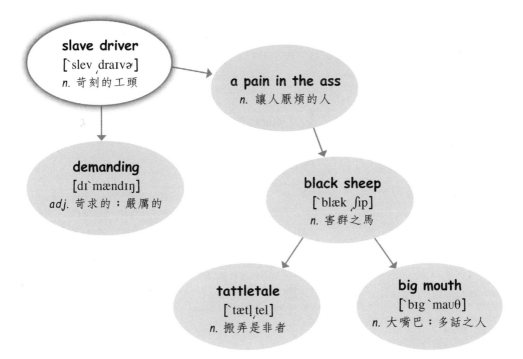

slave driver
[`slev ˌdraɪvɚ]
n. 苛刻的工頭

a pain in the ass
n. 讓人厭煩的人

demanding
[dɪ`mændɪŋ]
adj. 苛求的;嚴厲的

black sheep
[`blæk ʃip]
n. 害群之馬

tattletale
[`tætlˌtel]
n. 搬弄是非者

big mouth
[`bɪg `mauθ]
n. 大嘴巴;多話之人

hedonist
[`hidṇɪst]
n. 享樂主義者

freeloader
[`friˌlodɚ]
n. 白吃白喝的人

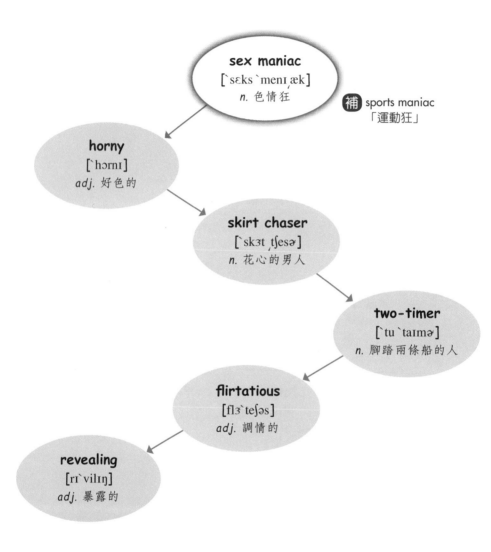

sex maniac
[`sɛks `menɪˌæk]
n. 色情狂

補 sports maniac
「運動狂」

horny
[`hɔrnɪ]
adj. 好色的

skirt chaser
[`skɝt ˌtʃesə]
n. 花心的男人

two-timer
[`tu `taɪmə]
n. 腳踏兩條船的人

flirtatious
[flɝ`teʃəs]
adj. 調情的

revealing
[rɪ`vilɪŋ]
adj. 暴露的

大師小叮嚀

✍ Maniac 是「極端狂熱者」，sex maniac 理所當然是「色情狂」了。

✍ Skirt 是「裙子」，chase 為「追趕」，追著裙子的人指的就是「花心男人」。例：My boyfriend is a skirt chaser.「我男友是個花心的男人。」。

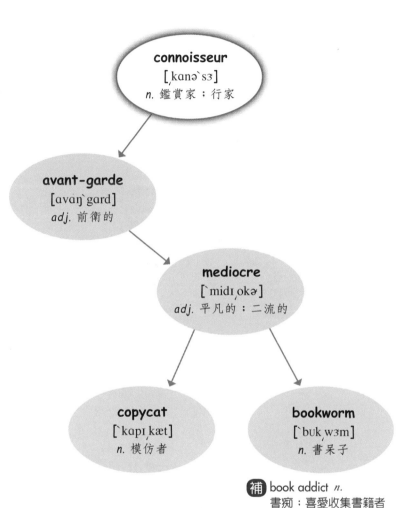

connoisseur
[ˌkɑnəˋsɜ]
n. 鑑賞家；行家

avant-garde
[ɑvɑŋˋgɑrd]
adj. 前衛的

mediocre
[ˋmidɪˌokə]
adj. 平凡的；二流的

copycat
[ˋkɑpɪˌkæt]
n. 模仿者

bookworm
[ˋbʊkˌwɜm]
n. 書呆子

補 book addict n.
書痴；喜愛收集書籍者

大師
小叮嚀 ┃ ✍ Avant-garde 源自法文。例：He is an avant-garde writer.「他是個前衛的作家。」。

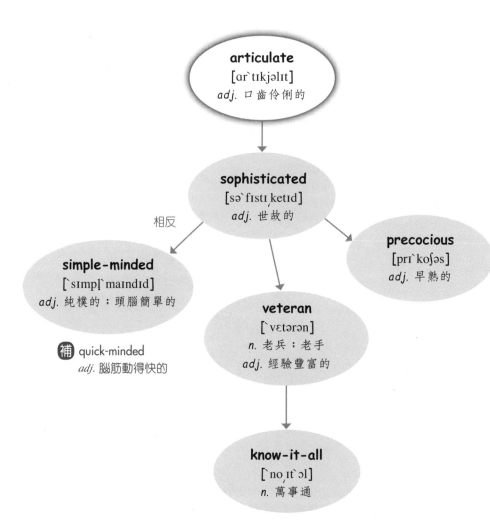

articulate
[ɑr`tɪkjəlɪt]
adj. 口齒伶俐的

sophisticated
[sə`fɪstɪˌketɪd]
adj. 世故的

相反

simple-minded
[`sɪmpl̩`maɪndɪd]
adj. 純樸的；頭腦簡單的

補 quick-minded
adj. 腦筋動得快的

precocious
[prɪ`koʃəs]
adj. 早熟的

veteran
[`vɛtərən]
n. 老兵；老手
adj. 經驗豐富的

know-it-all
[`no͵ɪt`ɔl]
n. 萬事通

 大師
小叮嚀

✐ Precocious 由 pre「在⋯⋯之前」和 cocious「認知」組成，意為「早熟的」。例：He is precocious and polite.「他早熟又有禮貌。」

✐ 如果要說某人為「萬事通小姐」或「萬事通先生」時，可以說 Miss Know-It-All 或 Mr. Know-It-All。

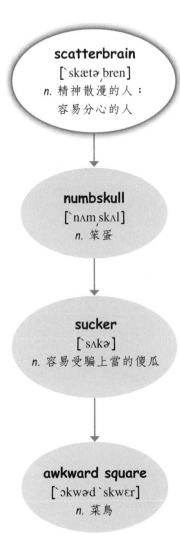

scatterbrain
[ˋskætəˏbren]
n. 精神散漫的人；
容易分心的人

numbskull
[ˋnʌmˏskʌl]
n. 笨蛋

sucker
[ˋsʌkə]
n. 容易受騙上當的傻瓜

awkward square
[ˋɔkwəd ˋskwɛr]
n. 菜鳥

大師
小叮嚀 | ✏ Awkward square 在大部分情況下可用 beginner「生手；初學者」來替換。

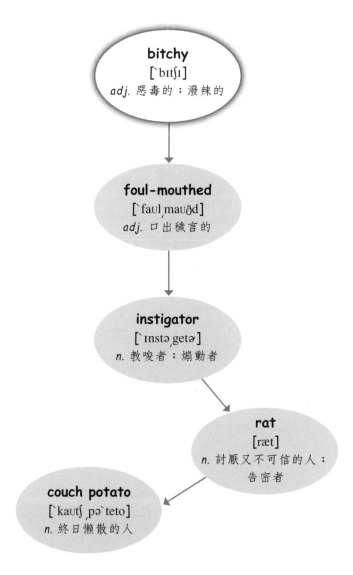

bitchy
[`bɪtʃɪ]
adj. 惡毒的；潑辣的

foul-mouthed
[`faʊl͵maʊðd]
adj. 口出穢言的

instigator
[`ɪnstə͵getə]
n. 教唆者；煽動者

rat
[ræt]
n. 討厭又不可信的人；
告密者

couch potato
[`kaʊtʃ͵pə`teto]
n. 終日懶散的人

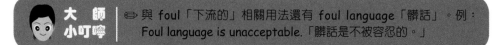

大師
小叮嚀｜☞ 與 foul「下流的」相關用法還有 foul language「髒話」。例：
Foul language is unacceptable.「髒話是不被容忍的。」

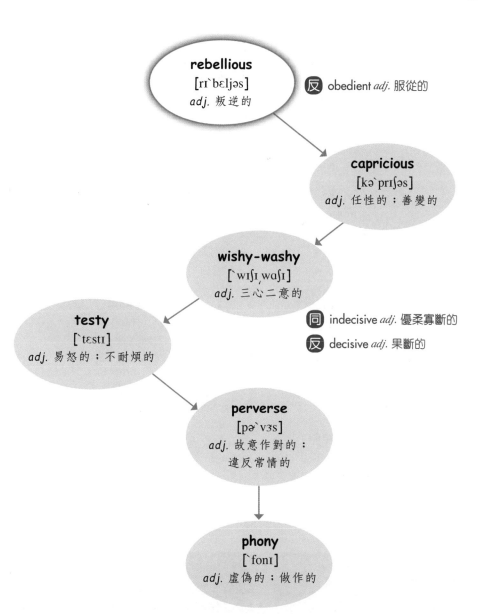

rebellious
[rɪˋbɛljəs]
adj. 叛逆的

反 obedient adj. 服從的

capricious
[kəˋprɪʃəs]
adj. 任性的；善變的

wishy-washy
[ˋwɪʃɪˏwɑʃɪ]
adj. 三心二意的

同 indecisive adj. 優柔寡斷的
反 decisive adj. 果斷的

testy
[ˋtɛstɪ]
adj. 易怒的；不耐煩的

perverse
[pɚˋvɝs]
adj. 故意作對的；
違反常情的

phony
[ˋfonɪ]
adj. 虛偽的；做作的

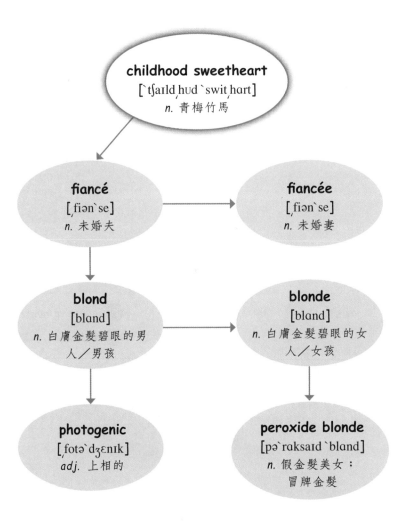

大師
小叮嚀

✏ Peroxide 是「雙氧水」。要將頭髮染成金色，常需先用雙氧水把深色頭髮漂淡再上色。

✏ 現在大多已用 blond 來指稱男女兩性，不再細分 blonde 和 blond。

✏ Photo 是「相片」，genic 是「有遺傳基因」之意。「有相片的基因」即為「上相」之意。

大師出馬

① Money, fame, and lots of free time can turn anyone into a **hedonist**.

金錢、聲譽和諸多閒暇能使任何人變成享樂主義者。

---

② Parents and teachers shouldn't shirk the responsibility of disciplining **rebellious** teenagers.

家長和師長都不應推卸教養叛逆青少年的責任。

(shirk the responsibility *ph.* 推卸責任)

---

③ Be a peacemaker instead of an **instigator** when coping with conflicts between your son and daughter-in-law.

處理兒子和媳婦的衝突時,一定要當和事佬而不是煽風點火者。

(cope with *ph.* 處理)

---

④ See that woman wearing that **revealing** backless dress? It's hard not to stare at her.

有看見那個穿著暴露露背裝的女生嗎?很難不盯著她瞧呢。

(backless *adj.* 露背的)

---

⑤ My grandmother thinks that Taipei is full of criminals, drunks and **sex maniacs**.

我奶奶覺得台北是個充滿罪犯、醉漢和色情狂的地方。

❻ You'd better stay away from Bob—he's a little **testy** this morning.
你最好離鮑伯遠一點，他今天早上有一點焦躁。

❼ My boyfriend may be **capricious**, but at least he isn't a **skirt chaser** like yours.
我男友或許善變，但至少他不像你男友是個花心大少。

❽ She's always making up **phony** excuses for being late.
她總是為遲到編造藉口。

❾ Mimiocorp are **copycats**. They often infringe on other people's patent rights and haven't had an original idea in ten years.
Mimiocorp 是抄襲者。他們經常侵犯他人的專利權，而且已經十年沒有原創構想了。
（infringe v. 侵犯　　patent right n. 專利權）

換你上場

學習成效知分曉！

☞ *Exercise* ......請依「Word Bank」的單字提示，在空格上填入適當字母，使橫、縱向表格都成為有意義的單字。

Word Bank

foul-mouthed, freeloader, rebellious, connoisseur, sex maniac, sophisticated, veteran, tomboy, demanding, skirt chaser

☞ *Answer key* ⋯⋯⋯⋯⋯⋯⋯⋯⋯⋯⋯⋯⋯⋯⋯⋯⋯⋯⋯⋯⋯⋯⋯⋯⋯⋯⋯⋯⋯

															f			
				c					s						r			
			f	o	u	l	-	m	o	u	t	h	e	d				
				n					p			o			e			
				n					h			m			l			
	r	e	b	e	l	l	i	o	u	s		b			o			
				i					i			o			a			
s	k	i	r	t	c	h	a	s	e	r		y			d			s
				s					t						e			e
			v	e	t	e	r	a	n						r			x
				u					c									m
				r					a									a
							d	e	m	a	n	d	i	n	g			i
									d									a
																		c

身體疾病
Physical Diseases

頭部、腦部

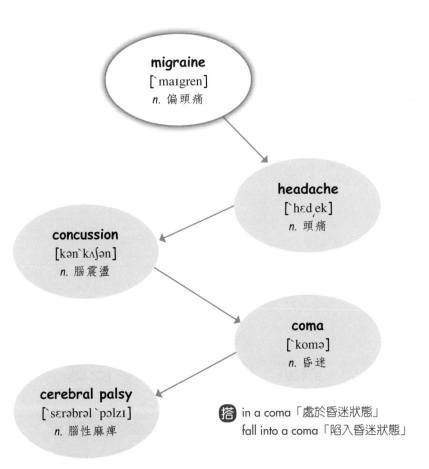

migraine
[ˋmaɪɡren]
n. 偏頭痛

headache
[ˋhɛdˏek]
n. 頭痛

concussion
[kənˋkʌʃən]
n. 腦震盪

coma
[ˋkomə]
n. 昏迷

cerebral palsy
[ˋsɛrəbrəl ˋpɔlzɪ]
n. 腦性麻痺

搭 in a coma「處於昏迷狀態」
fall into a coma「陷入昏迷狀態」

 大師小叮嚀 | ✐ Coma「昏迷」的使用範例如下：She was in a coma.「她處於昏迷狀態。」，She fell into a coma.「她陷入昏迷狀態。」

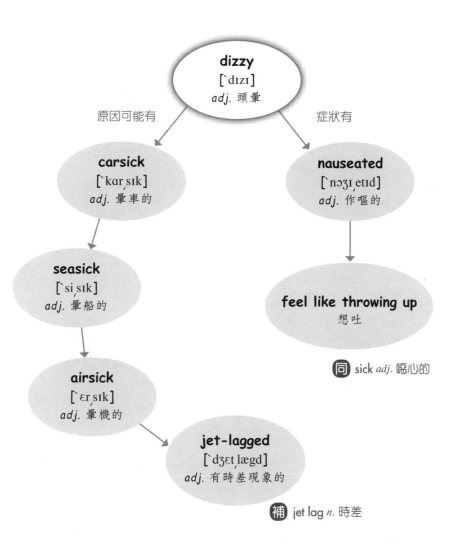

dizzy
[ˋdɪzɪ]
adj. 頭暈

原因可能有

症狀有

carsick
[ˋkɑrˏsɪk]
adj. 暈車的

nauseated
[ˋnɔzɪˏetɪd]
adj. 作嘔的

seasick
[ˋsiˏsɪk]
adj. 暈船的

feel like throwing up
想吐

airsick
[ˋɛrˏsɪk]
adj. 暈機的

同 sick *adj.* 噁心的

jet-lagged
[ˋdʒɛtˏlægd]
adj. 有時差現象的

補 jet lag *n.* 時差

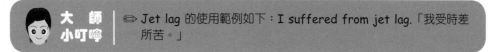

大師
小叮嚀 | ✑ Jet lag 的使用範例如下：I suffered from jet lag. 「我受時差所苦。」

眼睛

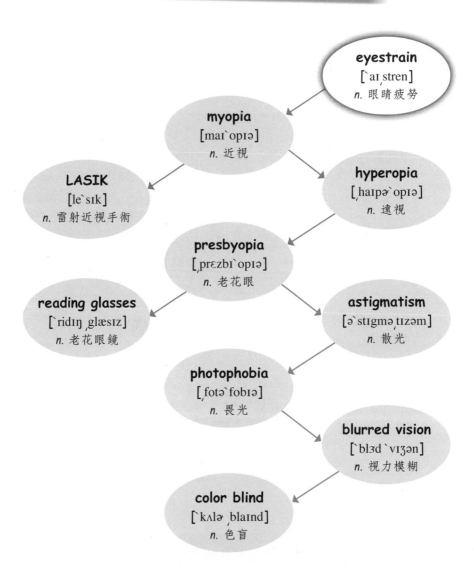

eyestrain
[`aɪ͵stren]
n. 眼睛疲勞

myopia
[maɪ`opɪə]
n. 近視

hyperopia
[͵haɪpəˋopɪə]
n. 遠視

LASIK
[le`sɪk]
n. 雷射近視手術

presbyopia
[͵prɛzbɪˋopɪə]
n. 老花眼

reading glasses
[`ridɪŋ ͵glæsɪz]
n. 老花眼鏡

astigmatism
[əˋstɪgmə͵tɪzəm]
n. 散光

photophobia
[͵fotəˋfobɪə]
n. 畏光

blurred vision
[`blɜd `vɪʒən]
n. 視力模糊

color blind
[`kʌlə ͵blaɪnd]
n. 色盲

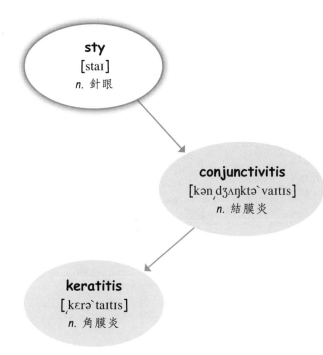

sty
[staɪ]
n. 針眼

conjunctivitis
[kənˌdʒʌŋktəˈvaɪtɪs]
n. 結膜炎

keratitis
[ˌkɛrəˈtaɪtɪs]
n. 角膜炎

大師
小叮嚀

✏ Myopia 也可稱作 nearsightedness，nearsighted 則是形容詞。
例：She is nearsighted.「她有近視。」

✏ Hyperopia 也可稱作 farsightedness，farsighted 則是形容詞。

✏ Blurred vision 的用法為：I have blurred vision.「我眼花了。」也可說成：My vision is blurred.

骨頭

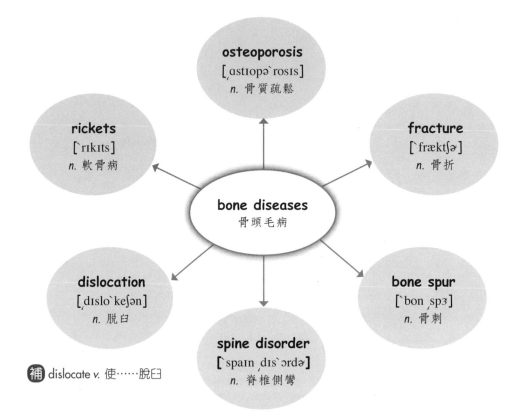

osteoporosis
[ˌɑstɪopəˈrosɪs]
n. 骨質疏鬆

rickets
[ˈrɪkɪts]
n. 軟骨病

fracture
[ˈfræktʃə]
n. 骨折

bone diseases
骨頭毛病

dislocation
[ˌdɪsloˈkeʃən]
n. 脫臼

bone spur
[ˈbon ˌspɝ]
n. 骨刺

spine disorder
[ˈspaɪn dɪsˈɔrdə]
n. 脊椎側彎

補 dislocate *v.* 使⋯⋯脫臼

大師
小叮嚀 | ✑ Dislocation 也可以如下表示：My shoulder is dislocated.
「我肩膀脫臼了。」

呼吸系統

cold
[kold]
n. 感冒

flu
[flu]
n. 流感

stuffy nose
[ˋstʌfɪ ˋnoz]
n. 鼻塞

補 stuffy *adj.* 塞住的

上呼吸道

pneumonia
[njuˋmonjə]
n. 肺炎

nosebleed
[ˋnoz͵blid]
n. 流鼻血

補 bleed *v.* 流血

bronchitis
[branˋkaɪtɪs]
n. 支氣管炎

asthma
[ˋæzmə]
n. 氣喘

補 asthmatic *n.* 氣喘患者

大師小叮嚀

- 流感（flu）比一般的感冒（cold）嚴重。
- Nosebleed 中的 bleed 可當動詞使用。例：Your nose is bleeding.「你在流鼻血。」
- Stuffy 為「塞住的」之意，也可用來指「頭昏腦脹」。例：My head is stuffy.「我的頭很昏。」

皮膚

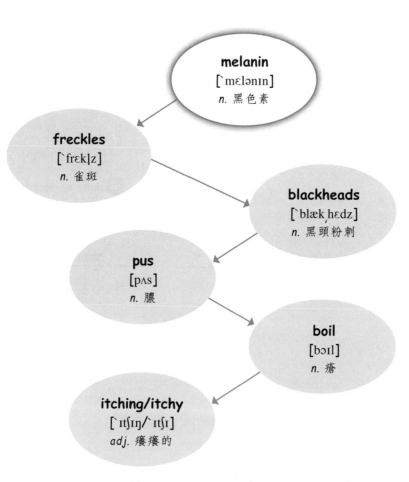

melanin
[`mɛlənɪn]
n. 黑色素

freckles
[`frɛkl̩z]
n. 雀斑

blackheads
[`blæk͵hɛdz]
n. 黑頭粉刺

pus
[pʌs]
n. 膿

boil
[bɔɪl]
n. 瘡

itching/itchy
[`ɪtʃɪŋ/`ɪtʃɪ]
adj. 癢癢的

 大師 小叮嚀 | ☞ 太陽中會有使皮膚變黑的 UV（ultraviolet [͵ʌltrə`vaɪəlɪt] 紫外線），但是皮膚中的 melanin 可保護我們免受陽光的傷害。

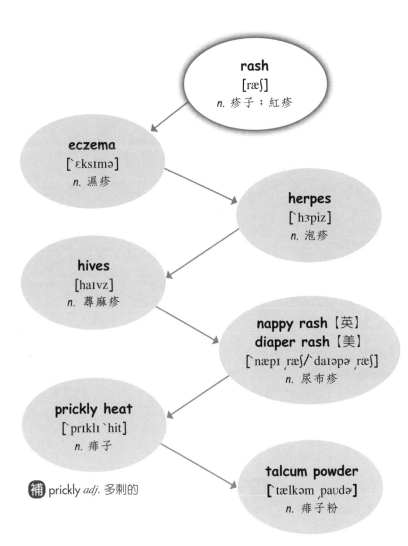

rash
[ræʃ]
n. 疹子；紅疹

eczema
[ˋɛksɪmə]
n. 濕疹

herpes
[ˋhɜpiz]
n. 泡疹

hives
[haɪvz]
n. 蕁麻疹

nappy rash【英】
diaper rash【美】
[ˋnæpɪ ͵ræʃ/ˋdaɪəpə ͵ræʃ]
n. 尿布疹

prickly heat
[ˋprɪklɪ ˋhit]
n. 痱子

補 prickly *adj.* 多刺的

talcum powder
[ˋtælkəm ͵paʊdə]
n. 痱子粉

 大師小叮嚀 ✍ 不管是濕疹、蕁麻疹還是尿布疹，紅紅一片的疹子都可稱為 rash。

心血管

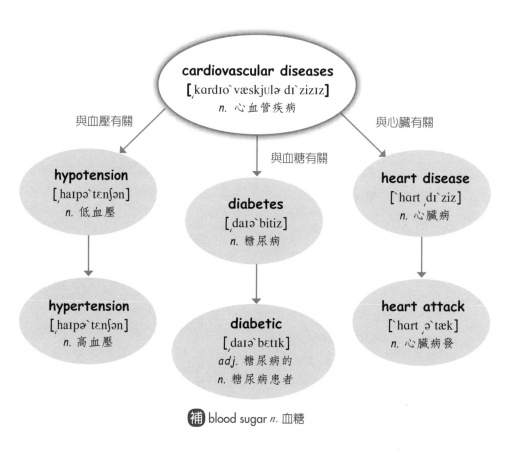

cardiovascular diseases
[ˌkɑrdɪoˋvæskjʊlə dɪˋzizɪz]
n. 心血管疾病

與血壓有關

與血糖有關

與心臟有關

hypotension
[ˌhaɪpəˋtɛnʃən]
n. 低血壓

diabetes
[ˌdaɪəˋbitiz]
n. 糖尿病

heart disease
[ˋhɑrtˌdɪˋziz]
n. 心臟病

hypertension
[ˌhaɪpəˋtɛnʃən]
n. 高血壓

diabetic
[ˌdaɪəˋbɛtɪk]
adj. 糖尿病的
n. 糖尿病患者

heart attack
[ˋhɑrtˌəˋtæk]
n. 心臟病發

補 blood sugar n. 血糖

 大師
小叮嚀

✍ 認識下列字根字首，對於記住這些單字很有幫助：cardio「心臟的」、vascular「血管的」。

✍ Heart attack 的使用範例如下：He had a heart attack last night.「他昨晚心臟病發。」

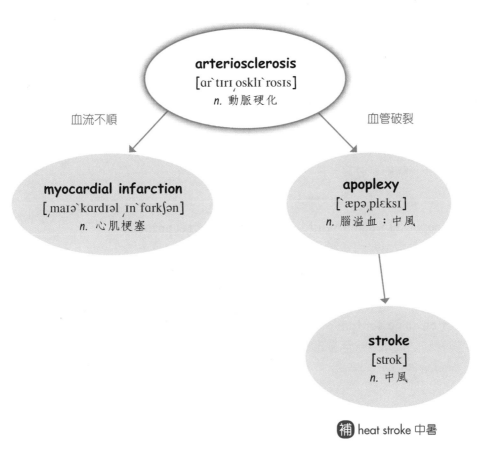

arteriosclerosis
[arˋtɪrɪˌosklɪˋrosɪs]
n. 動脈硬化

血流不順

血管破裂

myocardial infarction
[ˌmaɪəˋkardɪəlˌɪnˋfarkʃən]
n. 心肌梗塞

apoplexy
[ˋæpəˌplɛksɪ]
n. 腦溢血；中風

stroke
[strok]
n. 中風

補 heat stroke 中暑

 大師 小叮嚀　✎ 認識下列字根字首，對於記住這些單字很有幫助：arteri「動脈的」、myo「肌肉的」。

❶ I was jet-lagged and homesick during my first week in the States.
我到美國的第一個禮拜，不但為時差所苦又想家。

❷ Take a little break every hour when you use a computer in order to avoid eyestrain.
使用電腦每隔一小時就要休息一下，才不會眼睛疲勞。
（take a break *ph.* 休息一下）

❸ Menopausal women tend to suffer from osteoporosis.
停經婦女容易罹患骨質疏鬆症。
（menopausal *adj.* 停經的）

❹ Put on some suntan lotion to prevent freckles.
擦一些防曬油以避免長雀斑。
（suntan lotion *n.* 防曬油）

❺ Asthmatics are not able to play strenuous sports.
氣喘病患不能從事激烈運動。
（strenuous *adj.* 激烈的）

❻ Asians are luckier than Caucasians, because they have more **melanin** in their skin to protect them from sun damage.

黃種人比白種人幸運，因為他們的皮膚有較多黑色素來保護他們免於日曬傷害。

（Caucasian *n.* 白種人）

❼ Stay away from greasy foods that can cause **cardiovascular diseases**.

避免吃油膩的食物，會引發心血管疾病。

（greasy foods *n.* 油膩的食物）

❽ My mom noticed a **rash** on my leg. She's sensitive to that kind of thing since she has **eczema too**.

我母親發現我的腿起了紅疹。因為她自己也得了濕疹，所以對這類東西很敏感。

換你上場

⤷ *Exercise* ......將下列選項與正確的定義描述做配合。

Ⓐ melanin   Ⓑ stuffy nose   Ⓒ migraine   Ⓓ diabetic   Ⓔ concussion
Ⓕ stroke   Ⓖ cardiovascular diseases   Ⓗ pus   Ⓘ pimple   Ⓙ freckles

1. (　) Hypertension, hypotension, heart attack, and stroke all belong to this category.

2. (　) Small, dark spots on the face that are caused by exposure to the sun.

3. (　) A painful headache that makes you feel ill.

4. (　) What happens when blood vessels in the brain become blocked or burst.

5. (　) Dark pigment in our skin that helps prevent sun damage.

6. (　) The yellowish liquid in an infected wound.

7. (　) Skin problems that teenagers often endure due to oily skin.

8. (　) Someone who suffers from unstable blood sugar and must be careful about eating sweet foods.

9. (　) If someone feels dizzy, confused, and nauseated after a blow to the head, they may have one of these.

10. (　) If someone has difficulty breathing when he or she gets a cold, it's probably partly due to this.

⤷ *Answer key* ....

1. Ⓖ   2. Ⓙ   3. Ⓒ   4. Ⓕ   5. Ⓐ   6. Ⓗ   7. Ⓘ   8. Ⓓ   9. Ⓔ   10. Ⓑ

精神疾病

Mental Diseases

精神疾病

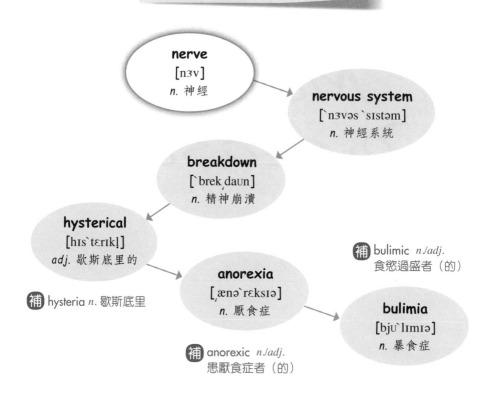

nerve
[nɜv]
n. 神經

nervous system
[`nɜvəs `sɪstəm]
n. 神經系統

breakdown
[`brek͵daʊn]
n. 精神崩潰

hysterical
[hɪs`tɛrɪkl̩]
adj. 歇斯底里的

補 hysteria n. 歇斯底里

anorexia
[͵ænə`rɛksɪə]
n. 厭食症

補 bulimic n./adj.
食慾過盛者（的）

bulimia
[bju`lɪmɪə]
n. 暴食症

補 anorexic n./adj.
患厭食症者（的）

大師小叮嚀

上述幾個補充字的使用範例如下：

☞ As soon as the band took the stage, mass hysteria erupted throughout the arena.
樂隊一上台，整場的群眾便開始歇斯底里。

☞ Bulimics often make themselves throw up or resort to laxatives to control their weight.
暴食症者常會催吐或使用瀉藥來控制體重。

☞ Many anorexics exercise far more than is normal.
許多厭食症者會比平常人過度運動。

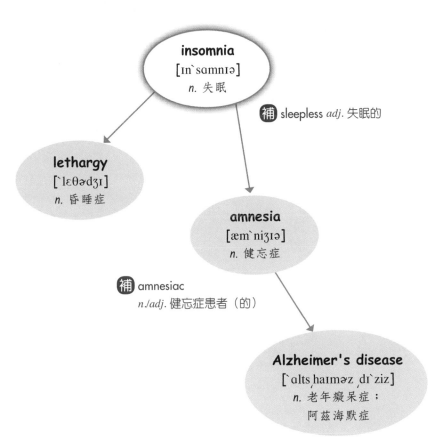

insomnia
[ɪn`sɑmnɪə]
n. 失眠

補 sleepless *adj.* 失眠的

lethargy
[`lɛθədʒɪ]
n. 昏睡症

amnesia
[æm`niʒɪə]
n. 健忘症

補 amnesiac
n./adj. 健忘症患者（的）

Alzheimer's disease
[`ɑltsˌhaɪməzˌdɪ`ziz]
n. 老年癡呆症；
阿茲海默症

 大師 小叮嚀 │ ✏ Amnesiac 可以如下使用：Amnesiacs may forget what they have said just seconds before. 「健忘症患者可能會忘記他們幾秒前說過的話。」

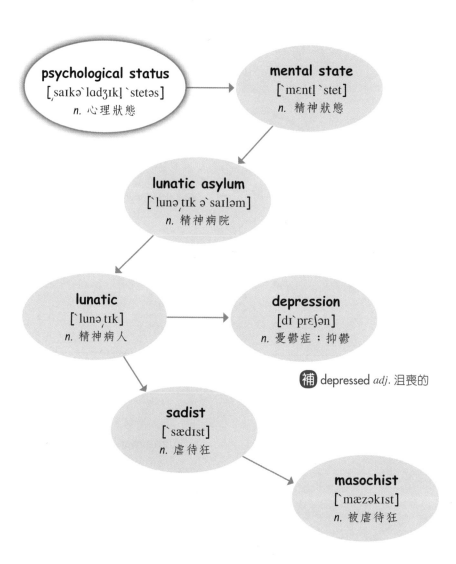

psychological status
[ˌsaɪkəˋladʒɪkl̩ ˋstetəs]
n. 心理狀態

mental state
[ˋmɛntl̩ ˋstet]
n. 精神狀態

lunatic asylum
[ˋlunəˌtɪk əˋsaɪləm]
n. 精神病院

lunatic
[ˋlunəˌtɪk]
n. 精神病人

depression
[dɪˋprɛʃən]
n. 憂鬱症；抑鬱

補 depressed *adj.* 沮喪的

sadist
[ˋsædɪst]
n. 虐待狂

masochist
[ˋmæzəkɪst]
n. 被虐待狂

**大師
小叮嚀** | ✍ Lunatic 原本跟 lunar「月亮」有關。狼人滿月時會變身，月亮讓人聯想到「瘋狂」，所以 lunatic 作為「精神病人」解。

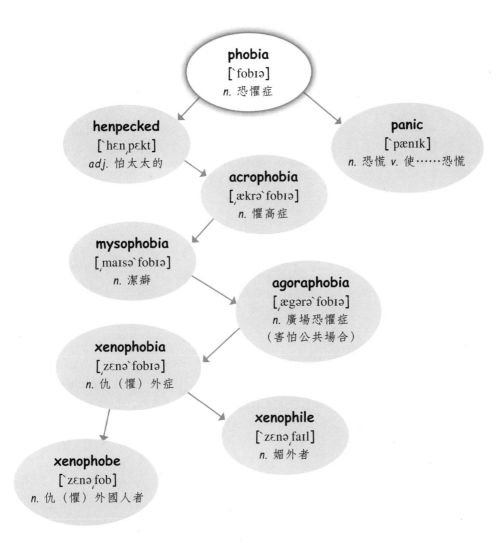

phobia
[`fobɪə]
n. 恐懼症

henpecked
[`hɛn͵pɛkt]
adj. 怕太太的

panic
[`pænɪk]
n. 恐慌 v. 使……恐慌

acrophobia
[͵ækrə`fobɪə]
n. 懼高症

mysophobia
[͵maɪsə`fobɪə]
n. 潔癖

agoraphobia
[͵ægərə`fobɪə]
n. 廣場恐懼症
（害怕公共場合）

xenophobia
[͵zɛnə`fobɪə]
n. 仇（懼）外症

xenophile
[`zɛnə͵faɪl]
n. 媚外者

xenophobe
[`zɛnə͵fob]
n. 仇（懼）外國人者

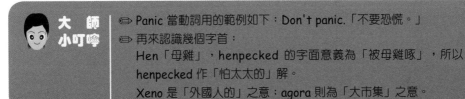

大師
小叮嚀

☞ Panic 當動詞用的範例如下：Don't panic. 「不要恐慌。」
☞ 再來認識幾個字首：
  Hen「母雞」，henpecked 的字面意義為「被母雞啄」，所以
  henpecked 作「怕太太的」解。
  Xeno 是「外國人的」之意；agora 則為「大市集」之意。

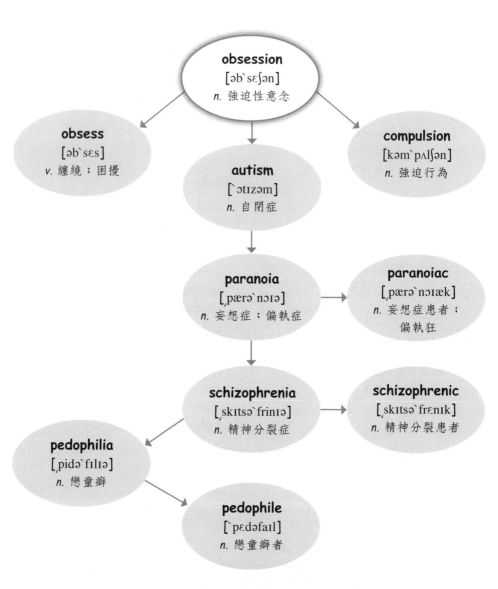

 大師小叮嚀 ☞ Ped 是 child 的字根；philia 則是「喜愛」，所以 pedophilia 指的就是「戀童癖」。

大師出馬

❶ The last thing you should do during an earthquake is become **hysterical**.
地震時你最不該做的就是歇斯底里。
（the last thing *ph.* 最不想要或最不喜歡的事物）

❷ Narcotics damage the human **nervous system**.
毒品損害人類的神經系統。
（narcotic *n.* 毒品）

❸ Repeatedly going on crash diets may lead to **anorexia**.
反覆地過度節食可能會導致厭食症。
（crash *adj.* 速成的　crash diet *n.* 過度節食）

❹ **Autism** is a mental disorder that impairs the sufferer's ability to respond to others.
自閉症是一種精神異常，會使患者無法與他人互動。
（disorder *n.* 失調　impair *v.* 損害）

❺ Unfair immigration laws are often driven by **xenophobia** rather than economic interests.
不公平的移民法通常都是由排外情結造成，而非經濟上的利益。

❻ Recurrent behavior, such as the repeated washing of hands, is one of the common symptoms of **mysophobia**.

重複性行為像是不斷洗手，就是潔癖的特徵之一。

（recurrent *adj.* 一再發生的；定期重複的）

❼ When she discovered that her child was missing, she called the police in a **panic**.

當她發現她的小孩走失，她慌張地報了警。

❽ My parents are **obsessed** with my shortcomings. They only see my weaknesses.

我的父母執著於我的短處，他們只看見我的缺點。

❾ Why are you taking so many classes? Are you a **masochist** or something?

你為什麼修這麼多課，你是被虐狂啊？

換你上場

Exercise ······ 將下列選項與正確的定義描述做配合

Ⓐ hysteria Ⓑ pedophilia Ⓒ lunatic Ⓓ acrophobia Ⓔ depression
Ⓕ autism Ⓖ anorexia Ⓗ agoraphobia Ⓘ henpecked

1. (　) Erratic eating patterns caused by a fear of weight gain

2. (　) Feelings of uneasiness when in places with lots of people

3. (　) Being sexually attracted to children

4. (　) Feelings of sadness and a lack of motivation

5. (　) A person whose behavior is unpredictable and annoying

6. (　) Married men who are nagged and dominated by their wives

7. (　) An irrational fear of heights

8. (　) Uncontrollable outbursts of anger or excitement

9. (　) A condition in which a person is unable to easily communicate emotion to others

Answer key ···

1. Ⓖ　2. Ⓗ　3. Ⓑ　4. Ⓔ　5. Ⓒ　6. Ⓘ　7. Ⓓ　8. Ⓐ　9. Ⓕ

PART 3

生活
LIFE

住 宅

Housing

房屋種類

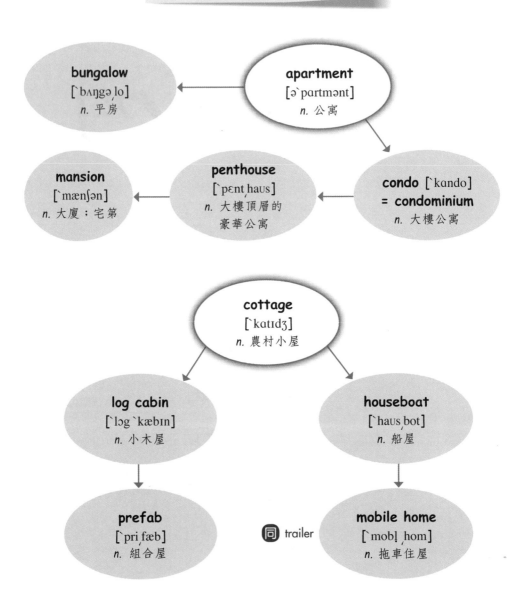

bungalow
[ˋbʌŋɡəˌlo]
n. 平房

apartment
[əˋpɑrtmənt]
n. 公寓

mansion
[ˋmænʃən]
n. 大廈；宅第

penthouse
[ˋpɛntˌhaʊs]
n. 大樓頂層的
豪華公寓

condo [ˋkɑndo]
= condominium
n. 大樓公寓

cottage
[ˋkɑtɪdʒ]
n. 農村小屋

log cabin
[ˋlɔɡ ˋkæbɪn]
n. 小木屋

houseboat
[ˋhaʊsˌbot]
n. 船屋

prefab
[ˋpriˌfæb]
n. 組合屋

同 trailer

mobile home
[ˋmobḷ ˌhom]
n. 拖車住屋

租屋、買屋

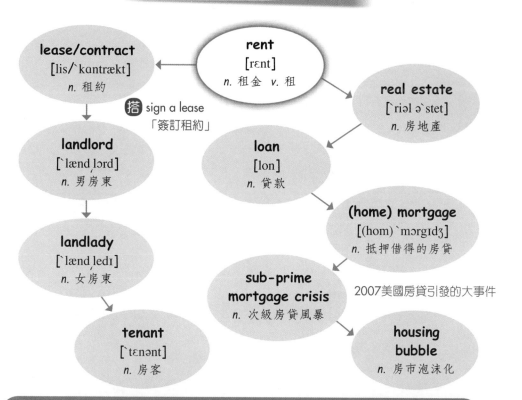

rent
[rɛnt]
n. 租金 *v.* 租

lease/contract
[lis/ˋkɑntrækt]
n. 租約

real estate
[ˋriəl əˋstet]
n. 房地產

搭 sign a lease
「簽訂租約」

landlord
[ˋlænd͵lɔrd]
n. 男房東

loan
[lon]
n. 貸款

landlady
[ˋlænd͵ledɪ]
n. 女房東

(home) mortgage
[(hom) ˋmɔrgɪdʒ]
n. 抵押借得的房貸

sub-prime mortgage crisis
n. 次級房貸風暴

2007美國房貸引發的大事件

tenant
[ˋtɛnənt]
n. 房客

housing bubble
n. 房市泡沫化

大師
小叮嚀

✏ Lease 和 rent 都有「出租」之意，用法也很相似：lease/rent sth. from sb. 「向某人租某物」；lease/rent sth. out to sb. 「出租某物給某人」。在美式英語中，lease 指的是較長期（通常一年以上）的契約。

1) Parts of the building are leased/rented out to students.
這棟房子的一部分出租給學生。

2) Who do you lease/rent the apartment from?
這間公寓你是跟誰租的？

✏ 「有八十萬的房貸」怎麼說？就是 have an $800,000 home loan。

✏ 「車貸」則是 car loan。

房屋各部分

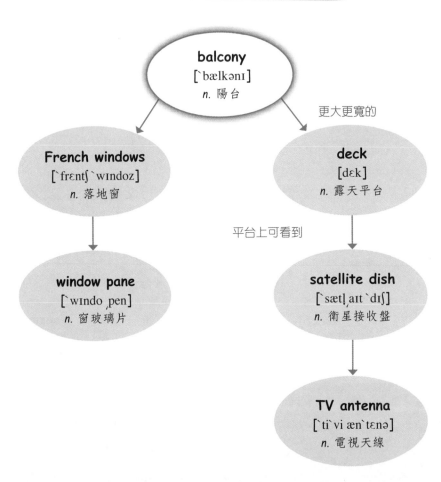

balcony
[`bælkənɪ]
n. 陽台

更大更寬的

French windows
[`frɛntʃ `wɪndoz]
n. 落地窗

deck
[dɛk]
n. 露天平台

平台上可看到

window pane
[`wɪndo ‚pen]
n. 窗玻璃片

satellite dish
[`sætḷ ‚aɪt `dɪʃ]
n. 衛星接收盤

TV antenna
[`ti`vi æn`tɛnə]
n. 電視天線

大師小叮嚀

☞ 獨立住屋入口處的門廊叫做 porch [portʃ]。

☞ 落地窗因為不只一片玻璃，所以 window 要用複數型。

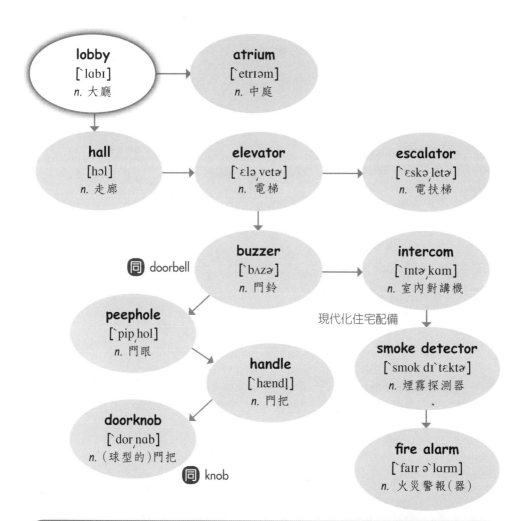

lobby
[ˋlɑbɪ]
n. 大廳

atrium
[ˋetrɪəm]
n. 中庭

hall
[hɔl]
n. 走廊

elevator
[ˋɛləˌvetə]
n. 電梯

escalator
[ˋɛskəˌletə]
n. 電扶梯

buzzer
[ˋbʌzə]
n. 門鈴

同 doorbell

intercom
[ˋɪntəˌkam]
n. 室內對講機

現代化住宅配備

peephole
[ˋpipˌhol]
n. 門眼

handle
[ˋhændl̩]
n. 門把

smoke detector
[ˋsmok dɪˋtɛktə]
n. 煙霧探測器

doorknob
[ˋdorˌnab]
n.（球型的）門把

同 knob

fire alarm
[ˋfaɪr əˋlarm]
n. 火災警報（器）

 大頭小叮嚀

- Detect (*v.*) 是「發現；察覺」，所以 smoke detector 可想而知是用來偵察煙霧的設備。
- Buzzer 和 doorbell 雖然同義，但搭配的動詞不同。「按門鈴」可以說 press the buzzer 或是 ring the doorbell。
- Peephole 的 peep (*v./n.*) 為「窺視；偷看」之意，而「偷窺狂」則是 peeping Tom。
- Doorknob 的 knob 指的就是「球形突出物」。

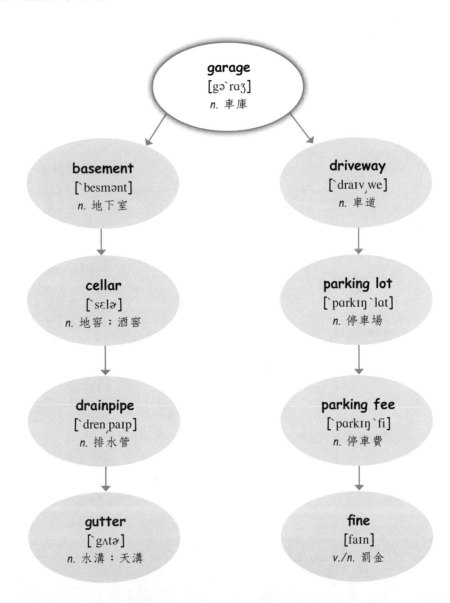

garage
[gə`rɑʒ]
n. 車庫

basement
[`besmənt]
n. 地下室

driveway
[`draɪˌwe]
n. 車道

cellar
[`sɛlə]
n. 地窖；酒窖

parking lot
[`pɑrkɪŋ `lɑt]
n. 停車場

drainpipe
[`drenˌpaɪp]
n. 排水管

parking fee
[`pɑrkɪŋ `fi]
n. 停車費

gutter
[`gʌtə]
n. 水溝；天溝

fine
[faɪn]
v./n. 罰金

 大師
小叮嚀 │ ✑「高額罰金」要如何表示呢？和 heavy 這個字搭配使用即可。例如：be fined (*v.*) heavily「被罰重金」；a heavy fine (*n.*)「高額罰金」。

大師出馬

1 The **real estate** broker found me an apartment with ridiculously high **rent**.

房仲業者幫我找了一間房租高得離譜的公寓。

（ridiculously *adv.* 荒謬地）

2 The **gutters** get flooded whenever a typhoon hits.

每次颱風來襲，水溝都會淹水。

（flood *v.* 淹沒）

3 I pressed the **buzzer**, but there was no answer.

我按了門鈴，卻沒人來應門。

4 The thief fled from the police by climbing down a **drainpipe**.

小偷沿著排水管爬下，逃開了警察。

（flee *v.* 逃走）

5 Check the **peephole** before you unlock the door.

開門前先從門眼確認一下。

6 **Smoke detectors** are a basic safety device that should be installed in every building.

煙霧探測器是基本的安全裝置，每棟大樓應該都要裝設。

（safety device *n.* 安全裝置）

❼ Run for your life if the **fire alarm** goes off.

要是火災警報器響了，就快逃命吧！

（*go off* ph. （警報）響起）

❽ Taking the **elevator** is a lot easier on my legs than taking the stairs.

坐電梯比起爬樓梯，我的腿會輕鬆得多。

（*take the stairs* ph. 爬樓梯）

❾ We couldn't get out because there was a car parked at the bottom of the **driveway**.

有輛車停在車道盡頭，我們出不去。

❿ Marven got **fined** for eating on the subway.

馬文因為在地鐵吃東西被罰款。

換你上場

學習成效知分曉！

⟳ **Exercise** ...... 根據你所聽到的對話完成填空。

Evelyn: Do you have any 1. 公寓 or houses for 2. 出租 ?

Landlady: Yes, I have a 3. 三層樓的房子 that includes basic furnishings and a 4. 衛星接收盤 .

Evelyn: There are just two of us.

Landlady: Oh, OK. Well, I also have a nice new apartment that you might be interested in. It's very modern and has almost everything you can 5. 想得到 , including an 6. 電梯 , an 7. 空調 , a 8. 煙霧探測器 , and a 9. 火災警報器 .

Evelyn: That's great! Does the door have a 10. 門眼 ? I am very 11. 注重安全 .

Landlady: It sure does. And you can use the 12. 室內對講機 to talk with the 13. 大門守衛 in the 14. 大廳 anytime you want.

Evelyn: Nice. By the way, I'm 15. 對蚊子過敏 , so is it OK if I install① an extra 16. 紗窗 on all the windows?

Landlady: That's fine.

Evelyn: Good. And does the building have parking?

Landlady: There's an 17. 地下停車場 , which charges② NT$500 per car monthly.

Evelyn: Sounds reasonable.③ 18. 我們要在哪裡簽約 ?

Answer key

1. apartments
2. rent
3. three-story house
4. satellite dish
5. think of
6. elevator
7. air conditioner
8. smoke detector
9. fire alarm
10. peephole
11. concerned about safety
12. intercom
13. doorman
14. lobby
15. allergic to mosquitoes
16. screen
17. underground parking lot
18. Where do we sign the lease

解析

① install (v.)「安裝」。從家具、機器、設備乃至電腦軟體的安裝都可以用 install。
② charge (v.) 收費
③ reasonable (adj.)（價錢）公道的；不貴的

中譯

艾芙琳： 妳有任何公寓或房屋要出租嗎？
房東太太：有啊，我有一間三層樓的房子，附基本家具和一個衛星接收盤。
艾芙琳： 我們只有兩個人。
房東太太：喔，好，那我有一間超棒的新公寓妳可能會有興趣。它非常現代化，幾乎擁有所有妳想得到的東西，包括電梯、空調、煙霧探測器和火災警報器。
艾芙琳： 太好了！那大門有沒有門眼？我很注重安全的。
房東太太：當然有。而且妳還可以隨時用室內對講機跟大廳的大門守衛聯繫。
艾芙琳： 真好！順便請問一下，我對蚊子過敏，所以我可不可以在所有窗戶加裝紗窗呢？
房東太太：可以。
艾芙琳： 好，這棟樓有停車場嗎？
房東太太：我們的大樓有地下停車場，收費是每部車每月 500 元。
艾芙琳： 聽起來很合理。我們要在哪裡簽約呢？

珠 寶
Jewelry

珠寶

jewelry
[`dʒuəlrɪ]
n. 珠寶

imitation jewelry
[ˌɪmə`teʃən `dʒuəlrɪ]
n. 假珠寶

18 karat gold
[`e`tin `kærət `gold]
n. 18K金

fine jewelry
[`faɪn `dʒuəlrɪ]
n. 真珠寶

24K gold/genuine gold
[`twɛntɪ ˌfor `kærət `gold/`dʒɛnjuɪn `gold]
n. 純金

pawn shop
[`pɔn `ʃap]
n. 當舖

gold bar
[`gold `bar]
n. 金條

pawnbroker
[`pɔn ˌbrokə]
n. 當舖老板

大師 小叮嚀 | ✏ 「22K金」的英文則是 22K gold，唸法是 22 karat gold。

108

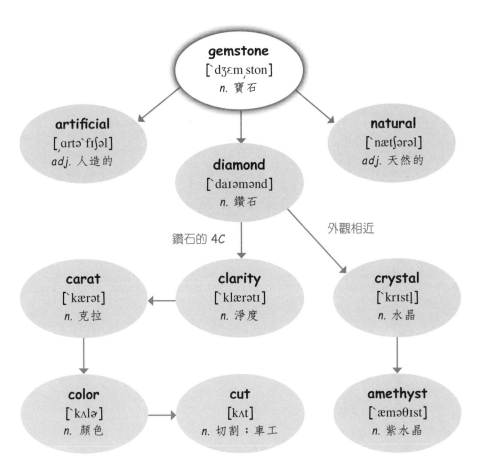

 大師 小叮嚀 ✎ 鑽石的 4C 指的就是：clarity「淨度」、carat「重量」、cut 「切工」、color「顏色」。

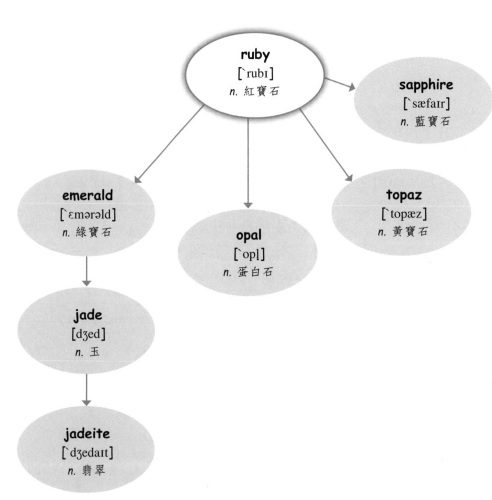

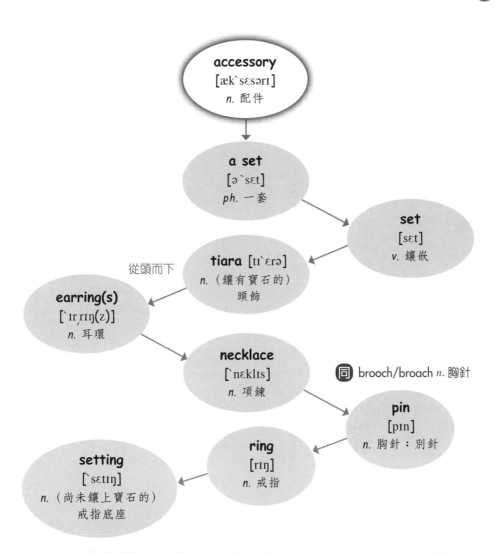

accessory
[æk`sɛsərɪ]
n. 配件

a set
[ə `sɛt]
ph. 一套

set
[sɛt]
v. 鑲嵌

從頭而下

tiara [tɪ`ɛrə]
n. （鑲有寶石的）
頭飾

earring(s)
[`ɪrˌrɪŋ(z)]
n. 耳環

necklace
[`nɛklɪs]
n. 項鍊

同 brooch/broach *n.* 胸針

pin
[pɪn]
n. 胸針；別針

ring
[rɪŋ]
n. 戒指

setting
[`sɛtɪŋ]
n. （尚未鑲上寶石的）
戒指底座

**大　師
小叮嚀**

- Brooch 是明確地指女用胸針或領針；而 pin 則泛指任何種類的別針。
- Set「鑲嵌」（常用被動式）：set A in B / set B with A「鑲 A 於 B 中」。例 1：I had the diamond set in my watch.「我把鑽石鑲在錶中。」例 2：The pendant is set with jadeite.「這個墜子鑲著翡翠。」

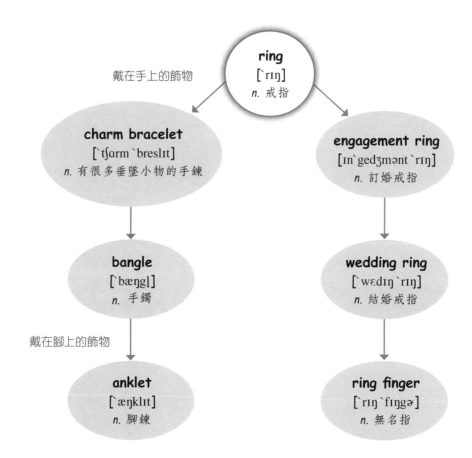

戴在手上的飾物

ring
[ˋrɪŋ]
n. 戒指

charm bracelet
[ˋtʃɑrm ˋbreslɪt]
n. 有很多垂墜小物的手鍊

engagement ring
[ɪnˋgedʒmənt ˋrɪŋ]
n. 訂婚戒指

bangle
[ˋbæŋgl̩]
n. 手鐲

wedding ring
[ˋwɛdɪŋ ˋrɪŋ]
n. 結婚戒指

戴在腳上的飾物

anklet
[ˋæŋklɪt]
n. 腳鍊

ring finger
[ˋrɪŋ ˋfɪŋgɚ]
n. 無名指

大師
小叮嚀

- Ring finger「無名指」是因我們常將戒指戴在無名指而得名。
- Charm bracelet 上頭的垂墜飾物就叫作 charm。
- 鼻環稱為 nose ring；而舌環則通常是 tongue stud。
- Wedding band 中的 band 指的是沒有裝飾、沒有寶石，只有一圈的素面戒指。

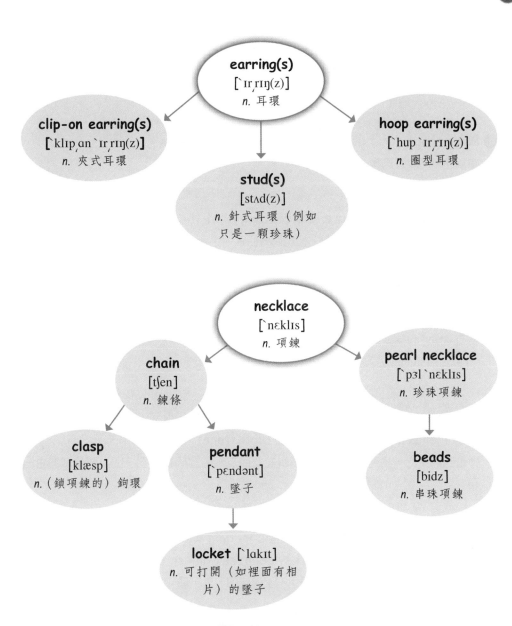

earring(s)
[`ɪr͵rɪŋ(z)]
n. 耳環

clip-on earring(s)
[`klɪp͵ɑn `ɪr͵rɪŋ(z)]
n. 夾式耳環

stud(s)
[stʌd(z)]
n. 針式耳環（例如
只是一顆珍珠）

hoop earring(s)
[`hup `ɪr͵rɪŋ(z)]
n. 圈型耳環

necklace
[`nɛklɪs]
n. 項鍊

chain
[tʃen]
n. 鍊條

pearl necklace
[`pɝl `nɛklɪs]
n. 珍珠項鍊

clasp
[klæsp]
n. （鎖項鍊的）鉤環

pendant
[`pɛndənt]
n. 墜子

beads
[bidz]
n. 串珠項鍊

locket [`lɑkɪt]
n. 可打開（如裡面有相
片）的墜子

**大師
小叮嚀**
✏ Hoop earrings 中的 hoop 指的就是「圈狀物」。
✏ Locket 就是有可放照片等的盒式垂墜，很普遍喔！

❶ **Pawn shops** don't usually accept **imitation jewelry**.
當舖通常不收假珠寶。

❷ **Artificial gemstones** are less dazzling—but they are cheaper.
人工寶石光彩比較沒那麼耀眼,但也比較便宜。
(dazzling *adj.* 燦爛耀眼的)

❸ A fine diamond with high **clarity** and a fine **cut** costs a fortune.
具有高淨度和完美車工的真鑽價值不菲。
(cost a fortune *ph.* 花費一大筆錢)

❹ You were born in May, right? Well, you should ask your girlfriend to buy you an **emerald** since that's your birthstone.
你是五月生的,對吧?那麼你應該叫你女朋友幫你買個綠寶石,因為那是你的生日石。

❺ The 2008 Beijing Olympic Games medals were made using different colors of **jade**, a mineral that symbolizes Chinese culture.
2008 北京奧運的獎牌是由不同顏色的玉做成的,玉石礦物象徵著中國的文化。
(medal *n.* 獎章;獎牌)

6 This is the most beautiful **engagement ring** ever! Of course I'll marry you!

這是我見過最美的訂婚戒指了！我當然願意和你結婚。

---

7 This **charm bracelet** has charms shaped like hearts.

這個垂墜手鍊的墜飾是心型的。

---

8 Since Ariel doesn't want to have her ears pierced, she can only wear **clip-on earrings**.

愛麗兒不想穿耳洞，所以她只能戴夾式耳環。

（have one's ears pierced *ph.* 穿耳洞）

---

9 Can you fix the broken **clasp** on my necklace?

你能修理我項鍊上壞掉的扣環嗎？

---

10 Ann keeps her grandmother's photo in the **locket** she wears around her neck.

安把她奶奶的照片保存在她戴在脖子上的小盒墜子裡。

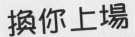

○→ *Exercise* ......根據你所聽到的對話完成填空。

Clerk: May I help you?

Customer: I want to get my mother some 1. 配件 for Mother's Day.

Clerk: Does she prefer 2. 純金 accessories or 3. 寶石 ? Oh, if she is more traditional, she might like a 4. 玉鐲 .

Customer: My mother has a very 5. 優雅的氣質 . 6. 珍珠 may be the best choice. Can I take a look at that pair of 7. 珍珠耳環 ?

Clerk: 8. 您的品味真好 ! They are one of our 9. 熱賣商品 . In fact, we have a whole 10. 套 , which includes studs, a 11. 項鍊 , and a 12. 胸針 .

Customer: Fabulous! I'll take them. Now I still need something for my 13. 婆婆 . 14. 她獨愛紅寶石 .[1] What would you 15. 推薦 ?

Clerk: We have two exquisite[2] 16. 紅寶石 over here; one is set in a 17. 戒指 , and the other in a 18. 垂墜項鍊 .

Customer: Wow! I'm afraid that I can't afford both. I think I'll just take the ring.

Clerk: Yes, ma'am. 19. 您需要包裝嗎 ?

Customer: Yes, please.

∽ Answer key

1. accessories
2. 24 karat gold
3. gemstones
4. jade bangle
5. elegant disposition
6. Pearls
7. pearl studs
8. You have good taste
9. bestsellers
10. set
11. necklace
12. brooch
13. mother-in-law
14. She is obsessed with rubies
15. recommend
16. rubies
17. ring
18. pendant
19. Would you like me to gift-wrap them for you

∽ 解析

① be obsessed with/by 對……著迷
② exquisite (*adj.*) 精美的；精巧的

∽ 中譯

店員：需要幫忙嗎？
顧客：我想買些飾品給媽媽當母親節禮物。
店員：她比較喜歡純金飾品還是寶石？噢，如果她比較傳統一點，她可能會喜歡玉鐲。
顧客：我媽媽的氣質很優雅，珍珠或許是最好的選擇。我能看看那副珍珠耳環嗎？
店員：您的品味真好！這是我們店裡的熱賣商品之一，其實我們有全套的商品，包含一對耳環、項鍊和胸針。
顧客：好極了！我買這套。現在我還得要買個東西送給我婆婆。她獨愛紅寶石，你有什麼可以推薦的嗎？
店員：我們有兩款精緻的紅寶石，一個鑲在戒指，另一個鑲在垂墜項鍊。
顧客：哇！兩樣都買我恐怕負擔不起。我帶戒指就好。
店員：好的，小姐。您需要包裝嗎？
顧客：是的，麻煩了。

廚房用具
Kitchenware

鍋類

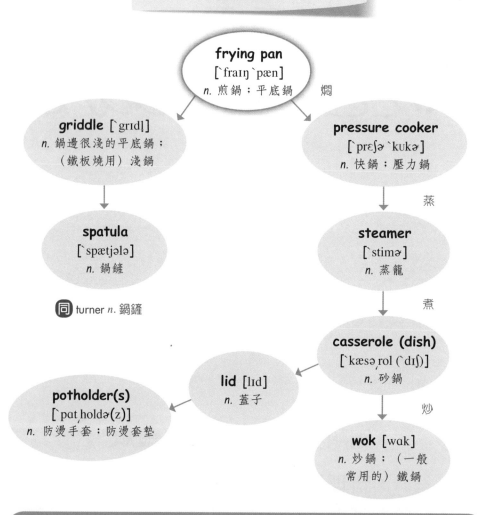

frying pan
[`fraɪŋ `pæn]
n. 煎鍋；平底鍋 　燜

griddle [`grɪdl̩]
n. 鍋邊很淺的平底鍋；
（鐵板燒用）淺鍋

pressure cooker
[`prɛʃɚ `kukɚ]
n. 快鍋；壓力鍋

spatula
[`spætjələ]
n. 鍋鏟

蒸

steamer
[`stimɚ]
n. 蒸籠

同 turner *n.* 鍋鏟

煮

casserole (dish)
[`kæsəˌrol (`dɪʃ)]
n. 砂鍋

lid [lɪd]
n. 蓋子

potholder(s)
[`patˌholdɚ(z)]
n. 防燙手套；防燙套墊

炒

wok [wak]
n. 炒鍋；（一般
常用的）鐵鍋

**大師
小叮嚀**

☞ 「爐子」是 stove 或 burner，但後者較常用來指稱香爐類的容器，例：incense burner「香爐」。

☞ 「防燙手套」也可稱為 oven mitt/glove 或 heat (resistant) glove。

料理器具

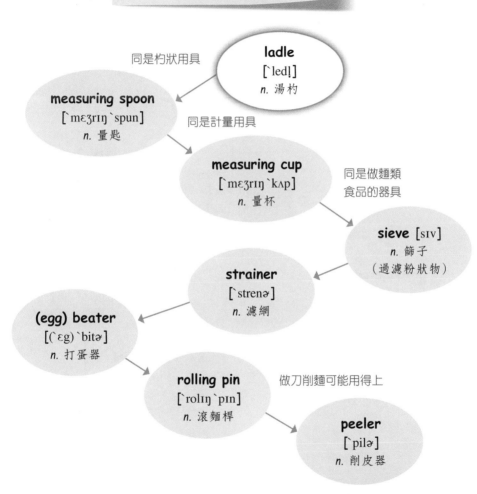

ladle
[`ledl`]
n. 湯杓

同是杓狀用具

measuring spoon
[`mɛʒrɪŋ `spun`]
n. 量匙

同是計量用具

measuring cup
[`mɛʒrɪŋ `kʌp`]
n. 量杯

同是做麵類
食品的器具

sieve [sɪv]
n. 篩子
（過濾粉狀物）

strainer
[`strenə`]
n. 濾網

(egg) beater
[(`ɛg) `bitə`]
n. 打蛋器

rolling pin
[`rolɪŋ `pɪn`]
n. 滾麵桿

做刀削麵可能用得上

peeler
[`pilə`]
n. 削皮器

大師小叮嚀 ✏ Strainer 和 sieve 該如何區分呢？
Strainer 是用來分離固態和液態食物，例如撈水餃的杓子或是廚房水槽使用的濾網；而 sieve 的洞孔較小，用來過濾粉狀物，分離大小顆粒。

廚房器具

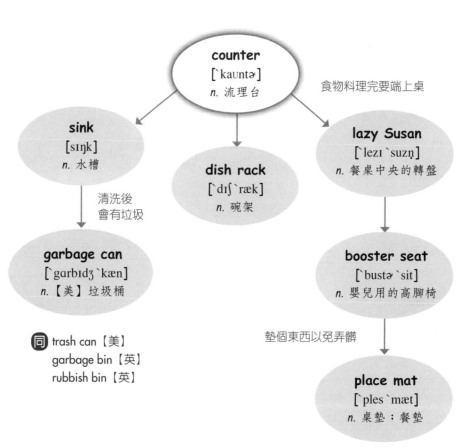

counter
[ˋkaʊntɚ]
n. 流理台

食物料理完要端上桌

sink
[sɪŋk]
n. 水槽

dish rack
[ˋdɪʃˋræk]
n. 碗架

lazy Susan
[ˋlezɪ ˋsuzn̩]
n. 餐桌中央的轉盤

清洗後
會有垃圾

garbage can
[ˋgɑrbɪdʒ ˋkæn]
n. 【美】垃圾桶

booster seat
[ˋbustɚ ˋsit]
n. 嬰兒用的高腳椅

墊個東西以免弄髒

place mat
[ˋples ˋmæt]
n. 桌墊；餐墊

同 trash can【美】
garbage bin【英】
rubbish bin【英】

杯壺類

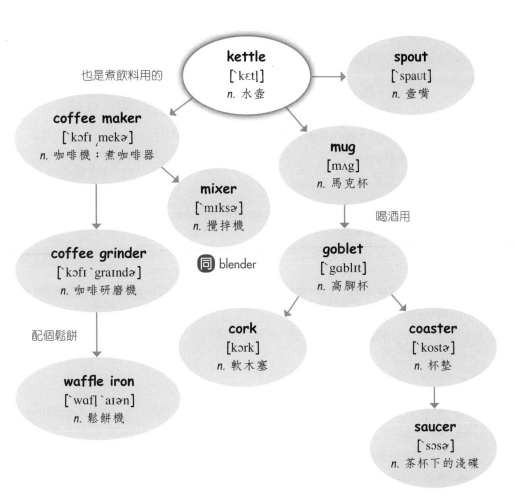

kettle
[`kɛtḷ]
n. 水壺

spout
[`spaʊt]
n. 壺嘴

也是煮飲料用的

coffee maker
[`kɔfɪ ˌmekə]
n. 咖啡機；煮咖啡器

mixer
[`mɪksə]
n. 攪拌機

mug
[mʌg]
n. 馬克杯

喝酒用

同 blender

coffee grinder
[`kɔfɪ `graɪndə]
n. 咖啡研磨機

goblet
[`gɑblɪt]
n. 高腳杯

cork
[kɔrk]
n. 軟木塞

coaster
[`kostə]
n. 杯墊

配個鬆餅

waffle iron
[`wɑfḷ `aɪən]
n. 鬆餅機

saucer
[`sɔsə]
n. 茶杯下的淺碟

大師小叮嚀 📖 喝香檳前「拔出軟木塞」的動作就是 pop the cork，pop 是「發出砰的聲響」之意。

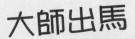

❶ Heat some oil in the **frying pan** before you throw in the garlic.

在你丟進蒜頭之前，倒一些油在煎鍋裡加熱。

（heat v. 加熱）

❷ How can you make pancakes without a **spatula**?

你沒有鍋鏟怎麼做煎餅？

❸ If you want to make noodles, it's useful to have a good **rolling pin**.

如果你要做麵，有根桿麵棍是很有用的。

❹ The kitchen **counter** is a mess, because my mom forgot to put the lid on the **blender**.

我媽忘了把果汁機的蓋子蓋上，現在廚房的流理台是一團糟。

（mess n. 混亂）

❺ We have a stainless steel **dish rack**, but I'm thinking about getting a wooden one.

我們有個不銹鋼碗架，但我考慮買個木製的。

（stainless steel n. 不銹鋼）

❻ My sister-in-law is planning to buy a **booster seat**, so her baby girl can join us at the dining table.
我弟妹計畫要買張嬰兒的高腳椅，好讓她的小女兒能和我們一起在餐桌用餐。

❼ We should empty the **trash can** every day to keep the kitchen from smelling.
我們應該每天清空垃圾桶，廚房才不會發臭。
（empty v. 倒空）

❽ The whistle on the **kettle** is broken, so you have to watch for the steam coming out of the **spout**.
水壺上的汽笛壞了，所以你要注意壺口冒出的水蒸汽。

❾ Please put a **coaster** under the glass or you'll leave a stain on the tea table.
請在玻璃杯下放一個杯墊，不然你會在茶桌上留下印子。
（stain n. 污跡）

❿ A candle-lit dinner would be more romantic with champagne in **goblets**.
搭配上斟有香檳的高腳杯，燭光晚餐會更浪漫。
（lit 為 light 的過去式和過去分詞）

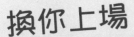

∽ *Exercise* ······根據你所聽到的對話完成填空。

Mother: All I have to do is put on a 1. 宴席 like the 2. 滿漢全席 at every 3. 家庭聚會 ① and everything will be just fine, right?

Daughter: That's why all the 4. 親戚 enjoy the yearly event so much, "master chef." The 5. 海蔘切丁 are ready on the 6. 砧板 .

Mother: Thank you. Please 7. 遞給 me the 8. 炒菜鍋 and the 9. 鍋鏟 , and I still need 10. 半茶匙的鹽 . Oh, can you check the 11. 蒸籠 first? I think the 12. 清蒸石斑 is almost done.

Daughter: OK. By the way, Jill is already setting the table. ②

Mother: She'd better be careful. The 13. 烤乳豬 is still hot from the 14. 烤箱 .

Daughter: You're right. I'll remind her. I'll also have her put the 15. 電磁爐 on the table to keep the 16. 餛飩湯 warm.

Mother: OK. She may need some 17. 防燙手套 , too. And don't forget the 18. 湯杓 for the soup.

Daughter: Mom! Aunt Gigi is here with Jamie. She brought some 19. 人參燉雞 in a 20. 壓力鍋 !

Mother: Super! Could you get out the 21. 嬰兒用高腳椅 for Jamie?

Daughter: Sure. I bet I can find her favorite 22. 卡通餐墊 , too!

✎ *Answer key* ....

1. banquet	9. turner/spatula	17. potholders
2. full Manchu-Han banquet	10. half a teaspoon of salt	18. ladle
3. family reunion	11. steamer	19. ginseng chicken soup
4. relatives	12. steamed grouper	20. pressure cooker
5. sea cucumber cubes	13. roast suckling pig	21. booster seat
6. cutting board	14. oven	22. cartoon place mat
7. hand	15. hot plate	
8. wok	16. wonton soup	

✎ 解析 ....

① reunion (*n*.) 團聚
② set the table 擺放餐具

✎ 中譯 ....

媽媽：每次家庭聚會，我都非得辦一個像滿漢全席的宴席就是了，對吧？

女兒：這就是為什麼所有的親戚都非常喜愛這個年度盛事啊，「大廚」！海蔘切丁已經準備好在砧板上了。

媽媽：謝謝。請把炒菜鍋和鍋鏟遞給我，另外我還要半茶匙的鹽。對了，妳先去看看蒸籠好嗎？我想清蒸石斑快好了。

女兒：好。順便跟妳說，吉兒已經在擺餐具了。

媽媽：她最好小心一點。烤乳豬剛出爐還很燙呢。

女兒：妳說的沒錯，我會提醒她。我也會叫她把電磁爐擺到桌上讓餛飩湯保溫。

媽媽：好，她可能還需要防燙手套。還有，不要忘了盛湯用的湯杓。

女兒：媽！琪琪阿姨和潔美已經到了。她用壓力鍋帶人參燉雞來！

媽媽：太好了！妳能把嬰兒用高腳椅拿出來給潔美嗎？

女兒：當然，我相信我還可以找到她最喜歡的卡通餐墊！

居家掃除
Household Cleaning

打掃用具

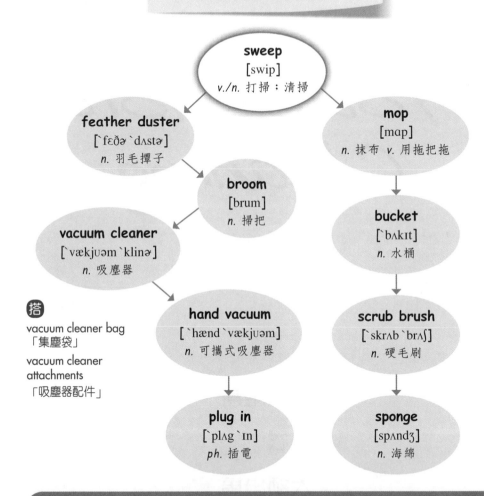

sweep
[swip]
v./n. 打掃；清掃

feather duster
[ˈfɛðɚ ˈdʌstɚ]
n. 羽毛撣子

mop
[mɑp]
n. 抹布 *v.* 用拖把拖

broom
[brum]
n. 掃把

vacuum cleaner
[ˈvækjuəm ˈklinɚ]
n. 吸塵器

bucket
[ˈbʌkɪt]
n. 水桶

hand vacuum
[ˈhænd ˈvækjuəm]
n. 可攜式吸塵器

scrub brush
[ˈskrʌb ˈbrʌʃ]
n. 硬毛刷

plug in
[ˈplʌg ˈɪn]
ph. 插電

sponge
[spʌndʒ]
n. 海綿

搭
vacuum cleaner bag
「集塵袋」

vacuum cleaner
attachments
「吸塵器配件」

大師小叮嚀

✏ 「用硬毛刷刷洗」就是 scrub (*v.*)。
例：scrub the bucket「刷水桶」。

✏ 「用吸塵器吸」就是 vacuum (*v.*)。
例：vacuum the carpet「用吸塵器吸地毯」。

✏ Vacuum cleaner attachments 可能有不同形狀或功能的吸頭等。

洗衣

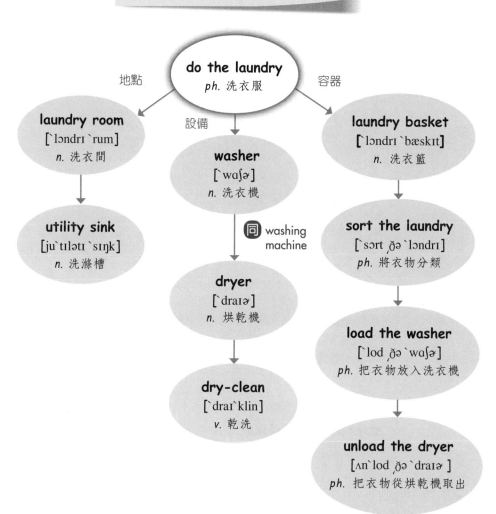

do the laundry
ph. 洗衣服

地點

設備

容器

laundry room
[`lɔndrɪ `rum]
n. 洗衣間

washer
[`waʃə]
n. 洗衣機

laundry basket
[`lɔndrɪ `bæskɪt]
n. 洗衣籃

utility sink
[ju`tɪlətɪ `sɪŋk]
n. 洗滌槽

同 washing machine

sort the laundry
[`sɔrt ðə `lɔndrɪ]
ph. 將衣物分類

dryer
[`draɪə]
n. 烘乾機

load the washer
[`lod ðə `waʃə]
ph. 把衣物放入洗衣機

dry-clean
[`draɪ`klin]
v. 乾洗

unload the dryer
[ʌn`lod ðə `draɪə]
ph. 把衣物從烘乾機取出

 大師小叮嚀 ✉ 「洗碗」的說法跟「洗衣服」相似，叫作 do the dishes，而「洗碗精」和「洗衣精」都是 detergent。

搭

hang up clothes to dry
「晾衣服」

hang out clothes to dry
「在室外晾乾衣服」

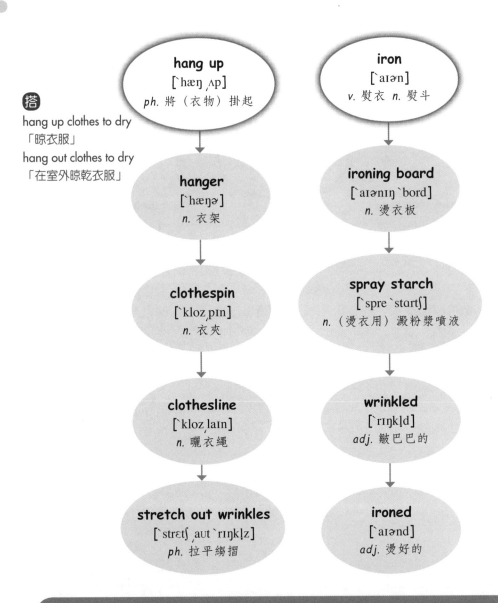

hang up
[`hæŋ͵ʌp]
ph. 將（衣物）掛起

iron
[`aɪən]
v. 熨衣 *n.* 熨斗

hanger
[`hæŋə]
n. 衣架

ironing board
[`aɪənɪŋ `bord]
n. 燙衣板

clothespin
[`kloz͵pɪn]
n. 衣夾

spray starch
[`spre `startʃ]
n.（燙衣用）澱粉漿噴液

clothesline
[`kloz͵laɪn]
n. 曬衣繩

wrinkled
[`rɪŋkḷd]
adj. 皺巴巴的

stretch out wrinkles
[`strɛtʃ ͵aut `rɪŋkḷz]
ph. 拉平縐摺

ironed
[`aɪənd]
adj. 燙好的

大　師
小叮嚀

✏ Spray (*n.*)「噴灑液；噴霧器」，例：「噴霧殺蟲劑」是 insect spray。
(*v.*)「噴灑」，例：「在自己身上噴香水」是 spray perfume on oneself。

大師出馬

❶ Is the **vacuum cleaner** **plugged in**?
吸塵器有插電嗎？

❷ Armed with only a **bucket** and **sponge**, I started washing my car.
只帶著水桶和海綿，我開始洗車。

❸ Can woolens be **dry-cleaned**?
毛料衣服能乾洗嗎？

❹ **Sorting laundry** involves more than separating clothes according to color and fabric type; one should also check for stains and damage.
衣物分類不是只根據顏色跟布料而已，還要檢查污漬和破損處。
(fabric *n.* 布料)

❺ It takes more than five minutes to **iron** a **wrinkled** dress properly.
要把一件皺巴巴的洋裝燙好，得花五分鐘以上。

❻ My mom always **hangs** laundry **up** to dry instead of using a clothes **dryer**.
我媽媽都是把洗好的衣服自然晾乾而不是用烘衣機。

❼ **Clothespins** are indispensable for hanging clothes.

曬衣夾在曬衣服時是不可缺少的。

（indispensable *adj.* 不可或缺的）

---

❽ You can spray water on **wrinkled** clothing and pull on them to **stretch out wrinkles**, or you can spray the clothes while **ironing** them.

你可以在皺巴巴的衣物上噴點水後拉平縐摺，或是在燙衣服的時候噴水。

換你上場

學習成效知分曉！

∞ *Exercise* ⋯⋯ 根據你所聽到的對話完成填空。

Husband: Honey, the kitchen floor needs a good 1. 刷洗 .

Wife: I know. But take a look at the 2. 曬衣繩 ! I 3. 洗衣服 all day yesterday! I even 4. 漂白 the white 5. 床單 , ① and 6. 燙平 several of your 7. 皺巴巴的 shirts. I think I deserve a day off. ②

Husband: I know you do, but I really need your help. You are an 8. 專家 at this stuff. Why don't we give the whole house a 9. 大掃除 together?

Wife: All right. 10. 我會很感激 if you'd be willing to ③ be in charge of ④ 11. 掃地 and 12. 刷洗 though.

Husband: No problem. I'll do the kitchen and bathroom floor first and then the yard.

Wife: Maybe you could also 13. 用吸塵器吸 the 14. 地毯 a little or 15. 用拖把拖 our bedroom.

Husband: Can I ask you something? What are you in charge of?

Wife: Getting everything ready. There are so many things you're going to need: the 16. 掃把 , the 17. 畚箕 , the 18. 吸塵器 , the 19. 水桶 , the 20. 硬毛刷 , and probably a 21. 海綿 and some 22. 抹布 too.

Husband: Yeah, anything else?

Wife: Oh! Well, I'd be happy to 23. 插電 the vacuum cleaner for you too!

Husband: You're too kind!

✍ *Answer key*

1. scrubbing	9. good cleaning	17. dust pan
2. clothesline	10. I would appreciate it	18. vacuum cleaner
3. did the laundry	11. sweeping	19. bucket
4. bleached	12. scrubbing	20. scrub brush
5. sheets	13. vacuum	21. sponge
6. ironed	14. carpet	22. rags
7. wrinkled	15. mop	23. plug in
8. expert	16. broom	

✍ 解析

① sheet (*n.*) 床單
② take ... off 休假（多久時間），例如：take one week off「請假一週」。
③ be willing to + V 願意……
④ in charge of + sth. 負責……

✍ 中譯

先生：親愛的，廚房地板需要好好刷洗一番了。

太太：我知道啊。不過看一下曬衣繩吧！我昨天洗了一整天的衣服！我還漂白了白色床單、燙了幾件你皺巴巴的襯衫。我想我應該可以休息一天。

先生：我知道妳可以，不過我真的需要妳的幫忙。妳是這方面的專家嘛。我們何不一起給整個房子好好來個大掃除。

太太：好吧。如果你願意負責掃地和刷洗的話，我會很感激的。

先生：沒問題。我會先弄廚房和浴室的地板，然後再打掃院子。

太太：或許你也可以用吸塵器吸一下地毯，或用拖把拖一下我們的臥房。

先生：我可以問妳一件事嗎？那妳要負責什麼？

太太：把所有東西準備好。你會需要很多東西的：掃把、畚箕、吸塵器、水桶、硬毛刷，可能還需要海綿和抹布。

先生：是喔！還有呢？

太太：喔！我也很樂意幫你把吸塵器的插頭插上！

先生：妳也太好心了吧！

電腦、通訊、消費者電子產品
Computers, Communication & Consumer Electronics

電腦

computer
[kəm`pjutɚ]
n. 電腦

Internet
[`ɪntɚˌnɛt]
n. 網際網路

shut down (the computer)
ph. 關機

同 turn off the computer

反 turn on the computer

wireless network
[`waɪrlɪs `nɛtˌwɝk]
n. 無線網路

crash
[kræʃ]
v./n. 當機

upload
[ʌp`lod]
v. 上傳（資料）

反 download v. 下載

lag
[læg]
v./n. 訊號延遲

instant telecommunication
[`ɪnstənt `tɛlɪkəˌmjunə`keʃən]
n. 即時通訊

bug
[bʌg]
n. 程式的錯誤

webcam
[`wɛbˌkæm]
n. 網路攝影機

video conference
[`vɪdɪˌo `kɑnfərəns]
n. 視訊會議

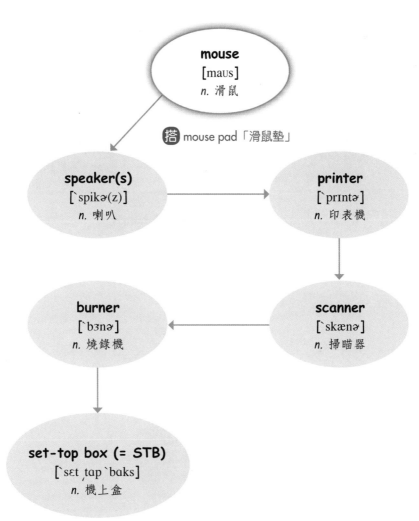

mouse
[maʊs]
n. 滑鼠

搭 mouse pad「滑鼠墊」

speaker(s)
[`spikɚ(z)]
n. 喇叭

printer
[`prɪntɚ]
n. 印表機

scanner
[`skænɚ]
n. 掃瞄器

burner
[`bɜnɚ]
n. 燒錄機

set-top box (= STB)
[`sɛt ˌtɑp `bɑks]
n. 機上盒

手機

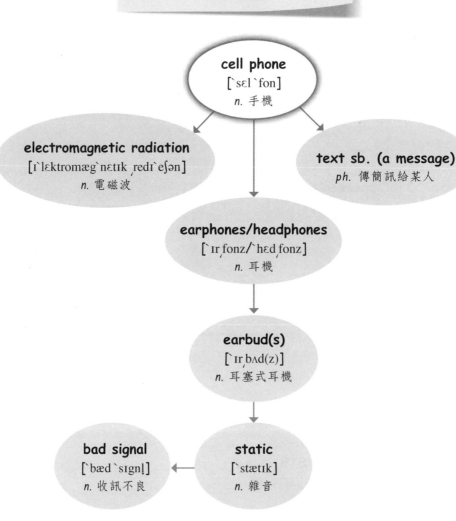

cell phone
[ˋsɛl ˋfon]
n. 手機

electromagnetic radiation
[ɪˋlɛktromægˋnɛtɪk ˏrediˋeʃən]
n. 電磁波

text sb. (a message)
ph. 傳簡訊給某人

earphones/headphones
[ˋɪrˏfonz/ˋhɛdˏfonz]
n. 耳機

earbud(s)
[ˋɪrˏbʌd(z)]
n. 耳塞式耳機

bad signal
[ˋbæd ˋsɪgnl̩]
n. 收訊不良

static
[ˋstætɪk]
n. 雜音

 大師 小叮嚀 ✍ 要表示「手機收訊不良」可以說：The signal is bad. 或 I'm getting poor reception.

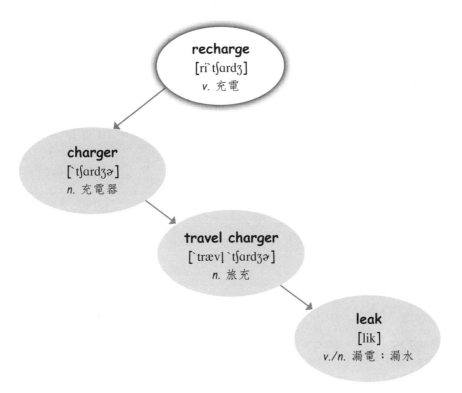

recharge
[ri`tʃardʒ]
v. 充電

charger
[`tʃardʒə]
n. 充電器

travel charger
[`trævl `tʃardʒə]
n. 旅充

leak
[lik]
v./n. 漏電；漏水

大師
小叮嚀

- 我們常使用的「充電電池」就是 rechargeable battery。
- 另外，recharge 也可用來表示精神上的充電，即休息一段時間以恢復精力，說法是 recharge one's batteries。例：Jacqueline took a trip to France to recharge her batteries.「賈桂琳到法國休息充電。」
- 「漏水的管子」就叫 (a) leaky pipe，leaky (adj.)「漏水的；漏電的」。

電話

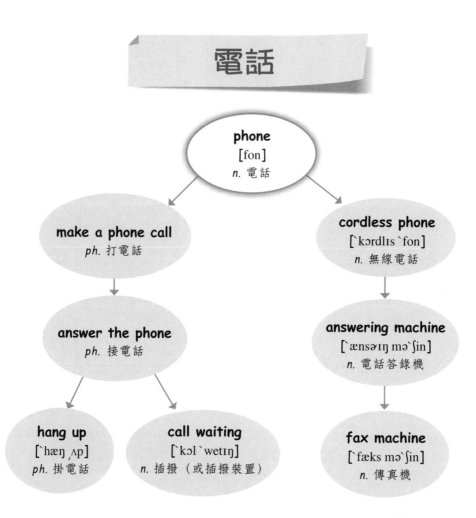

phone
[fon]
n. 電話

make a phone call
ph. 打電話

cordless phone
[ˋkɔrdlɪs ˋfon]
n. 無線電話

answer the phone
ph. 接電話

answering machine
[ˋænsɚɪŋ məˋʃin]
n. 電話答錄機

hang up
[ˋhæŋ ˄p]
ph. 掛電話

call waiting
[ˋkɔl ˋwetɪŋ]
n. 插撥（或插撥裝置）

fax machine
[ˋfæks məˋʃin]
n. 傳真機

大師
小叮嚀

- Hang up on sb. 就是「掛某人電話」之意。例：How could you hang up on me?「你怎麼可以掛我電話？」
- Do you have call waiting?「你電話有沒有插撥裝置？」。若要表示「等一下，我有插撥」，則可以說：Hold on, I've got someone else on the line.
- Fax machine 中的 fax 可當動詞「傳真」。例：I just faxed three pages to you.「我剛剛傳了三頁給你。」

電視

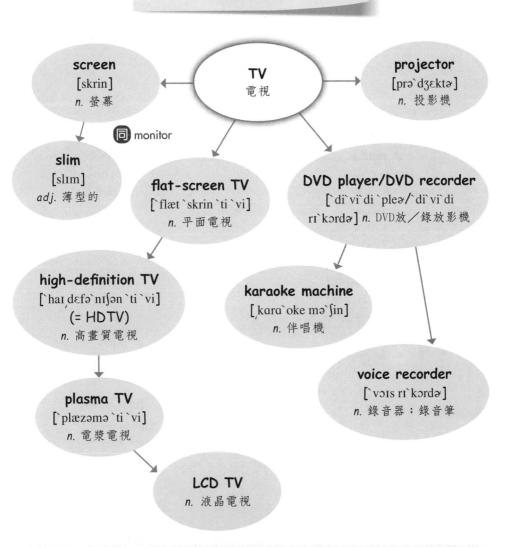

TV
電視

screen
[skrin]
n. 螢幕

同 monitor

slim
[slɪm]
adj. 薄型的

flat-screen TV
[ˋflæt ˋskrin ˋti ˋvi]
n. 平面電視

projector
[prəˋdʒɛktə]
n. 投影機

DVD player/DVD recorder
[ˋdi ˋvi ˋdi ˋpleə/ˋdi ˋvi ˋdi rɪˋkɔrdə] *n.* DVD放／錄放影機

high-definition TV
[ˋhaɪ͵dɛfəˋnɪʃən ˋti ˋvi]
(= HDTV)
n. 高畫質電視

karaoke machine
[͵karaˋoke məˋʃin]
n. 伴唱機

voice recorder
[ˋvɔɪs rɪˋkɔrdə]
n. 錄音器；錄音筆

plasma TV
[ˋplæzəmə ˋti ˋvi]
n. 電漿電視

LCD TV
n. 液晶電視

**大師
小叮嚀**

✐ LCD 是 liquid crystal display「液晶顯示」的縮寫字。
✐ High-definition 中的 definition 是「清晰度」之意。

音響

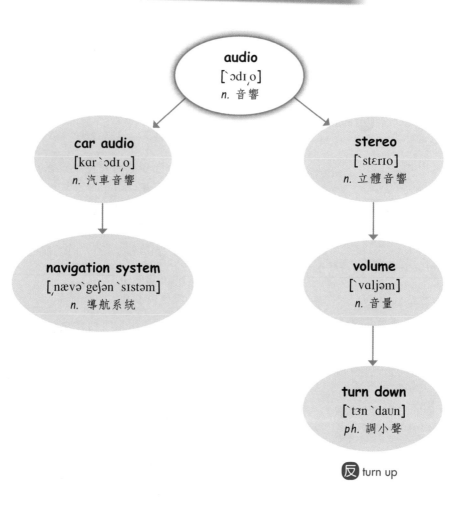

audio
[`ɔdɪ͵o]
n. 音響

car audio
[kar `ɔdɪ͵o]
n. 汽車音響

stereo
[`stɛrɪo]
n. 立體音響

navigation system
[͵nævə`geʃən `sɪstəm]
n. 導航系統

volume
[`valjəm]
n. 音量

turn down
[`tɜn `daʊn]
ph. 調小聲

反 turn up

 大師 小叮嚀 ✎ 如果要使 navigation system 的意義更明確，只要在前頭加上 car，變成 car navigation system 即可。

相機

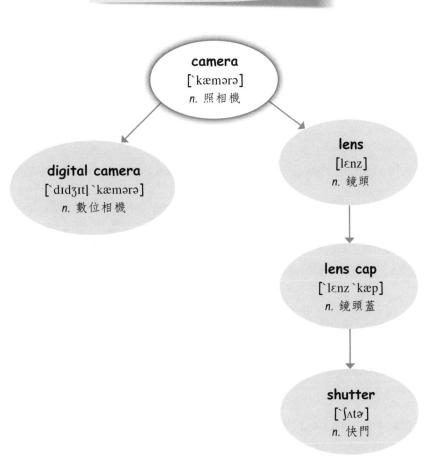

camera
[`kæmərə]
n. 照相機

digital camera
[`dɪdʒɪtḷ `kæmərə]
n. 數位相機

lens
[lɛnz]
n. 鏡頭

lens cap
[`lɛnz `kæp]
n. 鏡頭蓋

shutter
[`ʃʌtə]
n. 快門

大師
小叮嚀 ✏ 「快門」是 shutter，不過「按下快門」這個動作，用 press the button「按下按鈕」表示即可。

大師出馬

① The **computer** suddenly **crashed** while I was typing the final paper for my humanities class.

我在打人文課期末報告時,電腦突然當機了。

(humanities *n.* 人文學科)

② Philip's electric shaver needs to be **charged** before his trip to Taiwan.

菲利普的電動刮鬍刀在他到台灣之前要先充電。

③ **Leaky** batteries can be a real health hazard.

漏電電池對健康可能會造成嚴重的危害。

④ I don't hear anything but **static**. Either we have a **bad signal** or the **cell phone** itself is just lousy.

我除了雜音什麼都聽不見,不是我們的收訊不良就是手機本身就很爛。

⑤ People who live near high-voltage power lines might be exposed to dangerous levels of **electromagnetic radiation**.

住在高壓電線附近的人可能暴露在高危險量的電磁波中。

(high voltage *n.* 高壓 be exposed to *ph.* 被暴露在)

⑥ The newest **LCD TVs** have **slim**, high-definition screens.

最新的液晶電視螢幕既薄、畫質又好。

7 Are you crazy? How could you **hang up** on your boss!

你瘋了嗎？你怎能掛你老闆的電話！

---

8 Why didn't you **answer the phone**? I know you have **call waiting**.

你為什麼不接電話？我知道你有插撥裝置。

---

9 I'd like to **turn down** the television a little, but I can't find the remote.

我想把電視關小聲一點，可是我找不到搖控器。

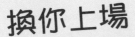

⊶ *Exercise* ......根據你所聽到的對話完成填空。

Husband: I 1. <u>已經預定了頂級的蜜月套房</u> in the best hotel in Tokyo for our 2.<u>結婚週年紀念</u> .

Wife: Wow! 3. <u>有多棒啊</u> ？

Husband: They've got a 4. <u>電漿電視</u> , a 5. <u>DVD 錄放影機</u> , and a 6. <u>伴唱機</u> in the room, and that's just for starters. You'll probably be more interested in the 7. <u>溫泉按摩浴缸</u> and 8. <u>蒸汽浴</u> .

Wife: Ooh, that does sound nice, especially since I have to do some business while we're there. Oh, that reminds me. Does the room have a 9. <u>傳真機</u> ？

Husband: I don't think so, but I'm sure you could use the one in the business center.

Wife: I can't wait to 10. <u>打包行李</u> ！

Husband: Remember to bring your 11. <u>手機</u> . That's why you got a 3G phone, right? So you could use it in Japan. It's expensive though, so maybe you could send 12. <u>簡訊</u> instead of calling.

Wife: Thanks for reminding me. I guess that means we'll need the 13. <u>旅充</u> to 14. <u>充電</u> it too. We should also bring our MP3 players and 15. <u>耳塞式耳機</u> , and let's bring the electronic dictionary in case we need to translate something. Oh, and you have to remember the 16. <u>伸縮鏡頭</u> for the 17. <u>數位相機</u> .

Husband: I heard from the 18. <u>旅行社</u> that we can rent a car with a 19. <u>導航系統</u> there.

Wife: Cool! We're going to have so much fun!

⟜ *Answer key*

1. have booked the best honeymoon suite
2. anniversary
3. How good is that
4. plasma TV
5. DVD recorder
6. karaoke machine
7. hot tub
8. sauna
9. fax machine
10. pack

11. cell phone
12. text messages
13. travel charger
14. recharge
15. earbuds
16. zoom lens
17. digital camera
18. travel agency
19. navigation system

⟜ 中譯

先生：我已經在東京最好的飯店預定了頂級的蜜月套房來慶祝我們的結婚週年紀念。

太太：哇！有多棒啊？

先生：他們的房間內有電漿電視、DVD 錄放影機和伴唱機，這只是剛開始呢，妳可能對溫泉按摩浴缸和蒸汽浴更感興趣。

太太：喔，那聽起來的確很棒，尤其是因為我們在那邊，我還得處理一些公事。喔，這倒提醒了我，房間內有傳真機嗎？

先生：我想沒有，不過我相信妳可以使用商務中心的。

太太：我等不及要打包行李了！

先生：記得帶妳的手機。這是妳為什麼買 3G 手機的原因，對吧？這樣妳就可以在日本使用它。不過很貴，所以或許妳發簡訊就好，不要打電話。

太太：謝謝提醒。我想那表示我們也需要帶旅充來充電。我們應該也要帶 MP3 和耳塞式耳機，還有電子辭典，以免我們需要翻譯東西。喔，你要記得帶數位相機的伸縮鏡頭喔。

先生：我聽旅行社說我們可以在那裡租到有導航系統的車。

太太：太好了！我們一定會玩得很開心！

PART 4

交 通
TRAFFIC

陸上交通
Traffic

馬路相關

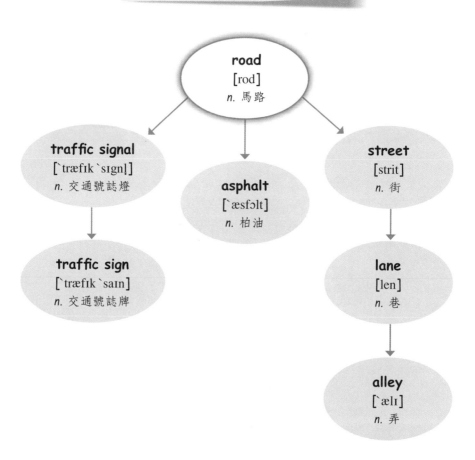

road
[rod]
n. 馬路

traffic signal
[`træfɪk `sɪgn̩]
n. 交通號誌燈

asphalt
[`æsfɔlt]
n. 柏油

street
[strit]
n. 街

traffic sign
[`træfɪk `saɪn]
n. 交通號誌牌

lane
[len]
n. 巷

alley
[`ælɪ]
n. 弄

大師小叮嚀

✐ Traffic signal 大多指的是燈號，如：traffic lights。紅綠燈也可稱為 stop lights。

✐ Traffic sign 則為交通標誌，是以圖、文字表達的指示牌。

✐ 在書寫地址時，可參考以下相對應的縮寫：Avenue: Ave.「大道」; Road: Rd.「路」; Street: St.「街」; Lane: Ln.「巷」。

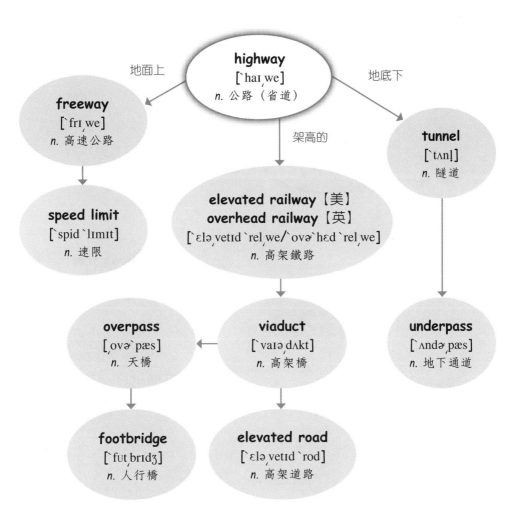

highway
[`haɪˌwe]
n. 公路（省道）

地面上 ─ **freeway**
[`frɪˌwe]
n. 高速公路

地底下 ─ **tunnel**
[`tʌn!]
n. 隧道

架高的 ─ **elevated railway【美】**
overhead railway【英】
[`ɛləˌvetɪd `relˌwe／ovəˈhɛd `relˌwe]
n. 高架鐵路

speed limit
[`spid `lɪmɪt]
n. 速限

overpass
[`ovəˌpæs]
n. 天橋

viaduct
[`vaɪəˌdʌkt]
n. 高架橋

underpass
[`ʌndəˌpæs]
n. 地下通道

footbridge
[`futˌbrɪdʒ]
n. 人行橋

elevated road
[`ɛləˌvetɪd `rod]
n. 高架道路

大師小叮嚀

✏ 北美的高速公路（freeway 或 expressway）在英國為 motorway。

✏ Overpass 在歐美指樓與樓之間、供行人穿越有遮蔽的天橋，常見於購物中心和醫院，也可稱為 skywalk。美國大峽谷的觀景步道也稱做 skywalk。

✏ Interchange「交流道」又稱做 junction。歐美的交流道分兩種：full access 和 restricted access。前者無限制，可上亦可下；後者有限制，只能上或下。

行人相關

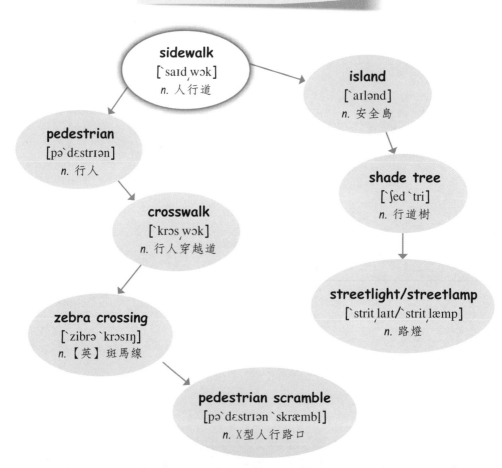

sidewalk
[`saɪdˌwɔk]
n. 人行道

island
[`aɪlənd]
n. 安全島

pedestrian
[pə`dɛstrɪən]
n. 行人

shade tree
[`ʃed `tri]
n. 行道樹

crosswalk
[`krɔsˌwɔk]
n. 行人穿越道

streetlight/streetlamp
[`stritˌlaɪt/`stritˌlæmp]
n. 路燈

zebra crossing
[`zibrə `krɔsɪŋ]
n.【英】斑馬線

pedestrian scramble
[pə`dɛstrɪən `skræmbļ]
n. X型人行路口

 **大師
小叮嚀**

✏ 北美的人行道稱為 sidewalk，英國人則稱作 pavement。

✏ Island「安全島」在英國稱為 refuge island。

✏ Pedestrian scramble 為在交叉路口供行人行走的 X 型黃色斑馬
線區塊，是在某一時段（通常為尖峰時段）為方便行人快速到達
斜對角，以免等兩次紅燈。

交通標誌

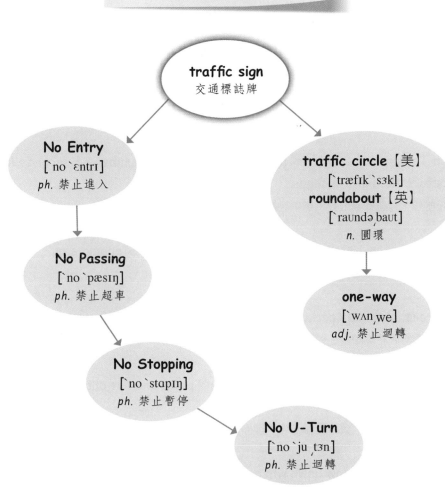

traffic sign
交通標誌牌

No Entry
[`no `ɛntrɪ]
ph. 禁止進入

traffic circle【美】
[`træfɪk `sɜk!]
roundabout【英】
[`raʊndəˌbaʊt]
n. 圓環

No Passing
[`no `pæsɪŋ]
ph. 禁止超車

one-way
[`wʌnˌwe]
adj. 禁止迴轉

No Stopping
[`no `stapɪŋ]
ph. 禁止暫停

No U-Turn
[`no `juˌtɜn]
ph. 禁止迴轉

大師小叮嚀 ✏ No Passing. 是美式用法，英式用法為 No Overtaking.

❶ Traffic signs come in all different shapes: circles, triangles, rectangles, and even pentagons and octagons.

交通標誌有很多不同形狀：圓形、三角形、長方形，甚至是五邊形和八角形。

（pentagon *n.* 五邊形　octagon *n.* 八邊形）

❷ In Taiwan, some **traffic lights** count down the number of seconds left before the light changes.

在台灣，有些紅綠燈會倒數號誌轉換前的剩餘秒數。

❸ Hey! You can't stop here. Don't you see that **No Stopping** sign?

嘿！你不能停在這裡。你沒看到那個「禁止暫停」標誌嗎？

❹ Streetlights help **pedestrians** and drivers to see better at night.

路燈讓行人和駕駛人在夜晚看得更清楚。

❺ In many parts of the city, scooters and bikes are not allowed to park on the **sidewalk**.

在市內很多地方，機車和腳踏車不能停放在人行道。

❻ All cars should slow down when passing the tollbooths on the **highway**.

所有車子在高速公路上經過收費站時應減速慢行。

❼ When you get to the end of the street, take the **footbridge** across the intersection and then head north.

當你走到街道盡頭，走人行橋通過十字路口，然後往北走。

換你上場

學 習 成 效 知 分 曉！

☞ *Exercise* ...... 根據你所聽到的對話完成填空。

Tina Chan
5F, No. 6, Ln. 302
Zhongshan Rd.
Yonghe 234

Marven Wu
8F, No. 6, Alley 45, Ln. 289
Sec. 2, Xinglong Rd.
Taipei 116

Tina: Are you going out? <u>1. 可不可以載我一程</u>？

Evelyn: Yes, I guess so. I'm just going to the supermarket to get some food for the party. Where do you want to go?

Tina: I'm just going to the post office <u>2. 在轉角</u>. I want to send this letter to Marven.

Evelyn: OK! <u>3. 妳可以順路搭我的車</u>.

(Evelyn is driving a car and Tina is sitting next to her.)

Tina: Why are we going so slow?

Evelyn: Because <u>4. 現在是尖峰時間</u>. Maybe we can get around this <u>5. 塞車</u> by getting on the <u>6. 快速道路</u>.

Tina: I hate this!

Evelyn: <u>7. 我們除了等以外什麼都不能做</u>. Look, there's a <u>8. 交通警察</u> directing traffic in the middle of the <u>9. 十字路口</u> now.

Tina:　I'm so jealous of <u>10. 那些行人</u>. I feel like a bird in a cage. I would have gotten there faster if I had walked.

Evelyn: <u>11. 耐心一點啦</u>！

☞ 中譯 ....

234 永和市中山路
302 巷 6 號 5 樓
Tina Chan 寄

116 台北市興隆路 2 段
289 巷 45 弄 6 號 8 樓
Marven Wu　收

Tina：　妳要出門嗎？可不可以載我一程？

Evelyn：是啊，沒錯！我要去超市買一些派對要用的東西。妳要去哪裡？

Tina：　我只是要去轉角的郵局，我要寄這封信給馬文。

Evelyn：沒問題啊！妳可以順路搭我的車。

（*Evelyn* 在開車，*Tina* 坐在她旁邊。）

Tina：　我們的速度怎麼這麼慢啊？

Evelyn：因為現在是尖峰時間。走快速道路，我們也許能避開塞車。

Tina：　我討厭這樣！

Evelyn：我們除了等以外什麼都不能做。妳看，有個交通警察正在十字路口中間指揮交通。

Tina：　我真妒嫉那些行人，我覺得好像籠中鳥一樣。如果我用走的，應該會更快到那邊。

Evelyn：耐心一點啦！

☞ *Answer key*

1. Can you give me a ride

2. on the corner

3. You can hitch a ride with me

4. it's rush hour

5. traffic jam

6. freeway

7. There's nothing we can do but wait

8. police officer

9. intersection

10. the pedestrians

11. Be patient

空中交通
Air Travel

機場

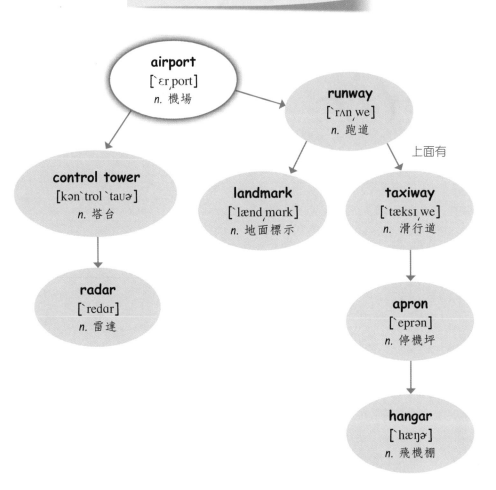

airport
[`ɛr͵port]
n. 機場

runway
[`rʌn͵we]
n. 跑道

上面有

control tower
[kən`trol `tauɚ]
n. 塔台

landmark
[`lænd͵mark]
n. 地面標示

taxiway
[`tæksɪ͵we]
n. 滑行道

radar
[`redar]
n. 雷達

apron
[`eprən]
n. 停機坪

hangar
[`hæŋɚ]
n. 飛機棚

大師小叮嚀 ☞ 飛機「起飛」是用 take off；「降落」是 land。

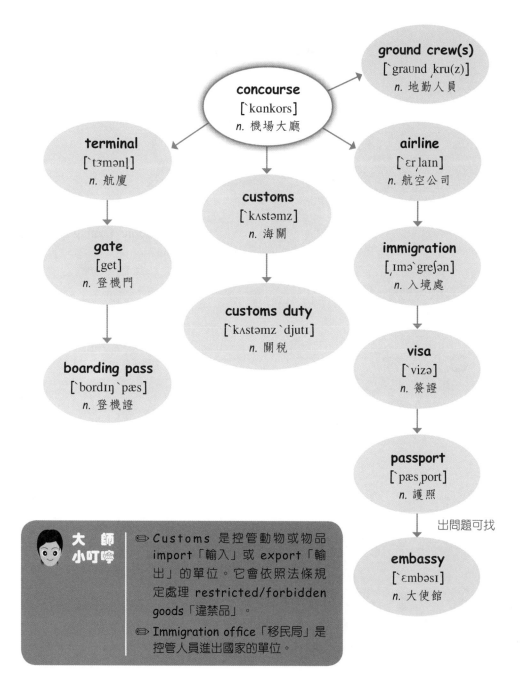

concourse
[ˋkɑnkors]
n. 機場大廳

ground crew(s)
[ˋgraʊnd ͵kru(z)]
n. 地勤人員

terminal
[ˋtɝmənl]
n. 航廈

customs
[ˋkʌstəmz]
n. 海關

airline
[ˋɛr͵laɪn]
n. 航空公司

gate
[get]
n. 登機門

immigration
[͵ɪməˋgreʃən]
n. 入境處

customs duty
[ˋkʌstəmz ˋdjutɪ]
n. 關稅

visa
[ˋvizə]
n. 簽證

boarding pass
[ˋbordɪŋ ˋpæs]
n. 登機證

passport
[ˋpæs͵port]
n. 護照

出問題可找

embassy
[ˋɛmbəsɪ]
n. 大使館

大頭小叮嚀

- Customs 是控管動物或物品 import「輸入」或 export「輸出」的單位。它會依照法條規定處理 restricted/forbidden goods「違禁品」。
- Immigration office「移民局」是控管人員進出國家的單位。

飛機相關

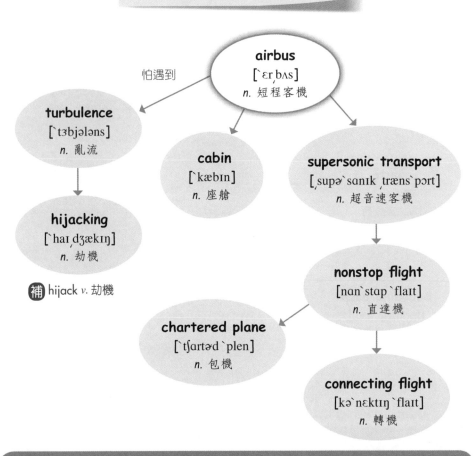

怕遇到

airbus
[ˋɛrˌbʌs]
n. 短程客機

turbulence
[ˋtɝbjələns]
n. 亂流

cabin
[ˋkæbɪn]
n. 座艙

supersonic transport
[ˌsupɚˋsɑnɪk ˌtrænsˋpɔrt]
n. 超音速客機

hijacking
[ˋhaɪˌdʒækɪŋ]
n. 劫機

 hijack v. 劫機

nonstop flight
[nɑnˋstɑp ˋflaɪt]
n. 直達機

chartered plane
[ˋtʃɑrtɚd ˋplen]
n. 包機

connecting flight
[kəˋnɛktɪŋ ˋflaɪt]
n. 轉機

大師小叮嚀

- 座艙等級的說法如下：first class「頭等艙」；business class 或 executive class「商務艙」；economy class「經濟艙」。

- Airsickness是「暈機」的名詞，airsick 是形容詞。例：I feel airsick.「我暈機了。」

- Aircraft hijacking 也可稱為 skyjacking。Hijacker (n.)「劫機者」，hijack (v.)「劫機」。例：The plane had been hijacked.「這架飛機被劫持了。」

機組人員

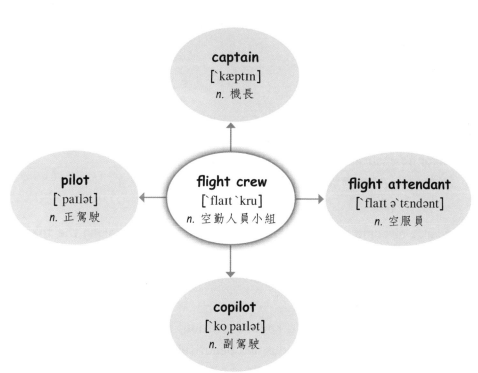

captain
[`kæptɪn]
n. 機長

pilot
[`paɪlət]
n. 正駕駛

flight crew
[`flaɪt `kru]
n. 空勤人員小組

flight attendant
[`flaɪt ə`tɛndənt]
n. 空服員

copilot
[`ko͵paɪlət]
n. 副駕駛

大師小叮嚀 ✍ Pilot「正駕駛」也可稱為 the first officer；copilot「副駕駛」也可稱為 the second officer。

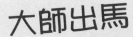 

❶ A **runway** is a strip of land at an **airport** for airplanes to take off and land on.

機場的跑道是讓飛機起飛、降落的長形陸地。

（strip *n.* 一塊；一條）

---

❷ The engineers are checking the wings and engines of the plane in the **hangar** to ensure the safety of the flight.

飛機維修員正在機棚裡檢查飛機的雙翼和引擎，以確保飛航安全。

---

❸ At large airports, it may take thirty minutes to travel along the **taxiway** to the **runway**.

在大型機場，光從滑行道到飛機跑道可能就得花上三十分鐘。

---

❹ Whether it's in a hotel, a railway station, or in an **airport terminal**, **concourses** are always spacious and beautiful.

不管是在飯店、車站或機場航廈，它們的大廳都很寬敞、漂亮。

（spacious *adj.* 寬敞的）

---

❺ China **Airlines** is the oldest airline company in Taiwan and it is known for its warm and friendly in-flight service and professional **pilots**.

中華航空是台灣歷史最悠久的航空公司，它以溫暖親切的機上服務和專業的機師而聞名。

❻ A **visa**, which is usually stamped or glued inside a **passport**, permits foreigners to formally enter the country.

簽證，通常蓋章或黏貼在護照內頁，是給外國人進入一國的正式許可。

（stamp v. 蓋上戳印　glue v. 黏貼）

❼ **Flight attendants** are trained to deal with all kinds of emergencies.

空服員被訓練處理任何緊急狀況。

❽ The common symptoms of **airsickness** are dizziness, nausea, and fatigue.

暈機最常見的症狀是頭暈目眩、噁心想吐和疲勞感。

（nausea n. 反胃作嘔　fatigue n. 勞累）

❾ **Hijackers** use passengers as hostages to force the flight to a given location.

劫機者將乘客當成人質來迫使飛機飛往指定的目的地。

（hostage n. 人質　force v. 強迫　given location n. 指定的目的地）

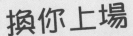

ↄ *Exercise* …… 根據你所聽到的對話完成填空。

(Tina and Evelyn are at the airport.)

Tina: Wow! The 1. 機場大廳 was built in fine style.

Evelyn: Did you 2. 再次檢查 your to-do list? I don't want you to leave anything you need at home.

Tina: 3. 放心啦 ! I'm sure I've got everything with me. Take out your 4. 護照 , we should 5. 辦理登機手續 . Let's go!

(After they have their boarding passes.)

Tina: The attendants were so nice; they were smiling the whole time when they were dealing with my stuff.

Evelyn: Yup. I've heard that, no matter what, the 6. 客服人員 for this 7. 航空公司 are very nice. You know what? I have thought of being a 8. 空姐 before. How about you?

Tina: Me?! Never! I'm not tall enough! And I 9. 會暈機 . Besides, 10. 碰到亂流我就會超緊張的 .

Evelyn: Well, maybe we should go by ship next time.

Tina: Oh, no! I forgot to bring my sunglasses! I can't sunbathe without them.

Evelyn: 11. 妳看吧，妳真是個糊塗蛋 . I told you to check everything before you left home.

Tina: Don't look at me like that! I can buy some in the 12. 免稅商店 . 13. 沒什麼大不了的啦 .

Evelyn: 14. 隨妳怎麼說 !

⟶ *Answer key* ··

1. concourse
2. double-check
3. Don't worry
4. passport
5. check in
6. customer service people
7. airline
8. flight attendant
9. get airsick
10. turbulence makes me nervous
11. See. You're always such a scatterbrain
12. duty free shop
13. It's not a big deal
14. Whatever you say

⟶ 中譯 ···

（*Tina* 和 *Evelyn* 在機場。）

Tina： 哇！這個機場大廳蓋得真漂亮！
Evelyn：妳有再次檢查妳的應帶物品清單嗎？我希望妳不要把該帶的東西忘在家裡了。
Tina： 放心啦！我確定我該帶的都帶齊了。拿出妳的護照，我們該去辦理登機手續了。走吧！

（她們拿到登機證之後。）

Tina： 那些服務人員好好喔！他們在幫我辦理的時候一直面帶微笑呢！
Evelyn：對啊！我聽說這家航空公司的客服人員不論什麼情況都非常親切。妳知道嗎？我曾經想過
要當空姐呢！妳有想過嗎？
Tina： 我？！從來沒有！我不夠高，而且我會暈機。還有，碰到亂流我就會超緊張的。
Evelyn：那，也許下次我們應該改搭船。
Tina： 喔，不！我忘了帶我的太陽眼鏡！沒有它們，我不能做日光浴！
Evelyn：妳看吧，妳真是個糊塗蛋。我早就跟妳說要在出門前檢查所有該帶的東西。
Tina： 別這樣看我嘛！我可以去免稅商店買一副啊！沒什麼大不了的啦。
Evelyn：隨妳怎麼說！

海上交通
Sea Transportation

船的種類

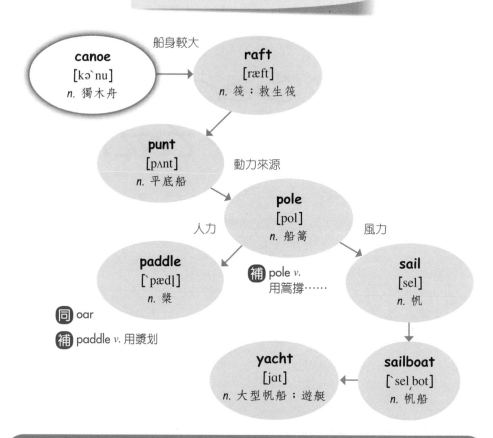

canoe
[kə`nu]
n. 獨木舟

船身較大

raft
[ræft]
n. 筏；救生筏

punt
[pʌnt]
n. 平底船

動力來源

pole
[pol]
n. 船篙

人力

paddle
[`pædl̩]
n. 槳

補 pole *v.*
用篙撐……

風力

sail
[sel]
n. 帆

同 oar

補 paddle *v.* 用槳划

yacht
[jɑt]
n. 大型帆船；遊艇

sailboat
[`sel͵bot]
n. 帆船

大師
小叮嚀

✍ Paddle 只有一枝，由划槳人（paddler）於中心支撐、左右划動使船前進，獨木舟屬於此類；oar 則有兩枝，通常固定在船上。

✍ Sailboat 是簡單型帆船；yacht 則指大型帆船（有船艙），後來也被用來指「遊艇」。

✍ Punt 的底是平的（常見航行於英國牛津和劍橋大學校內的小河中），用 pole 抵住河底使船前進。徐志摩《再別康橋》中的「尋夢，撐一支長篙，向青草更青處漫溯」描繪的正是用 pole 撐 punt 的情景。

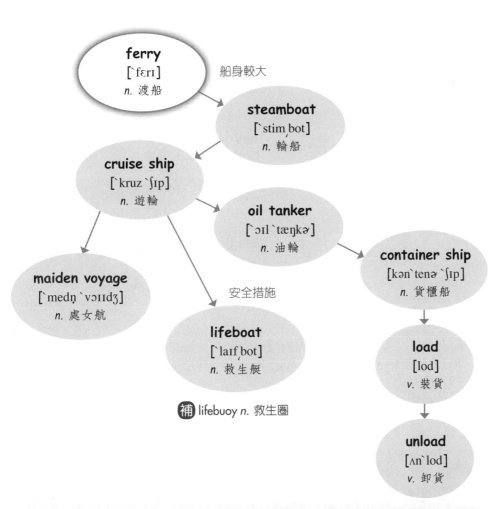

ferry
[`fɛrɪ]
n. 渡船

船身較大

steamboat
[`stim‚bot]
n. 輪船

cruise ship
[`kruz `ʃɪp]
n. 遊輪

oil tanker
[`ɔɪl `tæŋkɚ]
n. 油輪

container ship
[kən`tenɚ `ʃɪp]
n. 貨櫃船

maiden voyage
[`medṇ `vɔɪɪdʒ]
n. 處女航

安全措施

lifeboat
[`laɪf‚bot]
n. 救生艇

load
[lod]
v. 裝貨

unload
[ʌn`lod]
v. 卸貨

補 lifebuoy *n.* 救生圈

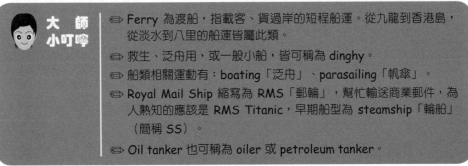

大師小叮嚀

✐ Ferry 為渡船，指載客、貨過岸的短程船運。從九龍到香港島，從淡水到八里的船運皆屬此類。

✐ 救生、泛舟用，或一般小船，皆可稱為 dinghy。

✐ 船類相關運動有：boating「泛舟」、parasailing「帆傘」。

✐ Royal Mail Ship 縮寫為 RMS「郵輪」，幫忙輸送商業郵件，為人熟知的應該是 RMS Titanic，早期船型為 steamship「輪船」（簡稱 SS）。

✐ Oil tanker 也可稱為 oiler 或 petroleum tanker。

船的各部分

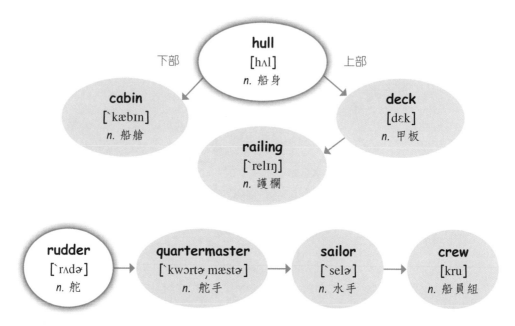

下部   hull [hʌl] n. 船身   上部

cabin [`kæbɪn] n. 船艙

deck [dɛk] n. 甲板

railing [`relɪŋ] n. 護欄

rudder [`rʌdə] n. 舵 → quartermaster [`kwɔrtə͵mæstə] n. 舵手 → sailor [`selə] n. 水手 → crew [kru] n. 船員組

 大師 小叮嚀

- Sailor 也可稱為 mariner，指在航海方面有專業知識的船員。 Crew 則指在飛機或船上工作的全體人員。

- 船上的艙等說法如下：stateroom「特等房」、grand/first-class cabin「頭等艙」、second-class cabin「二等艙」、third-class cabin「三等艙」。

- Chief officer 和 first officer 指的是「大副」，second officer 則是「二副」。

- Deck 除了指船上的地面外，也可指任何類似甲板的地方，如飛機或雙層公車的頂層。Deck chair 指的則是在海邊或泳池畔擺放的帆布摺疊躺椅。

- 相關俚語：to see how the wind blows「見風轉舵」

航海相關

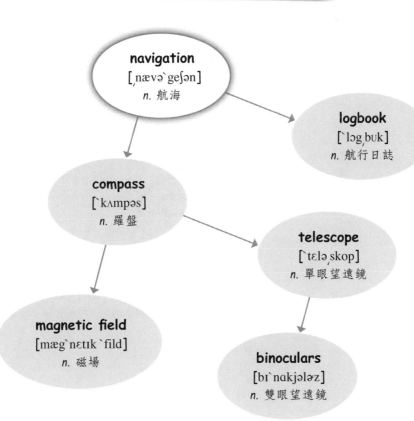

navigation
[ˌnævəˈgeʃən]
n. 航海

logbook
[ˈlɔgˌbʊk]
n. 航行日誌

compass
[ˈkʌmpəs]
n. 羅盤

telescope
[ˈtɛləˌskop]
n. 單眼望遠鏡

magnetic field
[mægˈnɛtɪk ˈfild]
n. 磁場

binoculars
[bɪˈnakjələz]
n. 雙眼望遠鏡

水上運動

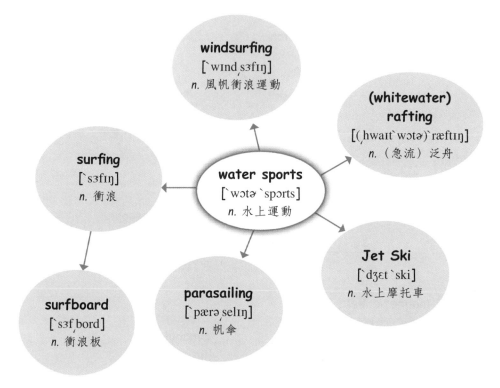

大師小叮嚀

☞ Windsurfing 是結合 sailing「風帆」和 surfing「衝浪」的水上運動。例：I'd like to go windsurfing.「我想去風帆衝浪。」或 I'd like to learn how to windsurf.「我想學如何風帆衝浪。」

☞ Jet Ski 是以水上摩托車的廠牌而得名。

大師出馬

單字用法看這邊！

❶ I **poled** the **punt** up the river and **paddled** the **canoe** down the river.
我以篙撐平底船逆流而上，再用槳划獨木舟順流而下。

❷ Even though the Titanic was the largest **steamer** in the world before she sailed and was touted as the safest ship ever built, she tragically sank into the ocean's depths on her **maiden voyage** in 1912.
雖然鐵達尼號在她以史上最安全的船為號召吸引顧客出航前，是當時世界上最大的輪船，她卻悲劇性地在 1912 年處女航中沉入海底深處。
（tout v. 招攬）

❸ A **lifeboat** is a boat designed to save people's lives when they get into trouble at sea. After the sinking of the Titanic, big ships such as **cruise ships** were required to have a sufficient number of lifeboats for all passengers on board.
救生艇是設計來拯救在海上遇上麻煩的人們。在鐵達尼號沉船後，諸如遠洋郵輪此類的大型船隻都必須有足夠數量的救生艇供船上乘客使用。
（on board ph. 在船上的）

❹ This lady's **cabin** is on the second level. Please show her the way.
這位小姐的艙房位於第二層，請帶她去。

❺ A **logbook** is a record of a voyage. They are often used to explain sea disasters in the same way that a black box is used to investigate airplane crashes.

航海日記是航行的記錄。它們常被用來說明海難原因，如同黑盒子被用來調查空難原因一般。

❻ A **compass** and **binoculars** are two great navigational tools for sailors. They use the former to determine direction and the latter to see distant objects.

羅盤和雙筒望遠鏡是水手們的二樣航海得力助手。他們用前者來決定方位，後者來看清遠方物體。

(navigational *adj.* 航行的)

換你上場

學習成效知分曉！

☞ *Exercise* ······ 根據你所聽到的對話完成填空。

(Tina and Evelyn are going on a trip to Japan by ship.)

Evelyn: This is my first time on a 1. 郵輪 ; everything is so new to me!

Tina: Me, too. It's my first time to stand on the 2. 甲板 and lean on the 3. 護欄 looking out to sea. I'm feeling like I'm Rose! *(Tina opens her arms.)*

Evelyn: Oh! Stop it! I don't think our ship has anything to do with the Titanic. *(Evelyn grabs the railing and is quiet for a while.)* Is this ship safe? I mean, does it carry enough 4. 救生艇 ?

Tina: 5. 放輕鬆一點嘛 . Ever since the Titanic sank in 1912, all big ships need to have enough lifeboats for all of the passengers.

Evelyn: Don't even mention that word!

Tina: 6. 好好好 , let's 7. 換個話題吧 ! Do you like 8. 水上活動 ?

Evelyn: I went 9. 泛舟 once. It was exciting but also a little dangerous.

Tina: Oh, yeah? I really like 10. 滑水 ! It makes me feel like I'm an ancient Chinese kung fu master who can walk on the surface of water.

Evelyn: You've got a wild imagination.

∽ *Answer key* ··

1. cruise ship
2. deck
3. railing
4. lifeboats
5. Relax/Take it easy
6. All right
7. talk about something else/change the subject
8. water sports
9. rafting
10. waterskiing

∽ 中譯 ··

（*Tina* 和 *Evelyn* 在前往日本的船上。）

Evelyn：這是我第一次坐郵輪，所有事都好新奇喔！

Tina： 我也是啊！這是我第一次站在甲板上倚著欄杆眺望大海，我覺得我好像 Rose 喔！（*Tina* 張開她的雙臂。）

Evelyn：喂，別再講了！我們這艘船和鐵達尼號一點關係都沒有！（*Evelyn* 抓著欄杆沉默了一會兒。）這艘船安全嗎？我是說……它有足夠的救生艇嗎？

Tina： 放輕鬆一點嘛。自從鐵達尼號在 1912 年沉船後，所有大型船隻都必須擁有足夠的救生艇供乘客使用。

Evelyn：別提那個名字！

Tina： 好好好，我們換個話題吧！妳喜歡水上活動嗎？

Evelyn：我泛舟過一次，很刺激可是也有點危險。

Tina： 是喔？我很喜歡滑水！它讓我覺得自己像中國古代的武術大師，可以在水面上行走。

Evelyn：妳的想像力太豐富了！

PART 5

教育
EDUCATION

校 園
Campus

學制

two-semester system
[`tu sə`mɛstɚ `sɪstəm]
n. 一年兩學期制

trimester system
[traɪ`mɛstɚ `sɪstəm]
n. 三學期制

four-quarter system
[`for `kwɔrtɚ `sɪstəm]
n. 一年四學期制

spring term
[`sprɪŋ ˏtɝm]
n. 春季班

summer term
[`sʌmɚ ˏtɝm]
n. 夏季班

大 師 小叮嚀

✐ 一年兩學期是台灣的一般學制。
✐ 三學期制是上、下學期加上夏季班。
✐ 四學期制則是上、下學期加上春季班和夏季班。

校友

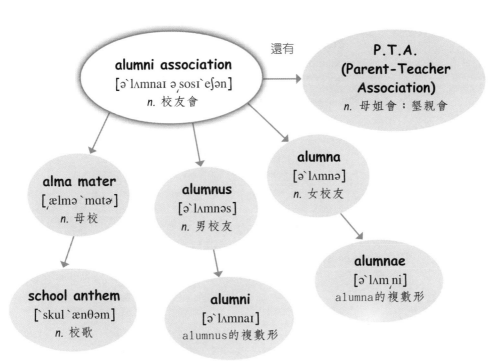

還有

alumni association
[ə`lʌmnaɪ əˌsosɪ`eʃən]
n. 校友會

**P.T.A.
(Parent-Teacher
Association)**
n. 母姐會；懇親會

alma mater
[`ælmə `matə]
n. 母校

alumnus
[ə`lʌmnəs]
n. 男校友

alumna
[ə`lʌmnə]
n. 女校友

school anthem
[`skul `ænθəm]
n. 校歌

alumni
[ə`lʌmnaɪ]
alumnus的複數形

alumnae
[ə`lʌm͵ni]
alumna的複數形

大師小叮嚀

- School anthem 也可稱為 school song；「國歌」則是 national anthem。
- Alumni 有時也可用來泛指男女校友。
- 「在校功課成績好」可用 do great in school 來表示。
- Summa cum laude [`sumə `kʌm `laudə] (*adv.*)「以優異成績畢業」，例：He graduated summa cum laude.「他以優異的成績畢業。」

學校相關

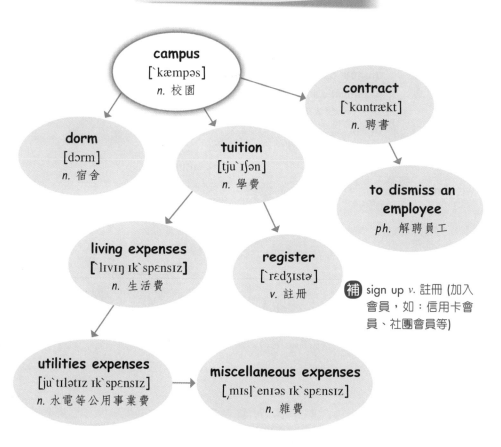

campus
[ˋkæmpəs]
n. 校園

contract
[ˋkɑntrækt]
n. 聘書

dorm
[dɔrm]
n. 宿舍

tuition
[tjuˋɪʃən]
n. 學費

to dismiss an employee
ph. 解聘員工

living expenses
[ˋlɪvɪŋ ɪkˋspɛnsɪz]
n. 生活費

register
[ˋrɛdʒɪstɚ]
v. 註冊

補 sign up *v.* 註冊 (加入
會員，如：信用卡會
員、社團會員等)

utilities expenses
[juˋtɪlətɪz ɪkˋspɛnsɪz]
n. 水電等公用事業費

miscellaneous expenses
[ˏmɪsḷˋenɪəs ɪkˋspɛnsɪz]
n. 雜費

大師
小叮嚀

✐ 註冊成為社團會員等的「註冊」，則用 sign up 這個字。
✐ 其他校園常用用語，補充如下：
I live on campus. 「我住校內。」
I live off campus. 「我住校外。」
I rent a place off campus. 「我在校外租房子。」

課堂相關

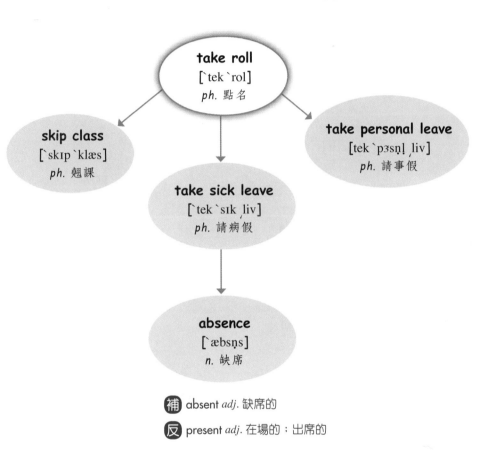

take roll
[ˋtek ˋrol]
ph. 點名

skip class
[ˋskɪp ˋklæs]
ph. 翹課

take sick leave
[ˋtek ˋsɪk ˌliv]
ph. 請病假

take personal leave
[tek ˋpɝsn̩ḷ ˌliv]
ph. 請事假

absence
[ˋæbsn̩s]
n. 缺席

補 absent *adj.* 缺席的

反 present *adj.* 在場的；出席的

功、過

cheat
[tʃit]
v. 作弊

demerit
[dɪˋmɛrɪt]
n. 記過

相反

merit
[ˋmɛrɪt]
n. 功；獎

三個大過就

prize
[praɪz]
n. 獎品

dismissed from school
ph. 被退學

withdraw from school
ph. 自動退學

citation
[saɪˋteʃən]
n. 獎狀

take leave of absence
ph. 休學

apply for a scholarship
ph. 申請獎學金

大師
小叮嚀

✏ 常用用語補充如下：
Don't cheat on the exam!「考試不要作弊！」
Are you going to apply for a scholarship?「你要申請獎學金嗎？」
Did the teacher take roll?「老師有點名嗎？」
I got a demerit.「我被記過了。」

教育

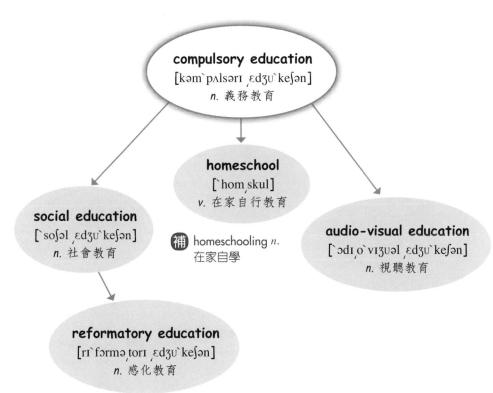

compulsory education
[kəm`pʌlsərɪ ˌɛdʒʊ`keʃən]
n. 義務教育

homeschool
[`hom͵skul]
v. 在家自行教育

social education
[`soʃəl ͵ɛdʒʊ`keʃən]
n. 社會教育

補 homeschooling *n.*
在家自學

audio-visual education
[`ɔdɪˏo`vɪʒuəl ͵ɛdʒʊ`keʃən]
n. 視聽教育

reformatory education
[rɪ`fɔrmə͵torɪ ͵ɛdʒʊ`keʃən]
n. 感化教育

大師
小叮嚀

✏ Homeschooling 在西方非常普遍，是指學齡兒童在家中接受教育，有別於學校教育。

考試

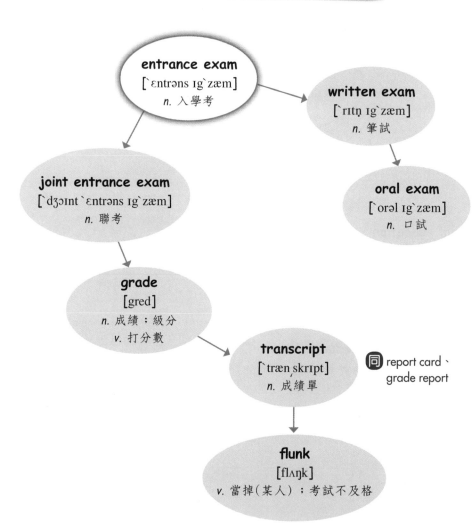

entrance exam
[ˋɛntrəns ɪgˋzæm]
n. 入學考

written exam
[ˋrɪtn̩ ɪgˋzæm]
n. 筆試

joint entrance exam
[ˋdʒɔɪnt ˋɛntrəns ɪgˋzæm]
n. 聯考

oral exam
[ˋorəl ɪgˋzæm]
n. 口試

grade
[gred]
n. 成績；級分
v. 打分數

transcript
[ˋtrænˏskrɪpt]
n. 成績單

🔲 report card、
grade report

flunk
[flʌŋk]
v. 當掉（某人）；考試不及格

修課

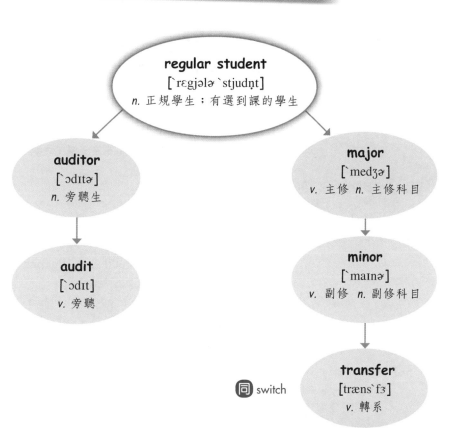

regular student
[ˋrɛgjələ ˋstjudn̩t]
n. 正規學生；有選到課的學生

auditor
[ˋɔdɪtə]
n. 旁聽生

audit
[ˋɔdɪt]
v. 旁聽

major
[ˋmedʒə]
v. 主修 *n.* 主修科目

minor
[ˋmaɪnə]
v. 副修 *n.* 副修科目

transfer
[trænsˋfɜ]
v. 轉系

同 switch

 大師小叮嚀

✏ Major 和 in 搭配使用，例：I'm majoring in English.「我主修英文。」

✏ English major (*n.*)「主修英文的學生」，例：I'm an English major.「我的主修是英文。」

✏ Transfer 的使用範例如下：He transferred from the Department of Japanese.「他是從日文系轉過來的。」Transfer 也可當「轉學生」名詞使用，但重音移至第一音節。

非課業類測驗

aptitude test
[ˋæptəˌtjud ˋtɛst]
n. 性向與能力測驗

補 aptitude *n.* 天資；才能

IQ (Intelligence Quotient)
[ɪnˋtɛlədʒəns ˋkwoʃənt]
n. 智商

EQ (Emotional Intelligence Quotient)
[ɪˋmoʃənḷ ɪnˋtɛlədʒəns ˋkwoʃənt]
n. 情緒智商

AQ (Adversity Quotient)
[ədˋvɝsətɪ ˋkwoʃənt]
n. 逆境智商

補 adversity *n.* 逆境；不幸

CQ (Creativity Quotient)
[ˌkrieˋtɪvətɪ ˋkwoʃənt]
n. 創意指數

大師出馬

❶ Do high **tuition** fees ensure high-quality education?
高學費確保高品質教育嗎？

❷ My parents paid my **tuiton**, but I still took a part-time job to cover my **living expenses**.
父母支付我的學費，但我還是做一份兼職工作來支付生活開銷。

❸ Miss Lee **took** two days **personal leave** to attend a funeral last week.
李小姐上星期請二天事假去參加喪禮。

❹ Christina **majored** in English and **minored** in international trade when she was in school.
克莉絲蒂娜在校時主修英文，輔修國際貿易。

❺ **EQ** is more important than **IQ** in competitive job markets.
在競爭的職場，情緒智商比智商還要重要。

❻ The **entrance exam** for graduate school includes an **oral exam** in addition to a **written exam**.
研究所入學考除了筆試還有口試。
（graduate school *n.* 研究所）

❼ In Taiwan, most senior high school students study in cram schools in order to raise their score on the **joint entrance exam**.
為了在聯考有更好的成績，台灣大部分的高中生都在補習班補習。

換你上場

學 習 成 效 知 分 曉!

Exercise ...... 根據你所聽到的對話完成填空。

Tina: Did you do well on your graduate school 1. 入學考 ?

Evelyn: Not really.

Tina: How come?

Evelyn: I didn't do well on the 2. 口試 .

Tina: What did the professors ask?

Evelyn: One of the three asked me to talk about my own 3. 缺點 . And the other two just made sarcastic remarks.

Tina: Don't worry. They were trying to test your 4. 情緒智商 . How did you reply?

Evelyn: I said that my mother always complains about my messy bedroom and that I felt nervous.

Tina: You got it right. Never 5. 露出馬腳 by saying "I'm lazy" or "my English is poor." Did you take any classes in cram schools?

Evelyn: No, I couldn't afford it.

Tina: What if you don't get accepted?

Evelyn: No big deal. 6. 不經一事, 不長一智 . Besides, 7. 校友 from my school will help me find a job after I graduate.

✐ *Answer key* ┈┈┈┈┈┈┈┈┈┈┈┈┈┈┈┈┈┈┈┈┈┈┈┈┈┈┈┈┈┈┈┈

1. entrance exam

2. oral exam

3. weaknesses

4. EQ

5. give yourself away

6. Live and learn. / A fall into the pit, a gain in your wit.

7. alumni

✐ 中譯 ┈┈┈

Tina： 妳研究所入學考考的好嗎？

Evelyn：不怎麼好。

Tina： 為什麼？

Evelyn：我的口試不順利。

Tina： 教授問了什麼問題？

Evelyn：其中一個要我談談自身的缺點，其他兩個只說了一些諷刺的話。

Tina： 不要擔心，他們只是想測試妳的情緒智商。妳怎麼回答？

Evelyn：我說我媽總是抱怨我的房間太亂，而且，我有一點緊張。

Tina： 這樣說就對了。千萬不要露出馬腳說「我很懶惰」或是「我的英文不好」。妳有到補習班補習嗎？

Evelyn：沒有，我負擔不起。

Tina： 如果妳沒有被錄取呢？

Evelyn：沒什麼大不了的。不經一事，不長一智。此外，我學校的校友在我畢業後會幫我找工作。

數 學

Mathematics

運算

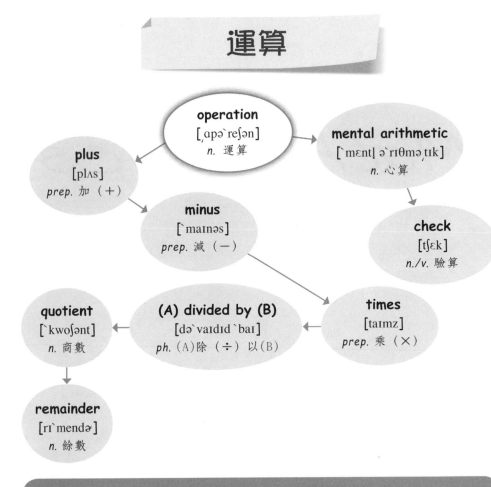

operation
[ˌɑpəˋreʃən]
n. 運算

plus
[plʌs]
prep. 加（＋）

mental arithmetic
[ˋmɛntḷ əˋrɪθməˌtɪk]
n. 心算

minus
[ˋmaɪnəs]
prep. 減（－）

check
[tʃɛk]
n./v. 驗算

quotient
[ˋkwoʃənt]
n. 商數

(A) divided by (B)
[dəˋvaɪdɪd ˋbaɪ]
ph. (A)除（÷）以(B)

times
[taɪmz]
prep. 乘（×）

remainder
[rɪˋmendə]
n. 餘數

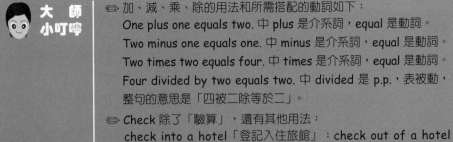

大師小叮嚀

✍ 加、減、乘、除的用法和所需搭配的動詞如下：
One plus one equals two. 中 plus 是介系詞，equal 是動詞。
Two minus one equals one. 中 minus 是介系詞，equal 是動詞。
Two times two equals four. 中 times 是介系詞，equal 是動詞。
Four divided by two equals two. 中 divided 是 p.p.，表被動，
整句的意思是「四被二除等於二」。

✍ Check 除了「驗算」，還有其他用法：
check into a hotel「登記入住旅館」；check out of a hotel
「付帳離開旅館」。

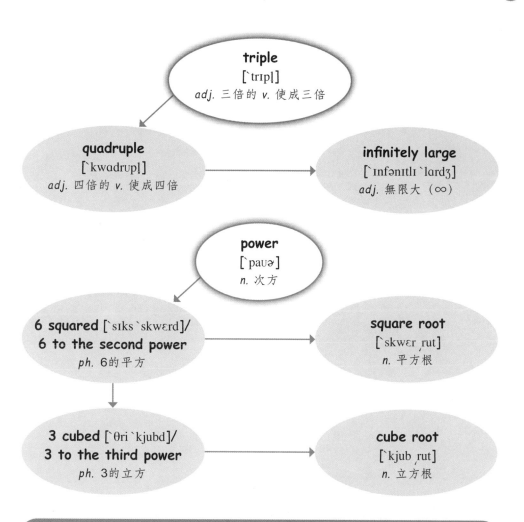

triple
[`trɪpl̩]
adj. 三倍的 *v.* 使成三倍

quadruple
[`kwadrʊpl̩]
adj. 四倍的 *v.* 使成四倍

infinitely large
[`ɪnfənɪtlɪ `lardʒ]
adj. 無限大（∞）

power
[`pauə]
n. 次方

6 squared [`sɪks `skwɛrd]/
6 to the second power
ph. 6的平方

square root
[`skwɛr ˌrut]
n. 平方根

3 cubed [`θri `kjubd]/
3 to the third power
ph. 3的立方

cube root
[`kjub ˌrut]
n. 立方根

 大師小叮嚀

✏ Triple 和 double 的使用範例如下：
I'll have a pepperoni and mushroom with double cheese, please.「我要一份義大利香腸蘑菇披薩，加上雙份起司，麻煩你。」
My salary has tripled.「我的薪水變成原來的三倍。」

✏ 平方根、立方根的表示範例如下：
The square root of 9 is 3.「9 的平方根是 3。」
The cube root of 8 is 2.「8 的立方根是 2。」

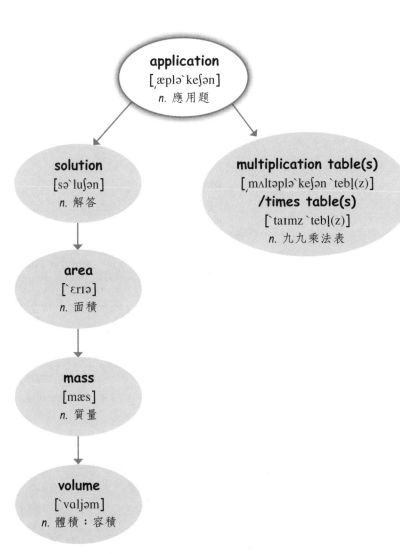

數字

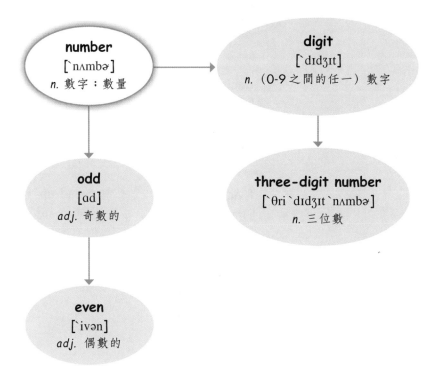

number
[ˋnʌmbɚ]
n. 數字；數量

digit
[ˋdɪdʒɪt]
n. (0-9 之間的任一) 數字

odd
[ɑd]
adj. 奇數的

three-digit number
[ˋθri ˋdɪdʒɪt ˋnʌmbɚ]
n. 三位數

even
[ˋivən]
adj. 偶數的

大師小叮嚀 | ✐ Number 和 digit 不同之處可舉例說明如下：
10 這個 number 含有兩個 digits：1 和 0。

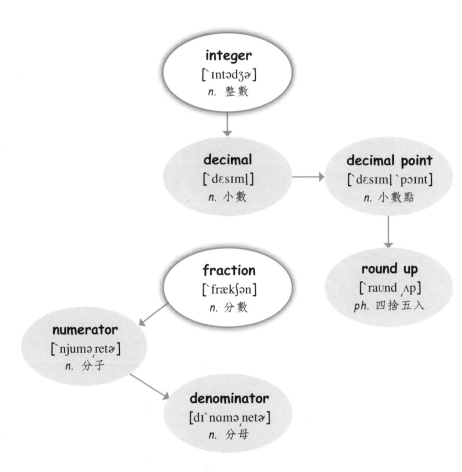

integer
[ˈɪntədʒɚ]
n. 整數

decimal
[ˈdɛsɪml̩]
n. 小數

decimal point
[ˈdɛsɪml̩ ˈpɔɪnt]
n. 小數點

round up
[ˈraʊnd ˌʌp]
ph. 四捨五入

fraction
[ˈfrækʃən]
n. 分數

numerator
[ˈnjuməˌretɚ]
n. 分子

denominator
[dɪˈnaməˌnetɚ]
n. 分母

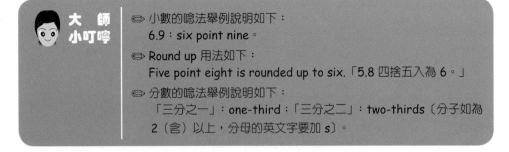

大師
小叮嚀

- 小數的唸法舉例說明如下：
  6.9：six point nine。
- Round up 用法如下：
  Five point eight is rounded up to six. 「5.8 四捨五入為 6。」
- 分數的唸法舉例說明如下：
  「三分之一」：one-third；「三分之二」：two-thirds〔分子如為 2（含）以上，分母的英文字要加 s〕。

學理

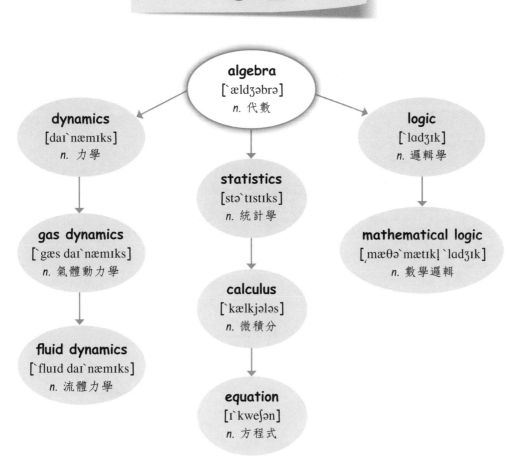

algebra
[ˋældʒəbrə]
n. 代數

dynamics
[daɪˋnæmɪks]
n. 力學

logic
[ˋlɑdʒɪk]
n. 邏輯學

statistics
[stəˋtɪstɪks]
n. 統計學

gas dynamics
[ˋgæs daɪˋnæmɪks]
n. 氣體動力學

mathematical logic
[͵mæθəˋmætɪk ˋlɑdʒɪk]
n. 數學邏輯

calculus
[ˋkælkjələs]
n. 微積分

fluid dynamics
[ˋfluɪd daɪˋnæmɪks]
n. 流體力學

equation
[ɪˋkweʃən]
n. 方程式

大師
小叮嚀

✏ Algebra 是含有 x 及 y（此處的 x 和 y 稱作為 variable「變數」）的學科。

✏ Statistics 除了統計學，亦可作「統計數據」(*pl.*) 解。例：I need to see the statistics before I make a decision.「我做決定之前需要看數據」，單數則為 statistic。

幾何

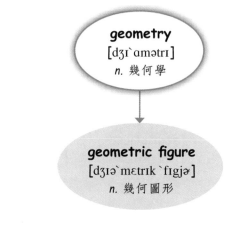

geometry
[dʒɪ`ɑmətrɪ]
n. 幾何學

geometric figure
[dʒɪə`mɛtrɪk `fɪgjə]
n. 幾何圖形

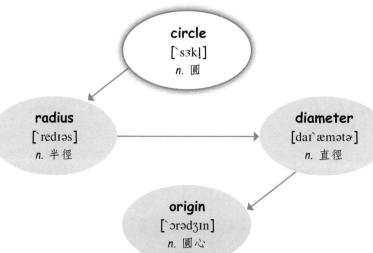

circle
[`sɜkl]
n. 圓

radius
[`redɪəs]
n. 半徑

diameter
[daɪ`æmətə]
n. 直徑

origin
[`ɔrədʒɪn]
n. 圓心

大師出馬

❶ I am not good at **mental arithmetic**.
我心算不好。

❷ The **equations** in **algebra** and **calculus** give me headaches.
代數和微積分中的方程式讓我頭疼。

❸ I spend about NT$120,000 per semester on tuition, utilities, and miscellaneous living expenses. **Plus** rent, the total amount is nearly NT$130,000.
我每學期大約花十二萬在學費、水電費和生活雜費,加上房租,總共花了將近十三萬。
(total *adj.* 總計的)

❹ My parents **tripled** my allowance after I entered college because of my increased living expenses.
我上大學之後,我父母把我的零用錢增加為三倍,因為我的生活費增加。
(allowance *n.* 零用錢)

❺ Could you teach me how to memorize the **multiplication tables**?
你可以教我怎麼背九九乘法表嗎?

❻ The **area** of Taiwan is 36,000 square kilometers, and the population is 23,000,000.
台灣的土地面積是三萬六千平方公里,人口則是二千三百萬。

換你上場

學 習 成 效 知 分 曉！

☞ *Exercise*

舉凡銀行交易、國際貿易到日常生活，數字扮演著極其重要的角色。不熟悉數字進位，有可能造成「千萬」的誤差。

英文中的數字單位只有 hundred「百」、thousand「千」、million「百萬」、billion「十億」、trillion「兆」。其他像是「萬」、「十萬」、「千萬」、「億」，則分以 10 thousand、100 thousand、10 million、100 million 表達。

多練習才能熟悉英文數字的用法。接著就來試試，你是否能看到數字馬上就說出英文唸法。

❶ 八萬
❷ 六十七萬
❸ 二百三十萬
❹ 二百三十萬七千
❺ 五千六百萬
❻ 一億
❼ 五十七億

☞ *Answer key*

❶ eighty thousand
❷ six hundred (and) seventy thousand
❸ two point three million
❹ two million three hundred (and) seven thousand
❺ fifty six million
❻ one hundred million
❼ five point seven billion

⊶ *Exercise* ‥‥‥ 根據你所聽到的對話完成填空。

Tina: I visited the museum yesterday.

Evelyn: Did you see anything good?

Tina: They had several interesting Picassos. They were all composed of many 1. 幾何圖形 .

Evelyn: He was so talented. Unlike my brother, Picasso transformed lifeless circles, triangles, and squares into vivid paintings.

Tina: What does your brother do?

Evelyn: He's a 2. 數學系學生 . He only cares about 3. 代數 and 4. 微積分 .

Tina: And 5. 方程式 , right?

Evelyn: 6. 夠了 . Give me a break.

Tina: 7. 沒那麼糟 . Look on the bright side. You don't have to worry about getting stuck on really hard 8. 數學問題 . There's always someone who can help you.

Evelyn: Yeah, but he's still so boring. You know, I heard that Picasso once said, "If only we could pull out our brain and use only our eyes."[1] I don't think my brother would agree.

↪ *Answer key* ────────────────────────

1. geometric figures
2. math major
3. algebra
4. calculus
5. equations
6. Enough already
7. It's not that bad
8. math problems

↪ 解析 ────────────────────────────

① If only we could pull out our brain and use only our eyes.「用感性去欣賞，而非用理性去看。」為畢卡索的名言。

↪ 中譯 ────────────────────────────

Tina： 我昨天去參觀博物館。

Evelyn：妳有沒有看到什麼好玩的展覽品呢？

Tina： 他們有幾幅有趣的畢卡索畫作。它們都是由幾何圖形所構成的。

Evelyn：他真的很有天賦。不像我弟弟，畢卡索把沒有生命的圓形、三角形和正方形轉化成栩栩如生的畫作。

Tina： 妳弟弟是做什麼的呢？

Evelyn：他是數學系學生。他只在乎代數和微積分。

Tina： 還有方程式，對不對？

Evelyn：夠了，饒了我吧。

Tina： 沒那麼糟。往好的方面看，妳不必擔心被艱澀的數學題困住，總是有人可以幫妳解題。

Evelyn：是啊，不過他還是很無趣。妳知道，我聽畢卡索說過：「用感性去欣賞，而非用理性去看。」我想他是不會認同的。

PART 6

娛　樂
ENTERTAINMENT

電 影
Movies and Films

電影種類

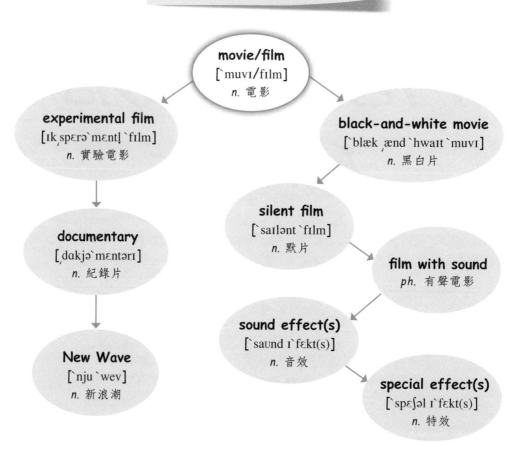

movie/film
[`muvɪ/fɪlm]
n. 電影

experimental film
[ɪkˌspɛrəˋmɛntl̩ ˋfɪlm]
n. 實驗電影

black-and-white movie
[ˋblæk ˏænd ˋhwaɪt ˋmuvɪ]
n. 黑白片

silent film
[ˋsaɪlənt ˋfɪlm]
n. 默片

documentary
[ˏdɑkjəˋmɛntərɪ]
n. 紀錄片

film with sound
ph. 有聲電影

New Wave
[ˋnju ˋwev]
n. 新浪潮

sound effect(s)
[ˋsaʊnd ɪˋfɛkt(s)]
n. 音效

special effect(s)
[ˋspɛʃəl ɪˋfɛkt(s)]
n. 特效

大師小叮嚀

New Wave（原法文 *La Nouvelle Vague*）是二次大戰後重建期的新思潮。各國皆有新浪潮，但以法國影響最為深遠，尤其是在電影界。當時一批新導演以創新手法拍攝出許多不同於以往風格且原創性高的影片，像是：楚浮（François Truffaut）的 *The 400 Blows*《四百擊》、高達（Jean-Luc Godard）的 *Breathless*《斷了氣》等。

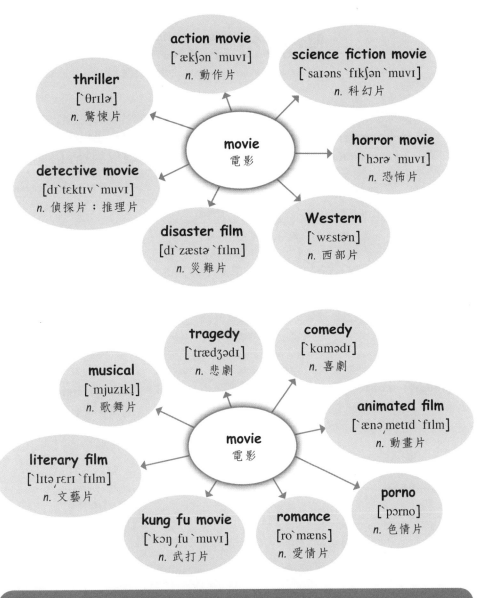

action movie
[`ækʃən `muvɪ]
n. 動作片

science fiction movie
[`saɪəns `fɪkʃən `muvɪ]
n. 科幻片

thriller
[`θrɪlə]
n. 驚悚片

horror movie
[`hɔrə `muvɪ]
n. 恐怖片

detective movie
[dɪ`tɛktɪv `muvɪ]
n. 偵探片；推理片

movie
電影

disaster film
[dɪ`zæstə `fɪlm]
n. 災難片

Western
[`wɛstən]
n. 西部片

tragedy
[`trædʒədɪ]
n. 悲劇

comedy
[`kɑmədɪ]
n. 喜劇

musical
[`mjuzɪkl]
n. 歌舞片

animated film
[`ænə‚metɪd `fɪlm]
n. 動畫片

movie
電影

literary film
[`lɪtə‚rɛrɪ `fɪlm]
n. 文藝片

porno
[`pɔrno]
n. 色情片

kung fu movie
[`kɔŋ fu `muvɪ]
n. 武打片

romance
[ro`mæns]
n. 愛情片

大師 小叮嚀
- Science fiction movie 也可稱為 sci-fi movie。
- Porno 是 pornographic movie 的縮寫，也可稱為 adult film 或 erotic（色情的）film。

電影從業人員

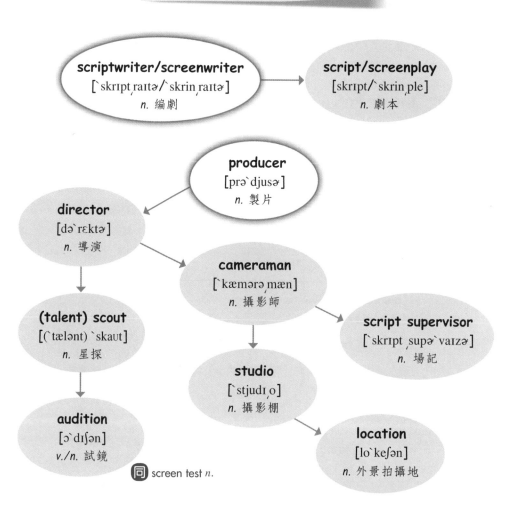

scriptwriter/screenwriter
[ˋskrɪptˏraɪtɚ/ˋskrɪnˏraɪtɚ]
n. 編劇

script/screenplay
[skrɪpt/ˋskrɪnˏple]
n. 劇本

producer
[prəˋdjusɚ]
n. 製片

director
[dəˋrɛktɚ]
n. 導演

cameraman
[ˋkæmərəˏmæn]
n. 攝影師

script supervisor
[ˋskrɪptˏsupɚˋvaɪzɚ]
n. 場記

(talent) scout
[(ˋtælənt) ˋskaʊt]
n. 星探

studio
[ˋstjudɪˏo]
n. 攝影棚

audition
[ɔˋdɪʃən]
v./n. 試鏡

同 screen test n.

location
[loˋkeʃən]
n. 外景拍攝地

大師
小叮嚀 ✏ Screenplay 又可分寫 original「原著」和 adapted「改編」兩種。

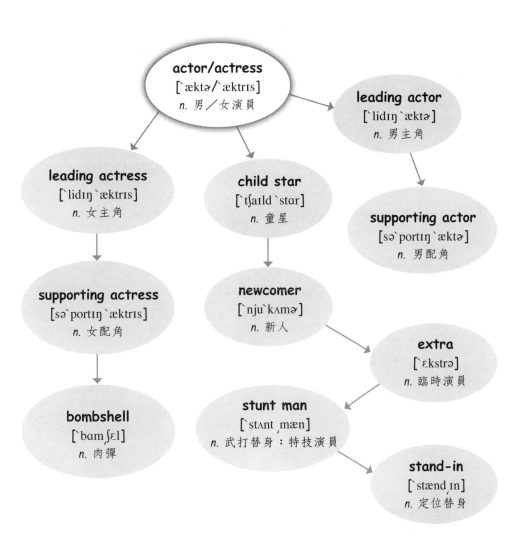

actor/actress
[ˋæktə/ˋæktrɪs]
n. 男／女演員

leading actor
[ˋlidɪŋ ˋæktə]
n. 男主角

leading actress
[ˋlidɪŋ ˋæktrɪs]
n. 女主角

child star
[ˋtʃaɪld ˋstar]
n. 童星

supporting actor
[səˋportɪŋ ˋæktə]
n. 男配角

supporting actress
[səˋportɪŋ ˋæktrɪs]
n. 女配角

newcomer
[ˋnjuˋkʌmə]
n. 新人

extra
[ˋɛkstrə]
n. 臨時演員

bombshell
[ˋbamˌʃɛl]
n. 肉彈

stunt man
[ˋstʌntˌmæn]
n. 武打替身；特技演員

stand-in
[ˋstændˌɪn]
n. 定位替身

大師小叮嚀

- Stunt man 又稱為 stunt performer。
- 電影拍攝前，代替演員站在表演位置設定佈景、光線的替身稱為 stand-in。電影的替身可分為兩種：stunt double 是危險動作的替身；而特殊技藝（如彈琴、歌唱、跳舞或裸戲）的替身則為 body double。

電影拍攝、後製

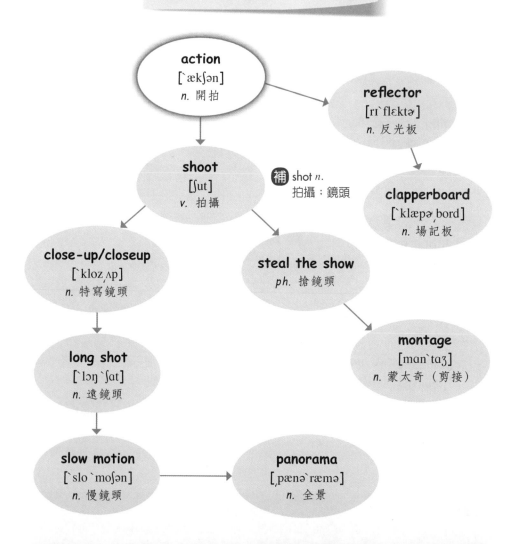

action
[`ækʃən]
n. 開拍

reflector
[rɪ`flɛktə]
n. 反光板

shoot
[ʃut]
v. 拍攝

補 shot *n.*
拍攝；鏡頭

clapperboard
[`klæpə͵bord]
n. 場記板

close-up/closeup
[`kloz͵ʌp]
n. 特寫鏡頭

steal the show
ph. 搶鏡頭

long shot
[`lɔŋ `ʃat]
n. 遠鏡頭

montage
[man`taʒ]
n. 蒙太奇（剪接）

slow motion
[`slo `moʃən]
n. 慢鏡頭

panorama
[͵pænə`ræmə]
n. 全景

大師小叮嚀 | ☞ Pan「移動攝影機拍攝全景」(*v.*) 是由 panorama 引申而來，例：the panorama of city life「都市生活的各種樣貌」。

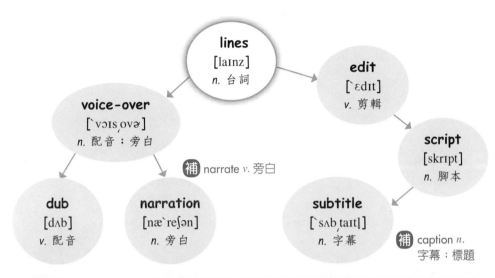

lines
[laɪnz]
n. 台詞

edit
[`ɛdɪt]
v. 剪輯

voice-over
[`vɔɪsˏovə]
n. 配音；旁白

補 narrate v. 旁白

script
[skrɪpt]
n. 腳本

dub
[dʌb]
v. 配音

narration
[næ`reʃən]
n. 旁白

subtitle
[`sʌbˏtaɪtl]
n. 字幕

補 caption n.
字幕；標題

◈ Voice-over 指的是電玩人物、玩偶（puppet）的配音，體育競賽現場戰況分析（live sport broadcast）、廣告（commercial）等的旁白也都屬此類。配音員則是 voice actor/actress 或 voice artist，跟演員一樣，配音也是一種表演藝術，配音員的聲音需要演技（voice acting）。

◈ Dub 指的是為動畫配音，或是替電影配上不同語言版本的發音，例如電影銷售至全球各國，某些國家會為影片配上本國語言，此項技術又稱為 ADR（automated dialogue replacement）。Dub 的使用範例如下：
Eddie Murphy dubbed the voice of the donkey in *Shrek*.
艾迪墨菲幫《史瑞克》裡的驢子配音。

◈ Narrate 的範例如下：
Do you know who's narrating this documentary? Her voice sounds familiar.
你知道誰幫這部紀錄片配旁白嗎？她的聲音聽起來很熟悉。

◈ Caption 指的是電視上的字幕。另外，招牌（signboard）、告示板（billboard）、商標或圖表上的文字或解說也稱為 caption。

◈ Subtitle 是電影字幕，有時佐以解釋以幫助耳聾或重聽的觀眾了解劇情（closed captioning）。DVD 內設的字幕選擇為 prerendered subtitles。

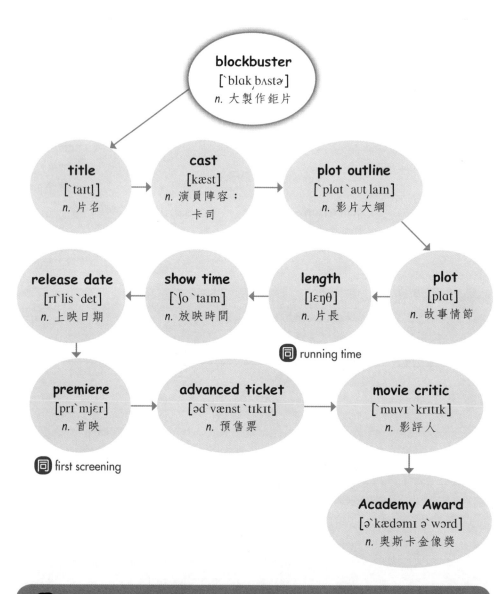

blockbuster
[ˋblɑk͵bʌstɚ]
n. 大製作鉅片

title
[ˋtaɪtl]
n. 片名

cast
[kæst]
n. 演員陣容；
卡司

plot outline
[ˋplɑt ˋaut͵laɪn]
n. 影片大綱

release date
[rɪˋlis ˋdet]
n. 上映日期

show time
[ˋʃo ˋtaɪm]
n. 放映時間

length
[lɛŋθ]
n. 片長

plot
[plɑt]
n. 故事情節

同 running time

premiere
[prɪˋmjɛr]
n. 首映

advanced ticket
[ədˋvænst ˋtɪkɪt]
n. 預售票

movie critic
[ˋmuvɪ ˋkrɪtɪk]
n. 影評人

同 first screening

Academy Award
[əˋkædəmɪ əˋwɔrd]
n. 奧斯卡金像獎

大師 小叮嚀

☞ 二輪戲院為 second-run theater；首輪為 first-run。露天戲院 為 open cinema，美國的汽車影院（坐在自己車內觀看露天大螢 幕）則為 drive-in theater。

☞ 奧斯卡小金人稱為 Oscar。

大師出馬

❶ *Steamboat Willie* was the first Mickey Mouse **film** that featured sound.
《蒸汽船威利》是米老鼠的第一部有聲電影。
（feature v. 以……為特色）

❷ The difference between a **musical** film and a stage musical is the use of lavish background scenery, which is difficult to create for the theater.
歌舞片和舞台音樂劇的不同在於華麗的背景，這對劇場來說是很難達成的。
（lavish adj. 華麗的）

❸ New **special effects** techniques have made **disaster films** much more spectacular.
新的特效技術讓災難片益加壯觀。
（spectacular adj. 壯觀的）

❹ **Experimental film** is one of the major genres of film-making.
實驗電影是電影製作的主要類型之一。

❺ An **audition** is used to evaluate the suitability of an **actor** or **actress** to perform a particular role.
試鏡是用來評量一位演員或女演員是否適合扮演某個特定角色。
（suitability n. 合適度）

❻ Different from **extras**, who are usually used in the background of a film, **stunt men** replace the **leading actors** in dangerous scenes.
和常用來當作電影背景的臨時演員不同，武打替身在危險場景代替主角上場。

❼ A **panorama** is a wide-angle view in painting, photography, film, or video.
「全景」是在繪畫、照片、電影或影帶上的一個廣角景象。
（wide-angle *adj.* 廣角的）

❽ Even though the leading actor and actress gave excellent performances, it was a young **newcomer** who **stole the show**.
儘管男女主角演得很出色，搶盡鋒頭的卻是一位新進演員。

❾ Tommy is a **voice actor** who does **voice-overs** in animated films and television commercials.
湯米是一個配音員，他幫動畫電影和電視廣告配音。

❿ When adapting a book into a **screenplay**, the **screenwriter** not only worries about satisfying picky readers, but also about pleasing the audience members who have never read the book.
把書改編成劇本時，編劇不但得費心讓挑剔的讀者滿意，還得取悅從沒看過這本書的觀眾。

⓫ Before watching a movie, I have a look at the **plot outline** and **cast**
看電影前，我會先看一下劇情大綱和演員名單。

⓬ *The Sound of Music* was the first film to defeat *Gone With the Wind* in ticket sales. It was a **blockbuster**, and played for more than a year in some first-run theaters.
《真善美》是第一部賣座超越《亂世佳人》的電影，它是部轟動的鉅片，在某些首輪戲院甚至播放超過一年。

換你上場

∽ *Exercise* ┈┈ 根據你所聽到的對話完成填空。

(Tina and Evelyn are chatting in a coffee shop.)

Evelyn: You look so happy! Did your 1. 白馬王子 give you a kiss?

Tina: Not exactly. But I just had a date with 2. 所有女人的夢中情人 , Mr. Darcy.

Evelyn: Oh, I see. You just saw the movie *Pride and Prejudice*. Right?

Tina: 3. 沒錯 ! I saw it on DVD. Have you seen it? It's the first 4. 愛情喜劇 in history and the best!

Evelyn: I read the novel a long time ago and really liked Mr. Darcy. How does he look in the movie? Does he look like how Jane Austen described him in the book?

Tina: Almost the same. 5. 兩位男女主角 are fine performers and 6. 飾演她姐妹的女配角 was great, too. But 7. 大體上說來 8. 比起電影，我比較喜歡原著 , because the book allows me to use my imagination.

Evelyn: You're right. 9. 我是哈利波特迷 , and I like the books better than the films, too. Even though 10. 大量特效 were used in the movies, the director ignored so many fascinating details.

Tina: My boyfriend hates reading. Since he never reads the books, he always thinks the movies are better.

Evelyn: What kinds of movies does he like?

Tina: You know, what men always like: 11. 科幻片、恐怖片或是有武打的動作片 . They'll watch anything as long as it has a little excitement.

Evelyn: Men! What are they thinking?

∽ *Answer key*

1. prince charming
2. every woman's dream
3. You got it
4. romantic comedy
5. Both the leading actor and actress
6. the supporting actress who played her sister
7. in general
8. I like the book better than the movie version
9. I'm a fan of *Harry Potter*
10. lots of special effects
11. science fiction movies, horror movies, or action movies with martial arts and fighting

∽ 中譯

（*Tina* 和 *Evelyn* 在咖啡館聊天。）

Evelyn：妳看起來好開心喔！是不是妳的白馬王子親了妳啊？

Tina： 不盡然啦！不過我剛剛跟所有女人的夢中情人達西先生約會。

Evelyn：喔，我知道了！妳剛看了電影《傲慢與偏見》，對吧！

Tina： 沒錯！我剛看完 DVD，妳看過了嗎？它是史上第一部愛情喜劇，也是最棒的！

Evelyn：我很久以前讀過小說，而且非常喜歡達西先生，他在電影裡看起來如何？看起來和珍‧奧斯汀在小說中描述的一樣嗎？

Tina： 幾乎一模一樣。兩位男女主角都是不錯的演員，飾演她姐妹的女配角也很棒。不過大體上說來，比起電影，我比較喜歡原著，因為原著可以讓我發揮想像力。

Evelyn：妳說的沒錯，我是哈利波特迷，比起電影，我也是比較喜歡書。雖然電影裡有大量特效，但導演省略了許多很棒的細節。

Tina： 我男朋友討厭看書。他從來沒看過這些書，所以他一直都覺得電影比較好看。

Evelyn：他喜歡看哪種類型的電影？

Tina： 妳知道的，男生都喜歡：科幻片、恐怖片或是有武打的動作片。只要是有一點點刺激的東西，他們就會喜歡。

Evelyn：天啊！真不知男生在想些什麼？

藝術

Art

繪畫

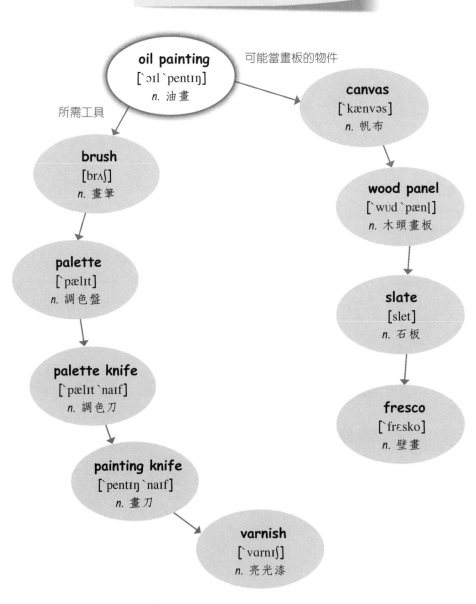

oil painting
[`ɔɪl `pentɪŋ]
n. 油畫

所需工具

brush
[brʌʃ]
n. 畫筆

palette
[`pælɪt]
n. 調色盤

palette knife
[`pælɪt `naɪf]
n. 調色刀

painting knife
[`pentɪŋ `naɪf]
n. 畫刀

varnish
[`vɑrnɪʃ]
n. 亮光漆

可能當畫板的物件

canvas
[`kænvəs]
n. 帆布

wood panel
[`wʊd `pænḷ]
n. 木頭畫板

slate
[slet]
n. 石板

fresco
[`frɛsko]
n. 壁畫

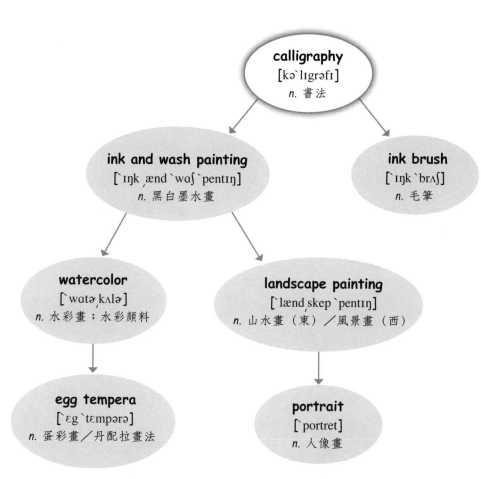

calligraphy
[kəˋlɪɡrəfɪ]
n. 書法

ink and wash painting
[ˋɪŋk ˏænd ˋwaʃ ˋpentɪŋ]
n. 黑白墨水畫

ink brush
[ˋɪŋk ˋbrʌʃ]
n. 毛筆

watercolor
[ˋwatɚˏkʌlɚ]
n. 水彩畫;水彩顏料

landscape painting
[ˋlændˏskep ˋpentɪŋ]
n. 山水畫(東)/風景畫(西)

egg tempera
[ˋɛɡ ˋtɛmpərə]
n. 蛋彩畫/丹配拉畫法

portrait
[ˋportret]
n. 人像畫

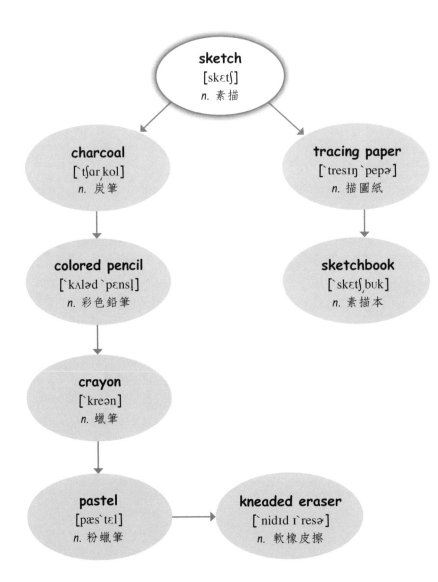

sketch
[skɛtʃ]
n. 素描

charcoal
[ˋtʃɑrˏkol]
n. 炭筆

tracing paper
[ˋtresɪŋ ˋpepɚ]
n. 描圖紙

colored pencil
[ˋkʌlɚd ˋpɛnsl]
n. 彩色鉛筆

sketchbook
[ˋskɛtʃˏbuk]
n. 素描本

crayon
[ˋkreən]
n. 蠟筆

pastel
[pæsˋtɛl]
n. 粉蠟筆

kneaded eraser
[ˋnidɪd ɪˋresɚ]
n. 軟橡皮擦

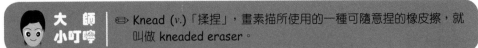

大師小叮嚀　✑ Knead (v.)「揉捏」，畫素描所使用的一種可隨意捏的橡皮擦，就叫做 kneaded eraser。

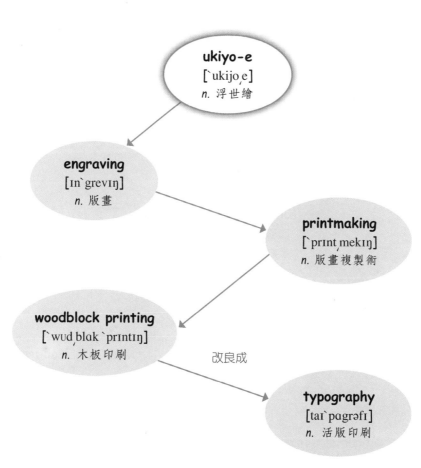

ukiyo-e
[`ukijo͵e]
n. 浮世繪

engraving
[ɪn`grevɪŋ]
n. 版畫

printmaking
[`prɪnt͵mekɪŋ]
n. 版畫複製術

woodblock printing
[`wʊd͵blɑk `prɪntɪŋ]
n. 木板印刷

改良成

typography
[taɪ`pɑgrəfɪ]
n. 活版印刷

大師小叮嚀 | ✏ Ukiyo-e 是日本的一種獨特繪畫藝術形式,源於 17 世紀,主要描繪人們日常生活和風景。

藝術風格

Gothic
[ˋɡɑθɪk]
n. 哥德式

依年代先後排列

Baroque
[bəˋrok]
n. 巴洛克

Renaissance
[rəˋnesṇs]
n. 文藝復興

Modernism
[ˋmɑdənˏɪzəm]
n. 現代主義

大　師
小叮嚀

- Gothic 原指建築風格，後來才延伸到繪畫與雕刻上。教堂的彩繪玻璃 (stained glass) 屬於此類。
- Baroque 是喜好華麗、誇張的一種藝術風格，作品呈現大量的對比，融合各種藝術形式。
- Renaissance 是於十四至十六世紀在歐洲發起的文化運動，作品表現人文主義思想，提倡科學，歌頌人體之美。文藝復興的三大藝術家分別為：米開朗基羅 (Michelangelo)、拉菲爾 (Raphael)、達文西 (da Vinci)。
- Modernism 始於十九世紀末，中心思想以科學邏輯為依據，設計上以簡單實用為主。

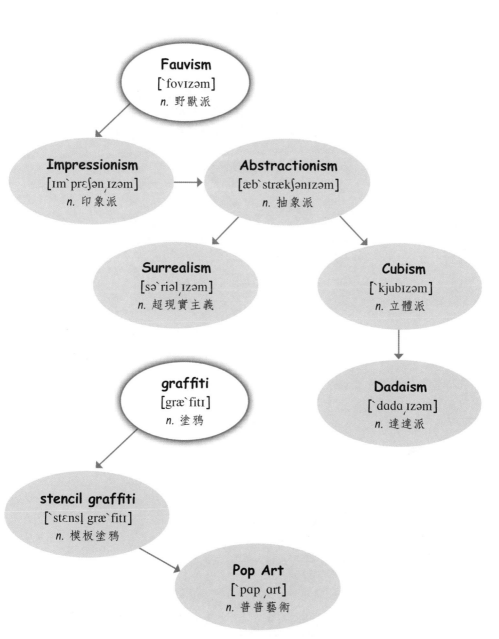

Fauvism
[ˋfovɪzəm]
n. 野獸派

Impressionism
[ɪmˋprɛʃənˏɪzəm]
n. 印象派

Abstractionism
[æbˋstrækʃənɪzəm]
n. 抽象派

Surrealism
[səˋriəlˏɪzəm]
n. 超現實主義

Cubism
[ˋkjubɪzəm]
n. 立體派

graffiti
[græˋfitɪ]
n. 塗鴉

Dadaism
[ˋdadɑˏɪzəm]
n. 達達派

stencil graffiti
[ˋstɛnsḷ græˋfitɪ]
n. 模板塗鴉

Pop Art
[ˋpɑp ˏɑrt]
n. 普普藝術

大師
小叮嚀

- ✑ Fauvism 於二十世紀初崛起，由於作品用色強烈大膽，線條揮灑自如，在 1905 年秋季沙龍中被評為「如野獸般狂野的畫法」而得名。代表畫家有：馬諦斯（Matisse）。

- ✑ Cubism 在二十世紀初開始活躍於藝壇。畫家利用不同的視點（viewpoint）將不同的面向同時表現，組合不同的素材來創造新主題，追求更真實的藝術。代表畫家有：畢卡索（Picasso）。

- ✑ Abstractionism 是於二十世紀興起的美術思潮，作品不以自然具體的對象為主體，轉而描繪不受拘束、無具體型態的事物。代表畫家有：康丁斯基（W. Kandinsky）。

- ✑ Impressionism 派別的畫家主張走出戶外在陽光底下寫生，重視光與影的變化，作品多喜歡描繪人物和自然風光，光影與色彩的融合為其特色。代表人物有：雷諾瓦（Renoir）、莫內（Monet）。

- ✑ Surrealism 藝術思潮受到佛洛伊德（Freud）出版《夢的解析》一書影響，對未知的淺意識感到好奇，作品充滿隱喻、暗示和似夢的描繪。代表人物有：達利（Dali）。

- ✑ Dadaism 於第一次世界大戰期間形成。受到戰爭的衝擊，人們對於以往的道德和美學都不具任何信心，眼下唯一存在的是自我的幻想，當時藝術家貶低傳統價值，達達主義實為一反藝術運動。作家杜象（Duchamp）在印有蒙娜麗莎（Mona Lisa）的圖片加上兩撇鬍子來反諷藝術，正是達達主義有名的作品。

- ✑ Pop Art 中的 pop 為 popular 的縮寫，指的是流行、通俗藝術，於二十世紀後期出現，旨在呈現日常生活的事物，作品更貼近生活，使人注意到自己周遭的事物。廣告、漫畫、商標都是作品。代表人物有：安迪‧沃荷（Andy Warhol）。

- ✑ Graffiti 是街頭藝術的一種，通常以噴漆（spray paint）或彩色顏料在牆上作畫，內容包羅萬象，是作者內心的抒發。

- ✑ Stencil graffiti 是 graffiti 的一種，差別在於模板（stencil）使用和噴漆方式，所以 stencil 的圖案容易複製。

手工藝

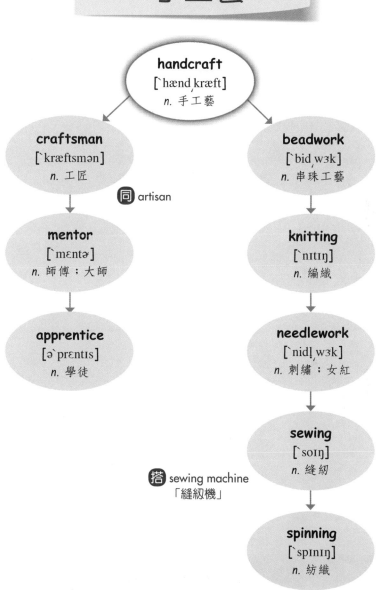

handcraft
[`hænd͵kræft]
n. 手工藝

craftsman
[`kræftsmən]
n. 工匠

同 artisan

mentor
[`mɛntə]
n. 師傅；大師

apprentice
[ə`prɛntɪs]
n. 學徒

beadwork
[`bid͵wɜk]
n. 串珠工藝

knitting
[`nɪtɪŋ]
n. 編織

needlework
[`nidl͵wɜk]
n. 刺繡；女紅

sewing
[`soɪŋ]
n. 縫紉

搭 sewing machine
「縫紉機」

spinning
[`spɪnɪŋ]
n. 紡織

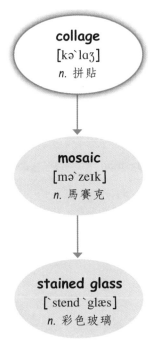

collage
[kə`lɑʒ]
n. 拼貼

mosaic
[mə`zeɪk]
n. 馬賽克

stained glass
[`stend `glæs]
n. 彩色玻璃

大師
小叮嚀 | ✐ Stained glass 也是馬賽克拼貼藝術的一種。

陶藝

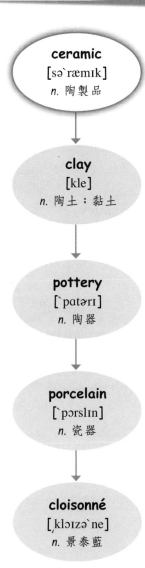

ceramic
[sə`ræmɪk]
n. 陶製品

clay
[kle]
n. 陶土；黏土

pottery
[`patərɪ]
n. 陶器

porcelain
[`pɔrslɪn]
n. 瓷器

cloisonné
[͵klɔɪzə`ne]
n. 景泰藍

木雕、雕刻

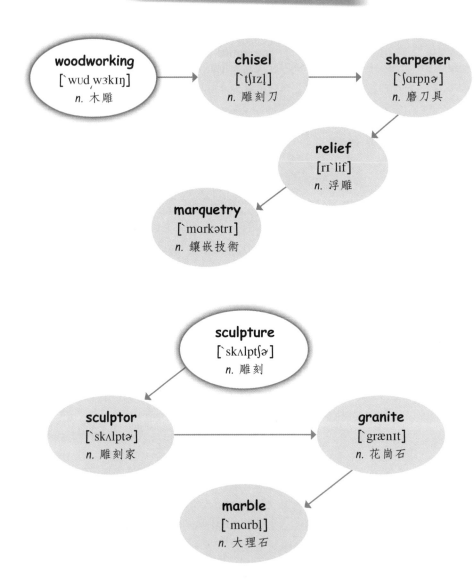

woodworking
[`wʊdˌwɜkɪŋ]
n. 木雕

chisel
[`tʃɪzl]
n. 雕刻刀

sharpener
[`ʃarpnɚ]
n. 磨刀具

relief
[rɪˋlif]
n. 浮雕

marquetry
[`markətrɪ]
n. 鑲嵌技術

sculpture
[ˋskʌlptʃɚ]
n. 雕刻

sculptor
[ˋskʌlptɚ]
n. 雕刻家

granite
[ˋgrænɪt]
n. 花崗石

marble
[ˋmarbl]
n. 大理石

大師出馬　單字用法看這邊！

❶ **Ukiyo-e**, which presented normal city life between the 17th and 20th centuries, is the main artistic genre of **woodblock printing** in Japan.

浮世繪畫風呈現十七到二十世紀間市井小民的生活，是日本重要的木版印刷藝術類型。

❷ **Egg tempera** appeared in the Middle Ages and was used in the main style of painting during that period. The paint is created by mixing dry powdered pigments and egg yolk.

蛋彩出現在中世紀，被使用在當時的主要繪畫風格中。顏料是由乾顏料粉和蛋黃混合而成。

（pigment *n.* 顏料　yolk *n.* 蛋黃）

❸ Painters who make **oil paintings** usually use a **palette** to mix colors and a **painting knife** to apply paint to the **canvas**.

油畫家通常用調色盤來混合顏色，用畫刀將顏料塗在帆布上。

❹ *The Last Judgement* painted on the Sistine Chapel ceiling by Michelangelo is one of the most famous **frescoes** of the High **Renaissance** period.

西斯汀教堂天花板上由米開朗基羅創作的《最後的審判》，是文藝復興極盛時期最有名的壁畫之一。

❺ Woodcutting and **engraving** are examples of two **printmaking** techniques.

木版雕刻和版畫是兩種版畫複製技術的範例。

❻ **Calligraphy**, in which characters are written with special **ink brushes**, is a significant art form in East Asia.

書法是東亞重要的一種藝術形式，用特別的毛筆來書寫字體。

(character *n.* 文字；字體)

❼ The **kneaded eraser** is made of a pliable material like gum, which does not leave behind eraser residue, and is used mostly by artists.

軟橡皮擦是用像橡膠一樣的軟性材料製成，不會留下殘屑，大部分為藝術家使用。

(pliable *adj.* 柔軟的　residue *n.* 殘餘；殘渣)

❽ **Beadwork** has recently become popular. Girls use needle and thread to string beads together to make bracelets, necklaces, or other types of jewelry.

串珠工藝最近很流行，女孩們用針線串珠製作手環、項鍊和其他種類的飾物。

❾ The man is shaping the **clay** as it turns on the wheel.

這個人正在幫輪上轉動的黏土塑形。

❿ Michelangelo's *David* is perhaps the most well-known **sculpture** of all time.

米開朗基羅的大衛像大概是史上最有名的雕像。

換你上場

➜ Exercise ......根據你所聽到的對話完成填空。

(Tina and Evelyn are having afternoon tea at a <u>1. 路邊咖啡座</u> .)

Evelyn: What's that on the wall? <u>2. 一定是有人腦袋不正常才會這麼做</u> .

Tina: That's <u>3. 街頭塗鴉啊</u> ! It's a type of <u>4. 街頭藝術</u> . It's usually made with <u>5. 畫筆</u> . Look! The one on the other wall is <u>6. 模板塗鴉</u> , which is made with <u>7. 模板</u> and <u>8. 噴漆</u> .

Evelyn: <u>9. 街頭藝術</u> ? You mean that's a genre of art? I think they're just <u>10. 在牆上胡亂畫一通</u> .

Tina: Ha! That's art! Some people like it and some don't. You know Monet, right? He's considered to be one of the greatest artists in history. But do you know what happened to him when he first exhibited his <u>11. 油畫畫作</u> *Impression* and *Sunrise*? He was satirized by the <u>12. 批評家</u> . They said that his painting only gave an impression of the scene, and that's how the term <u>13. 印象派</u> developed.

Evelyn: <u>14. 說到繪畫</u> , I must say that Matisse's work is really powerful. People say that his paintings are like wild beasts, and <u>15. 我非常認同</u> .

Tina: You like <u>16. 野獸派的</u> paintings? I used to like them, too, but after seeing the Dali <u>17. 特展</u> at the art museum, I became interested in <u>18. 超現實主義</u> . <u>19. 拼貼</u> was one of the techniques that artists from that period liked to use. Those artworks are so surprising!

Evelyn: I know that style of paintings. It's supposed to be an expression of the <u>20. 淺意識</u> , just like whatever is in your dreams.

Tina: That's right! I should draw a picture about my dream last night. Maybe I'll become an artist.

Evelyn: What was your dream about?

Tina: I was a billionaire and all my money was melting.

Evelyn: Well! 21. 那也太超現實了吧！

∽ *Answer key*

1. sidewalk cafe
2. It must have been done by someone who was completely out of his mind
3. graffiti
4. street art
5. brushes
6. stencil graffiti
7. stencils
8. spray paint
9. Street art
10. scribbles on the wall
11. oil paintings
12. critics
13. Impressionism
14. When it comes to paintings
15. I couldn't agree more
16. Fauvist
17. exhibit
18. Surrealism
19. Collage
20. unconscious
21. That's really surreal

∽ 中譯

（*Tina* 和 *Evelyn* 在路邊咖啡座喝下午茶。）

Evelyn：牆上那是什麼？一定是有人腦袋不正常才會這麼做。

Tina： 那是街頭塗鴉啊！街頭藝術的一種，通常用畫筆創作。看！另外那面牆上的是模板塗鴉，是用模板和噴漆製作的。

Evelyn：街頭藝術？妳是說它們是藝術的一種？我覺得它們只是在牆上胡亂畫一通。

Tina： 哈！這就是藝術，有人喜歡有人不喜歡。妳知道莫內，對吧！他是公認最頂尖的藝術家之一，但妳知道他第一次公開展覽他的畫作《印象》和《日出》時發生什麼事嗎？批評家挖苦他，說他的畫作傳遞的只是景物的「印象」，這也是印象派一詞的由來。

Evelyn：說到繪畫，我不得不說馬諦斯的畫作很強烈，人們說他的畫作就像野獸一般，我非常認同。

Tina： 妳喜歡野獸派的畫啊？我以前也很喜歡，不過自從在美術館看了達利特展後，我開始喜歡
　　　　超現實主義。拼貼是那個時期的藝術家愛用的技巧之一，那些作品都非常讓人驚豔！

Evelyn：我知道那種繪畫形式，那應該是一種淺意識的表現，就像妳夢裡出現的東西一樣。

Tina： 沒錯！我應該把我昨天夢到的東西畫出來，說不定我也會成為藝術家。

Evelyn：妳夢到什麼？

Tina： 我是個億萬富翁，我所有的錢都在融化。

Evelyn：呃，那也太超現實了吧！

電 玩
Video Games

電玩店

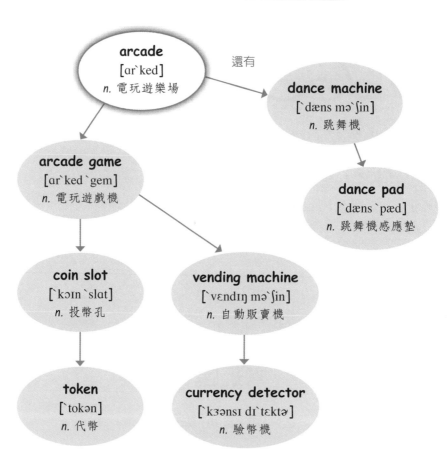

arcade
[ar`ked]
n. 電玩遊樂場

還有

dance machine
[`dæns mə`ʃin]
n. 跳舞機

dance pad
[`dæns `pæd]
n. 跳舞機感應墊

arcade game
[ar`ked `gem]
n. 電玩遊戲機

coin slot
[`kɔɪn `slɑt]
n. 投幣孔

vending machine
[`vɛndɪŋ mə`ʃin]
n. 自動販賣機

token
[`tokən]
n. 代幣

currency detector
[`kɜənsɪ dɪ`tɛktə]
n. 驗幣機

大師
小叮嚀

⇨ Arcade game 也可稱 arcade cabinet 或 arcade machine。
⇨ 自動販賣機有安裝驗幣機，以防有人投代幣。

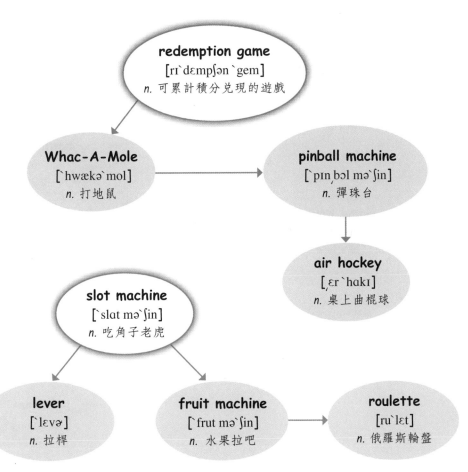

redemption game
[rɪ`dɛmpʃən `gem]
n. 可累計積分兌現的遊戲

Whac-A-Mole
[`hwækə`mol]
n. 打地鼠

pinball machine
[`pɪn͵bɔl mə`ʃin]
n. 彈珠台

air hockey
[͵ɛr `hakɪ]
n. 桌上曲棍球

slot machine
[`slat mə`ʃin]
n. 吃角子老虎

lever
[`lɛvə]
n. 拉桿

fruit machine
[`frut mə`ʃin]
n. 水果拉吧

roulette
[ru`lɛt]
n. 俄羅斯輪盤

電視遊樂器

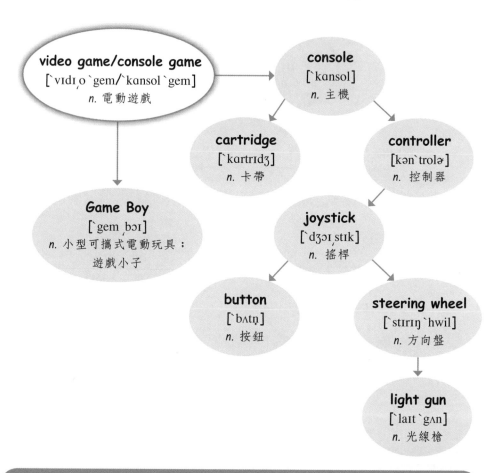

video game/console game
[`vɪdɪˏo `gem/`kansol `gem]
n. 電動遊戲

console
[`kansol]
n. 主機

cartridge
[`kartrɪdʒ]
n. 卡帶

controller
[kən`trolə]
n. 控制器

Game Boy
[`gem ˏbɔɪ]
n. 小型可攜式電動玩具；
遊戲小子

joystick
[`dʒɔɪˏstɪk]
n. 搖桿

button
[`bʌtn̩]
n. 按鈕

steering wheel
[`stɪrɪŋ `hwil]
n. 方向盤

light gun
[`laɪt `gʌn]
n. 光線槍

 大師 小叮嚀

☞ Console game 有別於 arcade game，console game 有遊戲主機，可以跟電視或相關機器連接，玩家可以在自家電視螢幕看到遊戲畫面，再外接 controller 就可以玩，與 video game 同。Arcade game 則是電玩店裡的大型遊戲台。

☞ Light gun 用於射擊遊戲（shooting game），是電玩的操縱器。

電腦遊戲

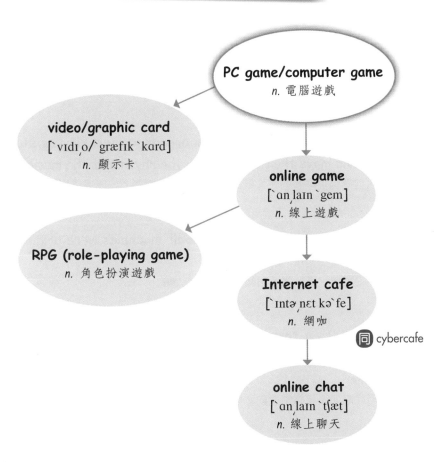

PC game/computer game
n. 電腦遊戲

video/graphic card
[ˋvɪdɪˏo/ˋgræfɪk ˋkard]
n. 顯示卡

online game
[ˋɑnˏlaɪn ˋgem]
n. 線上遊戲

RPG (role-playing game)
n. 角色扮演遊戲

Internet cafe
[ˋɪntɚˏnɛt kəˋfe]
n. 網咖

同 cybercafe

online chat
[ˋɑnˏlaɪn ˋtʃæt]
n. 線上聊天

大師 小叮嚀

✐ PC 即為 personal computer「個人電腦」。

✐ Handheld game console 為掌上型電玩，最早出現的是由日本 Nintendo（任天堂）公司研發的 Game Boy 遊戲機。

✐ RPG 為 role-playing game 的縮寫，是電玩遊戲的一種，玩家可以扮演遊戲中的角色，《魔獸世界》即為此類。

❶ Slot machines are a type of casino game. The player attempts to win money from the machine by pulling the **lever** on the side.
吃角子老虎是賭場遊戲的一種。玩家藉由扳下機器旁的拉桿，試圖從機器贏錢。

❷ Dance machines are a revolution in **arcade games**. Players stand on a **dance pad** and move their bodies with the rhythm of the music.
跳舞機是大型電玩遊戲機的一大革命。玩家站在跳舞墊上，隨著音樂節奏舞動身體。

❸ Like many other game machines, **pinball machines** were originally used for gambling.
跟很多其他遊戲機一樣，彈珠台最早是用來賭博的。

❹ If someone uses a **token** instead of a coin to buy something from a **vending machine**, the **currency detector** may reject it and return it to the consumer.
如果有人用代幣而不是錢幣從自動販賣機買東西，驗幣機會拒絕接受，並把它退還給顧客。

❺ Steering wheels and **light guns** are two kinds of **video game controllers**. The former are used for playing driving games, whereas the latter are for shooting games.
方向盤和光線槍是電玩操縱器的二種。前者用來玩駕駛遊戲；後者則用來玩射擊遊戲。

❻ In addition to controlling games, **joysticks** are also used for controlling machines like aircraft and tractors. Recently, small joysticks have even been adopted as controllers for mobile phones.

除了控制遊戲外，操作桿也可用來操縱像飛機或拖拉機等機器。近來，小型操作桿更被用來當作手機的操縱器。

（tractor *n*. 拖拉機；牽引機）

❼ After the Nintendo Company released the Game Boy, **handheld console games** grew in popularity.

自從任天堂公司推出 Game Boy 之後，掌上型電動遊戲機就蔚為一股風潮。

（release *v*. 發售；發行）

換你上場

⌐⊸ *Exercise* ······ 根據你所聽到的對話完成填空。

(Tina, Evelyn and Eric are at the 1. 電玩遊樂場 .)

Evelyn: Eric, what kind of games do you usually play? 2. 射擊遊戲 or 3. 賽車遊戲 ?

Eric: I used to play 4. 格鬥遊戲 . Do you know the *Street Fighter* series? It was a lot of fun!

Tina: I know. My brother really liked it, too, but I've never played the 5. 遊戲機 . I always play other games like 6. 打地鼠 . It's my favorite!

Eric: That's for girls! Even 7. 跳舞機 are more exciting than hitting a plastic mole.

Tina: That's not the only game I play. I'm also good at 8. 俄羅斯方塊 . I even 9. 得過最高分 10. 還把名字記錄在機器裡 . No one was able to 11. 打破我的紀錄 .

Evelyn: Ever since I won US$300 from a 12. 吃角子老虎 in Las Vegas, I play the slots every time I see one. And you know what? I'm always lucky.

Eric: 13. 這一切只跟機會有關吧 ! It's impossible for you to win every time.

Tina: Hey! There's one over there. Let's go get some 14. 代幣 and try it. Then we'll see how lucky you are.

Evelyn: OK. 15. 走吧 .

✑ *Answer key* ···

1. arcade
2. Shooting games
3. driving games
4. fighting games
5. arcade game
6. Whac-A-Mole
7. dance machines
8. Tetris

9. got the highest score
10. and was able to enter my name
11. knock it off the high score list
12. slot machine
13. That's bound to chance
14. tokens
15. Let's go

✑ 中譯 ··

（*Tina*、*Evelyn* 和 *Eric* 在電玩遊樂場。）

Evelyn： 艾瑞克，你平常都玩什麼遊戲？射擊遊戲還是賽車遊戲？

Eric： 我以前都玩格鬥遊戲，妳知道快打炫風那個系列嗎？那很好玩！

Tina： 我知道，我哥也很愛玩，不過我從來沒玩過遊戲機，我都是玩其他像打地鼠之類的遊戲。那是我的最愛！

Eric： 那是女生玩的遊戲！就連跳舞機都比打塑膠地鼠有趣。

Tina： 我不是只玩打地鼠啊！我也很擅長俄羅斯方塊，我還得過最高分，把名字記錄在機器裡，沒人可以打破我的紀錄呢！

Evelyn： 自從我在拉斯維加斯的吃角子老虎贏得三百美金，我每次只要看到拉吧機台都會玩一下，你們知道嗎？我每次都很幸運！

Eric： 這一切只跟機會有關吧！妳不可能每次都贏的。

Tina： 嘿！那邊有一台吃角子老虎，我們去換些代幣來試試，這樣我們就知道妳有多幸運了。

Evelyn： 好啊，走吧。

PART 7

自然
NATURE

占星學
Astrology

占星學

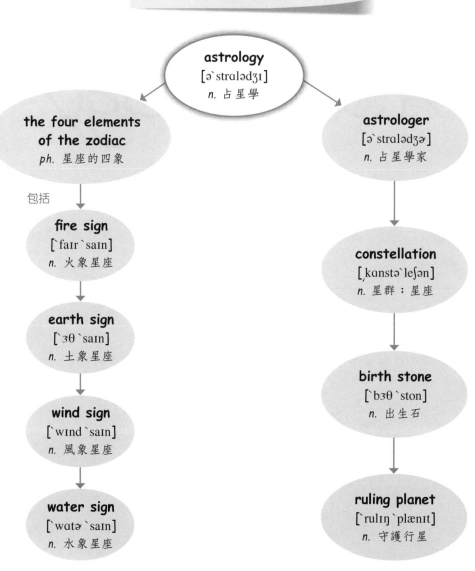

astrology
[ə`stralədʒɪ]
n. 占星學

the four elements
of the zodiac
ph. 星座的四象

astrologer
[ə`stralədʒɚ]
n. 占星學家

包括

fire sign
[`faɪr `saɪn]
n. 火象星座

earth sign
[`ʒθ `saɪn]
n. 土象星座

wind sign
[`wɪnd `saɪn]
n. 風象星座

water sign
[`watɚ `saɪn]
n. 水象星座

constellation
[ˌkanstə`leʃən]
n. 星群;星座

birth stone
[`bʒθ `ston]
n. 出生石

ruling planet
[`rulɪŋ `plænɪt]
n. 守護行星

星座特質

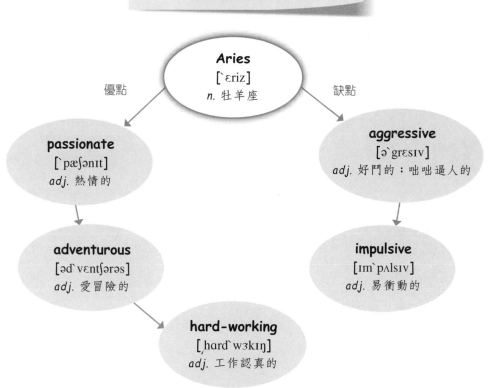

優點

Aries
[`ɛriz]
n. 牡羊座

缺點

passionate
[`pæʃənɪt]
adj. 熱情的

aggressive
[ə`grɛsɪv]
adj. 好鬥的;咄咄逼人的

adventurous
[əd`vɛntʃərəs]
adj. 愛冒險的

impulsive
[ɪm`pʌlsɪv]
adj. 易衝動的

hard-working
[ˌhard`wɜkɪŋ]
adj. 工作認真的

大師
小叮嚀

✎ Aries 和其他星座不同之處在於一個字有三種用法:
   a. 「人」(單複數同形):We have two Aries in my family.
      「我們家有兩個牡羊座。」
   b. 「星座」:Aries is the first sign of the zodiac.「牡羊座是
      十二星座裡的第一個。」
   c. 「形容詞」:She is a typical Aries boss.「她是一個典型的
      牡羊座老闆。」
✎ 有時候習慣直接用星座代表人稱使用,這在會話中是被允許的。

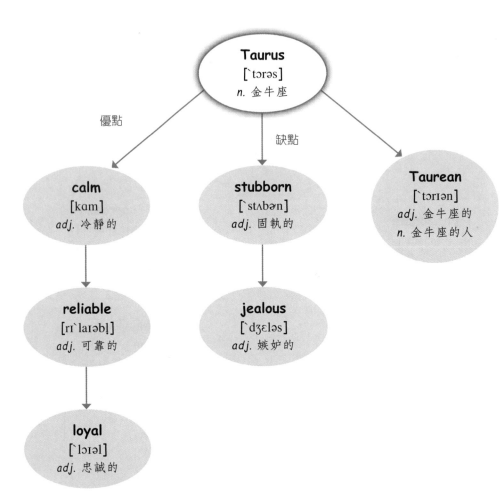

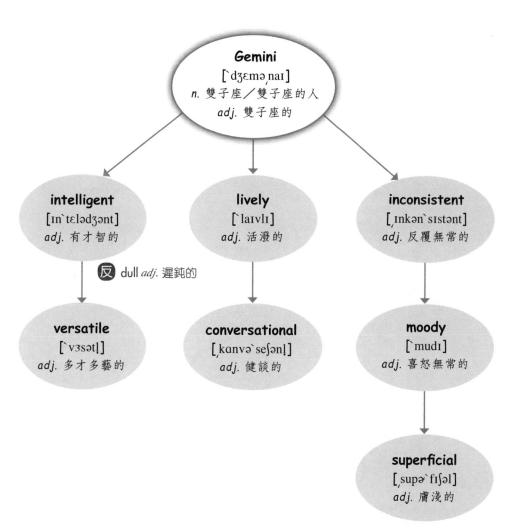

Gemini
[ˋdʒɛməˌnaɪ]
n. 雙子座／雙子座的人
adj. 雙子座的

intelligent
[ɪnˋtɛlədʒənt]
adj. 有才智的

反 dull *adj.* 遲鈍的

versatile
[ˋvɝsətḷ]
adj. 多才多藝的

lively
[ˋlaɪvlɪ]
adj. 活潑的

conversational
[ˌkɑnvɚˋseʃənḷ]
adj. 健談的

inconsistent
[ˌɪnkənˋsɪstənt]
adj. 反覆無常的

moody
[ˋmudɪ]
adj. 喜怒無常的

superficial
[ˌsupɚˋfɪʃəl]
adj. 膚淺的

259

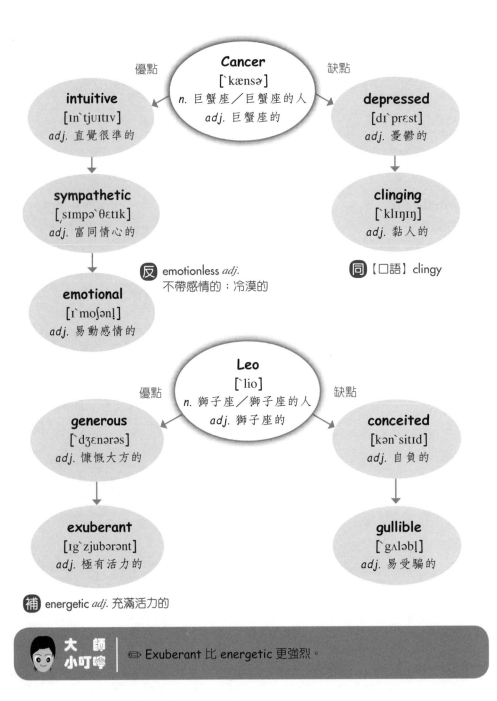

Cancer
[`kænsə]
n. 巨蟹座／巨蟹座的人
adj. 巨蟹座的

優點

缺點

intuitive
[ɪn`tjuɪtɪv]
adj. 直覺很準的

depressed
[dɪ`prɛst]
adj. 憂鬱的

sympathetic
[‚sɪmpə`θɛtɪk]
adj. 富同情心的

clinging
[`klɪŋɪŋ]
adj. 黏人的

反 emotionless adj.
不帶感情的；冷漠的

同 【口語】clingy

emotional
[ɪ`moʃənl]
adj. 易動感情的

Leo
[`lio]
n. 獅子座／獅子座的人
adj. 獅子座的

優點

缺點

generous
[`dʒɛnərəs]
adj. 慷慨大方的

conceited
[kən`sitɪd]
adj. 自負的

exuberant
[ɪg`zjubərənt]
adj. 極有活力的

gullible
[`gʌləbl]
adj. 易受騙的

補 energetic adj. 充滿活力的

大師
小叮嚀 | ✎ Exuberant 比 energetic 更強烈。

260

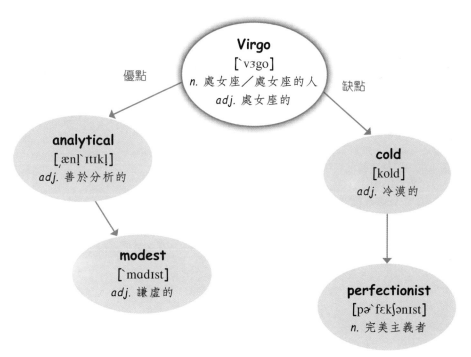

優點

Virgo
[`vɝgo]
n. 處女座／處女座的人
adj. 處女座的

缺點

analytical
[ˌænlˈɪtɪkḷ]
adj. 善於分析的

cold
[kold]
adj. 冷漠的

modest
[`mɑdɪst]
adj. 謙虛的

perfectionist
[pɚˈfɛkʃənɪst]
n. 完美主義者

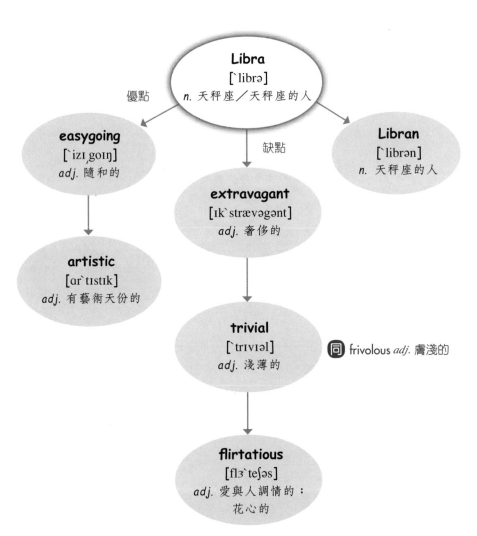

同 frivolous *adj.* 膚淺的

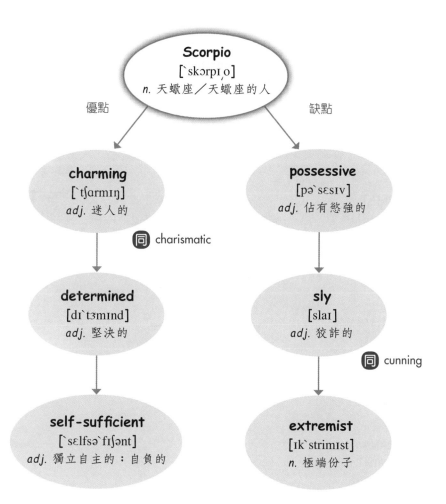

Scorpio
[ˋskɔrpɪˏo]
n. 天蠍座／天蠍座的人

優點　　　　　　　　　缺點

charming
[ˋtʃɑrmɪŋ]
adj. 迷人的

同 charismatic

possessive
[pəˋsɛsɪv]
adj. 佔有慾強的

determined
[dɪˋtɝmɪnd]
adj. 堅決的

sly
[slaɪ]
adj. 狡詐的

同 cunning

self-sufficient
[ˋsɛlfsəˋfɪʃənt]
adj. 獨立自主的；自負的

extremist
[ɪkˋstrimɪst]
n. 極端份子

大師
小叮嚀

✏ 和 Aries 的三種用法類似，Scorpio 有兩種用法，可用於「人」和「星座」，形容詞則為 Scorpionic，例：Scorpionic personality「天蠍座的個性」。

✏ Possessive 的用法：possessive of + 人「對某人有佔有慾」；possessive about + 物「對某物有佔有慾」。

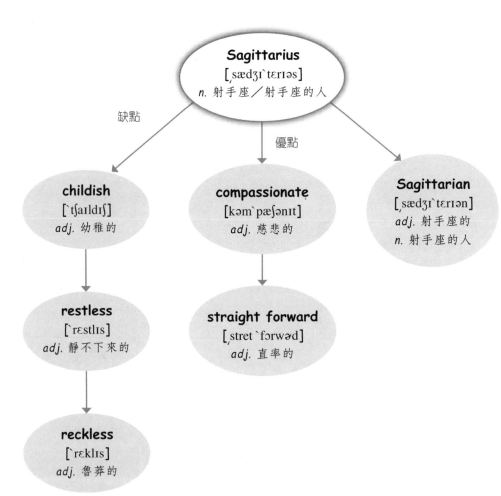

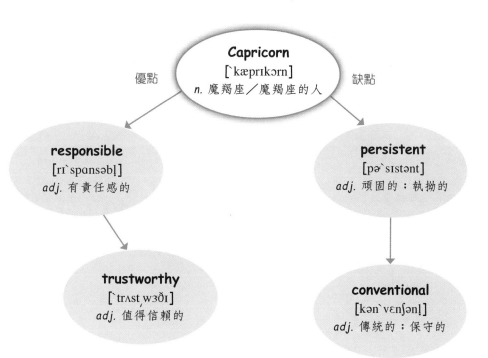

優點

缺點

Capricorn
[ˋkæprɪkɔrn]
n. 魔羯座／魔羯座的人

responsible
[rɪˋspɑnsəb!]
adj. 有責任感的

persistent
[pɚˋsɪstənt]
adj. 頑固的；執拗的

trustworthy
[ˋtrʌst͵wɝðɪ]
adj. 值得信賴的

conventional
[kənˋvɛnʃən!]
adj. 傳統的；保守的

大師
小叮嚀

- ✍ Capricorn 的形容詞是 Capricornean，例：a typical Capricornean look「典型的魔羯座長相」。

- ✍ Persistent 是指「執拗的」，帶有負面意味，例：a persistent salesman「令人厭煩的業務員」；若要形容人「不屈不撓」則可以使用 resolute。

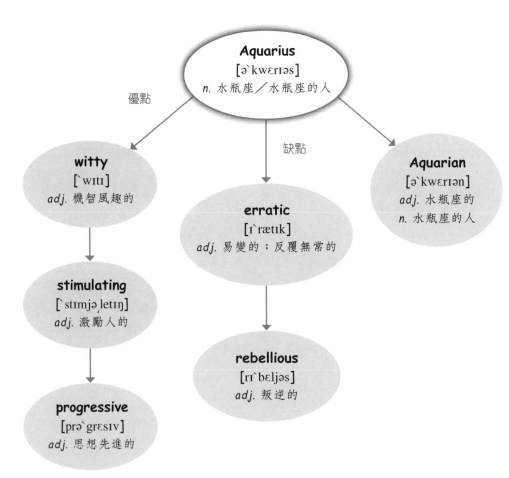

Aquarius
[ə`kwɛrɪəs]
n. 水瓶座／水瓶座的人

優點

缺點

witty
[`wɪtɪ]
adj. 機智風趣的

erratic
[ɪ`rætɪk]
adj. 易變的；反覆無常的

Aquarian
[ə`kwɛrɪən]
adj. 水瓶座的
n. 水瓶座的人

stimulating
[`stɪmjə͵letɪŋ]
adj. 激勵人的

rebellious
[rɪ`bɛljəs]
adj. 叛逆的

progressive
[prə`grɛsɪv]
adj. 思想先進的

大師
小叮嚀

✍ Erratic 是指一個人的言行善變，讓人捉摸不定，時有失常演出，
如：erratic behavior「反覆無常的行為」。

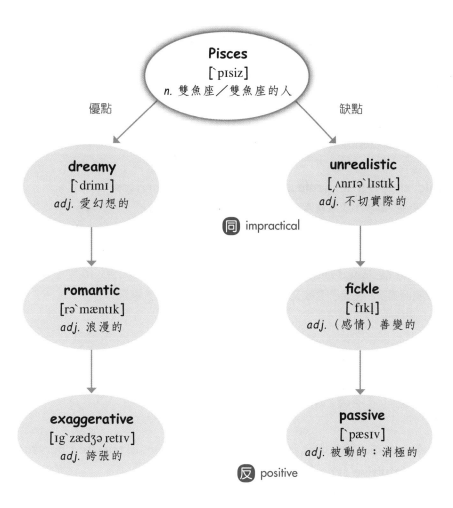

Pisces
[ˋpɪsiz]
n. 雙魚座／雙魚座的人

優點

缺點

dreamy
[ˋdrimɪ]
adj. 愛幻想的

unrealistic
[ˏʌnrɪəˋlɪstɪk]
adj. 不切實際的

同 impractical

romantic
[rəˋmæntɪk]
adj. 浪漫的

fickle
[ˋfɪkḷ]
adj. （感情）善變的

exaggerative
[ɪgˋzædʒəˏretɪv]
adj. 誇張的

passive
[ˋpæsɪv]
adj. 被動的；消極的

反 positive

 大師小叮嚀

✑ 和 Scorpio 一樣，Pisces 指人和星座，形容詞則是 Piscean，Piscean 亦可指雙魚座的人。

✑ Fickle 多被用來形容一個人對「友情」或「愛情」的善變與不忠。

大師出馬

單字用法看這邊！

❶ Sadly, it was John's fun-loving and **impulsive** nature that caused the failure of this marriage.

很遺憾，是約翰好玩和衝動的個性導致這樁婚姻的失敗。

❷ Children often act **jealously** when a new baby arrives.

新生兒到來時，小孩常會嫉妒。

❸ Students may find it difficult if an instructor's lectures are **inconsistent** with the assigned readings.

如果老師講課和指定的閱讀文章不一致，學生會很難進入狀況。

（instructor *n.* 大學講師）

❹ I didn't have a strong sense of security as a child, so I became quite **clingy**.

我小時候缺乏安全感，所以變得很黏人。

❺ My friend Sophia, who is a best-selling author, attributed her success to her **intuitive** sense of what readers want.

我朋友蘇菲亞是一個暢銷作家，她將她的成功歸功於她對讀者的期望有敏銳的直覺。

（attribute A to B 把 A 歸因於 B）

❻ If she wasn't so **conceited**, people might actually listen to Dr. Lee's ideas.

如果她沒有這麼自負，大家可能會聽李博士的意見。

7 The priest encouraged people to be **compassionate** and open their homes to the refugees.

牧師鼓勵大家發揮慈悲心，開放他們的家給難民。

8 Dealing with a **persistent** salesman who won't take no for an answer is annoying.

和鍥而不捨、不肯被拒絕的推銷員周旋是件惱人的事。

9 Tim is a gifted but **erratic** baseball player.

提姆是一位有天份但狀況不穩定的棒球選手。

10 Jamie is quite **possessive** about her toys. If anyone touches them, she screams.

潔美對於她的玩具有很強的佔有慾。如果有人摸它們，她就會尖叫。

11 Gary thinks that homosexual lovers have the right to get married, which in some places is a very **progressive** idea.

蓋瑞認為同性戀情侶有權利結婚，這個觀點在某些地方是非常先進的。

（homosexual *adj.* 同性戀的）

12 It's hard to plan our vacations very far in advance, because my husband is so **fickle**.

很難儘早規劃我們的假期，因為我丈夫非常善變。

換你上場

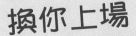

學習成效知分曉！

⟶ Exercise ······ 根據你所聽到的對話完成填空。

Evelyn: My new roommate is a 1. 自負的勢利鬼 . I can't stand her anymore. Are all 2. 獅子座的人 like that?

Tina: Some 2. 獅子座的人 do have a few 3. 令人討厭的特質 , but you have to admit that they are 4. 非常有活力 and 5. 大方 .

Evelyn: I 6. 比較喜歡跟處女座相處，因為他們勤奮又謙虛 .

Tina: But I heard that they're 7. 完美主義者 . And they can be so 8. 挑剔！①

Evelyn: Yeah, but at least they're 9. 獨立自主的 .

Tina: What other traits do you 10. 欣賞 ? For instance, what kind of guy are you looking for?

Evelyn: Well, I'd like him to be 11. 像金牛座一樣忠誠 , 12. 像雙子座一樣多才多藝 , as 13. 有創造力 as a Cancer, as 14. 謙遜 as a Virgo, 15. 討人喜歡 like a Libra, as 16. 迷人 as a Scorpio, 17. 樂觀 like a Sagittarius, and as 18. 有耐心 as a Capricorn.

Tina: Gee!② Where are you going to find a 19. 如意郎君 like that?

➣ *Answer key* ┄┄┄┄┄┄┄┄┄┄┄┄┄┄┄┄┄┄┄┄┄┄┄┄┄┄┄┄┄┄┄

1. conceited snob
2. Leos
3. unpleasant traits
4. exuberant
5. generous
6. prefer hanging out with Virgos, because they're diligent and modest
7. perfectionists
8. picky
9. self-sufficient

10. admire
11. as loyal as a Taurus
12. as versatile as a Gemini
13. creative
14. humble
15. pleasant
16. charming
17. optimistic
18. patient
19. Mr. Right

➣ 解析 ┄┄┄┄┄┄┄┄┄┄┄┄┄┄┄┄┄┄┄┄┄┄┄┄┄┄┄┄┄┄┄┄┄┄┄┄┄┄┄

① 在 And they can be so picky! 中,因為只是想像而非實際經驗,所以使用 can,有假設意味。
② Gee! (*interj.*) 天啊!(表示驚訝、憤怒等情緒)

➣ 中譯 ┄┄┄┄┄┄┄┄┄┄┄┄┄┄┄┄┄┄┄┄┄┄┄┄┄┄┄┄┄┄┄┄┄┄┄┄┄┄┄

Evelyn:我的新室友是一個自負的勢利鬼。我再也受不了她了,獅子座的人都跟她一樣嗎?
Tina: 有些獅子座的人的確有一些令人討厭的特質,但妳不得不承認他們是非常有活力又大方的。
Evelyn:我比較喜歡跟處女座相處,因為他們勤奮又謙虛。
Tina: 但我聽說他們是完美主義者。他們有可能非常挑剔!
Evelyn:或許吧,不過他們至少是獨立自主的人。
Tina: 妳還欣賞其他哪些特質?比如說,你在找什麼樣的對象?
Evelyn:嗯,我希望他能像金牛座一樣忠誠,像雙子座一樣多才多藝,像巨蟹座一樣有創造力,像處女座一樣謙遜,像天秤座一樣討人喜歡,像天蠍座一樣迷人,像射手座一樣樂觀,並且像魔羯座一樣有耐心。
Tina: 天啊!妳要上哪兒去找這樣的如意郎君啊?

天氣
Weather

天氣

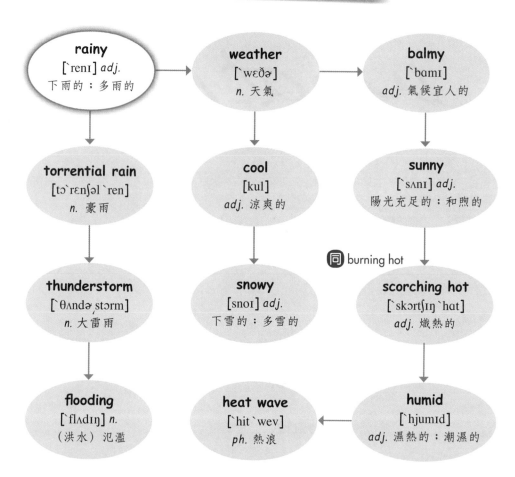

rainy
[ˋrenɪ] *adj.*
下雨的；多雨的

weather
[ˋwɛðɚ]
n. 天氣

balmy
[ˋbɑmɪ]
adj. 氣候宜人的

torrential rain
[tɔˋrɛnʃəl ˋren]
n. 豪雨

cool
[kul]
adj. 涼爽的

sunny
[ˋsʌnɪ] *adj.*
陽光充足的；和煦的

thunderstorm
[ˋθʌndɚˏstɔrm]
n. 大雷雨

snowy
[snoɪ] *adj.*
下雪的；多雪的

同 burning hot

scorching hot
[ˋskɔrtʃɪŋ ˋhɑt]
adj. 熾熱的

flooding
[ˋflʌdɪŋ] *n.*
（洪水）氾濫

heat wave
[ˋhit ˋwev]
ph. 熱浪

humid
[ˋhjumɪd]
adj. 濕熱的；潮濕的

大師小叮嚀　　☞ Sunny smile (*n.*) 陽光般的微笑。例：You have a sunny smile.
「你笑得好燦爛。」

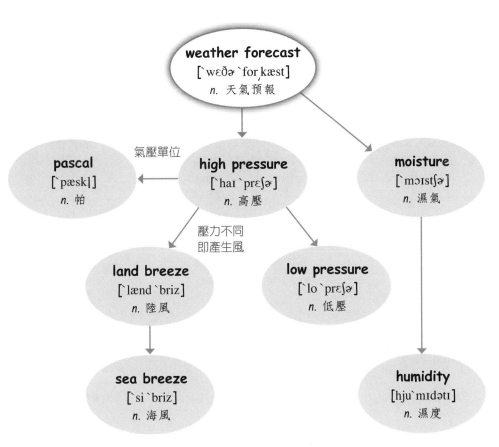

weather forecast
[ˋwɛðɚ ˋforˏkæst]
n. 天氣預報

氣壓單位

pascal
[ˋpæskḷ]
n. 帕

high pressure
[ˋhaɪ ˋprɛʃɚ]
n. 高壓

moisture
[ˋmɔɪstʃɚ]
n. 濕氣

壓力不同
即產生風

land breeze
[ˋlænd ˋbriz]
n. 陸風

low pressure
[ˋlo ˋprɛʃɚ]
n. 低壓

sea breeze
[ˋsi ˋbriz]
n. 海風

humidity
[hjuˋmɪdətɪ]
n. 濕度

大師
小叮嚀 ✏ 國際上統一用「百帕」（hectopascal）作為氣壓單位，1 帕等於
1 牛頓／米的平方。

氣候

climate
[ˋklaɪmɪt]
n. 氣候

climate change
[ˋklaɪmɪt ˋtʃendʒ]
n. 氣候變遷

tropical climate
[ˋtrɑpɪkļ ˋklaɪmɪt]
n. 熱帶氣候

dry season
[ˋdraɪ ˋsizņ]
n. 乾季

包含

久旱逢甘霖

El Niño
[ɛl ˋninjo]
n. 聖嬰現象

tropical cyclone
[ˋtrɑpɪkļ ˋsaɪklon]
n. 熱帶氣旋

monsoon
[manˋsun]
n. 季風；雨季

相反

La Niña
[la ˋninja]
n. 反聖嬰現象

subtropical
[sʌbˋtrɑpɪkļ]
adj. 亞熱帶的

equator
[ɪˋkwetə]
n. 赤道

大師 小叮嚀

☞ El Niño (西班牙文，意思是 the boy) 指嚴重影響全球氣候的太平洋熱帶海域的大風及海水的大規模移動。

☞ La Niña (西班牙文，意思是 the girl) 指赤道附近東太平洋水溫異常下降，導致氣候異常的現象。

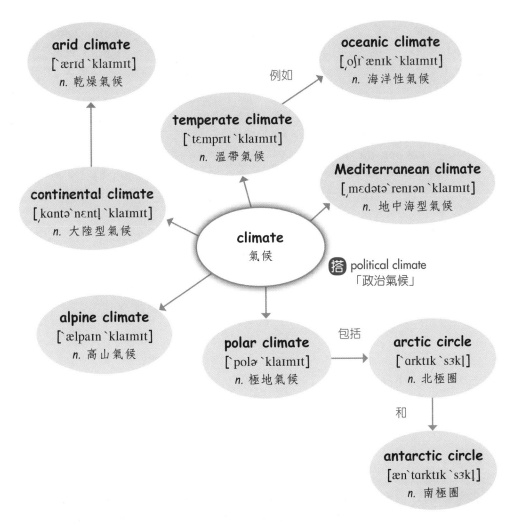

arid climate
[`ærɪd `klaɪmɪt]
n. 乾燥氣候

oceanic climate
[ˌoʃɪ`ænɪk `klaɪmɪt]
n. 海洋性氣候

例如

temperate climate
[`tɛmprɪt `klaɪmɪt]
n. 溫帶氣候

Mediterranean climate
[ˌmɛdətə`renɪən `klaɪmɪt]
n. 地中海型氣候

continental climate
[ˌkɑntə`nɛntḷ `klaɪmɪt]
n. 大陸型氣候

climate
氣候

搭 political climate
「政治氣候」

alpine climate
[`ælpaɪn `klaɪmɪt]
n. 高山氣候

polar climate
[`polə `klaɪmɪt]
n. 極地氣候

包括

arctic circle
[`ɑrktɪk `sɝkḷ]
n. 北極圈

和

antarctic circle
[æn`tɑrktɪk `sɝkḷ]
n. 南極圈

溫室氣體

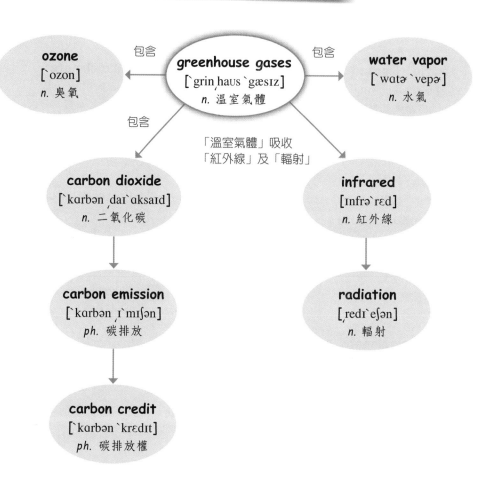

ozone
[`ozon]
n. 臭氧

包含 →

greenhouse gases
[`grin͵haʊs `gæsɪz]
n. 溫室氣體

← 包含

water vapor
[`watɚ `vepɚ]
n. 水氣

包含

「溫室氣體」吸收
「紅外線」及「輻射」

carbon dioxide
[`karbən ͵daɪ`aksaɪd]
n. 二氧化碳

infrared
[ɪnfrə`rɛd]
n. 紅外線

carbon emission
[`karbən ɪ`mɪʃən]
ph. 碳排放

radiation
[͵redɪ`eʃən]
n. 輻射

carbon credit
[`karbən `krɛdɪt]
ph. 碳排放權

大師小叮嚀

☞ 溫室氣體吸收紅外線輻射，地球整體的熱量平衡受到影響，導致溫室效應（greenhouse effect）及全球暖化（global warming）。

☞ Carbon credit 指的是國際間以金錢交易所購得的碳排放權。

大師出馬

① The **flooding**, which was caused by **torrential rain**, resulted in a tragic loss of human lives.

這一次豪雨所帶來的水災，造成了人員傷亡的悲劇。

② It's a little stuffy in here, isn't it? I think it's more **humid** in here than it is outside.

這裡有點通風不良，不是嗎？我想這裡比外面還要濕熱。

③ **Greenhouse gases** absorb **infrared radiation** and release heat. This is known as the greenhouse effect, and it contributes to global warming.

溫室氣體吸收紅外線輻射並釋放熱能，這被稱做溫室效應，導致了全球暖化。

④ This **heat wave** claimed sixty lives. It was the worst in the last fifty years.

這一波熱浪奪走了六十條人命，是近五十年來最嚴重的一次。

⑤ **El Niño** and **La Niña** have contributed to the decrease in harvest yields over the last decade.

聖嬰及反聖嬰現象造成近十年的農產收穫減少。

(yield *n.* 產量)

❻ Because Mediterranean climates are so sunny and balmy, many tourists are drawn to countries like Italy and Greece.

由於地中海型氣候陽光充足、氣候宜人，吸引許多遊客前往義大利、希臘等國旅遊。

（draw v. 吸引）

❼ Tropical areas around the equator nurture a great number of rain forests.

赤道周圍的熱帶地區培育了大片雨林。

（nurture v. 培育）

換你上場

學習成效知分曉！

❧ *Exercise* ......根據你所聽到的對話完成填空。

Tina: What are you doing?

Evelyn: I'm listening to a news program.

Tina: What's it saying?

Evelyn: That the U.S. president is trying to influence the 1. 二氧化碳排放 policies of some developing countries, like China and India.

Tina: I have heard that, too. The 2. 溫室效應 is caused by excessive 3. 二氧化碳 , and 4. 水氣 , which are the so-called 5. 溫室氣體 . This results in large-scale 6. 氣候變化 and 7. 地球暖化 .

Evelyn: 8. 不祥之兆已經浮現 . ①

Tina: I've been told that around seventy-five thousand species will disappear from the earth when a 9. 攝氏 0.1 度的 change occurs in the average temperature.

Evelyn: And the ice caps in the 10. 北極圈 and 11. 南極圈 are melting, resulting in a rise in 12. 海平面 .

Tina: As for climate changes, 13. 豪雨 and even 14. 洪水氾濫 will happen where there shouldn't be rainfall, 15. 宜人的 weather will be replaced by 16. 乾旱 , and the list goes on.

Evelyn: Keep in mind the wise saying, "17. 水能載舟，亦能覆舟 ." ② That is another side effect of urbanization. ③

❧ *Answer key* ···

1. carbon emissions
2. greenhouse effect
3. carbon dioxide
4. water vapor
5. greenhouse gases
6. climate changes
7. global warming
8. The writing is on the wall
9. 0.1 (zero-point-one) degree Celsius

10. arctic circle
11. antarctic circle
12. sea levels
13. torrential rains
14. flooding
15. balmy
16. droughts
17. The wind that blows out the candle also kindles the fire

❧ 解析 ···

① The writing is on the wall. 為聖經典故「牆上見字」，用以比喻「不祥之兆」。

② The wind that blows out the candle also kindles the fire.「吹熄燭火的風亦可以助長火勢。」用來比喻「水能載舟，亦能覆舟」。

③ urbanization (*n.*) 都市化

❧ 中譯 ···

Tina： 妳在做什麼啊？

Evelyn：我在聽新聞節目。

Tina： 它在說什麼？

Evelyn：新聞節目說美國總統想要干預開發中國家，像是中國、印度的二氧化碳排放管制政策。

Tina： 我也聽說過。溫室效應是由過多的二氧化碳和水氣所造成，這些氣體被稱為溫室氣體。這會造成大幅度的氣候變化和地球暖化。

Evelyn：不祥之兆已經浮現。

Tina： 我聽說平均攝氏溫度改變 0.1 度，會造成七萬五千種生物從地球上消失。

Evelyn：而且南北極圈的冰帽正在融化，造成海平面上升。

Tina： 至於氣候變化，不該下雨的地方會出現豪雨，甚至洪水氾濫；宜人的天氣將被乾旱取代，例子太多，不勝枚舉。。

Evelyn：切記「水能載舟，亦能覆舟。」這句至理名言，那是都市化的另一個後遺症。

動植物
Flora and Fauna

植物

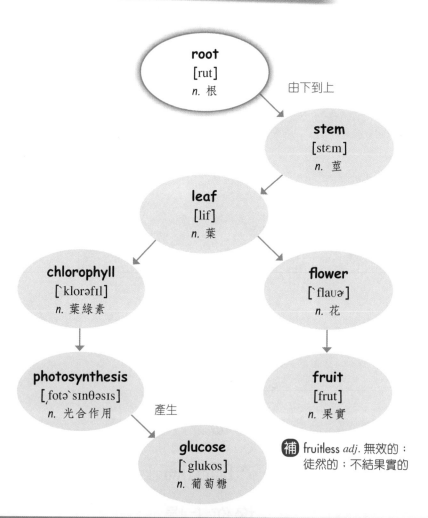

root
[rut]
n. 根

由下到上

stem
[stɛm]
n. 莖

leaf
[lif]
n. 葉

chlorophyll
[`klorəfɪl]
n. 葉綠素

flower
[`flauə]
n. 花

photosynthesis
[ˌfotə`sɪnθəsɪs]
n. 光合作用

產生

fruit
[frut]
n. 果實

glucose
[`glukos]
n. 葡萄糖

補 fruitless *adj.* 無效的；
徒然的；不結果實的

大師
小叮嚀

- Flora [`florə] *n.* 植物的總稱；fauna [`fɔnə] *n.* 動物的總稱。
- Photo：「光」；syn：「合成；集合」，所以光合作用叫做 photosynthesis。

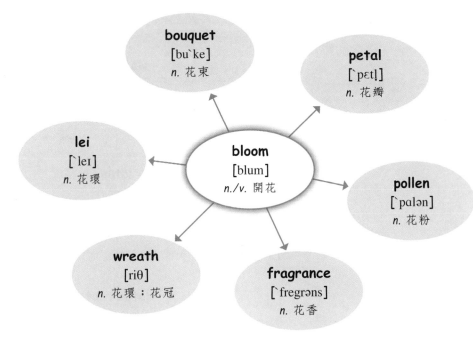

大師小叮嚀 | ✏ Lei 是套在脖子上，如夏威夷迎賓用的花環；wreath 則是戴在頭上的花冠，也可指非配戴用、用於慶祝或紀念的花環。

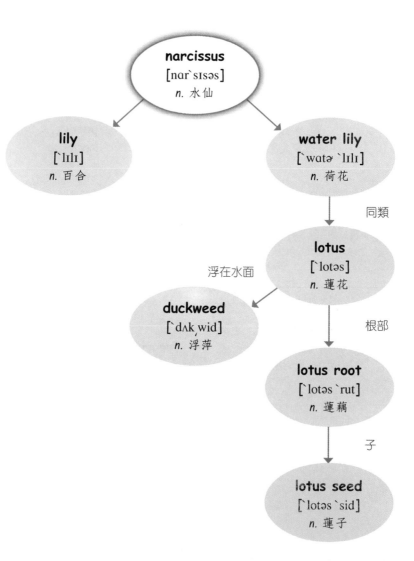

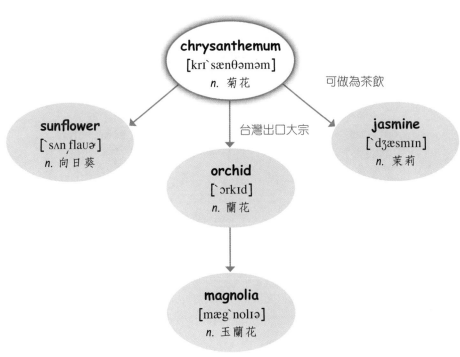

chrysanthemum
[krɪˋsænθəməm]
n. 菊花

可做為茶飲

sunflower
[ˋsʌnˌflauɚ]
n. 向日葵

台灣出口大宗

orchid
[ˋɔrkɪd]
n. 蘭花

jasmine
[ˋdʒæsmɪn]
n. 茉莉

magnolia
[mægˋnolɪə]
n. 玉蘭花

動物

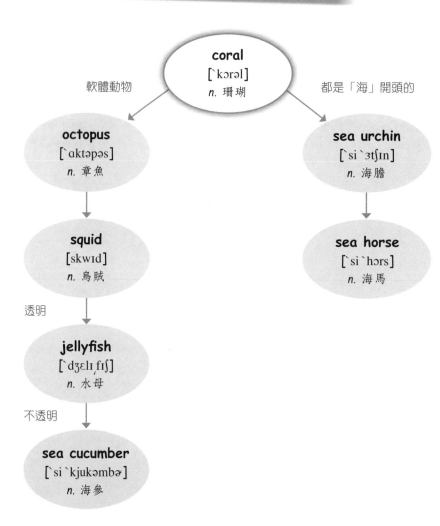

coral
[`kɔrəl]
n. 珊瑚

軟體動物

都是「海」開頭的

octopus
[`ɑktəpəs]
n. 章魚

sea urchin
[`si `ɝtʃɪn]
n. 海膽

squid
[skwɪd]
n. 烏賊

sea horse
[`si `hɔrs]
n. 海馬

透明

jellyfish
[`dʒɛlɪˏfɪʃ]
n. 水母

不透明

sea cucumber
[`si `kjukəmbɚ]
n. 海參

大師小叮嚀

○ Coral reef 是「珊瑚礁」。
○ Urchin 指的是「淘氣的孩子;頑童」。

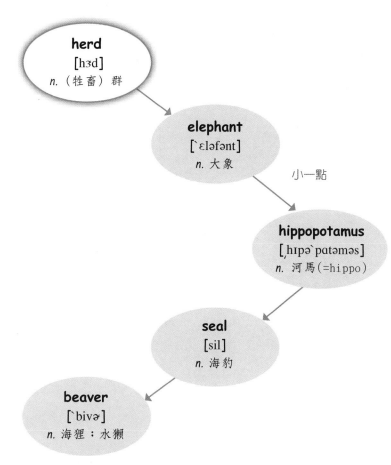

herd
[hɜd]
n.（牲畜）群

elephant
[ˋɛləfənt]
n. 大象

小一點

hippopotamus
[ˌhɪpəˋpatəməs]
n. 河馬（=hippo）

seal
[sil]
n. 海豹

beaver
[ˋbivə]
n. 海狸；水獺

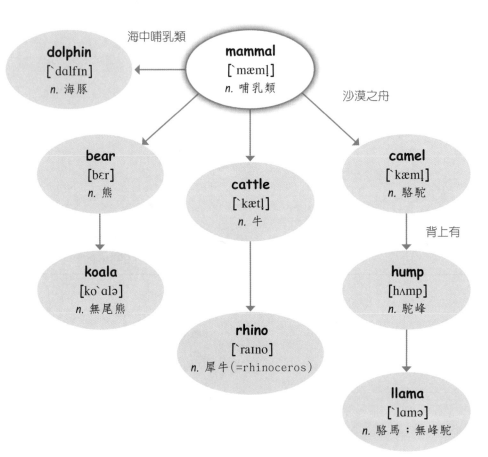

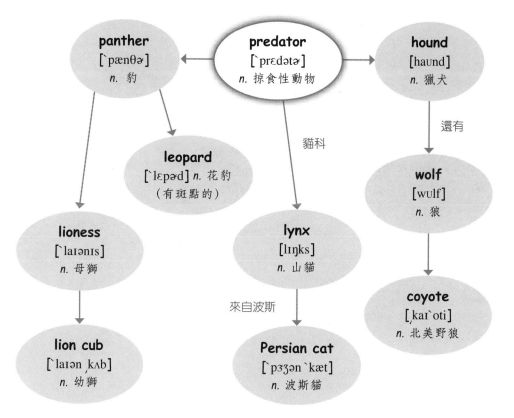

panther
[`pænθɚ]
n. 豹

predator
[`prɛdətɚ]
n. 掠食性動物

hound
[haʊnd]
n. 獵犬

leopard
[`lɛpəd] *n.* 花豹
（有斑點的）

貓科

還有

wolf
[wʊlf]
n. 狼

lioness
[`laɪənɪs]
n. 母獅

lynx
[lɪŋks]
n. 山貓

lion cub
[`laɪən ˏkʌb]
n. 幼獅

來自波斯

coyote
[ˏkaɪ`oti]
n. 北美野狼

Persian cat
[`pɝʒən `kæt]
n. 波斯貓

大師小叮嚀 | ✏ The old hound is the best.「老獵犬最有經驗。」即「薑是老的辣」。

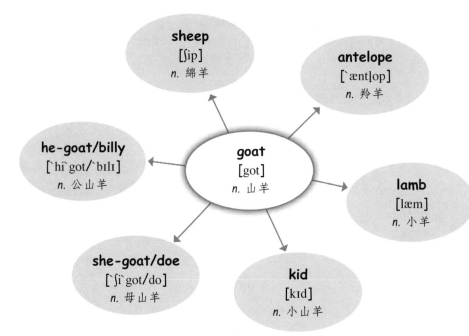

sheep
[ʃip]
n. 綿羊

antelope
[ˋæntlop]
n. 羚羊

he-goat/billy
[ˋhiˋgot/ˋbɪlɪ]
n. 公山羊

goat
[got]
n. 山羊

lamb
[læm]
n. 小羊

she-goat/doe
[ˋʃiˋgot/do]
n. 母山羊

kid
[kɪd]
n. 小山羊

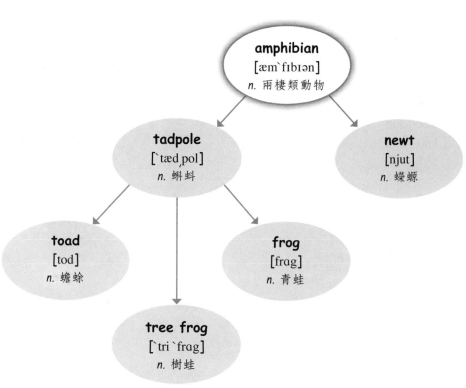

amphibian
[æmˋfɪbɪən]
n. 兩棲類動物

tadpole
[ˋtædˌpol]
n. 蝌蚪

newt
[njut]
n. 蠑螈

toad
[tod]
n. 蟾蜍

tree frog
[ˋtriˋfrɑg]
n. 樹蛙

frog
[frɑg]
n. 青蛙

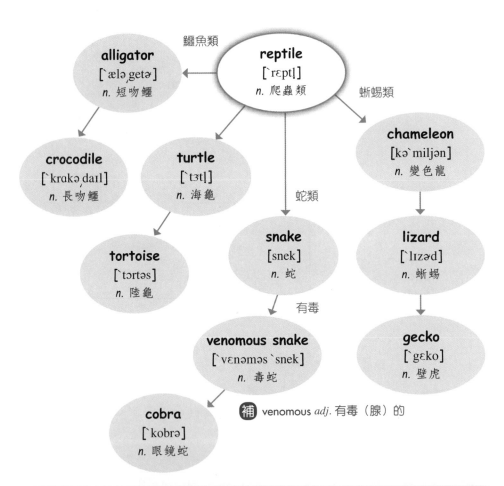

alligator
[ˈæləˌgetə]
n. 短吻鱷

鱷魚類

reptile
[ˈrɛptl]
n. 爬蟲類

蜥蜴類

chameleon
[kəˈmiljən]
n. 變色龍

crocodile
[ˈkrɑkəˌdaɪl]
n. 長吻鱷

turtle
[ˈtɝtl]
n. 海龜

蛇類

tortoise
[ˈtɔrtəs]
n. 陸龜

snake
[snek]
n. 蛇

lizard
[ˈlɪzəd]
n. 蜥蜴

有毒

venomous snake
[ˈvɛnəməs ˈsnek]
n. 毒蛇

gecko
[ˈgɛko]
n. 壁虎

cobra
[ˈkobrə]
n. 眼鏡蛇

補 venomous *adj.* 有毒（腺）的

大師小叮嚀

☞ Crocodile 與 alligator 不同之處在於嘴巴的長度，crocodile 的嘴巴比 alligator 長。

☞ Venom (*n.*)「（蛇、蜘蛛等的）毒液」；一般的毒藥是 poison；毒素則為 toxin，特指有害環境或健康的物質。

☞ Crocodile tears「假慈悲」，例：to cry crocodile tears「貓哭耗子假慈悲」。

大師出馬

❶ Butterfly **orchids** are expensive plants and need special care.
蝴蝶蘭是昂貴的植物，需要特別用心照料。

❷ **Flowers** and **fruits** are the reproductive organs of plants.
花及果實是植物的生殖器官。
（reproductive *adj.* 生殖的）

❸ I'm allergic to **pollen**.
我對花粉過敏。
（allergic to *ph.* 對……過敏）

❹ This perfume is made from dried rose **petals**.
這款香水是由乾燥的玫瑰花瓣所製成。

❺ Don't believe a word he says. Those are **crocodile tears** that he's crying.
不要相信他說的任何一句話，他是貓哭耗子假慈悲。

❻ A **leopard** cannot change his spots.
花豹脫不了身上的斑點。（即「江山易改，本性難移」。）

❼ The hibernating **snakes** began to move.
冬眠的蛇開始活動了。
（hibernate *v.* 冬眠）

❽ **Panthers** and lions are **predators**.
豹和獅子都是掠食性動物。

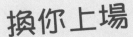 換你上場

∽ *Exercise* ······ 根據你所聽到的對話完成填空。

Evelyn: The weather is getting warm.

Tina:　Yeah, summer is almost here.

Evelyn: How have you been?

Tina:　Couldn't be better. I visited the arboretum with my parents yesterday.

Evelyn: With your parents? You're so 1. 孝順 . I went to the zoo in Mucha with my boyfriend last Sunday. We had so much fun. What did you see?

Tina:　There were some beautiful 2. 蓮花 and 3. 荷花 . They looked really healthy. How about you?

Evelyn: Let's see. We saw lots of 4. 兩棲類 like 5. 蠑螈 and 6. 樹蛙 , and we saw a 7. 母獅 taking care of her 8. 小獅子 .

Tina:　My parents felt as if they 9. 歷經時光倒流 .① We often went there when I was a kid.

Evelyn: Sounds like 10. 妳有個關係非常親密的家庭 .

Tina:　The Bible says, "11. 白髮是老年人的榮耀 ." You should spend more time with your parents.

Evelyn: But, I'm busy with work and they're getting old. Isn't it too late?

Tina:　Better late than never. Parents want nothing but their children's companionship.

↪ *Answer key* ···

1. filial
2. lotuses
3. water lilies
4. amphibians
5. newts
6. tree frogs
7. lioness
8. lion cub
9. had gone through a time warp
10. you have a really close-knit family
11. Gray hairs are the splendors of the old

↪ 解析 ···

① time warp (*n.*) 時間暫停；時光倒流

↪ 中譯 ···

Evelyn：天氣漸漸變暖了。

Tina： 是啊，夏天快來了。

Evelyn：妳最近好嗎？

Tina： 好得不得了。我昨天和我父母親去參觀植物園。

Evelyn：和妳父母？妳真孝順。上禮拜日我和我男友去木柵動物園。真好玩。妳看了些什麼？

Tina： 有很多美麗的蓮花和荷花，開得很茂盛。你們呢？

Evelyn：我想想，我們看到很多兩棲類，有蠑螈和樹蛙，還看到母獅照顧小獅子。

Tina： 我父母感覺好像歷經時光倒流。小時候他們常帶我去那裡。

Evelyn：聽起來妳有個關係非常親密的家庭。

Tina： 聖經說：「白髮是老年人的榮耀。」妳應該多花一點時間陪陪妳的父母親。

Evelyn：但我工作忙碌，他們也愈來愈老了。會不會太遲了？

Tina： 有開始就不會太遲。父母親想要的只是孩子的陪伴。

顏色與形狀
Colors and Shapes

顏色

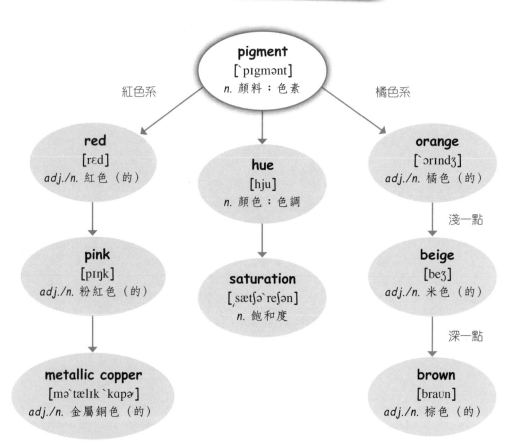

pigment
[`pɪgmənt]
n. 顏料；色素

紅色系

橘色系

red
[rɛd]
adj./n. 紅色（的）

hue
[hju]
n. 顏色；色調

orange
[`ɔrɪndʒ]
adj./n. 橘色（的）

淺一點

pink
[pɪŋk]
adj./n. 粉紅色（的）

saturation
[ˌsætʃəˋreʃən]
n. 飽和度

beige
[beʒ]
adj./n. 米色（的）

深一點

metallic copper
[məˋtælɪk ˋkɑpə]
adj./n. 金屬銅色（的）

brown
[braun]
adj./n. 棕色（的）

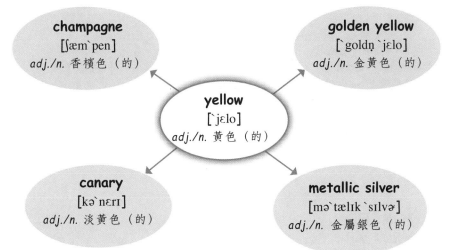

champagne
[ʃæm`pen]
adj./n. 香檳色（的）

golden yellow
[`goldn̩ `jɛlo]
adj./n. 金黃色（的）

yellow
[`jɛlo]
adj./n. 黃色（的）

canary
[kə`nɛrɪ]
adj./n. 淡黃色（的）

metallic silver
[mə`tælɪk `sɪlvɚ]
adj./n. 金屬銀色（的）

大師
小叮嚀 | ✏ 汽車車體反射出的金屬顏色即為 metallic，例：My car is metallic blue.「我的車是金屬藍色的。」

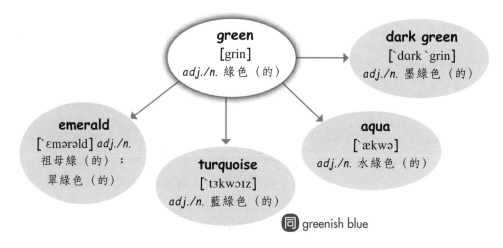

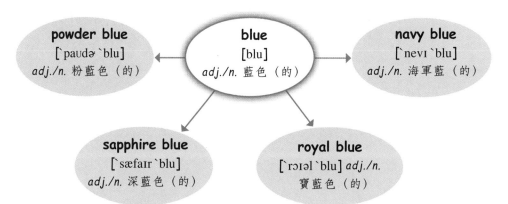

 大師 小叮嚀 | ✏ To dress in green「穿綠色的衣服」。

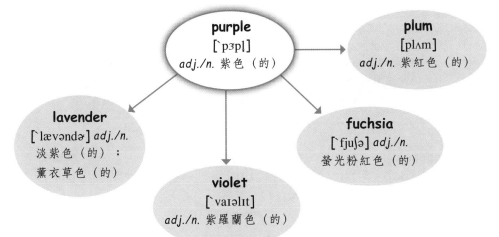

形狀

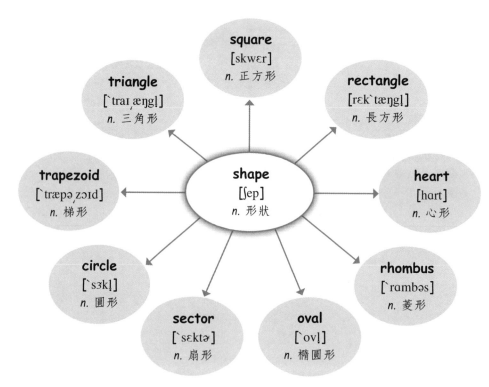

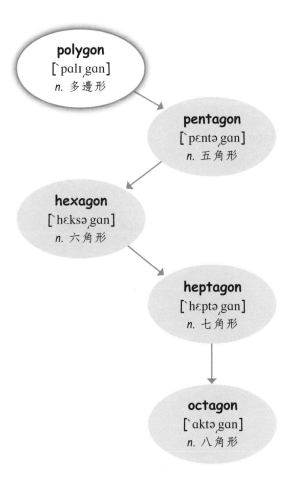

polygon
[ˋpɑlɪˏɡɑn]
n. 多邊形

pentagon
[ˋpɛntəˏɡɑn]
n. 五角形

hexagon
[ˋhɛksəˏɡɑn]
n. 六角形

heptagon
[ˋhɛptəˏɡɑn]
n. 七角形

octagon
[ˋɑktəˏɡɑn]
n. 八角形

大　師
小叮嚀

✎ 認識字首對記住這些單字很有助益：penta：「五」、hexa：「六」、hepta：「七」、octa：「八」、poly：「多；許多」、gon：「角形」。

✎ The Pentagon「美國五角大廈」，美國國防部所在地。

✎ 這些單字只要在字尾加上 "al" 即可構成形容詞。

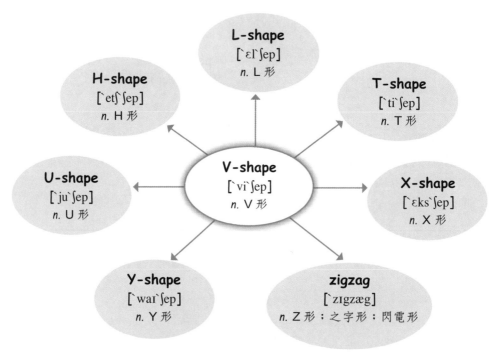

 大 師 小叮嚀 ✐ U-turn：（車輛）迴轉，例：We just passed the entrance. I guess you'll have to make a U-turn.「我們剛錯過入口，我想你得迴轉。」

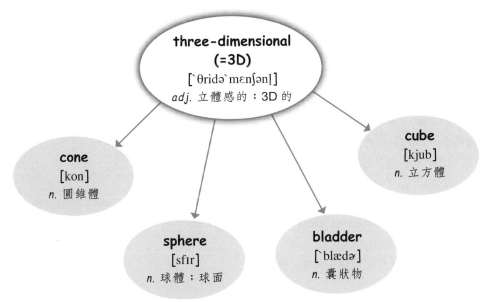

three-dimensional (=3D)
[ˋθrɪdəˋmɛnʃən!]
adj. 立體感的；3D 的

cone
[kon]
n. 圓錐體

cube
[kjub]
n. 立方體

sphere
[sfɪr]
n. 球體；球面

bladder
[ˋblædə]
n. 囊狀物

大師小叮嚀

✏ Traffic cone：交通錐。

✏ Ice cream cone：冰淇淋甜筒；cone：（盛冰淇淋的）錐形蛋捲筒。

大師出馬

❶ The goal posts in American football are described as "**H-shaped.**"
美式足球的球門是 H 形。
（describe v. 形成……的形狀）

❷ The clear **turquoise** sea reminds me of the good old days when I was a student in Ocean City, Maryland.
這清澈蔚藍的海洋勾起我在馬里蘭州海洋城讀書時的美好回憶。

❸ If you see someone driving in a **zigzag** pattern, call the police immediately.
如果你看到有人蛇行駕駛，要馬上報警。

❹ The earth isn't a perfect **sphere**; it's an oblate spheroid.
地球不是正圓的，而是個橢圓球體。
（oblate adj. 扁圓的　spheroid n. 球體）

❺ Snowflakes come in all sizes and patterns, but all of them are **hexagonal.**
雪花的大小和花樣有各種變化，但它們都是六角形。

❻ HSBC's logo is formed from six **triangles.**
匯豐銀行的商標由六個三角形組成。

❼ The sky is **sapphire blue** and the sun is **golden yellow.**
天空是深藍色的，而太陽是金黃色的。

❽ Your sports car is in **metallic silver.** It's so fancy.
你的跑車是金屬銀色的，好夢幻喔。

❾ **Saturation** refers to the intensity of a specific **hue.**
飽和度指的是某一顏色的強度。

換你上場

學習成效知分曉！

🔗 *Exercise* …… 連連看。

A. 形狀

heart •

oval •

pentagon •

octagon •

hexagon •

trapezoid •

B. 顏色

| brown · | · 藍綠色 |

| fuchsia · | · 淡紫色 |

| beige · | · 米色 |

| lavender · | · 螢光粉紅色 |

| turquoise · | · 棕色 |

| aqua · | · 海軍藍 |

| navy blue · | · 水綠色 |

↬ *Answer key* ⋯⋯⋯⋯⋯⋯⋯⋯⋯⋯⋯⋯⋯⋯⋯⋯⋯⋯⋯⋯⋯⋯⋯⋯⋯

A. 形狀

heart

oval

pentagon

octagon

hexagon

trapezoid

B. 顏色

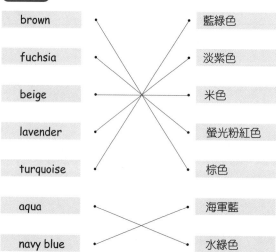

brown — 藍綠色

fuchsia — 淡紫色

beige — 米色

lavender — 螢光粉紅色

turquoise — 棕色

aqua — 海軍藍

navy blue — 水綠色

PART 8

新聞
NEWS

商業
Business

商業

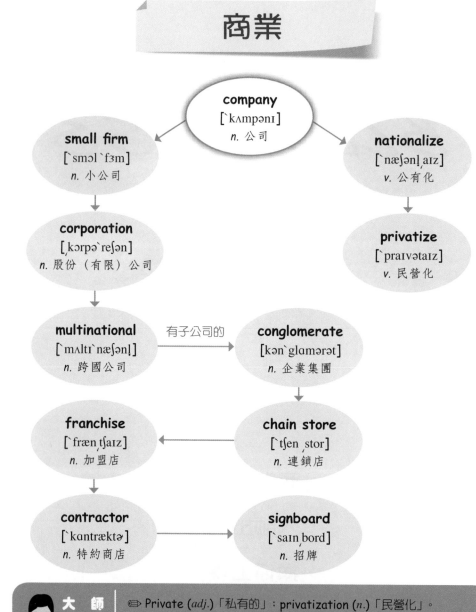

company
[ˋkʌmpənɪ]
n. 公司

small firm
[ˋsmɔl ˋfɝm]
n. 小公司

nationalize
[ˋnæʃənḷˏaɪz]
v. 公有化

corporation
[ˏkɔrpəˋreʃən]
n. 股份（有限）公司

privatize
[ˋpraɪvətaɪz]
v. 民營化

multinational
[ˋmʌltɪˋnæʃənḷ]
n. 跨國公司

有子公司的

conglomerate
[kənˋglɑmərət]
n. 企業集團

franchise
[ˋfrænˏtʃaɪz]
n. 加盟店

chain store
[ˋtʃenˏstor]
n. 連鎖店

contractor
[ˋkɑntræktɚ]
n. 特約商店

signboard
[ˋsaɪnˏbord]
n. 招牌

大師
小叮嚀

✐ Private (*adj.*)「私有的」；privatization (*n.*)「民營化」。
✐ National (*adj.*)「國有的」；nationalization (*n.*)「國有化」。

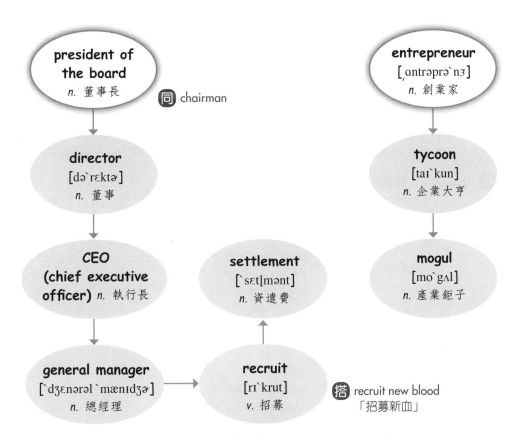

president of the board
n. 董事長

同 chairman

entrepreneur
[ˌɑntrəprə`nɝ]
n. 創業家

director
[də`rɛktə]
n. 董事

tycoon
[taɪ`kun]
n. 企業大亨

CEO (chief executive officer) *n.* 執行長

settlement
[`sɛtl̩mənt]
n. 資遣費

mogul
[mo`gʌl]
n. 產業鉅子

general manager
[`dʒɛnərəl `mænɪdʒə]
n. 總經理

recruit
[rɪ`krut]
v. 招募

搭 recruit new blood
「招募新血」

 大師小叮嚀

- ☞ 覺得 tycoon 和 mogul 難以區別嗎？
  前者通常專用於商業界，後者則可指各產業中的重要人物。
- ☞ President of board 中的 board 就是董事會。
- ☞ Recruitment (*n.*) 「招募」
  例：Volunteer recruitment for the 2008 Beijing Olympic Games began several years before the opening ceremony.
  「2008 北京奧運在開幕前幾年就開始招募義工。」

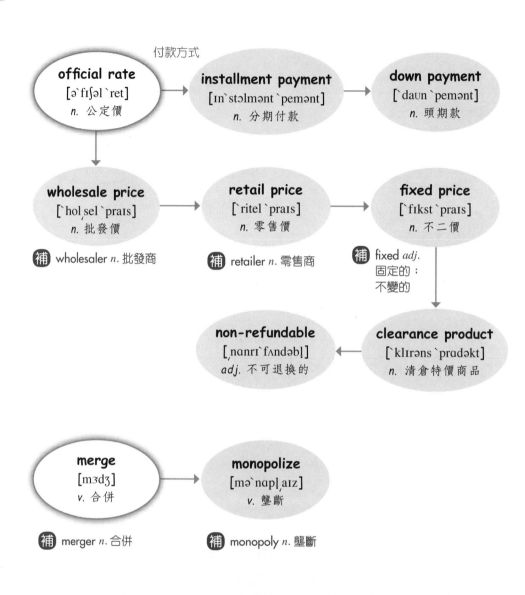

付款方式

official rate
[əˋfɪʃəl ˋret]
n. 公定價

installment payment
[ɪnˋstɔlmənt ˋpemənt]
n. 分期付款

down payment
[ˋdaʊn ˋpemənt]
n. 頭期款

wholesale price
[ˋholˏsel ˋpraɪs]
n. 批發價

補 wholesaler *n.* 批發商

retail price
[ˋritel ˋpraɪs]
n. 零售價

補 retailer *n.* 零售商

fixed price
[ˋfɪkst ˋpraɪs]
n. 不二價

補 fixed *adj.*
固定的；
不變的

non-refundable
[ˏnɑnrɪˋfʌndəbl̩]
adj. 不可退換的

clearance product
[ˋklɪrəns ˋprɑdəkt]
n. 清倉特價商品

merge
[mɝdʒ]
v. 合併

補 merger *n.* 合併

monopolize
[məˋnɑpl̩ˏaɪz]
v. 壟斷

補 monopoly *n.* 壟斷

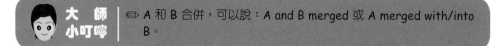

大師小叮嚀 ✎ A 和 B 合併，可以說：A and B merged 或 A merged with/into B。

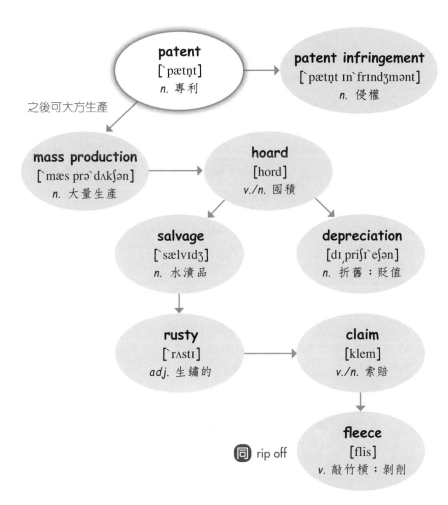

之後可大方生產

patent
[`pætn̩t]
n. 專利

patent infringement
[`pætn̩t ɪn`frɪndʒmənt]
n. 侵權

mass production
[`mæs prə`dʌkʃən]
n. 大量生產

hoard
[hord]
v./n. 囤積

salvage
[`sælvɪdʒ]
n. 水漬品

depreciation
[dɪ͵priʃɪ`eʃən]
n. 折舊；貶值

rusty
[`rʌstɪ]
adj. 生鏽的

claim
[klem]
v./n. 索賠

同 rip off

fleece
[flis]
v. 敲竹槓；剝削

大師
小叮嚀

✐ 請注意 patent 不同詞性的用法喔：(n.) 專利（權）；(adj.) 有專利的；(v.) 取得⋯⋯的專利權。Apply for a patent on sth. 「為⋯⋯申請專利」。

✐ （為某物）申請保險理賠怎麼說呢？就是 claim sth. on one's insurance，例：claim the stolen car on your insurance。也可以說 make an insurance claim，此時 claim 為名詞。

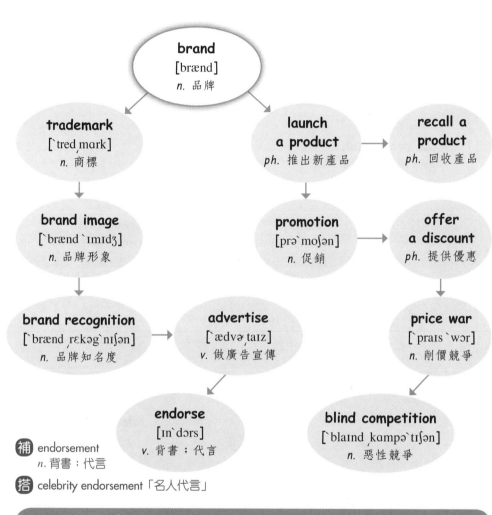

brand
[brænd]
n. 品牌

trademark
[`tred͵mark]
n. 商標

**launch
a product**
ph. 推出新產品

**recall a
product**
ph. 回收產品

brand image
[`brænd `ɪmɪdʒ]
n. 品牌形象

promotion
[prə`moʃən]
n. 促銷

**offer
a discount**
ph. 提供優惠

brand recognition
[`brænd ͵rɛkəg`nɪʃən]
n. 品牌知名度

advertise
[`ædvɚ͵taɪz]
v. 做廣告宣傳

price war
[`praɪs `wɔr]
n. 削價競爭

endorse
[ɪn`dɔrs]
v. 背書；代言

blind competition
[`blaɪnd ͵kampə`tɪʃən]
n. 惡性競爭

 endorsement
n. 背書；代言

搭 celebrity endorsement「名人代言」

> 大師小叮嚀
> ✍ 新產品的「推出」就用 launch (*v.*/*n.*)。
> ✍ 八折優惠怎麼說？就是 a discount of 20 percent 或 a 20 percent discount。
> 例：They offered me a 20 percent discount on a coat with a small stain. 「這件外套有個小汙點，店家給了我八折優惠。」
> ✍ 「代言人」就叫做 face。

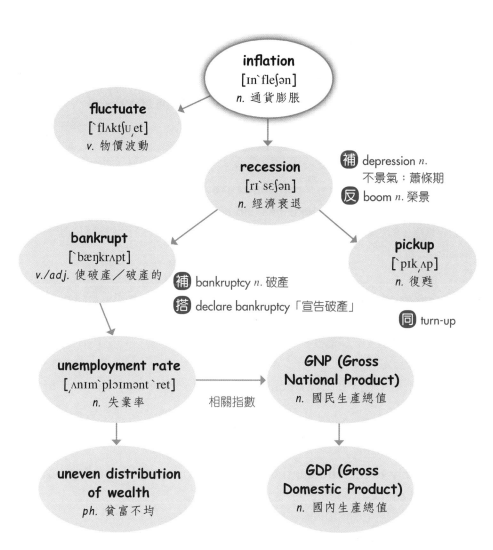

inflation
[ɪnˋfleʃən]
n. 通貨膨脹

fluctuate
[ˋflʌktʃʊˏet]
v. 物價波動

recession
[rɪˋsɛʃən]
n. 經濟衰退

補 depression n.
不景氣；蕭條期
反 boom n. 榮景

bankrupt
[ˋbæŋkrʌpt]
v./adj. 使破產／破產的

補 bankruptcy n. 破產
搭 declare bankruptcy「宣告破產」

pickup
[ˋpɪkˏʌp]
n. 復甦

同 turn-up

unemployment rate
[ʌnɪmˋplɔɪmənt ˋret]
n. 失業率

相關指數

GNP (Gross National Product)
n. 國民生產總值

uneven distribution of wealth
ph. 貧富不均

GDP (Gross Domestic Product)
n. 國內生產總值

大師
小叮嚀

✏ GNP = gross national product。
✏ GDP = gross domestic product。
✏ 「破產」常用 go bankrupt。
　　例：He went bankrupt in 2002.「他在 2002 年破產了。」

大師出馬

❶ I bought shares in the phone company when it was **privatized**.

我在電信公司民營化的時候買進它的股份。

（share *n.* 股份）

❷ The media **mogul** owns a **conglomerate** that has TV channels, radio stations, and publishes magazines and newspapers worldwide.

這個媒體鉅子的企業集團擁有電視頻道、廣播電台，並在全球發行雜誌和報紙。

（publish *v.* 發行）

❸ It is generally agreed that Microsoft has a **monopoly** on operating systems.

微軟是公認的操作系統壟斷者。

❹ The country's two biggest banks are set to **merge** by the end of the year.

這個國家最大的兩間銀行已經準備在年底前合併。

❺ Immediately after the earthquake, people started **hoarding** bottled water and canned food.

地震之後，大家馬上開始囤積瓶裝水和罐頭。

❻ You need to be careful when buying souvenirs, because some local stores have been **fleecing** tourists.

你買紀念品時要小心，因為有些當地商家會向遊客敲竹槓。

❼ Our new solar battery is protected by several local and international **patents**.

我們的太陽能電池在國內外都有專利保障。

(solar *adj.* 利用太陽光的)

❽ Defective food products should be **recalled** immediately in order to protect the health of consumers.

有瑕疵的食用性商品應該馬上回收，以保障消費者的健康。

(defective *adj.* 有缺陷的)

❾ My brother's cosmetics company secured many student customers with youthful **advertising** and low-priced products.

我哥哥的化妝品公司以充滿年輕活力的廣告和低價位的產品吸引了許多學生顧客。

❿ Nicole Kidman is no stranger to celebrity **endorsements**. She reportedly earned US$12 million in 2005 as the **face** of Chanel.

妮可・基嫚常為商品代言。據報她在 2005 年就因當香奈兒的代言人賺進了一千兩百萬美元。

(reportedly *adv.* 根據報導)

⓫ He went **bankrupt** during the Great **Depression**.

他在經濟大蕭條時破產了。

⓬ You may have noticed that Taiwan's **unemployment rate** has been increasing in recent years.

你可能發現到近年來台灣的失業率一直上升。

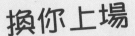

換你上場　學習成效知分曉！

↪ *Exercise* ‥‥‥‥ 根據你所聽到的對話完成填空。

Tina: I'm really excited about the 1. 推出 of our new line of rose 2. 護膚產品 . With the new 3. 專利成分 , there won't be a problem selling products even though they're 4. 大量生產 .

Evelyn: We shouldn't be too optimistic during a 5. 不景氣 . We're experiencing 6. 通貨膨脹 , 7. 物價波動 , and a low rate of 8. 消費 .

Patrick: I agree with you. The 9. 失業率 is climbing[①] and the 10. 國內生產毛額 is going the other way. We should try positive 11. 廣告 and 12. 行銷 to stimulate[②] the desire to purchase.

Tina: How about doing some 13. 大促銷 by offering 14. 折扣[③] on all of the products in our 15. 加盟店 ? After all, we're part of a 16. 跨國企業集團 and have ample[④] 17. 資金 .

Evelyn: But we'd better avoid a 18. 削價競爭 . That usually leads to 19. 惡性競爭 .

Patrick: I have two more suggestions: allow 20. 分期付款 for large purchases and withdraw the lousy 21. 概不退貨 policy.

Tina: We can also hire a celebrity to 22. 代言 our products.

Evelyn: Good. These great strategies, in addition to the strong 23. 品牌形象 , will definitely drum up business. [⑤]

Tina: We won't let the 24. 總經理 down. Let's go for it!

☞ *Answer key*

1. launch
2. skin care products
3. patented ingredients
4. mass produced
5. depression
6. inflation
7. price fluctuations
8. consumption
9. unemployment rate
10. GDP
11. advertising
12. marketing
13. heavy promotion
14. discounts
15. franchises
16. transnational conglomerate
17. capital
18. price war
19. blind competition
20. installment payments
21. non-refundable
22. endorse
23. brand image
24. general manager

☞ 解析

① climb (*v.*)（物價等）上升
② stimulate (*v.*) 刺激；激勵
　　例：stimulate economic growth「刺激經濟成長」。
③ 針對某產品提供某折扣常用：offer ... discount on sth.，注意介系詞用 on。
④ ample (*adj.*) 大量的；充裕的
⑤ drum up business「創造業績」，drum up sth. 就是「使⋯⋯興隆」的意思。

☞ 中譯

Tina： 我們新推出的玫瑰護膚系列讓我好興奮喔。有專利成分護航，就算大量生產也不用擔心會滯銷。

Evelyn： 時代不景氣，我們也不能太樂觀。現在還有通貨膨脹、物價波動和低消費率的問題。

Patrick： 我贊成妳的說法。最近失業率攀升，國內生產毛額下降，我們應該用積極的廣告及行銷來刺激買氣。

Tina： 我們辦個大促銷，在各加盟店做全館折扣如何？反正我們公司是跨國集團，資金充裕。

Evelyn： 但我們最好避免削價競爭，這常會帶來惡性競爭。

Patrick：我還有兩個建議：對大量購買開放分期付款，以及撤銷概不退貨的愚蠢策略。

Tina： 我們還可以邀請名人為產品代言。

Evelyn： 很好。有了這些策略，再加上有力的品牌形象，一定能夠創造業績。

Tina： 我們不會讓總經理失望的。加油吧！

銀行和金融
Banking and Finance

銀行

account
[ə`kaunt]
n. 帳戶;帳目

deposit
[dɪ`pazɪt]
v./n. 存款

withdraw
[wɪð`drɔ]
v. 提款

balance
[`bæləns]
n. 結餘

credit card
[`krɛdɪt `kard]
n. 信用卡

debit card
[`dɛbɪt `kard]
n. 提款卡

如果密碼錯誤

invalid
[ɪn`vælɪd]
adj. 無效的

password
[`pæs͵wɝd]
n. 密碼

搭 enter the password
「輸入密碼」

cash
[kæʃ]
v. 兌現 n. 現金

vault
[vɔlt]
n. 金庫

traveler's check
[`trævləz `tʃɛk]
n. 旅行支票

serial number
[`sɪrɪəl `nʌmbə]
n. 序號

大師小叮嚀 ✍ 「查詢餘額」就是 check one's balance,例:I'd better check my balance at the ATM.「我最好到提款機查詢一下餘額。」

金融

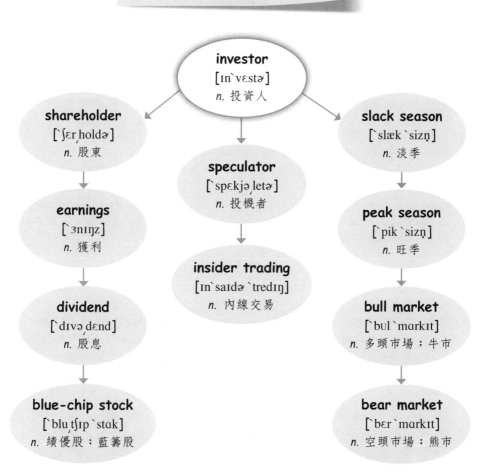

investor
[ɪn`vɛstə]
n. 投資人

shareholder
[`ʃɛr͵holdə]
n. 股東

speculator
[`spɛkjə͵letə]
n. 投機者

slack season
[`slæk `sizn̩]
n. 淡季

earnings
[`ɝnɪŋz]
n. 獲利

insider trading
[ɪn`saɪdə `tredɪŋ]
n. 內線交易

peak season
[`pik `sizn̩]
n. 旺季

dividend
[`dɪvə͵dɛnd]
n. 股息

bull market
[`bul `markɪt]
n. 多頭市場;牛市

blue-chip stock
[`blu ͵tʃɪp `stak]
n. 績優股;藍籌股

bear market
[`bɛr `markɪt]
n. 空頭市場;熊市

**大 師
小叮嚀**

✍ Peak season 的 peak 就是「高峰、頂點」。

✍ 多頭市場是指行情看漲的市場;空頭市場是指行情看跌的市場。
例:Most investors are optimistic in a bull market and hysterical in a bear market.「大多數的投資人在多頭市場中態度積極,在空頭市場中卻歇斯底里。」

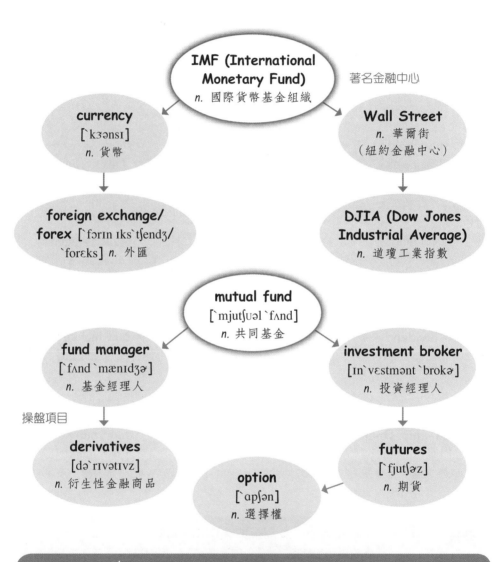

IMF (International Monetary Fund)
n. 國際貨幣基金組織

著名金融中心

currency
[ˋkɝənsɪ]
n. 貨幣

Wall Street
n. 華爾街
（紐約金融中心）

foreign exchange/
forex [ˋfɔrɪn ɪksˋtʃendʒ/
ˋforɛks] *n.* 外匯

DJIA (Dow Jones Industrial Average)
n. 道瓊工業指數

mutual fund
[ˋmjutʃʊəl ˋfʌnd]
n. 共同基金

fund manager
[ˋfʌnd ˋmænɪdʒɚ]
n. 基金經理人

investment broker
[ɪnˋvɛstmənt ˋbrokɚ]
n. 投資經理人

操盤項目

derivatives
[dəˋrɪvətɪvz]
n. 衍生性金融商品

option
[ˋɑpʃən]
n. 選擇權

futures
[ˋfjutʃɚz]
n. 期貨

大師
小叮嚀

☞ 香港恆生指數：Hang Seng Index。
☞ 台灣加權指數：TWI (TSEC Weighted Index，TSEC = Taiwan Stock Exchange Corporation「台灣證券交易所」)。

大師出馬

1 My husband's success in investing is reflected in his bank **balance**.
從我先生的銀行餘額可看出他投資的成功。

2 You can **cash traveler's checks** at banks in most countries.
在大部分國家的銀行，你都可以兌現旅行支票。

3 To protect the property of its customers, a bank's **vault** should be impregnable.
銀行金庫理當十分牢固才能保障客戶的財產。
（impregnable *adj.* 堅不可摧的）

4 In a bear **market**, **shareholders** anxiously hope for a recovery in share value.
空頭市場裡，股東們都焦急地盼望股價回升。
（anxiously *adv.* 焦急地）

5 **Dividends** will be sent to shareholders within ten days of the end of the fiscal year.
股息會在會計年度結束後十日內發給股東。
（fiscal year *n.* 會計年度）

6 **Wall Street**, a narrow street in New York City, is considered to be the heart of the American financial market.
華爾街是紐約市的一條狹窄街道，卻是公認的美國金融市場核心。
（financial market *n.* 金融市場）

❼ The **Dow Jones Industrial Average** plunged ninety points in less than an hour this afternoon.

今天下午道瓊工業指數不到一小時就大跌了 90 點。

（plunge v. 急降）

❽ I need some local **currency**, because many store-owners don't accept **credit cards**.

我需要一些本地貨幣，因為很多店家不收信用卡。

❾ The shrewd **fund manager** is renowned for his accurate forecasts.

這位精明的基金經理人以他精準的預測享負盛名。

（shrewd adj. 精明的；敏銳的　renowned adj. 有名望的）

換你上場

學習成效知分曉！

➔ *Exercise* ⋯⋯根據你所聽到的對話完成填空。

Tina: 1. 投資 is practically a universal activity nowadays. Since I've recently started receiving my 2. 退休金 , I'm going to give it a shot.①

Evelyn: It's an important thing to learn. Retired people often suffer from the effects of 3. 貶值 and 4. 通貨膨脹 .

Tina: I'm totally on board. ② But how do I start?

Evelyn: Go talk to an 5. 投資經理人 at a bank!

Tina: I can't believe my ears!③ Aren't bank services limited to accepting 6. 存款 and making 7. 貸款 ? 8. 提領 money from 9. 自動提款機 is the only thing I do at the bank.

Evelyn: You're so out of the loop!④ Banking services directed at individuals have expanded⑤ to include 10. 退休金與退休生活規劃 , 11. 保險 and investment products, issuing⑥ 12. 衍生性金融商品, and the list goes on.

Tina: Do you think their services are reliable?

Evelyn: Yes, My broker is very professional and always has time to advise me in both the 13. 淡季 and the 14. 旺季 . Do you want to hear something really great? My decision to buy 15. 績優股 in January has already resulted in significantly ⑦ higher earnings ⑧ for the year.

Tina: Wow! So you've become one of the 16. 暴發戶 , like all those 17. 投機者 I see on TV.

Evelyn: Not yet, but maybe some day. And do remember to invest honestly! Many people have gone to jail for 18. 內線交易 . We should really learn from their mistakes.

⌇➔ *Answer key* ⌇⌇

1. Investing	10. pension and retirement planning
2. pension	11. insurance
3. depreciation	12. derivatives
4. inflation	13. slack season
5. investment broker	14. peak season
6. deposits	15. blue chips
7. loans	16. nouveau riche
8. Withdrawing	17. speculators
9. the ATM	18. insider trading

⌇➔ 解析 ⌇⌇

① give it a shot = give it a try「試試看」

② on board 贊成

③ I can't believe my ears! 難以相信自己的耳朵，意思就是「你說什麼？我真不敢相信！」

④ loop是圈或環，所以 out of the loop（在圈圈的外面），就是「消息不靈通」囉！

⑤ expand (*v.*) 擴大；擴張

⑥ issue (*v.*) 發行（舉凡報紙、雜誌、郵票、貨幣、股票的發行都用 issue）

⑦ significantly (*adv.*) 顯著地　significant (*adj.*) 重大的；顯著的

⑧ earnings (*n.*) 利潤；收益

⌇➔ 中譯 ⌇⌇

Tina：　現在幾乎人人都做投資。最近我開始領退休金了，也打算試試看。

Evelyn：學習是很重要的。退休的人往往因為通貨膨脹和貨幣貶值而大受損失。

Tina：　我完全贊同。但我該怎麼開始呢？

Evelyn：去找銀行的投資經理人啊！

Tina：　我真不敢相信！銀行不是只有存款跟貸款服務嗎？我到銀行都只會從提款機領錢而已耶。

Evelyn：妳真是太落伍了！銀行針對個人的服務已經擴大到退休金與退休生活規劃、保險與投資產品、發行衍生性金融商品，還有很多呢！

Tina：　妳認為他們的服務可靠嗎？

Evelyn：是啊！我的經理人非常專業，而且在淡旺季都會撥空給我建議。妳想聽一件很棒的事嗎？
　　　　我一月份買的績優股已經幫我今年賺了極高的利潤。
Tina：　哇！那妳也跟電視上那些投機者一樣成了暴發戶啦！
Evelyn：現在還不是，也許以後吧。但是做投資要正正當當！很多人都因為內線交易而坐牢。我們
　　　　真的應該引以為戒。

醫學
Medicine

醫學

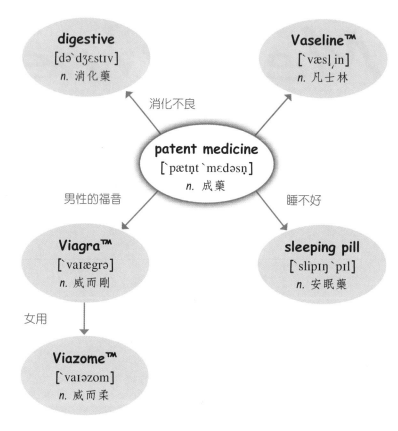

digestive
[də`dʒɛstɪv]
n. 消化藥

Vaseline™
[`væslˌ in]
n. 凡士林

消化不良

patent medicine
[`pætn̩t `mɛdəsn̩]
n. 成藥

男性的福音

睡不好

Viagra™
[`vaɪægrə]
n. 威而剛

sleeping pill
[`slipɪŋ `pɪl]
n. 安眠藥

女用

Viazome™
[`vaɪəzom]
n. 威而柔

大師小叮嚀 ✎ 家禽（poultry）和家畜（livestock）如果不是野放的，多少都含有抗生素（antibiotic）和生長激素（growth hormone），會致癌（carcinogenic），少吃為妙。

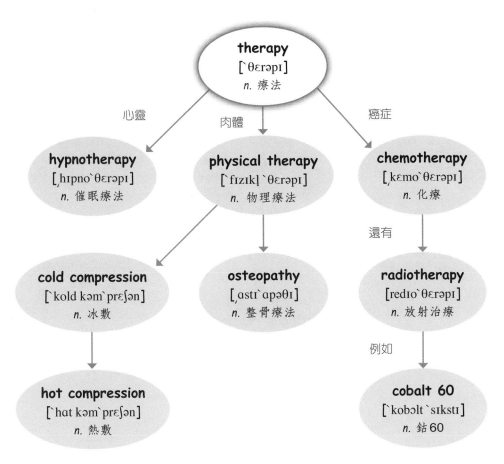

therapy
[ˋθɛrəpɪ]
n. 療法

心靈　　肉體　　癌症

hypnotherapy
[ˏhɪpnoˋθɛrəpɪ]
n. 催眠療法

physical therapy
[ˋfɪzɪk!ˋθɛrəpɪ]
n. 物理療法

chemotherapy
[ˏkɛmoˋθɛrəpɪ]
n. 化療

還有

cold compression
[ˋkold kəmˋprɛʃən]
n. 冰敷

osteopathy
[ˏɑstɪˋɑpəθɪ]
n. 整骨療法

radiotherapy
[redɪoˋθɛrəpɪ]
n. 放射治療

例如

hot compression
[ˋhɑt kəmˋprɛʃən]
n. 熱敷

cobalt 60
[ˋkobɔlt ˋsɪkstɪ]
n. 鈷 60

大師小叮嚀

✍ Osteo-：「骨頭」的字首。

✍ Hypnotize (*v.*) 對⋯⋯施催眠術，例：Is the patient hypnotized?「病人被催眠了嗎？」

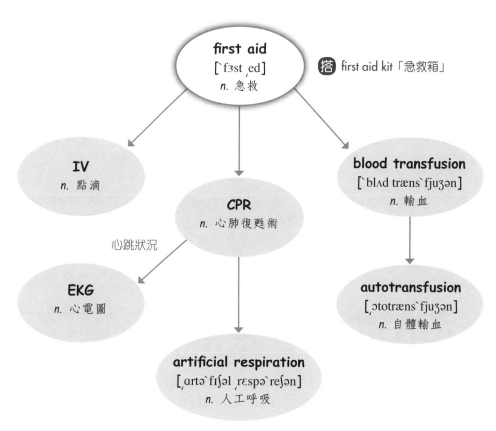

first aid
[ˋfɝst ˏed]
n. 急救

搭 first aid kit「急救箱」

IV
n. 點滴

CPR
n. 心肺復甦術

blood transfusion
[ˋblʌd trænsˋfjuʒən]
n. 輸血

心跳狀況

EKG
n. 心電圖

autotransfusion
[ˏototrænsˋfjuʒən]
n. 自體輸血

artificial respiration
[ˏartəˋfɪʃəl ˏrɛspəˋreʃən]
n. 人工呼吸

 大師
小叮嚀 | ✍ IV 的使用範例如下：I was too nauseous to eat, so the doctor gave me an IV.「我反胃吃不下飯，所以醫生幫我打點滴。」

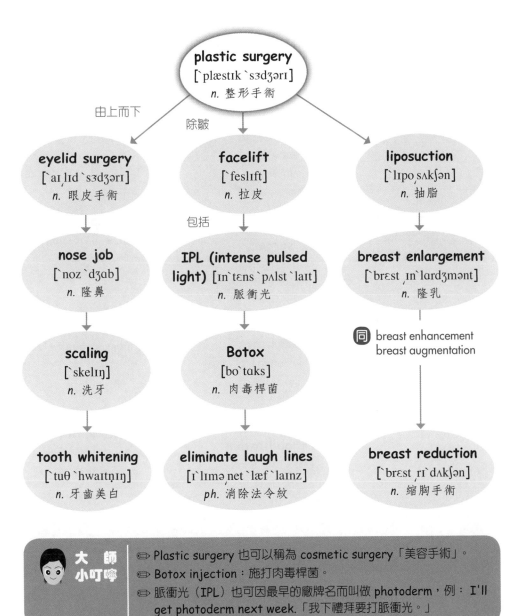

341

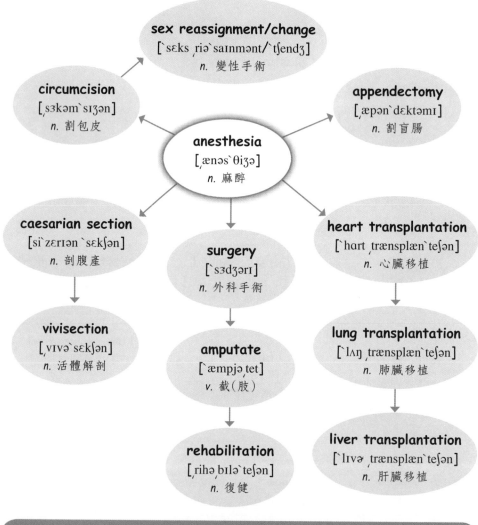

sex reassignment/change
[ˋsɛks͵riəˋsaɪnmənt/ˋtʃendʒ]
n. 變性手術

circumcision
[͵sɝkəmˋsɪʒən]
n. 割包皮

appendectomy
[͵æpənˋdɛktəmɪ]
n. 割盲腸

anesthesia
[͵ænəsˋθiʒə]
n. 麻醉

caesarian section
[sɪˋzɛrɪən ˋsɛkʃən]
n. 剖腹產

surgery
[ˋsɝdʒərɪ]
n. 外科手術

heart transplantation
[ˋhart͵trænsplænˋteʃən]
n. 心臟移植

vivisection
[͵vɪvəˋsɛkʃən]
n. 活體解剖

amputate
[ˋæmpjə͵tet]
v. 截（肢）

lung transplantation
[ˋlʌŋ͵trænsplænˋteʃən]
n. 肺臟移植

rehabilitation
[͵rihə͵bɪləˋteʃən]
n. 復健

liver transplantation
[ˋlɪvə͵trænsplænˋteʃən]
n. 肝臟移植

大師小叮嚀

✐ Caesarian section 原名是「帝王式切開術」，因為傳說凱撒大帝（Caesar）是經由剖腹產所生的，也可以稱為 C-section。

✐ Anesthesia 分為：local anesthesia「局部麻醉」；general anesthesia「全身麻醉」。

✐ Vivisection 中的 vivi 是「活的」、section 為「切開」。

大師出馬

❶ Morphine is sometimes used to relieve pain during **surgery**
外科手術中有時會用嗎啡作為止痛劑。
（relieve v. 釋放；解放）

❷ Facelift surgeries are typically performed under **local anesthesia**
拉皮手術通常是在局部麻醉的情況下完成。

❸ Liposuction surgeries not only remove body fat but also blood and many other liquids from the body.
抽脂手術移除的不僅是體脂肪，還有血液和許多其他液體。

❹ Take some **digestives** if you suffer from indigestion.
消化不良的話就吃一些消化藥。

❺ I'd like to have a more prominent nose, so I'm thinking about getting a **nose job**.
我想要鼻子更挺一點，所以我正考慮去隆鼻。

❻ Don't have a **breast enlargement** just to please someone else.
不要為了討好誰而去隆乳。

❼ CPR may help a victim of cardiac arrest to regain consciousness.
心肺復甦術可以幫助心跳停止的病人恢復意識。
（cardiac arrest ph. 心搏停止）

換你上場

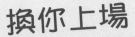

學習成效知分曉！

⟶ **Exercise** ...... 根據你所聽到的對話完成填空。

Doctor: Do your broken legs hurt?

Patient: Thanks, doctor. They feel OK after I took those 1. 止痛藥 .

Doctor: Good. You can gradually take fewer of them. You put your life at risk when you rode in that motorcycle race without wearing knee protectors and shin guards. Fortunately, new developments in 2. 整骨療法 have kept you from becoming an 3. 截肢病患 .

Patient: Did I lose a lot of blood?

Doctor: Yes, you did. We had to give you 4. 心肺復甦術 , a blood 5. 輸血 and nutrients through an 6. 點滴 . Be careful not to knock it over, OK?

Patient: I'll be careful. Will I need to go through 7. 復健 ?

Doctor: Of course. It's called 8. 物理療法 , and it will help restore your muscles and bones.

Patient: Will it be difficult?

Doctor: Inevitably. Hopefully you've learned a lesson from all this.

∽ *Answer key* ⋯⋯⋯⋯⋯⋯⋯⋯⋯⋯⋯⋯⋯⋯⋯⋯⋯⋯⋯⋯⋯⋯⋯⋯⋯⋯⋯⋯

1. pain killers
2. osteopathy
3. amputatee
4. CPR
5. transfusion
6. IV
7. rehabilitation
8. physical therapy

∽ 中譯 ⋯⋯⋯⋯⋯⋯⋯⋯⋯⋯⋯⋯⋯⋯⋯⋯⋯⋯⋯⋯⋯⋯⋯⋯⋯⋯⋯⋯⋯⋯⋯⋯⋯⋯⋯

醫生：你骨折的兩條腿還痛嗎？

病人：吃完止痛藥就不痛了，謝謝你，醫生。

醫生：那不錯，你可以漸漸減少藥量了。不戴上護膝和護脛就參加摩托車比賽，你真是在玩命。幸好現在整骨技術發達，你才能免於成為截肢病患。

病人：我流了很多血嗎？

醫生：是啊，我們需要幫你做心肺復甦術、輸血，還打點滴補充營養。小心別撞翻了，好嗎？

病人：我會的。我還要做復健嗎？

醫生：那當然。這叫物理療法，可以恢復你的肌肉還有骨頭。

病人：我會吃很多苦頭嗎？

醫生：免不了的。希望你能因此得到教訓。

法律
Law

法律

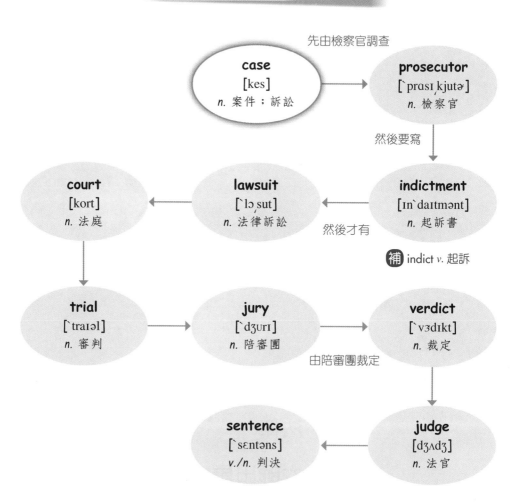

先由檢察官調查

case
[kes]
n. 案件；訴訟

prosecutor
[ˋprɑsɪˌkjutɚ]
n. 檢察官

然後要寫

court
[kort]
n. 法庭

lawsuit
[ˋlɔˌsut]
n. 法律訴訟

然後才有

indictment
[ɪnˋdaɪtmənt]
n. 起訴書

補 indict *v.* 起訴

trial
[ˋtraɪəl]
n. 審判

jury
[ˋdʒʊrɪ]
n. 陪審團

verdict
[ˋvɝdɪkt]
n. 裁定

由陪審團裁定

sentence
[ˋsɛntəns]
v./n. 判決

judge
[dʒʌdʒ]
n. 法官

大師
小叮嚀 ✏ 在西方國家是由陪審團（jury）來裁定（verdict），然後由法官來宣判（sentence）。

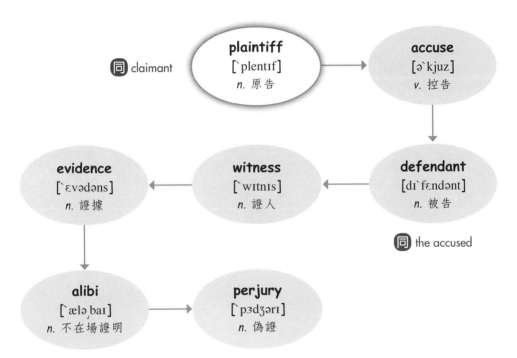

同 claimant

plaintiff
[`plentɪf]
n. 原告

accuse
[ə`kjuz]
v. 控告

evidence
[`ɛvədəns]
n. 證據

witness
[`wɪtnɪs]
n. 證人

defendant
[dɪ`fɛndənt]
n. 被告

同 the accused

alibi
[`ælə͵baɪ]
n. 不在場證明

perjury
[`pɝdʒərɪ]
n. 偽證

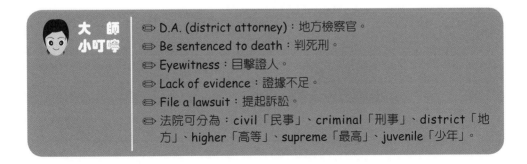

大師小叮嚀

- D.A. (district attorney)：地方檢察官。
- Be sentenced to death：判死刑。
- Eyewitness：目擊證人。
- Lack of evidence：證據不足。
- File a lawsuit：提起訴訟。
- 法院可分為：civil「民事」、criminal「刑事」、district「地方」、higher「高等」、supreme「最高」、juvenile「少年」。

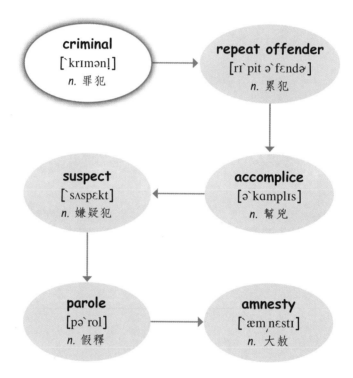

criminal
[`krɪmənḷ]
n. 罪犯

repeat offender
[rɪ`pit ə`fɛndə]
n. 累犯

suspect
[`sʌspɛkt]
n. 嫌疑犯

accomplice
[ə`kamplɪs]
n. 幫兇

parole
[pə`rol]
n. 假釋

amnesty
[`æm͵nɛstɪ]
n. 大赦

大師
小叮嚀

相關用法舉例如下：

- Jack is on parole. 「傑克正在假釋期間。」
- Announce (an) amnesty for somebody：宣布大赦某人。

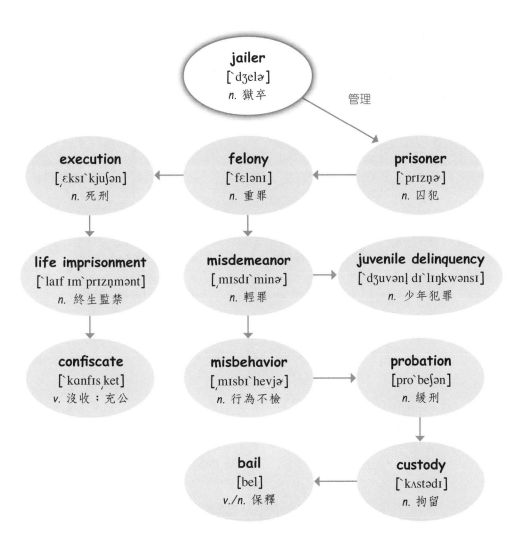

jailer
[`dʒelə]
n. 獄卒

管理

execution
[ˌɛksɪ`kjuʃən]
n. 死刑

felony
[`fɛlənɪ]
n. 重罪

prisoner
[`prɪznə]
n. 囚犯

life imprisonment
[`laɪf ɪm`prɪznmənt]
n. 終生監禁

misdemeanor
[ˌmɪsdɪ`minə]
n. 輕罪

juvenile delinquency
[`dʒuvənḷ dɪ`lɪŋkwənsɪ]
n. 少年犯罪

confiscate
[`kanfɪsˌket]
v. 沒收；充公

misbehavior
[ˌmɪsbɪ`hevjə]
n. 行為不檢

probation
[pro`beʃən]
n. 緩刑

bail
[bel]
v./n. 保釋

custody
[`kʌstədɪ]
n. 拘留

**大師
小叮嚀**

相關用法舉例如下：

✍ He was bailed out by his father. 「他被父親保釋出來。」

✍ Tom is going to stand trial for murder. 「湯姆將因謀殺而面臨
審判。」

✍ In custody：被拘留。

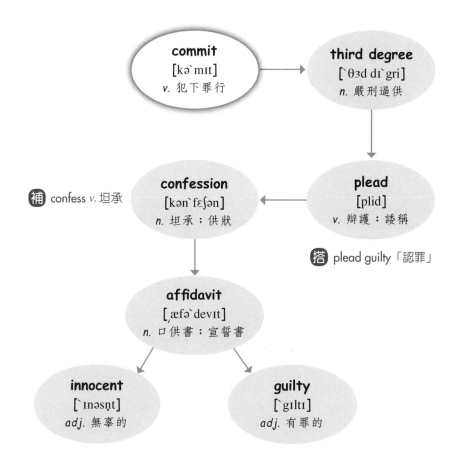

commit
[kə`mɪt]
v. 犯下罪行

third degree
[`θɝd dɪ`gri]
n. 嚴刑逼供

補 confess v. 坦承

confession
[kən`fɛʃən]
n. 坦承；供狀

plead
[plid]
v. 辯護；謊稱

搭 plead guilty「認罪」

affidavit
[ˌæfə`devɪt]
n. 口供書；宣誓書

innocent
[`ɪnəsn̩t]
adj. 無辜的

guilty
[`gɪltɪ]
adj. 有罪的

大師小叮嚀

相關用法舉例如下：

☞ I plead (not) guilty to the charge. 「我（不）承認那項指控。」

☞ I don't know whether he is guilty or innocent. 「我不知道他到底是有罪還是無辜的。」

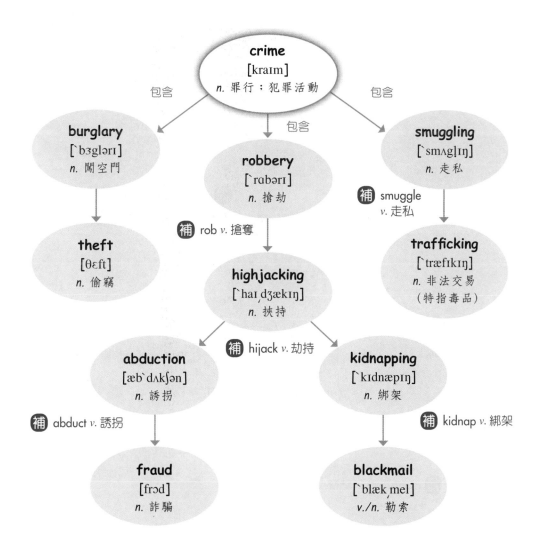

crime
[kraɪm]
n. 罪行;犯罪活動

包含

包含

包含

burglary
[ˋbɝglərɪ]
n. 闖空門

robbery
[ˋrɑbərɪ]
n. 搶劫

smuggling
[ˋsmʌglɪŋ]
n. 走私

補 smuggle *v.* 走私

theft
[θɛft]
n. 偷竊

補 rob *v.* 搶奪

trafficking
[ˋtræfɪkɪŋ]
n. 非法交易
(特指毒品)

highjacking
[ˋhaɪˏdʒækɪŋ]
n. 挾持

補 hijack *v.* 劫持

abduction
[æbˋdʌkʃən]
n. 誘拐

kidnapping
[ˋkɪdnæpɪŋ]
n. 綁架

補 abduct *v.* 誘拐

補 kidnap *v.* 綁架

fraud
[frɔd]
n. 詐騙

blackmail
[ˋblækˏmel]
v./n. 勒索

大師
小叮嚀
✍ 以下三個相關單字也要牢記:kidnapper「綁匪」、hostage「人質」、ransom「贖金」。

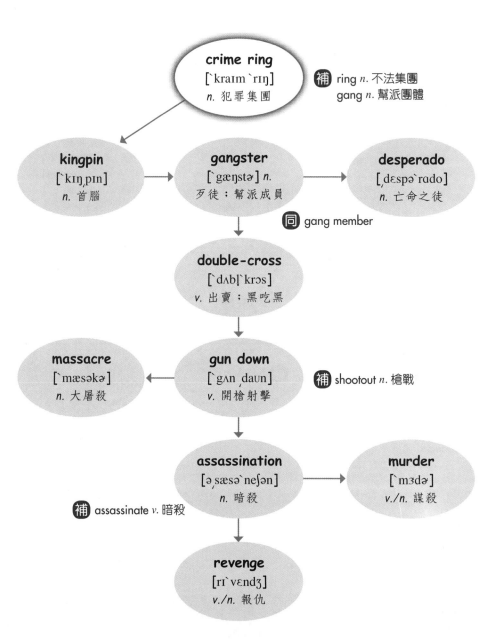

crime ring
[`kraɪm `rɪŋ]
n. 犯罪集團

補 ring n. 不法集團
gang n. 幫派團體

kingpin
[`kɪŋ,pɪn]
n. 首腦

gangster
[`gæŋstə] n.
歹徒；幫派成員

desperado
[,dɛspə`rado]
n. 亡命之徒

同 gang member

double-cross
[`dʌbḷ`krɔs]
v. 出賣；黑吃黑

massacre
[`mæsəkə]
n. 大屠殺

gun down
[`gʌn ,daʊn]
v. 開槍射擊

補 shootout n. 槍戰

assassination
[ə,sæsə`neʃən]
n. 暗殺

murder
[`mɝdə]
v./n. 謀殺

補 assassinate v. 暗殺

revenge
[rɪ`vɛndʒ]
v./n. 報仇

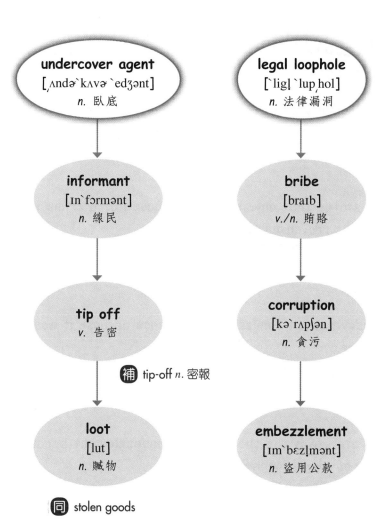

undercover agent
[ˌʌndəˈkʌvə ˈedʒənt]
n. 臥底

legal loophole
[ˈligl̩ ˈlupˌhol]
n. 法律漏洞

informant
[ɪnˈfɔrmənt]
n. 線民

bribe
[braɪb]
v./n. 賄賂

tip off
v. 告密

補 tip-off *n.* 密報

corruption
[kəˈrʌpʃən]
n. 貪污

loot
[lut]
n. 贓物

embezzlement
[ɪmˈbɛzl̩mənt]
n. 盜用公款

同 stolen goods

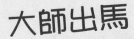

❶ The serial killer was **sentenced** to **life imprisonment** without **parole**.

這名連續殺人犯被判無期徒刑，且不得假釋。

（serial *adj.* 連續的）

❷ The law states that anyone who is **accused** of a **crime** is presumed **innocent** until proven **guilty**.

法律明定，任何被告在證明有罪之前都視同無辜。

（presume *v.* 假定；認為）

❸ The **affidavit** is not admissible as **evidence** because it was filed after the deadline.

這份口供是在期限後才取得，因此不予採納。

（admissible *adj.* 可採納的）

❹ The secretary was not charged with **embezzlement** because he took advantage of a **legal loophole**.

那個秘書鑽法律漏洞，並未被控盜用公款。

（be charged with *ph.* 被指控）

❺ Two innocent bystanders were **gunned down** on the street in a gang **shootout**.

兩名無辜的路人在幫派街頭槍戰中中彈身亡。

❻ The thief **double-crossed** his partners and **tipped off** the police about their next **burglary**.
那名竊賊出賣他的同夥，告訴警方他們計畫的下樁竊案。

❼ He was taken into **custody** and later indicted for drug **trafficking** and **murder**.
他被拘留，隨後因涉嫌毒品交易和謀殺被起訴。

❽ After the **jury** delivered a guilty **verdict**, the **defendant's** attorney announced his intention to file an appeal with the supreme **court**.
陪審團判決有罪後，被告的律師宣稱他準備上訴到最高法院。

❾ The defendant's request for **bail** was refused because of a previous conviction.
那名被告之前的罪行使得他申請保釋被駁回。

❿ The accused **pleaded** not guilty to the charge and presented an iron-tight **alibi**.
被告不承認那項指控，並提出強而有力的不在場證明。

⓫ The **gang members** were already gone by the time the police arrived, so it's likely that someone in the department **tipped** them **off**.
警察趕到時歹徒們已經逃跑了，看來極可能局裡有人通風報信。

換你上場

學習成效知分曉！

∽ *Exercise* ……根據題目的定義，從下列單字中找出正確的字填上。

jury	witness	confiscate	blackmail	kidnap
fraud	murder	in custody	plaintiff	trafficking
alibi	misbehavior	amnesty	suspect	

1. _____ : the crime of killing a person, especially with intent.

2. _____ : a person who files a lawsuit against another person.

3. _____ : to seize a person by force and demand a ransom in exchange for releasing that person.

4. _____ : the buying and selling of illegal things, such as guns, drugs, and endangered animals.

5. _____ : the state of being kept injail, especially while one is awaiting trial.

6. _____ : to seize by some authority.

7. _____ : the defense of having been elsewhere at the time and place of a criminal act.

8. _____ : a person who is believed to have committed a crime.

9. _____ : the act of an authority, such as a government, by which a pardon is granted to a large group of individuals.

10. _____ : the person in a law court who tells the jury and judge what she or he knows about the case.

☞ *Answer key* ··

1. murder
2. plaintiff
3. kidnap
4. trafficking
5. in custody
6. confiscate
7. alibi
8. suspect
9. amnesty
10. witness

宗教

Religion

宗教

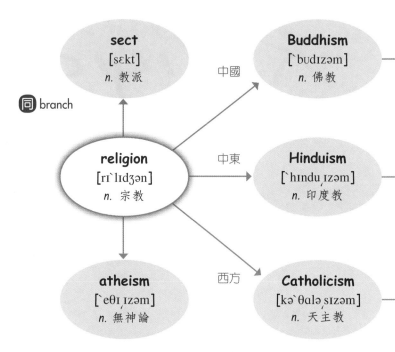

sect
[sɛkt]
n. 教派

同 branch

religion
[rɪ`lɪdʒən]
n. 宗教

中國

Buddhism
[`budɪzəm]
n. 佛教

中東

Hinduism
[`hɪndu͵ɪzəm]
n. 印度教

atheism
[`eθɪ͵ɪzəm]
n. 無神論

西方

Catholicism
[kə`θalə͵sɪzəm]
n. 天主教

大師
小叮嚀

- 有 -ism 字尾的名詞表示某種主義、學說、行為特徵……等。
- 將字尾 -ism 改成 -ist，即表示尊崇或視某主義為主要行為依據的人。例：Taoism「道教」 → Taoist「道教徒」；atheism「無神論」 → atheist「無神論者」。
- 天主教和基督教的聖經幾乎完全一樣，但是天主教比較注重祭典儀式、比較尊奉瑪利亞；基督教則比較儉樸、尊奉耶穌。
- 猶太教的聖經沒有新約，因為他們不相信新約中所提的耶穌就是舊約中所預言的救世主（Messiah），執意認為救世主應該如君王般華麗地降臨，而非生活貧困的木匠。

源自中國

Taoism/Daoism
[ˋtaʊˏɪzəm/ˋdaʊˏɪzəm]
n. 道教

Shinto
[ˋʃɪnto]
n. 日本神道教

Chinese folk religion
n. 中國民間信仰

還有

Islam
[ˋɪsləm]
n. 伊斯蘭教

Sikhism
[ˋsikɪzəm]
n. 錫克教

Christianity
[ˏkrɪstʃɪˋænətɪ]
n. 基督教

Judaism
[ˋdʒudɪˏɪzəm]
n. 猶太教

補 Christian *n.* 基督徒
Protestant *n.* 新教徒

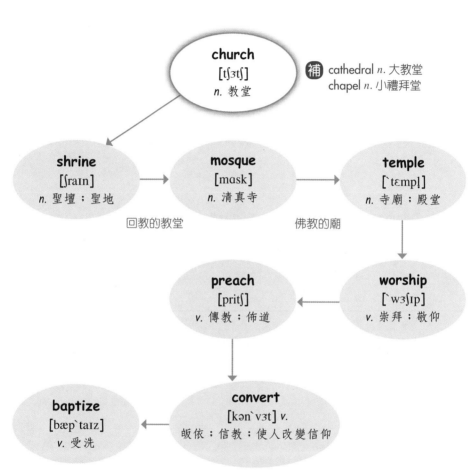

church
[tʃɝtʃ]
n. 教堂

補 cathedral *n.* 大教堂
chapel *n.* 小禮拜堂

shrine
[ʃraɪn]
n. 聖壇；聖地

mosque
[mɑsk]
n. 清真寺

回教的教堂

temple
[ˋtɛmpl̩]
n. 寺廟；殿堂

佛教的廟

preach
[pritʃ]
v. 傳教；佈道

worship
[ˋwɝʃɪp]
v. 崇拜；敬仰

baptize
[bæpˋtaɪz]
v. 受洗

convert
[kənˋvɝt] *v.*
皈依；信教；使人改變信仰

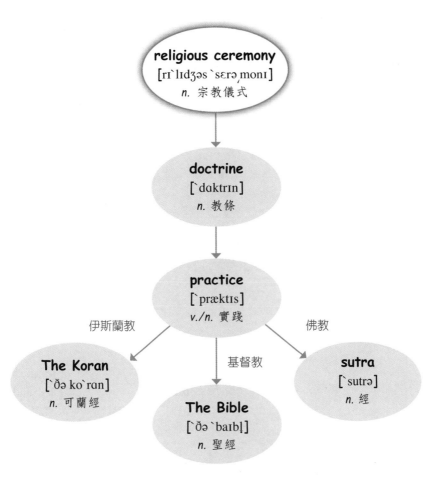

religious ceremony
[rɪ`lɪdʒəs `sɛrə͵monɪ]
n. 宗教儀式

doctrine
[`dɑktrɪn]
n. 教條

practice
[`præktɪs]
v./n. 實踐

伊斯蘭教

The Koran
[`ðə ko`ran]
n. 可蘭經

基督教

The Bible
[`ðə `baɪbļ]
n. 聖經

佛教

sutra
[`sutrə]
n. 經

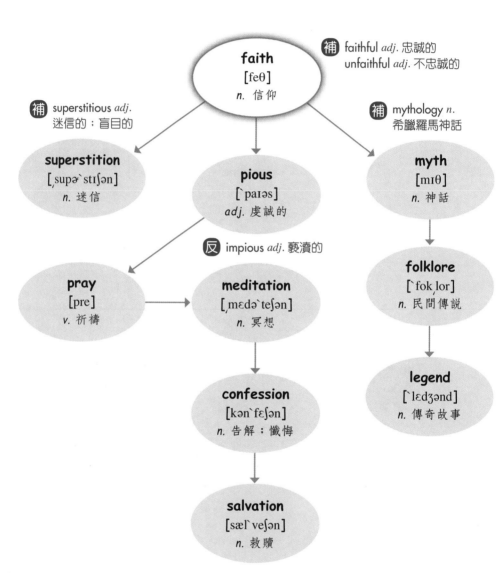

補 faithful *adj.* 忠誠的
unfaithful *adj.* 不忠誠的

faith
[feθ]
n. 信仰

補 superstitious *adj.*
迷信的；盲目的

補 mythology *n.*
希臘羅馬神話

superstition
[ˌsupəˋstɪʃən]
n. 迷信

pious
[ˋpaɪəs]
adj. 虔誠的

myth
[mɪθ]
n. 神話

反 impious *adj.* 褻瀆的

pray
[pre]
v. 祈禱

meditation
[ˌmɛdəˋteʃən]
n. 冥想

folklore
[ˋfokˌlor]
n. 民間傳說

confession
[kənˋfɛʃən]
n. 告解；懺悔

legend
[ˋlɛdʒənd]
n. 傳奇故事

salvation
[sælˋveʃən]
n. 救贖

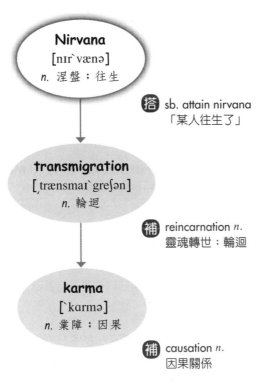

Nirvana
[nɪr`vænə]
n. 涅盤；往生

搭 sb. attain nirvana
「某人往生了」

transmigration
[ˌtrænsmaɪ`greʃən]
n. 輪迴

補 reincarnation *n.*
靈魂轉世；輪迴

karma
[`kɑrmə]
n. 業障；因果

補 causation *n.*
因果關係

 大師出馬

❶ Though he claims to be an **atheist**, he turns to **religion** from time to time for comfort.

他自稱無神論者，卻還是不時向宗教尋求慰藉。

（claim v. 宣稱　turn to ph. 轉向……）

❷ The **Bible** is to Christians what **the Koran** is to Muslims.

聖經對基督徒的重要性，就如同可蘭經對穆斯林一樣。

❸ The **sect** was short-lived, because the preachers didn't **practice** what they **preached**.

這個教派僅維持短暫的時間，因為那些佈道者說一套做一套。

❹ After suffering a personal tragedy, she **converted** to **Buddhism** to seek inner peace.

經歷自身的悲劇後，她皈依佛教以尋求內心平靜。

（inner adj. 內心、內在的）

❺ The **pious** woman knelt down and **prayed** silently to God.

那位虔誠的婦人跪下，默默向上帝禱告。

❻ Some Chinese people are quite **superstitious**. They may, for example, consider the number four to be unlucky.

有些中國人十分迷信。舉例來說，有人會認為「四」是一個不吉利的數字。

❼ Whenever he feels upset, he tries to calm down by **meditation**.
每當他心煩意亂，都會以冥想來沉靜思緒。

❽ The idea of **transmigration** has great significance in both **Hinduism** and Buddhism.
輪迴在印度教和佛教具有極大的意義。

❾ She told me that she found personal **salvation** through reading the Bible.
她告訴我她在讀聖經時找到個人救贖。

❿ Chinese customs and culture are closely bound to **folk religion**.
中國習俗與文化和民間信仰有密切的關係。
（be bound to ... *ph.* 和……有密切關係）

換你上場

學習成效知分曉！

🔗 *Exercise* ⋯⋯ 請根據提示完成字謎。

DOWN「垂直」

　1. 天主教的　2. 經　4. 新教徒　5. 回教　6. 猶太教　7. 可蘭經　8. 冥想

　11. 清真寺　13. 神道

ACROSS「水平」

　1. 皈依　3. 教堂　7. 業障　9. 無神論　10. 因果關係　12. 輪迴　14. 教條　15. 救贖

⟡ *Answer key*

C	O	N	V	E	R	T				S					
A								C	H	U	R	C	H		
T			P							T			I		
H			R		J		K	A	R	M	A		S		
O			O		U		O		A				L		
L			T		D		R		M				A		
I			E		A		A	T	H	E	I	S	M		
C	A	U	S	A	T	I	O	N		D					
			T		S					I		M			
	T	R	A	N	S	M	I	G	R	A	T	I	O	N	
	N		H						A		S				
D	O	C	T	R	I	N	E		T		Q				
	N								I		U				
S	A	L	V	A	T	I	O	N		O		E			
			O						N						

社　會
Society

新聞、媒體

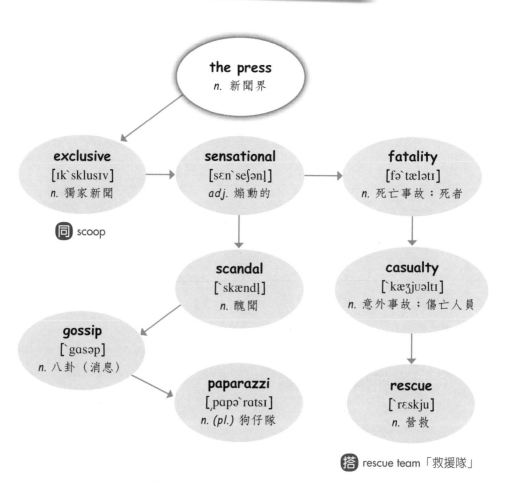

the press
n. 新聞界

exclusive
[ɪk`sklusɪv]
n. 獨家新聞

同 scoop

sensational
[sɛn`seʃənl̩]
adj. 煽動的

fatality
[fə`tælətɪ]
n. 死亡事故；死者

scandal
[`skændl̩]
n. 醜聞

casualty
[`kæʒjuəltɪ]
n. 意外事故；傷亡人員

gossip
[`gasəp]
n. 八卦（消息）

paparazzi
[͵papə`ratsɪ]
n. (pl.) 狗仔隊

rescue
[`rɛskju]
n. 營救

搭 rescue team「救援隊」

大師小叮嚀

- 三人死亡：three fatalities。
- 15 人傷亡（包括受傷和死亡）：fifteen casualties。
- Paparazzi 的單數為 paparazzo。

疾病

AIDS
(Acquired Immune
Deficiency Syndrome)
n. 愛滋病

HIV (Human
Immunodeficiency Virus)
n. 愛滋病毒

也可能致命

SARS (Severe Acute
Respiratory Syndrome)
n. 嚴重急性呼吸道綜合症

含有

coronavirus
[kə`ronəˌvaɪrəs]
n. 冠狀病毒

補 corona *n.* 冠狀部位

感情

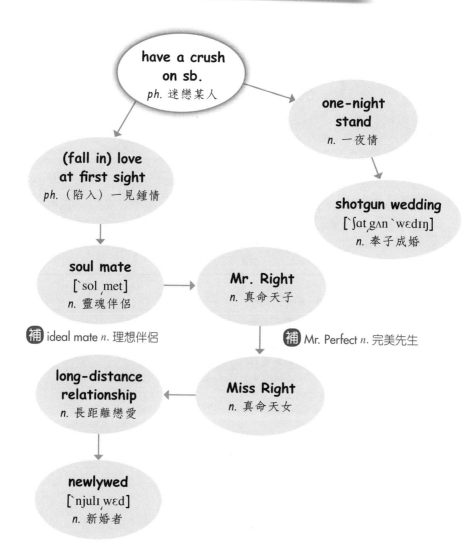

have a crush on sb.
ph. 迷戀某人

one-night stand
n. 一夜情

(fall in) love at first sight
ph.（陷入）一見鍾情

shotgun wedding
[`ʃɑt͵gʌn `wɛdɪŋ]
n. 奉子成婚

soul mate
[`sol ͵met]
n. 靈魂伴侶

Mr. Right
n. 真命天子

補 ideal mate *n.* 理想伴侶

補 Mr. Perfect *n.* 完美先生

long-distance relationship
n. 長距離戀愛

Miss Right
n. 真命天女

newlywed
[`njulɪ͵wɛd]
n. 新婚者

常見議題

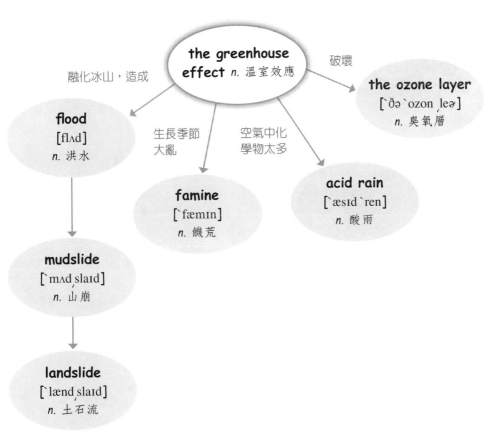

融化冰山，造成

the greenhouse effect *n.* 溫室效應

破壞

the ozone layer
[ˋðə ˋozon ˏleə]
n. 奧氧層

flood
[flʌd]
n. 洪水

生長季節大亂

空氣中化學物太多

famine
[ˋfæmɪn]
n. 饑荒

acid rain
[ˋæsɪd ˋren]
n. 酸雨

mudslide
[ˋmʌdˏslaɪd]
n. 山崩

landslide
[ˋlændˏslaɪd]
n. 土石流

大師 小叮嚀

✐ 和溫室效應相關的議題為全球暖化（global warming）。
✐ 聖經裡有名的洪水故事你可能聽過，裡面的諾亞方舟就叫做 Noah's ark。

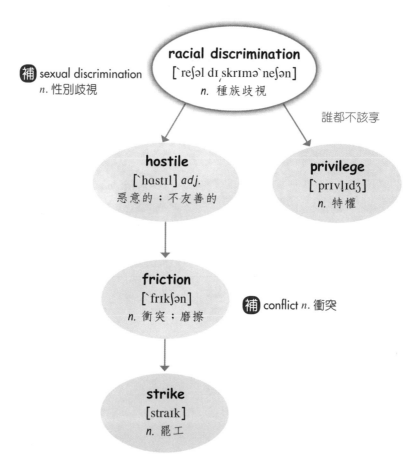

補 sexual discrimination
n. 性別歧視

racial discrimination
[ˋreʃəl dɪˌskrɪməˋneʃən]
n. 種族歧視

誰都不該享

hostile
[ˋhastɪl] adj.
惡意的；不友善的

privilege
[ˋprɪvḷɪdʒ]
n. 特權

friction
[ˋfrɪkʃən]
n. 衝突；磨擦

補 conflict n. 衝突

strike
[straɪk]
n. 罷工

景點

National Palace
Museum
n. 國立故宮博物院

National Museum
of History
n. 國立歷史博物館

Taiwan
Museum
n. 國立台灣博物館

National Taiwan
Democracy Memorial Hall
n. 國立台灣民主紀念館

Sun Yat-sen
Memorial Hall
n. 國父紀念館

Taipei Fine
Arts Museum
n. 台北市立美術館

世界四大博物館

**The Metropolitan
Museum of Art**
n. 紐約大都會博物館

↓

**National
Palace Museum**
n. 故宮博物院

↓

**The
Louvre** [`ðə `luvə]
n. 羅浮宮

↓

**The
British Museum**
n. 大英博物館

**大　師
小叮嚀**

✏ 學生出國玩之前，可以辦一張國際學生證（ISIC = International
Student Identity Card），不論交通還是參觀博物館等景點，
都可以享有優惠喔！

✏ 羅浮宮於每月的第一個星期日可免費入場。

✏ 大英博物館可免費入場。

大師出馬

❶ Many museums in the UK, including **the British Museum**, are free to all visitors.

英國有許多博物館都免收門票，包括大英博物館。

---

❷ The Jade Cabbage in the **National Palace Museum** has two grasshoppers on it that symbolize fertility.

故宮裡的翠玉白菜上有兩隻蚱蜢，象徵多子多孫。

（fertility *n.* 繁殖力）

---

❸ The glass pyramid at the entrance to **the Louvre** was designed by the Chinese-American architect I. M. Pei.

羅浮宮門口的玻璃金字塔是由美籍華人貝聿銘先生所設計。

（pyramid *n.* 金字塔）

---

❹ **Racial discrimination**, a common problem in many workplaces, must be addressed by the business community.

種族歧視的問題存在於許多工作場合，商界一定要正視。

---

❺ After a successful preliminary negotiation, the air traffic controllers agreed not to call a **strike**.

在初步薪資協商成功後，這些航管人員同意不罷工了。

（preliminary *adj.* 初步的）

❻ Is it so hot because **the greenhouse effect** is worsening?

天氣那麼熱是因為溫室效應越來越嚴重了嗎?

（worsen v. 日益嚴重）

❼ I don't understand why he has such a **hostile** attitude toward me.

我不明白他為什麼對我充滿敵意。

❽ The brave firefighters **rescued** many people from the burning building.

英勇的消防隊員們從燃燒的建築裡救出許多人。

❾ **The press** should use its power as a watchdog to uncover important information, and comminicate it to the public.

新聞界應該善用它的力量扮演監督的角色,發掘重要的資訊傳遞給大眾。

（watchdog n. 監視　uncover v. 發掘）

換你上場

學習成效知分曉！

✍ *Exercise* ⋯⋯ 請根據提示完成字謎。

DOWN「垂直」

　1. 傷亡人員　3. 饑荒　5. 洪水　7. 特權

ACROSS「水平」

　2. 醜聞　4. 八卦消息　6. 新婚者　8. 罷工　9. 惡意的　10. 營救

⌁ *Answer key* ⋯⋯⋯⋯⋯⋯⋯⋯⋯⋯⋯⋯⋯⋯⋯⋯⋯⋯⋯⋯⋯⋯⋯⋯⋯

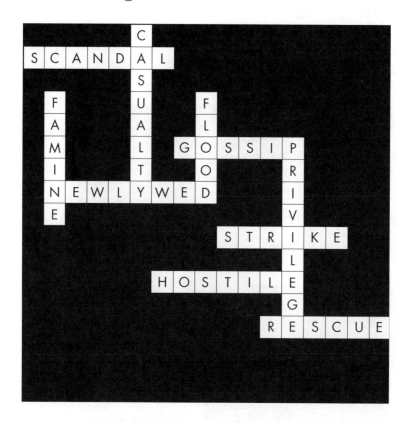

政治
Politics

政治

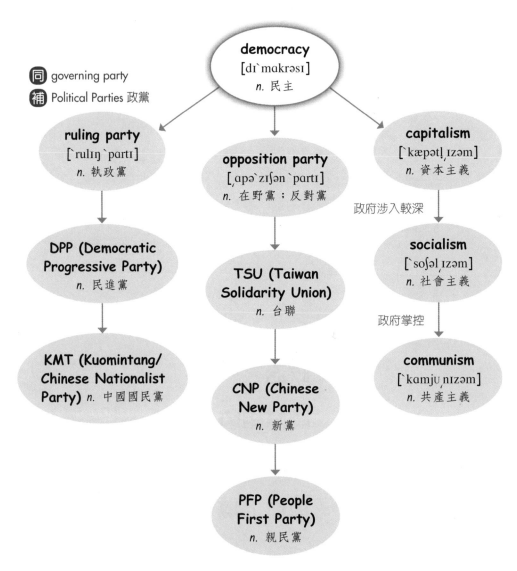

同 governing party

補 Political Parties 政黨

democracy
[dɪ`makrəsɪ]
n. 民主

ruling party
[`rulɪŋ `partɪ]
n. 執政黨

opposition party
[ˌɑpə`zɪʃən `partɪ]
n. 在野黨;反對黨

capitalism
[`kæpətḷˌɪzəm]
n. 資本主義

政府涉入較深

DPP (Democratic Progressive Party)
n. 民進黨

TSU (Taiwan Solidarity Union)
n. 台聯

socialism
[`soʃəlˌɪzəm]
n. 社會主義

政府掌控

KMT (Kuomintang/ Chinese Nationalist Party) n. 中國國民黨

CNP (Chinese New Party)
n. 新黨

communism
[`kamjuˌnɪzəm]
n. 共產主義

PFP (People First Party)
n. 親民黨

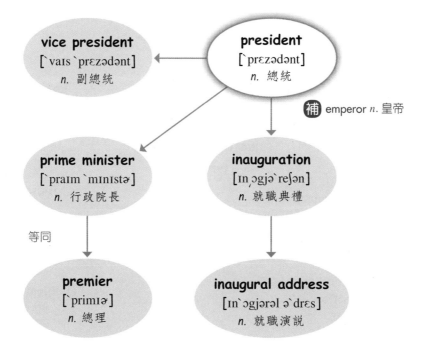

vice president
[`vaɪs `prɛzədənt]
n. 副總統

president
[`prɛzədənt]
n. 總統

補 emperor n. 皇帝

prime minister
[`praɪm `mɪnɪstə]
n. 行政院長

inauguration
[ɪnˌɔgjə`reʃən]
n. 就職典禮

等同

premier
[`primɪə]
n. 總理

inaugural address
[ɪn`ɔgjərəl ə`drɛs]
n. 就職演說

大師
小叮嚀

✍ 各國依其政治體制及職責而有「行政院長」和「總理」的不同稱謂，但二者地位大致相同。

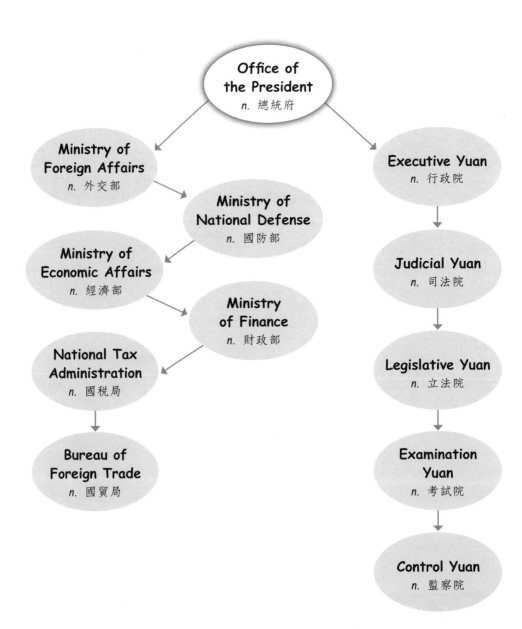

Office of the President
n. 總統府

Ministry of Foreign Affairs
n. 外交部

Ministry of National Defense
n. 國防部

Ministry of Economic Affairs
n. 經濟部

Ministry of Finance
n. 財政部

National Tax Administration
n. 國稅局

Bureau of Foreign Trade
n. 國貿局

Executive Yuan
n. 行政院

Judicial Yuan
n. 司法院

Legislative Yuan
n. 立法院

Examination Yuan
n. 考試院

Control Yuan
n. 監察院

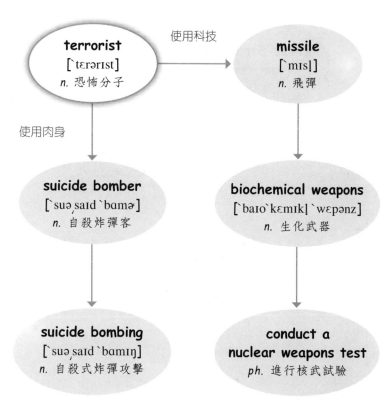

terrorist
[ˋtɛrərɪst]
n. 恐怖分子

使用科技

missile
[ˋmɪsḷ]
n. 飛彈

使用肉身

suicide bomber
[ˋsuəˌsaɪd ˋbɑmɚ]
n. 自殺炸彈客

biochemical weapons
[ˋbaɪoˋkɛmɪkḷ ˋwɛpənz]
n. 生化武器

suicide bombing
[ˋsuəˌsaɪd ˋbɑmɪŋ]
n. 自殺式炸彈攻擊

**conduct a
nuclear weapons test**
ph. 進行核武試驗

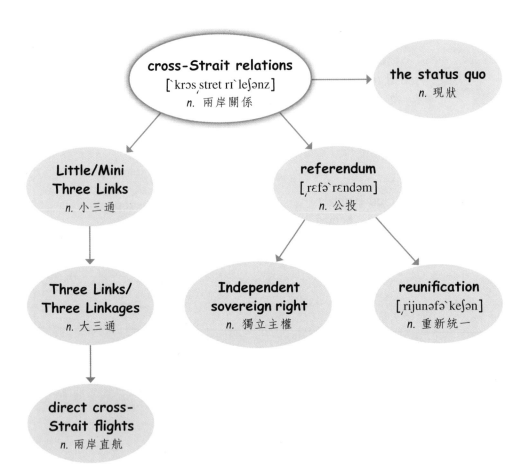

✎ 大三通（the Three Links）指的是：direct postal「郵政」、transportation「交通」和 trade「貿易」。

✎ 小三通（the Mini Three Links）指的是：金馬地區與大陸福建沿海的三通。

美國兩黨政治

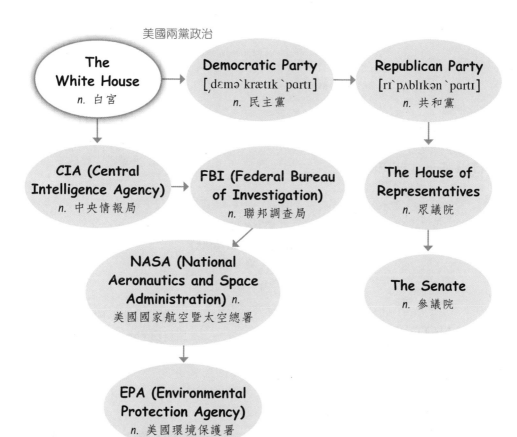

The White House
n. 白宮

Democratic Party
[ˌdɛməˈkrætɪk ˈpɑrtɪ]
n. 民主黨

Republican Party
[rɪˈpʌblɪkən ˈpɑrtɪ]
n. 共和黨

CIA (Central Intelligence Agency)
n. 中央情報局

FBI (Federal Bureau of Investigation)
n. 聯邦調查局

The House of Representatives
n. 眾議院

NASA (National Aeronautics and Space Administration) n.
美國國家航空暨太空總署

The Senate
n. 參議院

EPA (Environmental Protection Agency)
n. 美國環境保護署

大師小叮嚀

✑ 「議會」有不同說法：

a. 英國體制的 Houses of Parliament 包括 the House of Lords 「上議院」和 the House of Commons「下議院」。

b. 美國體制的國會 Congress 包括 the Senate「參議院」和 the House of Representatives「眾議院」。

c. 台灣體制為 the Legislative Yuan「立法院」。

d. 國會議員在美國稱為 Congressperson（senator 或 representative），在台灣為 legislator「立法委員」，在英國則為 Member of Parliament。

國際組織

G8
(The Group of Eight)
n. 八大工業國
領袖高峰會議

WHO (World Health
Organization)
n. 世界衛生組織

The UN
(United Nations)
n. 聯合國

NATO (North Atlantic
Treaty Organization)
n. 北大西洋公約組織

The EU
(European Union)
n. 歐盟

The EFTA (European
Free Trade Association)
n. 歐洲自由貿易協會

大師
小叮嚀

✎ Coalition/alliance「聯盟」。英國是歐盟的一份子，但不屬於歐元區（Euro Area），而使用英鎊（the pound sterling）。

✎ 八大工業國組織（G8），包括美國、日本、英國、德國、法國、義大利、加拿大、俄羅斯。

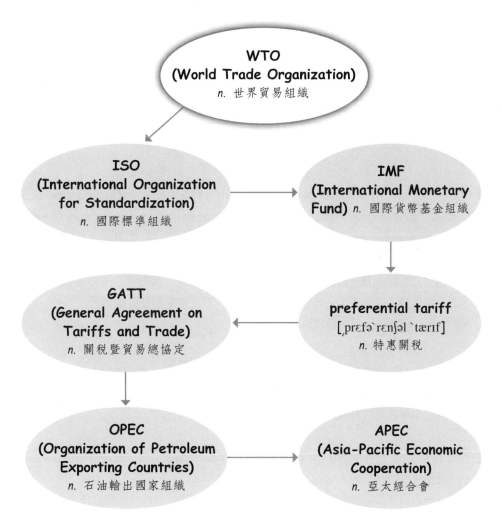

❶ The **CIA**, a government organization in the United States, collects information about other countries and also engages in covert actions all over the world.
美國政府機構裡的中央情報局蒐集其它國家的情報，並在全球進行秘密行動。
（government organization *n.* 政府機構　covert *adj.* 暗地的）

❷ **NATO** is an international organization of nations, including the U.S., Canada, Britain, and twenty-three European countries, which have all agreed to support one another in the event one of the participating countries is attacked.
北大西洋公約組織是一個國際組織，包括美國、加拿大、英國和二十三個歐洲國家，他們達成協議，如果其中一個會員國遭受攻擊，其它國家都會挺身而出。
（participating country *n.* 會員國）

❸ **NASA** is the agency responsible for spacecraft and space exploration programs in the U.S.
美國太空總署負責研發太空梭和太空漫遊計劃。

❹ The **EU** is an organization of European countries that have joint policies on trade, agriculture, and finance.
歐盟為一歐洲國家的聯合組織，這些國家有共同的貿易、農業及金融政策。
（joint *adj.* 聯合的）

❺ The Japanese **emperor** is the symbol of Japan.
日本天皇是日本的象徵。

❻ The **President** gave a brilliant **inaugural address**.

總統做了一場很棒的就職演說。

❼ **Suicide bombing** is a ruthless form of armed violence.

自殺式炸彈攻擊是一種無情的武裝暴力。

（armed violence *n.* 武裝暴力）

❽ North Korea **conducted a nuclear weapons test** last week.

上週北韓進行核武試驗。

❾ To maintain **the status quo** means to keep things the way they are now.

維持「現狀」就是指讓事情保持不變。

❿ The **IMF** is an international organization that monitors the global financial system.

國際貨幣基金組織是一個監督全球金融系統的國際機構。

（monitor *v.* 監督　financial system *n.* 金融系統）

換你上場

學習成效知分曉！

👁️ *Exercise* ······ 你知道下列組織的英文名稱為何嗎？請與方框中的選項配對。學會這些字，看報紙就再也不會一頭霧水了喔！

(a) NATO	(b) APEC	(c) EU	(d) UN	(e) WHO
(f) WTO	(g) ISO	(h) EFTA	(i) OPEC	(j) IMF

❶ 歐盟 ·· [　]

❷ 國際貨幣基金組織 ··· [　]

❸ 世界衛生組織 ·· [　]

❹ 聯合國 ·· [　]

❺ 歐洲自由貿易協會 ··· [　]

❻ 石油輸出國家組織 ··· [　]

❼ 世界貿易組織 ·· [　]

❽ 北大西洋公約組織 ··· [　]

❾ 亞太經合會 ·· [　]

❿ 國際標準組織 ·· [　]

👁️ *Answer key* ···

❶ c ❷ j ❸ e ❹ d ❺ h ❻ i ❼ f ❽ a ❾ b ❿ g

經濟
Economics

經濟

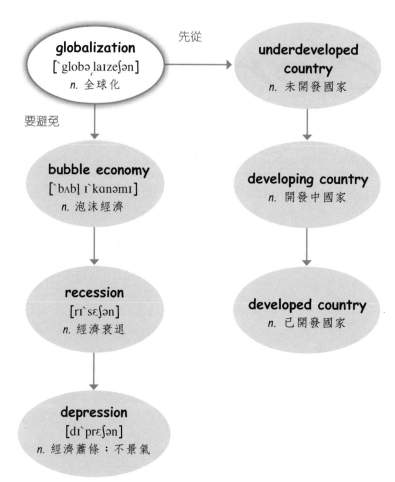

先從

globalization
[`globə͵laɪzeʃən]
n. 全球化

underdeveloped
country
n. 未開發國家

要避免

bubble economy
[`bʌb͵l ɪ`kanəmɪ]
n. 泡沫經濟

developing country
n. 開發中國家

recession
[rɪ`sɛʃən]
n. 經濟衰退

developed country
n. 已開發國家

depression
[dɪ`prɛʃən]
n. 經濟蕭條；不景氣

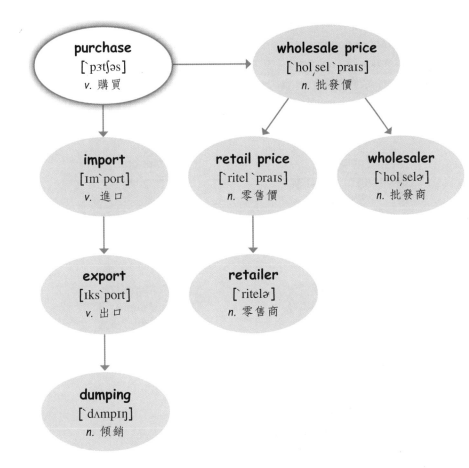

purchase
[`pɜtʃəs]
v. 購買

wholesale price
[`holˌsel `praɪs]
n. 批發價

import
[ɪm`port]
v. 進口

retail price
[`ritel `praɪs]
n. 零售價

wholesaler
[`holˌselɚ]
n. 批發商

export
[ɪks`port]
v. 出口

retailer
[`ritelɚ]
n. 零售商

dumping
[`dʌmpɪŋ]
n. 傾銷

大師
小叮嚀

✑ 注意下列三字的重音位置：

economy [ɪ`kanəmɪ] (n.) 經濟。

economics [ˌikə`namɪks] (n.) 經濟學。

economist [ɪ`kanəmɪst] (n.) 經濟學者。

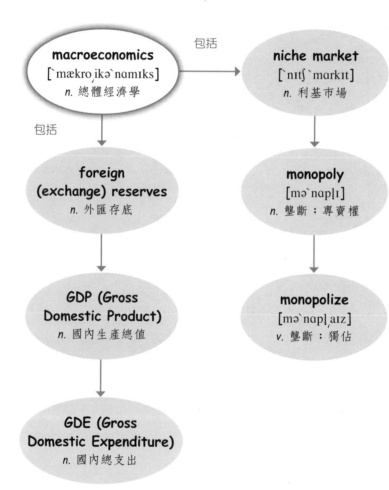

macroeconomics
[ˋmækroˏɪkəˋnamɪks]
n. 總體經濟學

包括

niche market
[ˋnɪtʃ ˋmarkɪt]
n. 利基市場

包括

foreign
(exchange) reserves
n. 外匯存底

monopoly
[məˋnaplɪ]
n. 壟斷；專賣權

GDP (Gross
Domestic Product)
n. 國內生產總值

monopolize
[məˋnaplˏaɪz]
v. 壟斷；獨佔

GDE (Gross
Domestic Expenditure)
n. 國內總支出

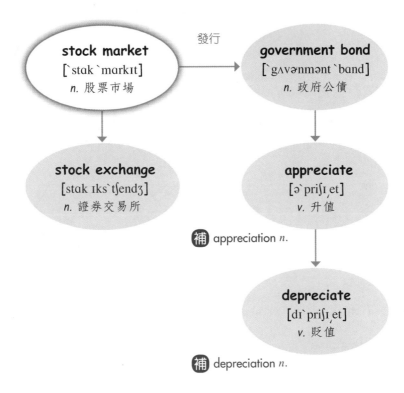

stock market
[`stɑk `mɑrkɪt]
n. 股票市場

發行

government bond
[`gʌvənmənt `bɑnd]
n. 政府公債

stock exchange
[stɑk ɪks`tʃendʒ]
n. 證券交易所

appreciate
[ə`priʃɪˌet]
v. 升值

補 appreciation n.

depreciate
[dɪ`priʃɪˌet]
v. 貶值

補 depreciation n.

大師
小叮嚀

幣值升、貶值的說法如下：

✏ New Taiwan dollar depreciated against the U.S. dollar.
「新台幣對美元下跌。」

✏ The RMB has appreciated 9 percent against the U.S. dollar.
「人民幣對美元已漲 9%。」

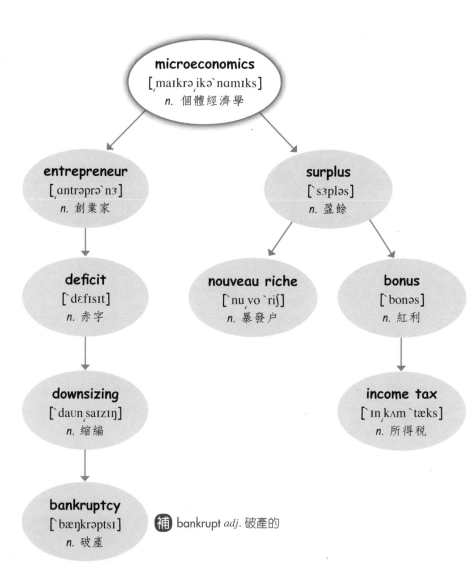

microeconomics
[ˌmaɪkrəˌikəˋnamɪks]
n. 個體經濟學

entrepreneur
[ˌɑntrəprəˋnɝ]
n. 創業家

surplus
[ˋsɝpləs]
n. 盈餘

deficit
[ˋdɛfɪsɪt]
n. 赤字

nouveau riche
[ˋnuˌvoˋriʃ]
n. 暴發戶

bonus
[ˋbonəs]
n. 紅利

downsizing
[ˋdaʊnˌsaɪzɪŋ]
n. 縮編

income tax
[ˋɪnˌkʌmˋtæks]
n. 所得稅

bankruptcy
[ˋbæŋkrəptsɪ]
n. 破產

補 bankrupt adj. 破產的

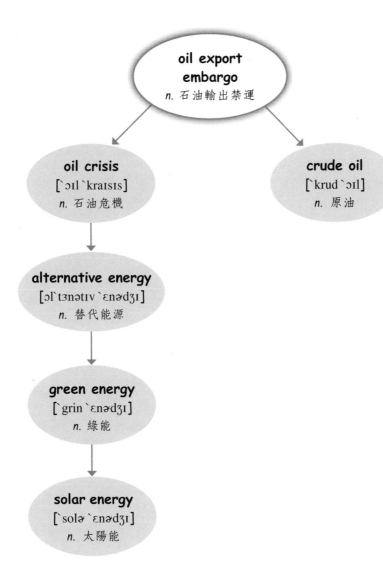

oil export embargo
n. 石油輸出禁運

oil crisis
[`ɔɪl `kraɪsɪs]
n. 石油危機

crude oil
[`krud `ɔɪl]
n. 原油

alternative energy
[ɔl`tɜnətɪv `ɛnədʒɪ]
n. 替代能源

green energy
[`grin `ɛnədʒɪ]
n. 綠能

solar energy
[`solə `ɛnədʒɪ]
n. 太陽能

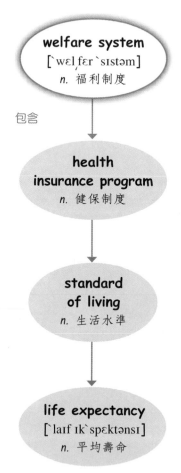

包含

welfare system
[`wɛl,fɛr `sɪstəm]
n. 福利制度

health
insurance program
n. 健保制度

standard
of living
n. 生活水準

life expectancy
[`laɪf ɪk`spɛktənsɪ]
n. 平均壽命

搭 the average life expectancy of women
「女性平均壽命」

大師出馬

❶ I spend nearly US$500 on **imported** food every month.
我每個月花將近 500 美元在進口食品上。

❷ Some fabrics are sold to **retailers**, but most are purchased by clothing manufacturers.
有些布料會賣給零售商，但大多數還是由成衣製造商購買。
(fabric *n.* 布)

❸ I want to know more about the challenges facing India as it undergoes **globalization**.
我想更了解印度如何面對全球化的挑戰。

❹ Taiwan is the fifth-largest holder of **foreign exchange reserves** in the world.
台灣的外匯存底排名世界第五。
(holder *n.* 持有者；保持者)

❺ The London Stock Exchange, founded in 1801, is one of the largest **stock exchanges** in the world.
倫敦證券交易所創立於 1801 年，是世界上最大的證交所之一。

❻ You must define your **niche market** before deciding on your marketing strategy.

擬定行銷策略前你必須先找出利基市場。

（marketing strategy *n.* 行銷策略）

❼ He declared **bankruptcy** after becoming unable to pay off his credit card debt.

在無力償還卡債後他宣布破產。

❽ Inflation is rising rapidly; the dollar is **depreciating**.

通貨膨脹迅速；美金正在貶值。

換你上場

學 習 成 效 知 分 曉！

✎ *Exercise* ······ 請根據提示完成字謎。

DOWN「垂直」

1. 平均壽命 3. 進口 4. 出口 6. 壟斷 7. 紅利

ACROSS「水平」

2. 全球化 4. 創業家 5. 股票 7. 破產

⌇ *Answer key* ⋯⋯⋯⋯⋯⋯⋯⋯⋯⋯⋯⋯⋯⋯⋯⋯⋯⋯⋯⋯⋯⋯⋯⋯⋯⋯⋯⋯

```
                                          L
      G L O B A L I Z A T I O N
                          M             F
        E N T R E P R E N E U R
        X                 O             E
        P                 R             X
  S T O C K               T             P
        R         M                     E
        T         O                     C
            B A N K R U P T C Y
        O         O                     A
        N         P                     N
        U         O                     C
        S         L                     Y
                  Y
```

Notes

國家圖書館出版品預行編目資料

翻譯大師教你記單字. 進階篇 / 詹婷婷, 解鈴容, 吳岳峰 作
－－ 初版. －－ 臺北市：貝塔, 2008.06
　面： 公分
　ISBN 978-957-729-696-2（平裝附光碟片）

　1. 英語　2. 詞彙

805.12　　　　　　　　　　　　　　　　97009094

翻譯大師教你記單字——進階篇

主　　編 / 郭岱宗
作　　者 / 詹婷婷、解鈴容、吳岳峰
執行編輯 / 陳家仁

出　　版 / 貝塔出版有限公司
地　　址 / 台北市 100 館前路 12 號 11 樓
電　　話 / (02) 2314-2525
傳　　真 / (02) 2312-3535
客服專線 / (02) 2314-3535
客服信箱 / btservice@betamedia.com.tw
郵撥帳號 / 19493777
帳戶名稱 / 貝塔出版有限公司

總 經 銷 / 時報文化出版企業股份有限公司
地　　址 / 桃園縣龜山鄉萬壽路二段 351 號
電　　話 / (02) 2306-6842

出版日期 / 2011 年 4 月初版四刷
定　　價 / 320 元
ISBN：978-957-729-696-2

翻譯大師教你記單字——進階篇

喚醒你的英文語感！

請對折後釘好，直接寄回即可！

100 台北市中正區館前路12號11樓

 貝塔語言出版 收
Beta Multimedia Publishing

 寄件者住址 □□□

貝塔語言出版
Beta Multimedia Publishing

讀者服務專線 (02) 2314-3535　讀者服務傳真 (02) 2312-3535
客戶服務信箱 btservice@betamedia.com.tw
www.betamedia.com.tw

謝謝您購買本書！！

貝塔語言擁有最優良之英文學習書籍，為提供您最佳的英語學習資訊，您填妥此表後寄回（免貼郵票），將可不定期免費收到本公司最新發行之書訊及活動訊息！

姓名：＿＿＿＿＿＿＿＿＿　性別：☐男 ☐女　生日：＿＿＿年＿＿＿月＿＿日

電話：（公）＿＿＿＿＿＿＿　（宅）＿＿＿＿＿＿＿＿＿（手機）＿＿＿＿＿＿＿＿

電子信箱：＿＿＿＿＿＿＿＿＿＿＿＿＿＿＿＿＿＿＿＿＿＿＿＿＿＿＿＿＿＿

學歷：☐高中職含以下　☐專科　☐大學　☐研究所含以上

職業：☐金融　☐服務　☐傳播　☐製造　☐資訊　☐軍公教　☐出版
　　　☐自由　☐教育　☐學生　☐其他

職級：☐企業負責人　☐高階主管　☐中階主管　☐職員　☐專業人士

1. 您購買的書籍是？＿＿＿＿＿＿＿＿＿＿＿＿＿＿＿＿＿＿＿＿＿＿＿

2. 您從何處得知本產品？（可複選）

　☐書店 ☐網路 ☐書展 ☐校園活動 ☐廣告信函 ☐他人推薦 ☐新聞報導 ☐其他＿＿＿

3. 您覺得本產品價格：

　☐偏高 ☐合理 ☐偏低

4. 請問目前您每週花了多少時間學英語？

　☐不到十分鐘 ☐十分鐘以上，但不到半小時 ☐半小時以上，但不到一小時
　☐一小時以上，但不到兩小時 ☐兩個小時以上 ☐不一定

5. 通常在選擇語言學習書時，哪些因素是您會考慮的？

　☐封面 ☐內容、實用性 ☐品牌 ☐媒體、朋友推薦 ☐價格 ☐其他＿＿＿

6. 市面上您最需要的語言書種類為？

　☐聽力 ☐閱讀 ☐文法 ☐口說 ☐寫作 ☐其他＿＿＿

7. 通常您會透過何種方式選購語言學習書籍？

　☐書店門市 ☐網路書店 ☐郵購 ☐直接找出版社 ☐學校或公司團購 ☐其他＿＿＿

8. 給我們的建議：＿＿＿＿＿＿＿＿＿＿＿＿＿＿＿＿＿＿＿＿＿＿＿

＿＿＿＿＿＿＿＿＿＿＿＿＿＿＿＿＿＿＿＿＿＿＿＿＿＿＿＿＿＿＿＿

＿＿＿＿＿＿＿＿＿＿＿＿＿＿＿＿＿＿＿＿＿＿＿＿＿＿＿＿＿＿＿＿

喚醒你的英文語感！

Get a Feel for English !